AN OBSTINATE VANITY

For Jean,
Enjoy!
Keddie Hughes.

BY

KEDDIE HUGHES

Copyright © Keddie Hughes 2016
This book is sold subject to the condition that it shall not, by way of trade or otherwise, be lent, resold, hired out, or otherwise circulated without the publisher's prior consent in any form of binding or cover other than that in which it is published and without a similar condition including this condition being imposed on the subsequent publisher.
The moral right of Keddie Hughes has been asserted.
ISBN-13: 978-1523965830
ISBN-10: 1523965835

For Bob.

This is a work of fiction. Names, characters, businesses, organizations, places, events and incidents either are the product of the author's imagination or are used fictitiously. Any resemblance to actual persons, living or dead, events, or locales is entirely coincidental.

CONTENTS

Chapter 1 .... *1*
Chapter 2 .... *15*
Chapter 3 .... *27*
Chapter 4 .... *44*
Chapter 5 .... *58*
Chapter 6 .... *76*
Chapter 7 .... *91*
Chapter 8 .... *101*
Chapter 9 .... *113*
Chapter 10 .... *122*
Chapter 11 .... *134*
Chapter 12 .... *143*
Chapter 13 .... *159*
Chapter 14 .... *172*
Chapter 15 .... *184*
Chapter 16 .... *195*
Chapter 17 .... *207*
Chapter 18 .... *213*
Chapter 19 .... *221*
Chapter 20 .... *231*
Chapter 21 .... *244*
Chapter 22 .... *253*
Chapter 23 .... *269*
Chapter 24 .... *280*
Chapter 25 .... *293*
Chapter 26 .... *304*
Chapter 27 .... *314*
Chapter 28 .... *319*
Chapter 29 .... *325*
Chapter 30 .... *330*

Chapter 31 .... *333*
Chapter 32 .... *338*
Chapter 33 .... *345*
Chapter 34 .... *361*
Epilogue *371*

"Vanity is becoming a nuisance, I can see why women give it up, eventually. But I'm not ready for that yet."

- Margaret Atwood

Chapter 1

Beth joined the stream of mid-morning travellers as they fanned out to their various platforms as if choreographed. She imagined people might register the cut of her hair and suit, the restraint of her kitten heels, her confident step, and think she was a businesswoman going into the office a little later than usual. Some might even regard her as the sort of woman who was skilfully navigating her looks through middle age; at least they might if they took no more than a passing glance.

She stepped into the last carriage. It was almost empty. She chose a window seat. A girl was slumped diagonally opposite her. She was wearing gold studded sandals with diamanté bows, footwear that Beth thought seemed designed to attract attention, yet she had withdrawn from the world, arms crossed, white buds in her ears, her head tucked onto her chest like a sleeping bird.

As the carriage filled up, Beth became aware of a subtle change of atmosphere around her, a check in the step as people approached before moving past. Two men were standing by the door, looking down at their feet, in weary anticipation of a journey spent standing, yet the seats beside and opposite her were empty. She felt both furious and forlorn. She had never considered herself beautiful, thank God, was sorry for those women who did and were so quickly judged because of it, but the speed of her transformation from a reasonably attractive forty-four year old woman to someone who people avoided sitting beside, was bewildering.

She had been given a diagnosis. Bell's Palsy. A paralysis of the facial nerve probably triggered by the virus that had kept her off work for the past week. Bell's Palsy. She had tried to say it out loud but her lips and tongue had thickened around the 'b' and 'p'. She wondered if Mr Bell had taken any cruel pleasure in seeing those afflicted with his disease struggle so much to pronounce it. There was no cure. Doctor Rorke said most cases of Bell's Palsy get better on their own. It was likely to be temporary, she said, offering the prognosis like a gift.

She caught sight of the twisted side of her face in the window. *LIKELY TO BE TEMPORARY*, she repeated to herself, taunting her reflection, but it stared back at her, indifferent. She was unhappily drawn to the numb cheek, poking, prodding, bullying it to return to its familiar self. It was a compulsive preoccupation, in the same way your tongue can exhaust itself exploring a hole in a tooth.

She had called Ainslie as soon as she had left the surgery and told him she would be in later that morning. 'It would take more than a bout of flu and a frozen cheek to keep me away.' She used a tone of voice that she had perfected over the years, one that extracted the drama out of things.

She thought about the day ahead; a short meeting

with Ainslie to debrief the week she'd been off; the afternoon chairing the judging panel of the Young Entrepreneur Competition; and later in the evening, working on a bid proposal for Rubikon's Research and Development Centre. Going through the day's routine felt as comforting as counting money.

The train was about to leave when a woman and a child bundled their way towards her. Beth estimated the girl to be about four or five but was so overweight she could pass for a child much older. Her cheeks ballooned, squashing her features into a permanently cross expression; a perfect rosebud mouth sucked on a lollipop, her lips moving in and out as rhythmically as an anemone. Her mother was an adult-sized version of the same physiognomy and was struggling to put a buggy in the overhead rack, her jumper rucking up exposing lardy flesh. Beth thought that the child would be better off if she did more walking, but could see she needed to intervene if they were ever going to sit down and settle. "Can I help you with that?" she offered, getting up.

"No thanks," replied the mother brusquely. "Sit down, Ailsa," she commanded. The girl sat in the seat next to Beth; she had taken the lollipop out of her mouth and was staring, her lips making a perfect 'O', the inside of her mouth scarlet as if inflamed.

"Ailsa. It's not nice to stare," said the woman loudly. Beth knew this was intended to amplify her rudeness whilst appearing to excuse it. The mother sat opposite and glowered as if Beth had no right to be in a public place, then jabbed the sleeping girl beside her awake. "D'you mind if my wee girl changes seats with you?" The girl rumbled from sleep, got up, and moved without demur.

Mother and daughter were now sitting side by side, across from her, appraising Beth with hostility. The mother eventually looked away, rummaged in her bag for a magazine and retreated into it. The girl however, continued to stare as if time was suspended. Beth leaned forwards, stuck out her tongue and fluttered the tip at her. The girl let out a scream, tugged at her mother's sleeve and began to cry. Beth gazed out of the window, the outer suburbs of Edinburgh flying past her, and felt oddly lifted by the exchange.

***

The office was a ten-minute walk from Queens Street Station but she had only gone a hundred yards when a gathering of clouds rolled in from the Clyde, obliterating the sun as instantly as a light switch. Her left eye began to weep as the gusty spring wind picked up. She dabbed it with her hanky. What a bloody nuisance. She felt the first spots of rain and slipped into a doorway, hunkered down, emptying the contents of her bag onto the ground: makeup bag, paper hankies, mobile phone, straws, wallet, eye drops, co-codamol and prednisone tablets. No umbrella.

She felt as if she had been hit by a terrible blow; her head slumped in her hands and she thought with astonishment that she might cry. She stood up before that impulse had time to settle. The steady drizzle had gathered momentum and raindrops dripped off the door mantel as solid as glass beads. The minutes slid by, the rain relentless; she felt caught in an unfamiliar grip of indecision, an unpleasant and pointless dithering.

A sound behind her roused her. She turned but the doorway was five metres deep and she could see nothing in the darkness, then a shuffling noise or shallow breathing. Something or someone was behind her. Adrenalin zipped through her, her eyes instantly adjusting to the gloom. A figure was emerging from a pile of clothing; glints of silver became the outline of a shopping trolley. The person was folding up cardboard and then placing bedding on top, as gently as laying a coverlet over a baby. Two black bin bags billowed out in the small space, before being flipped over the trolley and tied shut in one practised movement. Beth felt she was trespassing on some intimate ritual.

At first she thought it was a child but as the figure came towards her she could see it was a girl, her skin as pale as wax and on her neck was a black tattoo, shaped like a large lozenge, looking like a hellish hole in her gullet. An oversized coat, dark wool and matted, sat on her skinny shoulders. She began to thread her arms through the sleeves and the tattoo on her neck expanded and contracted with her movements like a black mouth. Early twenties, thought Beth, probably a user or a runaway, though she thought she hadn't been on the streets for long; there was a faint smell of soap, mixed with damp cardboard coming from her.

"I'm involved with a charity for homeless women. They could help you," said Beth.

The girl stared at her, her face alive with incredulity. "Fuck off you silly cow," she said and squeezed past her, diving into the rain, head down, trolley barging into a thickening flow of pedestrians. Beth was momentarily stunned by her rudeness and the speed of her escape. The pavements were slick, treacherous, but she didn't hesitate to run out after her. By the time Beth caught up with her, she was soaked, her hair plastered to her face.

She caught the sleeve of her coat and the girl turned, shaking her off. "I said fuck off!" she shouted. The dark stain of the neck tattoo seemed blacker, more ominous in the daylight. They stood facing each other in the drumming rain. *She's right*, thought Beth. *She doesn't need help, any more than I do*, but there was something about her that made her reluctant to let her go. Beth pulled a note from her wallet. A twenty. More than she intended but she threw it on top of her trolley. "Now you can fuck off!" she said. The girl took the money without speaking and pushed roughly past her. Beth watched as she navigated the trolley through the crowded pavement as skilfully as a fighter pilot dodging enemy fire.

She tightened the belt on her trench coat; her shoulders damp, her hair dripping. A taxi with a yellow light came towards her and she held out her arm to hail it. She was already late for the meeting with Ainslie.

"More money than bloody sense," and she turned to see a middle aged man approaching her. "It wouldna be so bad if it was coming from your own pocket but it's coming from mine."

The taxi was slowing down in front of her. She was baffled by what the man was talking about. He was alongside her now and shoved a newspaper in her face. "Giving money to street scum. I've taken a photo of you and that girl on my phone so you canna deny it."

His face was fizzing with hostility. The photograph was mesmerising. Taken three months ago when she was first appointed as Chief Executive. "And you can fuck off too!" she shouted, opening the cab door and sliding inside the back seat before he realised he had been insulted and had lost his paper.

"The Agency, Waterloo Street," she said to the driver. She wanted to disappear into the warm fug of the taxi, but only for a moment. The paper demanded to be read. Things must be faced.

She read the headline again: 'Beth Colquhoun, newly appointed boss of The Agency earns more than the Prime Minister'. She scanned the article. She was pleased they had got her salary right. £185,000. It went on to complain about recent pay freezes for nurses, teachers and firemen, real people doing real work, not overpaid bureaucrats, unaccountable for nothing and to no one. She looked again at her face in the photo, seeing the bright confidence of a woman in her prime, her mouth sculpted by lipstick, the snaggletooth of her right incisor and a small scar on her lip, the only blemishes. She folded the damp paper and put it in her briefcase, welcoming the small ball of fury that had begun to grow inside her.

The Victorian façade of The Agency building stood impassively in the rain. She looked up and saw boxes were piled against unwashed windows. A scattering of cigarette butts like putrid confetti littered the pavement outside of the main entrance. She had only been away a week and already standards had slipped. She swiped her name badge and the glass doors slid apart, her heels clacking on the marble tiles of the reception. The interior was glass, steel, and purple Perspex; she thought the fittings looked flimsy and transient, no match against the solidness of the stone exterior and the weight of its history.

Flora, her assistant, was sitting at the reception desk, preoccupied with her phone. She dropped her briefcase on the counter. Flora looked up, startled. "Beth! You gave me a fright..." and on seeing her face, her eyes widened. "I mean... Sorry Beth... God you look... my auntie looked like that after her stroke too," her stare a mixture of boldness and malice.

"I'm sorry to hear that. Luckily for me, this is only going to be temporary," said Beth with a cheerful authority intended to signal the conversation about her health was over.

Flora was undeterred. "I was told you'd be off work for ages," she said.

Beth registered the note of disappointment. "I wouldn't want to miss the young entrepreneur of the year competition. It's one of The Agency's highlights isn't it?"

"Yes, it's a big day. We must all look our best," said Flora.

"Indeed we must," replied Beth, effortlessly allowing the barb to slide off her.

She could see Flora had her 'important visitors' face on; a slavering of foundation applied so thickly that an eruption of spots on her chin looked like blistered paint. Her hair hung around her shoulders, framing her face in a thick fringe; her eyelashes were heavy with mascara. "So let's get rid of the cigarette butts out the front shall we?" said Beth, inclining her head towards the door.

Flora blinked like a malevolent doll. "Don't blame me. It was the trade delegation from Latvia. I wanted to tell them smoking at the front door was against the new rules but Desmond Davies said it would be culturally insensitive. Culturally insensitive. Those were his very words."

The mention of Desmond Davies ruffled her to irritation. "Get it cleaned up before the contestants arrive," she said pleasantly.

"OK," said Flora. Beth smiled, which she suspected came out as a grimace and stepped past her towards the lift. She got out at the fifth floor and looked down the glass atrium. She could see the corner of the reception area where Flora sat. Her head was bent. She hadn't moved.

"Beth!" exclaimed Ainslie in his silky voice. "Great to have you back." He was walking towards her holding out his hand. She shook it. It was a little too warm, a little too moist. He made no effort hide his shock.

"It looks worse than it is. I've been told the paralysis will be gone by the end of the week. I'm fine," she said. Desmond Davies was already in her office, making himself at home.

"Of course you are," said Ainslie, allowing her to go in ahead of him.

"There's a couple of things that came in when you were off that we need to talk about and agree an approach," said Ainslie in his 'let's pretend everything is normal' voice.

Desmond was looking at her, helplessly fascinated. His tiny frame, emaciated from exercise and macrobiotic food, was getting smaller; she thought he was shrinking into himself, diminished by his failed ambition. She stared back at him; pink patches of embarrassment had begun to form at his jawline and he looked away. She felt both victorious and defeated. She would need to think of better ways to deal with people's curiosity than staring them into submission. "OK. Let's make it short then," she said, "the contestants are due in at one." She leant her left cheek against her palm and hoped it had lifted enough to match the other side.

"Have you seen this?" asked Desmond, handing her a copy of the newspaper. Beth retrieved her own copy and laid it alongside his. Hers was damp and tatty, Desmond's pristine. *It could be a metaphor for the differences in their physical appearance*, she thought.

"On the plus side, it gives us a good opportunity to tell our side of the story. Beth has reduced management numbers by 40 percent and made £1.5 million in savings," said Ainslie. She thought Ainslie's collar was tight, his suit jacket pulled around the buttons and she wondered if he might be overdoing the late night dinners and whisky drinking at the golf club.

"My journalist contact tells me this is only the start of a Beth Colquhoun backlash. They're going to bring up your non-exec position at Rubikon next," said Desmond. Beth could see his skin was shiny from the Vaseline he smeared over his face each morning before cycling to work; it made his pallid face look like a polished corpse. "Rubikon paid you £50,000 in the first three months of this year as a non-exec director. It makes you, us, The Agency, vulnerable to all sorts of suggestions, conflicts of interest, too little time on the job, that sort of thing," he added. Spittle had gathered at both edges of his mouth. He could barely hide his enthusiasm for this, thought Beth. She gave him a scornful look, but he didn't seem to register it. Then she realised he was looking at the paralysed side of her face and was mirroring that lack of life in his own expression.

"Remind who this Rubikon lot are?" asked Ainslie.

"One of the biggest life science companies in Asia. They manufacture compounds for drugs, food additives, agricultural foodstuffs," replied Desmond.

"They made a nine billion dollar profit last year and want to build a new Research & Development centre," said Beth. "I've been a non-exec director with them since 2007 when I was Industry Attaché in Singapore. I intend to use every bit of influence I have to persuade them to build that centre here in Scotland. It would mean thousands of jobs and millions of pounds flowing into the economy. I don't think I need to be apologetic about that."

Desmond was shaking his head. "We've seen it all before. Twenty-five years ago we invested the entire Agency budget in attracting multinational electronic companies to Scotland. We even called ourselves Silicon Glen. How many are left today? None. How many jobs? None. We need to focus on local people, growing local businesses."

"Like this Young Entrepreneur Competition," chipped in Ainslie. "Desmond has worked very hard on it. Each year it's getting bigger. We're thinking of approaching STV to televise it next year. It would be like a cross between *Dragons Den* and *The Apprentice*."

"Good idea but how are you promoting it this year?"

"It's mentioned on the website," replied Desmond.

Beth snorted. "The website looks like it hasn't been updated in years. Our hit rate is abysmal. What about Facebook? Twitter? YouTube? Social media will help raise our profile and give us a way to connect with the people of Scotland in a dynamic, powerful way." Desmond looked as if she had hit him with her wet newspaper.

"You're right of course," soothed Ainslie, "and I'm sure you'll get all these new things up and running in due course."

"For your information," said Desmond, "this competition is very high profile. There will be a big spread in the newspapers tomorrow. People will see how effective The Agency is in developing new businesses."

"Honestly," said Beth, rolling her eyes, "you think this competition will regenerate the Scottish economy? Six kids with a projection of what? Twenty grand profit each?"

"It's like planting seeds. We need to nurture and see them grow. Any one of these young people could be the next Mark Zuckerman," said Desmond.

Beth could hear his voice straining to keep control, red blotches around his jaw were spreading to his neck. "Zuckerberg," she corrected. "The problem is we don't have time to wait for seeds to grow. Read the paper. People are fed up with public money being spent on a bunch of bureaucrats with nothing to show. They want results. I want results. Now." Desmond's expression was venomous.

"OK, OK," said Ainslie, "you're both right. We must have organic growth in addition as large scale inward investment."

Ainslie was like an emulsifier, thought Beth, able to mix things together that wouldn't mix without him. Desmond was collecting his papers, short movements betraying his pique. "So can we agree that Beth keeps a low profile on the Rubikon work, at least until they've made their interest in Scotland official?" asked Desmond. His voice had resumed its usual mixture of confidence and self-importance, his complexion returned to its pale composure.

Beth suddenly felt tired, her tongue was like a wad of stuffing in her mouth. "Fine," she mumbled as she watched Desmond walk away in that tidy measured step of his.

Ainslie was looking at her kindly. "Be careful Beth, he would make an awkward enemy."

"You didn't hire me to be careful, Ainslie. If you remember you said radical change was needed." A cup of coffee had materialised; she longed to drink it but would need to get a straw from her handbag and was at a loss to know how to do this without evoking his pity.

Ainslie was looking at her closely, his expression concerned. "You've been working day and night since you got here. I think you should take it easier. No job is worth sacrificing your health for."

How dare he offer advice on how to live? thought Beth. *A wife in the suburbs whom he hasn't touched for years; three grown up children, all living abroad who value him more as a bank than a father; and a call girl and drink habit that are slowly giving him the look of a sad old codger.* "Take it easy? Of course I will. Once we've landed the Rubikon deal," said Beth. Ainslie smiled in defeat. "But tell me honestly, Ainslie, do you believe Desmond when he says this is the start of a Beth Colquhoun backlash?"

"You've ruffled a few feathers. The whisky men didn't take kindly to your speech at their annual trade dinner," said Ainslie mildly.

"Frankly they're in denial. A Japanese whisky has been just been voted the world's best. That should be a wake-up call for us all but particularly them," answered Beth.

"Maybe, but if I've learned one thing about dealing with people it's the importance of trust. Take time to get to know the folks here, so they can get to know you in return. As Chairman of The Agency you have my full support. I'm here to cover your back. You can rely on that, you know."

She wondered why he needed to tell her that if there was any doubt. "On a happier note, here's the list of the finalists for the Young Entrepreneur Competition. Three women, three men," he said proudly.

She smiled at his clumsy attempt to change a conversation. "Thanks Ainslie. Now will you go and make yourself a nuisance elsewhere? I must look a fright. I need time and a minor miracle to get myself looking presentable."

Ainslie looked at her in a way that made her feel queasy. "Of course you do, my dear."

Chapter 2

The blades dipped in and out of the water as Dougie pulled hard to clear the shoreline. It was a glorious morning. The wind ceaseless but kind, the sun silvering the sea far out in the bay, the low tide leaving the black sand streaked with rivulets the colour of mercury. The waves were as gentle as a breath, birds pecking and dancing at the edges. A few cows from Billy's farm were grazing on the tangles of kelp that had been washed up on the beach; it would be dried out and stinking by the next high tide. He felt a swell of disappointment that Benjy was so taken with the stuff. Who would have thought his bonny boy would be a finalist in the Young Entrepreneur of the Year Competition with his plans to grow it commercially?

The breeze stiffened as he rowed further out into the bay, his hair flying across his face so that he had to stop and pull it back into a ponytail. He took a moment to watch a hooded crow flying low across the dark pebbled water before starting to row again. He reached the native oyster beds first and lifted a basket from the middle line and examined their flat smoothness. They were almost a year old and thriving, but give them another two years and they would be magnificent.

He dipped a bottle in the water and took a sample. The levels of bacteria had risen in the past week and these oysters were tender compared with the other varieties, but he enjoyed giving them the extra care, like nurturing a delicate child that had the potential to be more successful than the rest of their siblings if given the right levels of time and encouragement.

He headed out to the twenty rail rows of seeded Pacific Oysters at the furthest edge of the farm. They came as adolescents from McNair's fisheries in Portree and Dougie brought them on to maturity. He scooped up one of the mesh baskets; twenty or so elongated whorls lay at the bottom. He lifted one out, easily 60mm, and made a mental note to move them to the harvest beds to be hardened off. He shucked it open, removing the beard with his thumb and slid it down his throat. It was the taste of the sea. An evocation of all the beauty around him – sensuous, luxurious. Everything smelly seaweed was not.

He could see the office Portakabin perched on the dunes, the Cuillin hills beyond. He shut his eyes. At first you might think it was quiet but the quietness had many layers: the hum of an outboard motor in the distance, the faint squeal of the shags out on the colony, the rasp of the breeze, the soft slap of the waves against the boat. Dougie enjoyed drifting along with the tide of life, tossed by the occasional wave, needing neither rudder nor compass. It was a mystery to him why his son would want to have his hand on the tiller of life and go faster than anyone else. Dougie doubted it would make him any happier.

He must have been sitting in the boat for some

time before a faint sound of shouting reached him. He could see Sally dancing on the shore, yelling at him through cupped hands, though he couldn't make out what she was saying. He turned reluctantly to pull the rip cord, hearing the outboard splutter into life, and steeled himself for trouble.

"The car's broken down!" she shouted, her words coming out of her fast and breathy. "What'll we do?"

"The first thing we do is calm down," said Dougie, dragging the boat clear of the water but all the time thinking hard. "I'll speak to him," he said, marching up to the office and dialling his number from the landline.

"Benjy lad, what's up? The AA man's arrived? Says the car needs towing. Can only take you as far as Tyndrum? There's a train that goes to Glasgow from there. You've still got time. It's only just past eight. Call us when you get there. Good luck son," and he hung up.

"D'you think he'll make it?" asked Sally.

"I do," he replied, but Sally seemed worried. Her heavy glasses gave her the look of someone who permanently fretted, thought Dougie. She was tall and heavy boned with hands as large as his. Her face was broad with a Slavic quality that could be beautiful but she made no effort with her appearance. Her complexion had been roughened by the weather. She'd tied her dirty blonde hair back in a clasp as a careless afterthought. It was a mystery to Dougie that Benjy, who had the pick of the girls on the island, had been so determined to choose her.

"I'll put the kettle on," she said. Dougie could see

she wanted to please. Perhaps that's what Benjy liked in her.

"Where's the lab report from last Monday's sample?" he asked.

She returned with the report and a cup of tea. Dougie studied it carefully. "I think we should run an extra test for vibrio parahaemolyticus," he said, giving her a test tube of water from his pocket. "Here's a sample I took this morning. If it's still not good, we'll have to speak to Benjy about it, but not a word to anyone else meantime. Even a hint of a problem could send those foodies at the Four Sisters running for cover," he said.

Her eyes were like small marbles behind her glasses. "I suppose that's the good thing about the seaweed project isn't it? It seems easier to grow; it's gone crazy in the trial section that Benjy's set up and the Four Sisters want it just as much as the oysters," she said.

"Oysters cannot be compared with seaweed, Sally. Oysters are the jewels of the sea. Seaweed is ugly, smelly detritus. Anyhow, oysters aren't difficult to grow if you know what you're doing," he said, although he knew there was little to be done if naturally occurring bacteria got out of hand.

"But why not take the easier option if you have the choice?" she asked, and he thought she was sounding more like Benjy each day and he wasn't sure he liked it.

"I'm off to open up the shop. Young Entrepreneur Competition or not, we've got a business to run," said Dougie.

"Doesn't Fiona normally open up on Fridays?"

"Not today," replied Dougie tartly, "you'll be OK here by yourself?"

"Benjy wants me to transfer the coding data onto the new billing system. Then I've got to set up a blog so he can tell everyone about the competition."

"It's good to be busy," said Dougie.

"He's going to win, Dougie. I know it even if you don't," she said as she turned back to her desk.

***

The town was waking up as Dougie made his way down the hill, people opening up shops, sweeping down pavements. It had a beguiling sort of prettiness that was both authentic and preserved. Everybody knew they needed the visitor trade but for the next few weeks, before the season geared up properly, they could pretend tourism was just a sideline.

John appeared on the brow of the hill. That police uniform of his kept gathering new bits and pieces of equipment, thought Dougie. His walk had taken on the sway of a swagger, his waist belt weighed down with radios and transmitters.

"Benjy get off OK this morning?" he asked.

"Everything's fine," replied Dougie, thinking it best to keep the details of the car breakdown to himself. "I've left Sally in charge, best to keep her busy."

"She's just like her mum, born worriers," he replied. Not for the first time, Dougie had the impression that John was evaluating his suitability as a father-in-law to Sally; a faint curl of distaste played about his mouth as he took in the white-haired ponytail, the denim shirt, the old jeans.

"We're all very proud of Benjy, Dougie. Most youngsters want to leave the island and those that stay don't have his ambition. Without people like him Skye's in danger of turning into a tourist only zone, a Scottish Disneyland," he said.

"Aye, he's always had a mind of his own," said Dougie.

"You're being modest, man. You've been mother and father to that boy. Not many men would have sacrificed themselves in the way you have. He's a credit to you."

Dougie felt a flush of irritation. There was nothing heroic about him. When Benjy's mother, Mei, had died he had no visa or permission to stay in Thailand. Stranded in a strange country with an infant son, he had come home to Skye and accepted Uncle Danny's offer of a labouring job on the oyster farm. When Danny died and left him and Benjy the farm, he'd been as surprised as anyone how quickly Benjy had taken to it.

"You're all coming tomorrow night? For Benjy's party?" asked Dougie.

"Of course. I hope we'll be celebrating a winner as well as a birthday boy," John said, shaking Dougie's hand warmly, "and I hope you don't mind me saying but Mharie and I would be delighted if a date for the wedding was announced too."

Dougie could see his eyes lighting up with anticipation. He adjusted the waist belt on his uniform, shaking down the bits of equipment like an overweight cockerel settling his feathers. "They're young. There's no rush," said Dougie.

John flung his head back and laughed. "That's what they'll put on your gravestone, Dougie McKinnon. Here lies a man who was never in a rush."

Dougie nodded and smiled. He could think of worst things to be said about a person.

"They've been sweethearts ever since primary school. Engaged for over a year. I think they know what they want by now," added John.

Dougie shrugged. He had long given up trying to influence Benjy about any of his choices but at the same time he knew first love doesn't always last forever.

He waved John goodbye and walked on down the main street, past the general store. He stopped and stared at the headline of the newspaper. No sooner had he been thinking about first love when Beth Colquhoun's face was looking right at him. 'Newly appointed Scottish Agency boss earns more than the Prime Minister'. There was the same strong jawline, full mouth, brown eyes the colour of milk chocolate and that wonderful dark red hair now curled expensively around her shoulders. She looked older of course and was thinner, but perhaps more handsome than he remembered her.

The story he told himself was that she was an old flame long since snuffed out, yet the more he had told himself that, the more he knew it wasn't true. It had been a seismic first love with a seismic ending to match. He had kept her in his sights in the intervening years in the same way an antelope keeps an eye on a lion. It had been easy enough. She was one of the new breed of career women that was forever in the papers or on TV: first the big job in London advising Tony Blair, then in Singapore and now back in Scotland heading up The Agency.

He had thought about telling Benjy about her but decided against it. Unlike Sally he was realistic about Benjy's chances of winning. He would be up against a lot of university-educated types, and what was the point of stirring up the past if he didn't need to? He looked again at the photograph and had the impression Beth was looking beyond the camera, looking at him directly and asking, *Are you out there Dougie? Do you still think of me?* He turned away, a sense of unease settling on him like an early morning mist.

He walked up the steep hill at the back of the town and then down the short driveway to the Oyster Shack. Benjy had rented it from the owners of the distillery when they no longer needed it for storing barley. He had transformed it into what he called a destination shop. They had started by selling their own oysters and locally farmed mussels and salmon. Now they had expanded into game, wet fish, and delicatessen.

In the spring sunshine, Dougie could see the outside needed a fresh coat of paint. Benjy might call it shabby chic but to Dougie it was plain scruffy after a hard winter. In a rush of enthusiasm he wondered if he might make a start on it today, but almost as quickly as he thought it, the notion disappeared.

He moved round to the back of the shed in the lea of the hill. Fiona was leaning against the wall, looking out towards the bay. She was wearing her favourite cardigan, the length of a coat, full of bobbles and snags. She had pulled it tight around her, outlining the generous curve of her shoulders and hips; the heels of her boots were worn down at the sides. She turned to face him. "Benjy get up in time this morning?" she asked.

The whole world is worried about Benjy, he thought. "I didn't expect you to be here," he said, taking in her round face, doughy from lack of sleep, her eyes pink from crying. He felt a familiar tug of pity and something else. Not love anymore, but a deep sense of care.

"Look Dougie, about last night," she began. He had a sudden dread that it would start up again, the tears, the pleading, the despair.

He interrupted, "I've been trying to tell you for months we need a break from each other."

"We're good together. We can work this out," she said.

Dougie felt stricken. He couldn't think of what to say.

"OK, I agree we take a wee breather but that doesn't mean I can't work in the shop. If Benjy wins that competition you'll be busier than ever. You'll be needing the help," she said.

Some instinct told him this was a bad idea but he felt heartened by her offer, it seemed like an improvement on the tearful lashings of last night. "It's good of you to think about us," he said. Tears had begun to swim in her eyes. She hugged him hard. He smelt her familiar smell, a mix of lavender and musk; her body soft and generous; but he no longer responded to it. He knew, in that moment, that however much he cared for her, she would always love him more.

He broke off as gently as he could and walked towards the shop, unlocking the padlock. The metal grill zipped upwards, clattering. A smell of malted barley exhaled from the walls. He watched Fiona busying herself in the ritual of opening up; taking out the polystyrene boxes from the fridge and placing them in the cooler display, arranging the jars on the shelf at the back of the counter. He thought he could see her prettiness beginning to bloat into middle age; how quickly that can happen to a woman and how unfair.

"Benjy's asked me to sing a few numbers at the party tomorrow. You don't mind?" she asked. He thought then there was a certain female quality in her courage that was characterised by enduring pain, of making the best of out of things. He admired it and at the same time resented it. It would be easier to let go of a lesser person.

"I don't mind," he said.

"Has he asked you to play?" she asked.

"No doubt I could be persuaded to get the fiddle out if I'm pestered enough," he said. Fiona smiled. He could feel its warmth trying to reach out to him.

The phone rang and she quickly answered it. "Benjy. For you."

Dougie took the phone and bowed his head as he listened. "OK," he said, replacing the receiver in its cradle.

"What did he say?" asked Fiona.

"His phone's nearly out of battery. He wants me to call The Agency to tell them he's going to be late."

"Late?"

"Aye, it's a miracle he's getting there in the first place. The car broke down over an hour ago."

Dougie walked to the front of the shop, slotting the cash register tray into its place. He could feel disapproval radiating out from Fiona.

"What are you waiting for?" she demanded.

"What's the point in calling? If he gets there, he'll be able to talk himself into a chance to present and if he doesn't get there, he doesn't get there." Dougie could feel the atmosphere between them cooling.

"If I didn't know better, Dougie McKinnon, I would think you didn't want him to get there, didn't want him to win. That you might be a bit jealous of him, threatened by his new ideas," she said.

He had long learned that the best way to deal with storm was to let it rage until it blew itself out. He watched as Fiona marched into the back office, pulled down the telephone directory and leaf through the pages. She began to dial a number. "OK. OK," he said, taking the receiver from her.

He was surprised when the phone was answered right away. He explained who he was and what had happened to Benjy. Next, a young woman came on. He repeated the story and was put on hold again. There was no music, just the crackle of a waiting line and the sound of his heart in his chest. Perhaps the next voice would be Beth's, that husky voice with an edge of warmth and brittleness. He felt a moment of dismay. He hadn't prepared himself and didn't know what he would say to her, but just as he decided to hang up, he heard the receiver being picked up. It was the same girl again.

"Dr Colquhoun says we can wait till 2.45pm. I'm afraid if he's going to be later than that, he won't be able to present," she said.

"That's very good of you," said Dougie.

Fiona had folded her arms across her chest and was looking smug.

"Happy now?" he asked, his tone harsh. Her arms dropped by her side, her eyes widened in hurt and he wondered, not for the first time, if sometimes he wasn't a very nice man.

Chapter 3

Excitement floated upwards from the central atrium. From above, Beth could see the competitors and staff from The Agency milling around below like a shoal of happy fish, darting and flashing from one corner of the room to the other. She wanted to shout down to them, to tell them to enjoy every second of this feeling of happiness because, in her experience it will never be equaled. Problems and self-doubt would make their appearance soon enough; even the winner would find that the aftermath of victory fraught with difficulties. The sad truth, she realised, is that only in the anticipation of happiness is there pure happiness.

She could see Flora moving between the contestants, her head bobbing, the sweep of hair about her shoulders. Desmond was shaking hands and weaselling his way around like an eager schoolboy. Neil Phillips had also turned up, corralled in a corner by three young women. She was pleased he had agreed to be one of the judges; his economics programme on Sunday morning TV as well as his work at the university added to his kudos. Their night out together two weeks ago might also have helped with his diary management. A photographer was marshalling them all into a picture. Flora was persuaded to join them. It didn't take much.

Beth smoothed down her skirt and picked off a hair from the sleeve of her jacket. She had recovered her poise from the bedraggled woman who had walked in a couple of hours earlier. She had even convinced herself that her fallen face could add to her gravitas as long as she avoided excessive smiling. She had prepared some strategies for the stares and had rehearsed a couple of rejoinders intended to reassure concern and satisfy curiosity. No, it doesn't hurt much, likely to be temporary, an unfortunate result of a viral infection, that sort of thing.

Neil and Desmond were deep in conspiratorial conversation when she made her appearance. Neil stepped forward to shake her hand, dry, firm. His eyes crinkled in a kindly way; his sandy hair, cut short, stood up in tufty clumps. He was looking at her steadily, his worry unmasked. "Do you mind if I ask…" he started.

"Of course not. I had a touch of flu last week. Was feeling much better. Then I woke up yesterday to find half of my face was paralysed. A neurologist in Edinburgh told me it's a reaction to a virus and likely to be temporary," she said, maintaining eye contact.

She saw him relax, taken in by her confidence and said in that melodious voice that was so popular with his female fans, "I'm so glad."

"I'm looking forward to this, aren't you?" she asked, and realised as she said it that it was true.

Walking into the melee of young people was as exhilarating as running into surf. She made a point of repeating each of their names, giving her attention in intense flattering bursts. There was something unexpected and wonderful about their apparent lack of interest in her physical appearance. They were all too taken up with themselves to care about anyone else.

"One last photo before we all go in," shouted the photographer as he chivvied them into position; he placed Beth in the front row, centre.

"Smile," he said. Beth stared ahead, straight-faced.

"Good morning ladies and gentlemen," she announced as they all settled in the boardroom. "It's an honour as chief executive of The Agency to welcome you to the final of our Young Entrepreneur of the Year competition. On behalf of the judging panel, Dr Neil Phillips, Economics Professor at Glasgow University, and Desmond Davies our Chief Financial Officer, we welcome you. We started with over 1,000 entries and after many months of careful selection, it is you who have been selected by your local chambers of commerce as being the best of the best."

The 'b's came out better than she had hoped; she dabbed the side of her eye, still dry. "You are the future of Scotland's economic vibrancy." She paused, vibrancy was a step too far, her tongue had come to a standstill; she could see a couple of puzzled looks. She took a breath to calm herself. "Mr Davies will take us through the logistics."

She pretended to give Desmond her full attention as he went through the process – the strict time limit of fifteen minutes per pitch with five minutes Question and Answer. He emphasised they would be judged purely on the impact on their presentation today. The winner would receive £25,000 and the resources of the marketing and financial planning team at The Agency.

A frisson of nervous energy bolted through the crowd; they glanced at each other for reassurance and the tension intensified. He finished by explaining that after the winner was announced, there would be drinks and a light buffet. "Although there will be a winner," he said, pausing for dramatic effect, "you should all regard yourselves as winners today."

Beth felt mildly nauseated by this clichéd claptrap. There is only one winner. Fact. They will get £25,000. Fact. The rest will get nothing. Fact. She thought if she had been speaking she would have been clear about that. Desmond put all six names of the contestants in a box and asked Neil to draw the first name. Neil attempted to lighten the mood by a joke about a raffle and valuable prizes.

"Benjy McKinnon!" he announced triumphantly. She looked towards the two young men suited, shaven and scrubbed.

"He's no' here," said one of them.

"The rules are clear," said Desmond, "no show, no go." Beth thought he was pleased with his fatuous rhyme.

Neil predictably was taking the softer line. "Surely we can wait, let one of the others go in his place?"

McKinnon; she felt a jag of memory but discounted it quickly. McKinnon was a common name.

Desmond shifted uncomfortably in his seat. "Your call Beth," he said under his breath. *He thinks he's deferring to my authority*, thought Beth, but she knew it was his way of avoiding a decision that he may want to question at a later date. "Choose someone else, we'll wait," she said quietly, and Neil retrieved another name from the box.

The heat in the room became stultifying as the afternoon progressed. Beth struggled to keep her attention as the disappointing predictability of the presentations made their weary progress. *There must be a template on the internet*, she thought; one that homogenised their approach into mediocrity. Background, main goals of the project, projected revenue, ROI bottom line impact. Conclusion was a repeat of the main objectives. Very tidy and not remotely how business works.

The voices of the presenters had taken on a mixture of breathy nervousness and dull monotone as if the darkened room and brightly coloured graphs had given them the comfort of anonymity. Her head had begun to feel tenderised as if she hasn't slept for days, the tingling in her face was like barbed wire being lightly dragged across her skin. She hoped the pain was a sign that the feeling in her face was returning to normal, like the pins and needles you get when an arm or leg recovers from numbness.

Flora appeared at the door, gesturing to attract her attention and she beckoned her in. At the sight of Flora sneaking into the room, the young man in mid presentation stumbled on his words. Flora whispered in her ear, "Benjy McKinnon's father is on the phone. The car's broken down. He's asking if we'll wait for him."

"Tell him we'll give him the last slot at 2.45pm. We can't wait any longer than that," replied Beth. Flora scurried out. "Apologies for that," she said to the young man, shadowed behind the beam of light from the projector, "we'll add on a couple of minutes to your time." He gulped and tried to regroup but it was hopeless, thought Beth. It was hopeless before the interruption. McKinnon. It was a common name.

When all five of the competitors had finished, Desmond announced a short break. Impatience began to seep into the room and although the competitors were the model of politeness, Beth knew that what began as sympathy towards Benjy McKinnon had become an unspoken unfairness about having to wait. It was 2.40pm. He had five minutes max.

Her face pain was becoming more of a distraction. Foolish of her to think she could manage without taking painkillers. She excused herself to go the ladies'. The mirror stretched the length of the room. She leaned into it. Her left eye stared back, unblinking, the colour of raw meat. It looked worse than this morning. A lot worse. She tilted her head back and squeezed some eye drops into it but with no blink mechanism most of it dribbled down her face.

She heard the muffled chatter of girls outside the door and slipped the eye drops into her bag. Two of the competitors came in, exchanging shy glances with her. She watched as one wetted her finger and stroked her eyebrow, outlining the perfect curve of her eye socket. The other had produced a small tub of lip salve and was applying gloss to her lips; how beautiful their flawless complexions, thought Beth, and how careless their awareness of it.

She retreated into one of the cubicles before the comparison between them had time to ferment into bitterness. The other two cubicle doors closely quickly afterwards. *Bang. Bang.* She sat there holding her breath, feeling as guilty as if she was doing something illegal. Silence hung in the air, as if they were all too embarrassed to make a sound. Beth flushed the toilet and swallowed two painkillers. They slipped down her throat without water.

"Beth! Are you in here? Benjy McKinnon's arrived!" Flora's voice was at full volume. Beth felt both caught out and found as she leant her lifeless cheek against the stainless steel of the cubicle door. "OK!" she shouted back as the sound of the flush subsided.

She walked towards the boardroom feeling like she had begun to hover above the ground. Desmond was shouting at a knot of people who had gathered in the corridor outside the boardroom. "Come in! Come in!" he cajoled, but there was a bottleneck where a tall young man stood, greeting people as if he was the host of a party.

"Hiya. I'm Benjy McKinnon," she heard him announce. "Sorry for being late." But there was no regret in his voice or manner. She took a moment to observe him. Tall, as graceful as a cat with a tousle of black hair, a shadow of fuzz on his top lip, his eyes the colour of nutmeg, almond shaped and unmistakeably Asian. He had pushed the sleeves of his suit jacket above his elbows and she saw his veins standing proud of his dark, creamy skin as he offered his hand to her. "Dr Colquhoun, I've been looking forward to meeting you," he said with a confidence that could either be arrogance or nerves.

She felt momentarily disoriented and it took her a

second to realise that, although she had dismissed the notion that Benjy McKinnon might be Dougie's son, she was disappointed this boy looked nothing like Dougie. Apart from his height there was no resemblance whatsoever. "You very nearly didn't meet me," she said more sharply than she intended.

"Yeah. A nightmare start but thanks for waiting," he said, apparently immune to her frosty tone.

Neil Phillips was at his shoulder. "D'you need a few minutes to settle yourself Benjy?"

"Nah, though a coffee would be nice," he said, looking at Flora, who slipped away to minister to the latecomer with an enthusiasm that Beth had never been able to command in the girl herself.

"Right," said Desmond, "let's get re-started!" and the room settled into an expectant hush. Benjy buried his head under the table, connecting his laptop to the projector. Beth felt her disappointment compounded. More charts, more graphs that point unerringly upwards.

Benjy's first slide was a picture of an industrial building in flames. There was a startle of interest from the audience as they took in the blurry image of twisted girders, aluminium foil flapping in the wind, a plume of black smoke billowing upwards and outwards at an unnatural horizontal angle.

Benjy's soft accent provided a quiet commentary: "March 2011, Reactor number 4 in Fukushima sustained massive damage following the tsunami. Unlike Chernobyl, much of the nuclear waste went directly into the sea or was channelled into the sea via the river that runs underground the length of the reactor. Since 2011, the area has been hit by several more earthquakes, further destabilising the site. Unconfirmed reports say that there are now three melted cores. As recently as this year, the beleaguered operator of the plant, TEPCO, admitted that leakage into the sea has continued ever since the initial explosions."

He then cut to a picture of a loch surrounded by castellated mountains, a cobalt sky, and summer clouds. A jolt of recognition hit Beth, both painful and delightful.

"This is Loch Coruisk on the Isle of Skye. If you look closely you can see the submerged crates in the far right hand corner where my Great Uncle Danny started an oyster farm over 50 years ago."

There was a collective moving forward as the group peered closely at the picture. Beth was both frozen to the spot and acutely awake. Dougie had been born in Skye but she had no memory of an Uncle Danny or an oyster farm. Her mind clicked frantically. Dougie spent some years in Asia after they split up. Benjy's mother could have been someone that he met there? Or maybe adopted as a baby there? Benjy was showing the next photo of the shell of the nuclear power station and the Skye picture together. "So ladies and gentlemen," he said, his voice even softer, "out of disaster comes opportunity."

"You've lost me there," said one of the boys.

"The thing that connects the two my friend is this: *Porphyra haitanensis*," he said, showing a picture of a stringy line of red kelp. The air of mystification deepened but he said nothing for several seconds, an absurd extravagance in a fifteen-minute pitch, thought Beth, though she could see the audience were gripped.

"The global market for seaweed is 14.7 billion tonnes and growing. It's as important to the Japanese as porridge oats is to us yet the people of Japan are distrustful of their atomic scientists who claim their seas are not contaminated. They are looking for safe places to grow their seaweed and Loch Coruisk is a very safe place."

"What return could you expect from an initial investment of £25,000 if you win the prize today?" asked Desmond. "Your presentation has been short of numbers so far," he said, sounding both encouraging and critical.

"How long is a piece of string, Mr Davies? Or should I say, how long is a piece of kelp?" That brought a chuckle of laughter from one or two of the competitors and Beth found herself joining in, enjoying the feel of Desmond's disapproving look. "The global market for edible seaweed is worth over two billion US dollars per year. They estimate that it will take twenty years for the Fukushima Reactor to be safe and for the water to be clear of contamination. That gives us time to get a piece of the action."

"Mr McKinnon," interjected Neil Phillips, "are you familiar with the work of Kathleen Drew Baker in this field?" Benjy shook his head, his tousle of hair, blue black, catching light of the room. "She was a remarkable British scientist whose discovery about the life cycle of seaweed in the 1940s helped greatly to increase production in Japan. But the point of my question is, do you understand anything about the production methods required to produce seaweed in commercial quantities?" asked Neil.

Typical of a polymath, thought Beth, genetically programmed to show off how much he knows about the most obscure subjects. She had a brief moment of regret about allowing their date the other week to go further than planned.

"I've been experimenting with the cultivation of natural spores in the loch to spawn the plants on ropes but that's only ever going to be enough to supply the likes of local restaurants. I now need to scale production using techniques like freezing and fixed nets. I don't know how to do that but I'm a fast learner, with a feel for the sea and a love of its creatures. That's a good start I reckon," he said.

"A start, yes, but frankly," began Desmond before Beth cut him off.

"Benjy, what vision do you have for this business – say in the next five years?"

He thought for a moment. "There's no reason why I couldn't make it big. In the same way the Japanese have been successful in whisky, we Scots could be just as successful in seaweed."

"But how do you intend to break into the Asian market, Benjy? Traditionally that's been difficult if not impossible for non-Asian companies," asked Desmond, irritated at Beth's interruption.

Benjy seemed momentarily taken aback. "I was hoping you'd help me. Dr Colquhoun was the Industry Attaché for the British Government in Singapore for the past five years wasn't she? I reckon you must have quite a few contacts?" He was looking at Beth now. She had his full attention. There was nothing in his face that reminded her of Dougie. Not a facial tic; not his colouring; not his confident way of speaking. And yet. And yet.

"Ah, maybe not then," he said, misreading her silence. "I've had an email from a Mr Takashama who's interested. It would be a shame if he backed me, not The Agency."

He bit his lip. Beth wondered if he thought he had gone too far, though Desmond appeared not to have heard and was peering into his smart phone.

"Thank you Mr McKinnon, your time is up."

The boardroom table was littered with spent coffee cups and half-drunk glasses of water. A drift of pencils had found their way into the middle of the table. Neil was leaning back in his chair, sucking the end of a pen. He looked up in mild interest as Desmond announced, "Rachel Cunningham's software project is the obvious winner. Impressive girl, impressive plan." Beth could see both of them thinking that wasn't all that was impressive about her.

"I liked the seaweed lad," said Neil.

"So can we agree it's down to those two?" said Beth. Fingers of exhaustion had begun to grip her skull; the painkillers had worn off, her eye was blazing. She had a sudden need for the thing to be over.

"He had ideas and energy but no business plan," said Desmond. She was astonished. It was hard to believe that anyone with a business brain would be taken in by the formulaic bar charts and projections of the other contestants.

"His proposal was the only one to come from the Islands. We need new industries if these parts of the country are to thrive. We've plenty of people who can help him with the business plan. That's the easy part. The passion and commitment, that's something different," argued Neil.

They both looked at her now. Her mind had stuck in a groove that was repeating in her head. Was this Dougie's son or wasn't it? She had no evidence connecting him with Dougie yet she couldn't let go of the possibility. And even if he was? Should she say something? Admit a possible connection? And what would that connection be? Her first love? With a man she hasn't seen for over twenty years? Did that even count as a connection?

"I agree they are both worthy winners," she said carefully. Desmond seemed pleased, thought Beth. *He's probably thinking I'll vote for the woman.* "A difficult decision but on balance my vote is for Rachel. A positive role model for women, a good contributor to the growing IT industry in Dundee, a well thought out plan," she concluded.

"Excellent!" said Desmond, animated in a way that exaggerated his rodent features.

"Can we at least give Benjy McKinnon a special mention? A runner-up prize perhaps? Some help with a business plan?" asked Neil.

"There's only one winner Neil, I'm sorry," she said. He gave her that look that was familiar, a look that if translated would say 'you're a hard woman'; a look he would never give a man. She wanted to add that there were other grants Benjy could apply for but she needed to ration her speech, her lips and tongue were aching from the effort of talking.

"I'll tell the caterers to clear up this mess and get the room ready for the announcement and the drinks and nibbles," said Desmond. He was as happy as if he was arranging a party for his own daughter.

***

"Dr Colquhoun," one of the girls began, her voice so earnest it had become a whine, "if you could give me some feedback as to why I didn't win. Some advice I could learn from?" The girl was looking at her expectantly. "Dr Colquhoun?" she repeated.

Beth saw the girl's downy skin, her mouth like bruised fruit and felt a pulse of envy. *Who cares about any of this when you are blessed with youth and perfect skin?* she thought. "Competitions are subjective. You must learn to be resilient. Keep trying," she said.

The girl was about to burst into tears but remembered her manners and whispered, "Thank you."

She watched her head towards Neil. *She'll get more sympathy there; more salve; more nonsense that there was a silver bullet in business.* Her eye was watering freely now, her hanky permanently scrunched in her hand. The dabbing and the wiping were becoming so automatic she wondered if they would become established tics like Desmond's clearing of his throat, or the way that Neil loosened his shirt collar as if the room was too warm.

"Hello." She turned to face Benjy. She looked into his dark honey-coloured eyes and was at a loss to know what to say. But there was no need, he had already begun talking.

"I'm gutted about losing. Tomorrow's my birthday. I've arranged a party at the local hotel but the only thing I cared about celebrating was winning this. I didn't hear the winner's presentation. She must have smashed it to beat me." There it was again, that mixture of small boy vulnerability and adolescent overconfidence.

"At least you've Mr Takashama to fall back on," she replied. Her tongue now felt like it had filled the left side of her mouth and was sticking to her gums and teeth.

"I didn't make that up. I did get an email from him," he said, "although I hoped it would be you that would help me break into Asia. I keep reading in the papers about the importance you attach to business to think globally." His expression was a mixture of defiance and curiosity. She wondered if he had read today's papers and was about to challenge her about her salary too.

"Your parents must be very proud of you," she said quietly. He seemed wary, as if trying to work out what her interest in his family might be, then just as quickly his demeanour cleared as if deciding that this was the sort of thing people of her generation ask people of his generation.

"Aye, though my dad thinks seaweed is smelly, mucky stuff."

"So what will happen to the oyster farm if you diversify into seaweed?" she asked.

"There's Dad and Sally," he replied. "They're more than capable."

Sally. A wife. Of course.

"He's a bit of a romantic, my dad, keen to keep up the family tradition rather than trying anything new," he said, and in that moment she knew with absolute certainty that this tall Asian boy was Dougie's son. She would go home and check it online but it was a foregone conclusion. She had found Dougie without looking for him.

"Well done Benjy! I'll make no secret of the fact that for me, you were the winner today," said Neil jovially, pushing into the conversation.

"Not everyone agreed with you, Dr Phillips," he said. Beth raised her right eyebrow, intending it to be quizzical but suspected it just looked odd.

"Don't let this put you off, Benjy. You've got a great idea there," said Neil, and Beth found herself nodding in agreement.

"Look, why don't you come and visit?" said Benjy, reaching into his inside pocket and giving them both his business card. "I'd love to show you round. You haven't been to any of the islands yet have you Dr Colquhoun?"

"It's my plan to visit all of Scotland's regions in due course," she said.

"Make sure Skye's your first stop and make it soon eh?" he said, and in response to their smiles added, "What d'you expect? You told me not to give up."

They watched him disappear into the crowd. "Fancy a trip to Skye, Beth?" asked Neil. "It's one of my favourite places on Earth," he said, his voice dropping low.

She had searched for Dougie before, had trawled the internet for any mention of him and asked the one or two university friends she still kept in touch with, but without success. She now had Benjy's card. Here was his address, an invitation to visit. Was this a serendipitous coincidence, destiny conspiring them to meet? She touched her dead cheek. Any meeting would have to wait till this thing had cleared up. He might be married but she couldn't bear the thought of meeting up and not looking her best.

"Finding talking difficult," she said quietly. "Time to head home."

"Pity. I was going to ask you to join me at the new tapas bar in Byers Road tonight. I think we both enjoyed ourselves the other week didn't we?" he said.

She ignored his hopeful face. "Sorry Neil. I need to rest. I've got a conference call with Rubikon later," she said.

"Shame. But take it easy, Beth. Don't overdo it."

She felt her irritation rise and knew she needed to leave before it got the better of her. She squeezed his arm and took one final look at the room. It was alive with conversation and residual excitement. The victorious Rachel Cunningham was laughing, her head thrown back. Her long white neck was as muscular as a swan and for the first time that day Beth remembered the homeless girl with the neck tattoo. She decided she would look in on the doorway on her way home, half hoping to see her and half hoping she had spent the twenty pounds wisely and found somewhere better to sleep.

Chapter 4

Dougie's glass had been empty for fifteen minutes. He looked over to the bar where Fiona was putting up a happy birthday sign, the kind that strung out individual letters in sparkly colours and was ignoring him.

"So Dad, what d'you think?"

Dougie snapped to attention like a schoolboy who'd been caught daydreaming. "Go through that again, son," he asked, and this time successfully caught Fiona's eye and held up his empty pint glass to her.

"Honestly Dad, it's only 6 o'clock," sighed Benjy. "What I'm saying is that I lost the competition because I didn't give them numbers."

Dougie saw Benjy's brow had furrowed, his eyes creased with disappointment. "Maybe the universe is telling you to give the seaweed idea a miss," he offered. Fiona came over to their table and placed a fresh pint in front of him, lightly brushing his shoulder as she took the empty glass away.

"Unlike you Dad, I don't believe in cosmic direction. What I need to do is regroup, refocus, get stronger."

"I had a look at the native oysters yesterday. So

few of the producers are growing them these days. If you want to diversify the business, what about increasing their production?"

"There's no way I'm giving up on the seaweed, Dad. It's a two billion dollar opportunity that's ours for the taking, especially not for an oyster that's a bugger to grow, even in your loving hands."

"There's wisdom in settling for what you've got. Ambition can screw people up. It can wreck their health."

"Settling for what you've got can also be bad for your health," said Benjy, looking pointedly at Dougie's beer. "My mind's made up."

"So what's next?" asked Dougie, draining his second glass and wiping the froth from his mouth with the back of his hand.

"I've invited Beth Colquhoun and the other judges to come to Skye. Show them round. Give them all the numbers they could ever want," said Benjy.

Dougie felt a momentary loss of balance on hearing Beth's name. "What makes you think they'd come? They've seen your idea and reckoned others were better."

"They were interested in me. Beth even asked about you."

"Me? She asked about me? By name?" asked Dougie, clearing his throat, feeling his heart jump in his chest.

"Obviously not by name. She doesn't know you. She wanted to know about the family business and how we would cope if we expanded into large-scale seaweed production."

Dougie felt disquiet settle on him. If Beth had spent time talking with Benjy about his family it wouldn't take her long to work out who he was.

"What's she like?" asked Dougie.

"Her secretary didn't have a good word to say about her."

"You were chatting up the secretary?" laughed Dougie.

"It's a well-known fact you find out about an organisation by talking to the workers, not the bosses," said Benjy.

"Ah, so you weren't flirting, you were doing research? Don't worry I won't tell Sally," said Dougie, hoping to lift the mood but Benjy was serious.

"They call Beth the Terminator."

"The Terminator?" said Dougie, wondering how the feisty nature he had known as a student had fermented into something so harsh.

"She sacked a lot of people when she first got the job. Probably long overdue. People like Flora feel threatened by that. It doesn't help that Beth looks a bit like the Terminator," he added.

"Her photo in the paper was nice, if you like that groomed, business lady look," he said.

"She's had a stroke or something. Part of her face is paralysed and her eye looks terrible. It sort of hangs off her face," said Benjy.

"That must be hard for someone in her position, you know, being a public figure," said Dougie, feeling his sense of imbalance deepen to dizziness.

"She's confident and after a while you don't notice it much. I have exactly the kind of business idea that could help her be successful. I reckon if I'm persistent enough, I can make her believe that too."

"Don't get your hopes up. I wouldn't want you to be disappointed," said Dougie.

"Talking of getting your hopes up and being disappointed, Sally tells me you've split up with Fiona."

"More like an amicable pause," said Dougie, and he turned to smile at Fiona who was polishing glasses behind the bar. She smiled back.

"For someone who wants an easy life, you make it very difficult for yourself when it comes to women."

"Not at all. I keep it simple. Nothing too heavy. The only thing that matters is you and me. Always has been, always will be," said Dougie.

"Don't make out I'm the reason for you guys splitting up. For what it's worth, Dad, I'd be happy if you married Fiona. She's a lovely person as well as one of the best saleswomen we've ever had in the shop."

"Where's all this talk about marriage coming from, Benjy? Have you and Sally decided to set a date?"

"There's too much going on with the business for that. Sally agrees, she's totally supportive," he said.

"Her dad said something about hoping for an announcement about a wedding date tonight so I think you've got some work to manage expectations in that department."

Fiona came over and asked them if they would like something to eat. She could easily rustle up a sandwich for them. Her gaze towards Dougie was so loving that Benjy lifted his eyebrow towards Dougie.

"No thanks Fiona," said Benjy, "I have to get back to the office but I'm sure Dad will take you up on your offer," he said, smiling at Dougie's discomfiture. Fiona turned and went back to the bar. Dougie was momentarily distracted by the sway of her hips.

"Before you go, Benjy," said Dougie pulling out a small package from his coat pocket, "a wee birthday present for you."

Benjy took the small parcel reluctantly as if it was dangerous. He felt the contents through the wrapping paper and Dougie smiled, remembering how much he enjoyed spinning out the suspense of opening presents as a wee boy. "Go on, get on with it!" he said.

Benjy unpeeled the paper and stared at the object in his lap.

"D'you like it?" asked Dougie.

Benjy held the knife up to the light. The blade flashed. His fingers stroked the smoothness of the boxwood handle.

"It's French. The world's best shucking knife," added Dougie, pleased but surprised to see how moved Benjy was with the gift.

"It's the engraving on the handle, Dad. It's a kelp design isn't it?" asked Benjy. Dougie felt a dash of surprise; he hadn't taken much notice of the handle. He took the knife from Benjy and examined the design more closely but all he could see was a band of squiggly lines.

"It's amazing how they've made something as ugly as seaweed look so good," said Dougie cheerfully. "Look after it and your children and their children will also be able to use it."

"I'll treasure it always," said Benjy, and they embraced.

Dougie could smell his familiar smell, feel his broad strong back and had to breathe deeply, his feelings of love threatening to overwhelm him. "I'm so very proud of you," he whispered before letting him go.

"See you later," smiled Benjy, "and Dad, please take it steady with the drink, you've got a long night ahead of you."

Dougie waited until he had shut the door before looking over to Fiona and signalling for a top up.

Three hours later and Dougie had settled into the comfort of the evening bonhomie, the only wrinkle being Fiona who seemed to be getting friendlier as the night progressed. She was wearing a new blouse; gold satin with a low cleavage caught in a flouncy bow, her creamy breasts on show. He had the uncomfortable sensation that this was for his benefit, that things were regressing back to them being a couple and he didn't know how to stop the slide without causing upset.

Benjy was at the bar surrounded by his friends, most of whom he had known since childhood. Dougie marvelled at the easy way he had with people he was so different from; standing a foot taller than most of them with his exotic looks and black hair.

He was laughing now, his head back, the bob of his Adam's apple breaking the smoothness of his neck. He was part of the gang of local kids yet his ambition set him apart from them; a Scottish lad with a passion for his homeland and at the same time looked like he came from somewhere else.

Sally had sidled up to his side and threaded her arm through his in a possessive gesture. She was wearing the same navy sweater she had been wearing all day. She had loosened her hair around her shoulders in a nod to the party but it had gone lanky in the heat. For a moment Dougie was surprised how cross he felt and couldn't decide whether it was because Sally made so little effort to look nice, or because Benjy didn't seem to care.

Sally's parents were standing at the other side of the bar. Mharie was wearing a tight-fitting dress, downing a gin and tonic. Seeing Dougie look her way, she winked at him and then nudged her husband John as if to tell him that he had to keep his eye on her. He wondered if Benjy had ever taken a good look at Sally's mum and worried that she might be a portent of what was to come.

Then John embraced her so warmly and without embarrassment that Dougie felt a punch of jealousy. Of course he understood the attraction of Sally and her family to Benjy – the unconditional love, the support, their unflagging faith in him. He made a resolution, in the way that you do when you've had a few pints, to be nicer to Sally, so there would be no distance between them, just one seamless extended family to support Benjy.

He drifted to the back door. The night air was

sobering. The sky was studded with the flinty light of stars. He could taste the salty tang of the sea. Life was like a river, he thought, you went along with the different character of the flow.

His childhood in Skye was like a spring rising up, uncertain but full of hope. His twenties had the rushing speed of a young river: university in Glasgow and the strength of his first love with Beth. Then came the rapids: breaking up with Beth, meeting Mei in Thailand, Benjy's birth and Mei's death. His thirties marked a time of maturing, the river settling down as Benjy grew up, the oyster farm establishing itself. Now, in his mid-forties, he was about to move into the welcome flow of the wide estuary.

Benjy could go off on his great kelp adventure and find his way through his own rapids, but he wasn't going with him. He was going to enjoy a calmer life, his reward for having survived the vicissitudes of earlier currents. There was still the chance of the occasional ripple and unexpected eddy of course. He would need to deal with Fiona and the outside chance of meeting Beth, but the volume of water was too great to be troubled or diverted. It would continue to move, inexorably, towards the sea beyond.

He walked down to the edge of the garden that bordered the loch. The tide was in and the black water lapped at the rocky edge. The wind chilled off the waves, the sky so dark it felt like a solid thing. He suddenly had the impression that he was not alone. He stood still and saw an outline of a man coming towards him. He walked with the sort of ease you would expect from a friend but stopped a few feet in front of him. Too dark to see his face, his shadow had a quality of stillness that made Dougie feel suddenly afraid.

"Hello," he called out, "you OK there?" But the figure didn't reply or move. Stood immobile. So immobile that Dougie thought perhaps it wasn't a person at all but a tree, a trick of the light. Yet there was a quality of being observed that he couldn't shake off. He was torn between going forward to find out who this was or to retreat back to the party. No contest. He turned to walk back to the pub when he felt the lightest of touches on his shoulder. It spread through his body as powerfully as if he had been jabbed by one of Billy's cattle prods.

"What the hell...?" he said, turning.

"I'm looking for Mr McKinnon," said a voice so cultured that it was like the mother of pearl inside an oyster shell.

"You've just scared the shit out of him," retorted Dougie, squinting in the gloom to make out the face of the man. He was much shorter than Dougie but then again most people were. He smelt the woody scent of expensive aftershave.

"Good evening Mr McKinnon. My name is Mr Takashama. I believe you are expecting me."

They walked into the pub and in the honey glow Dougie could see that Mr Takashama had a smooth complexion, the sort that didn't need shaving every day. His black hair was slickened with oil, the source of the smoky perfumed smell. His round glasses had black frames and gave him the look of an Asian monk. He could have been any age from thirty to sixty. He was looking at Dougie expectantly. There might even have been a gesture of disappointment in his expression.

"You've come far?" asked Dougie, knowing this was inadequate but unable to think of anything better to say.

"From your offices, by the beach," answered Mr Takahashi, again with a tone that seemed to suggest that Dougie should already know this.

"Not too far then," said Dougie.

"No one was there. I saw the lights so I walked towards them. I thought this might be Mr McKinnon's house."

"Call me Dougie," he said, holding out his hand and immediately regretting it, perhaps he should have bowed instead. "Although my son would say I'm here often enough for this to be my home, it is, in fact, the Long Inn Hotel. Now what can I get you to drink, Mr Taka..."

"Some water thank you," replied the small man, looking around at the crush of people.

Dougie had to bend over to hear him. "Can I interest you in a malt whiskey with your water? Our local distillery's world famous."

"Mr McKinnon, I came to talk business. Perhaps we can find somewhere quieter?"

"This is my son's 22nd birthday party and that's more important than any business I can name," said Dougie, rocking back on his heels and taking a better look at this little man. "Anyhow, what business would you want with me, and on a Saturday night as well?"

"Dad," said Benjy, suddenly at his side.

Dougie turned. "Benjy this is Mr Taka... Mr Taka..."

"Takashama," the man replied, and turned to face Benjy. The difference in their height and the similarity of their features was almost comical. His son was like a blown up version of the smaller man.

"Mr Takashama!" shouted Benjy. "How fantastic! I wasn't expecting you."

"I emailed you yesterday saying I had shortened my London trip and was coming today," he said in perfect English, a little clipped in tone, "but I see you are busy. If you had replied to my email yesterday, I could have avoided this misunderstanding."

"I was in Glasgow yesterday. Bit of a nightmare day. I'm sorry I didn't get your email. But look, you're here now. Please stay. In the morning we can show you the seaweed operation and go over some numbers," said Benjy.

"That's kind but I think..."

"Where are you staying?" interrupted Dougie.

"I have a room at The Four Sisters," replied Mr Takashama, "the restaurant is famous, even in Singapore," he said.

"The food's good here too," said Dougie, "and a fraction of the price. Benjy'll get you a seat by the fire."

Dougie went to the bar. "Charm offensive required," he said, leaning over towards Fiona. "Some Asian businessman has turned up out of the blue. Is a bit upset about the absence of a welcoming party." Fiona craned her neck to where Benjy and Mr Takashama were standing.

"I imagine he's hungry," said Fiona, "and looking at the state of his trousers, I think his feet might be wet."

And so it was that after half an hour, Mr Takashama was sitting by the open fire, eating their oysters. Dougie watched as he sluiced them down with a malt whisky chaser. He thought the haggis, chips, and black pudding that Fiona brought afterwards was a bit on the heavy side but Mr Takashama had purred with delight and eaten the lot. *Surprising how much food a small man can eat*, thought Dougie.

His socks, two petite strands of cashmere wool, were draped over the back of a chair drying against the warmth of the flames. The band had been playing a set of pop tunes and there were a few people dancing. There was an expectant hush as Benjy stepped forward to the microphone.

"Thanks to everyone for coming tonight. And a special welcome to Mr Takashama who's come all the way from Singapore." Heads turned and nodded in his direction. "As most of you know I lost the Young Entrepreneur Competition in Glasgow yesterday and I don't mind telling you I was upset. But Dad's always told me you're rich when you've got friends and family, and as I look around me tonight, I realise at the tender age of twenty-two, I'm a millionaire already." There were hoots of derision, though Dougie felt a lump in his throat and had to look away. He could see Mr Takashama was riveted. "Now I've asked the lovely Fiona to sing us a few songs. Please put your hands together for her."

Dougie saw Fiona pushing her way from the back of bar. The flush on her face had extended down to her chest and her eyes sparkled as she stepped up to the microphone. She closed her eyes. The first note flew from her throat.

There is a blackbird sits on yon tree

Some says it is blind and it cannae see

And so is my true love tae me.

The crowd were ecstatic in their applause and Fiona bowed low, her hair tumbling over her head and as she lifted her eyes she swept it aside, looking straight at Dougie. Mr Takashama seemed agitated.

"You OK?" asked Dougie and the man smiled. He could see the glint of a gold filling.

"Would you permit me?" Dougie was momentarily flummoxed, thinking that Mr Takashama was asking to proposition Fiona. He had been keeping pace with him on the Talliskers but there was no sign of inebriation.

"Would you permit me to sing?" repeated Mr Takashama.

"I'm sure we would," said Dougie. Fiona shrugged and made a space for him.

Mr Takashama stood in front of the microphone with the same stillness that Dougie had felt when he first met him. He took a few deep breaths as the crowd settled and quietened, half in curiosity and half in confusion. Then came a plaintive sound, hardly human, between a Muslim chant to prayers and an anguished cry. It was electrifying. Not music exactly, more an articulation of raw emotion. Discordant, just on the edge of pastiche, but there was something keening, beautiful, terrifying about it. Mr Takashama had no need of a microphone. Dougie knew little about singing and even less about Japanese folk singing but he reckoned this needed virtuosic skill. The applause at the end of it was extended but Mr Takashama resisted all entreaties to sing another as he padded his way back to his seat in his bare feet.

"In Japan we have a saying that folk music is where the heart's home lives," he said quietly, "it touches the deepest spirit with us."

"So were you singing about home?" asked Dougie.

"I was born in a small village in Kyushu, an island in the south, but I left as a young man and have never returned. Unlike you, Dougie McKinnon, I don't have a home. You do. It is here. With your son and with your wife, Fiona. Both so talented."

Dougie nodded, thinking it would be easier to explain the finer details of his love life later. Mr Takashama was looking into the fire, preoccupied. There was a pause before he spoke: "I've decided to stay for a few days."

"Benjy'll be delighted," said Dougie, "now, let's get you another drink. After all that singing you'll be needing something to wet your whistle."

Chapter 5

Beth suspected the pamphlet had been placed deliberately so she would see it. The face of a teenage boy, horribly disfigured by burns smiled at her; it was both shocking and fascinating. The strap line beneath the picture said, 'helping you face disfigurement.' She picked it up then dropped it quickly as if she'd been stung by it.

Dr Rorke's consulting room was in one the grand terraces in Edinburgh's New Town. It had a lumbering, cavernous quality that gave the impression of money and masculinity. Gratifyingly, Beth felt a rash of hot and cold pins dancing on her chin and right cheek, the pressure in her head tightening. In the past when she went to a doctor, which wasn't often, her symptoms would magically lessen as she waited, as if telling her that she was bothering the doctor unnecessarily. Not today.

The door opened and Dr Rorke invited her into another room. She had the scrubbed, fresh-faced complexion of a fourteen-year-old; a rash of pale freckles dusted her nose. Her lips were a little on the thin side in Beth's opinion, but magnificent, lightly glossed. The doctor shook her hand with a firmness that was just this side of impatience.

"Sorry to keep you waiting. A busy morning," she said, inviting Beth to sit opposite her. "So how can I help?"

Beth took a deep breath, surprised by how shaky she felt. "I'm worried that my Palsy's getting worse. The paralysis is spreading. The left side is no better and I'm getting pins and needles on the right side now. The headaches are more frequent and more severe." She thought that saying this out loud would settle her but she found herself blinking back tears. She took her hanky and dabbed her eye. "And this left eye. It never stops."

The doctor reached into a drawer, pulled on latex gloves and walked round to Beth's side, gently moving her hair and tucking it behind her ear. She examined her face intently; a look that went beyond seeing Beth as a person. "I can see the paralysis is still more or less total on the left side. How's your speech?"

"Better, or maybe I've just got better at avoiding troublesome consonants," replied Beth. The doctor nodded. "Open your mouth," she asked, and with her gloved fingers probed and pulled her lips and gums, then returned to her side of the desk and wrote something down. "So you came to see me, when was it? A fortnight ago?"

"Seventeen days," said Beth, suppressing an unexpected flutter of panic, "it's been seventeen days and it's getting worse."

The doctor moved her eyelid down over her eye. When she let it go, it snapped up like a roller blind. "Are you lubricating and taping this eye at night?" she asked.

"Yes, and eye drops throughout the day," said Beth.

"You've finished the course of steroids?"

"Yes. They didn't make any difference," Beth replied.

"How about sleeping?" The doctor was now making tapping movements across her hairline.

"Fine," said Beth, although it wasn't true. She woke most days in the early hours; the worry demon taunting her by stacking up every concern of her life into a tower of imminent catastrophe. She would eventually fall asleep after what seemed like hours of developing contingency plans, and then wake, disoriented with fatigue and disappointment; when she prodded her face and knew nothing was changed.

"I explained to you that these things usually get better on their own. It's still early days," Dr Rorke said, unpeeling the latex gloves from her fingers.

Beth felt something break inside her then. "I'm here because you're meant to be the best in the field. I was hoping for something more than 'let's just wait and see.'" She could hear her voice rising.

"Mrs Colquhoun…" began the doctor.

"Please understand," said Beth, her sense of desperation rising, impossible to check, "I'm good at putting on a brave face. I tell myself worse things happen to people. Every day. But I'm not here, Dr Rorke, to give you that brave face. I'm here to tell you I'm worried. I'm frightened about what's happening to me."

"Mrs Colquhoun, I understand this is upsetting and that for someone in your position…"

"I'm not married!" said Beth, her voice rising, pleased to see a blush suffuse the doctor's peachy skin. "Look, there must be tests you can run. Scans, bloods tests. I don't know. Investigate what's going on."

"You are presenting symptoms that are classic Bell's Palsy. The best treatment is to keep yourself healthy, minimise stress, allow your body to heal. Yes, there are tests we could run."

"Good," interrupted Beth, "I'm glad we can agree on that then." She felt her body was as brittle as dry wood.

The doctor paused for a minute as if considering her options. "In all likelihood you'll be seeing an improvement in the next two or three weeks. If you haven't, then yes, we can arrange further tests. But I have to warn you."

"Two or three weeks? I'd hoped we could have sorted something sooner," interrupted Beth, but there was a determined look in the doctor's eye that Beth recognised from her own repertoire of eye contact; it meant there was no further negotiation.

"My advice to you is to rest, try to take the stress out of your life," said the doctor kindly.

"You're asking me to take stress out of my life whilst insisting I wait two or three weeks doing nothing?" said Beth, but Dr Rorke wasn't listening. She was writing a prescription instead.

"Here's something stronger for the headaches. They're powerful so follow the dosage carefully. Also best to avoid alcohol."

Beth felt a jab of guilt that she had shouted at her,

but it wasn't enough to stem her impatience. "So we'll have the same conversation we're having now in two weeks and realise all we've done is waste time?"

"I think we'll be having a very different conversation in two weeks' time," said the doctor, smiling thinly.

***

Dusk had fallen when the train arrived into Glasgow, drizzle fell like a thin curtain and lights blinked prettily. Beth walked briskly, head down, her umbrella in front pushing her way through the rain. She disliked being late although she knew it was unlikely that Alec would be on time. Even as a child, he was allergic to punctuality.

She passed the doorway where she had met the homeless girl with the throat tattoo and looked in. It had become a ritual every time she passed by, but this evening as with every day since, it was empty. Small puddles had collected at the front of the passage. She smelled a note of ammonia and fried food, and hoped that the girl was somewhere warm and dry. It was a prayer that often came to her; to hope that no one would have to sleep on the streets on a night like this.

The restaurant was tucked in a backstreet, its art deco sign an original from the 1930s. She thought its shabbiness might be considered stylish but like much of the city she felt it could do with a good clean. The waitress was young, groomed, and stared at Beth with an odd expression that combined both blankness and curiosity. "And how are you this evening?" she asked pleasantly.

"I've got a headache," replied Beth. The waitress

took her coat and turned on her heel, her pert bottom wrapped tight in an ankle-length apron, and led Beth into the main room. "Your table's this way," she said cheerily.

"May I offer you a suggestion?" asked Beth. The girl stopped and turned.

"Of course," she replied, smiling her sweet waitressy smile.

"When you ask someone how they are, at least do them the courtesy of listening to their reply, otherwise don't ask," she said, matching the girl's sweet tone.

The girl's face froze satisfyingly. "I'm s-s-sorry?" she stuttered, more of a question than an apology but Beth was making her way towards her table. Alec, surprisingly had already arrived.

"Do they really think anyone is taken in by that sham of customer service? I'd rather be properly ignored," she said, but Alec barely registered her arrival. He was absorbed in reading the menu; eyes cast downwards, lips pursed, plump fingers gripping the edges of the laminated card. *He's like a well-fed seal*, thought Beth, his bald head a pointy dome, his black eyes twinkling, his small ears pinned back at the side of his head.

"Ah, Beth!" He got up to kiss her. On the good side. She could smell the recent cigarette he'd smoked.

"This damn face is making me crabby," she said and then qualified, "well, even more crabby than usual." He poured her a glass of wine; she saw the bottle was already two thirds empty.

"No thanks," she said, pushing her glass over to his side, "just some water and a straw. I'm afraid I can't manage drinking without a straw these days."

He settled back into his chair and was examining her closely. "D'you think you've gone back to work too soon?"

"It's a nuisance, Alec, that's all. Should go away by itself in a couple of weeks. The doctor's not worried so neither should we be," said Beth, marvelling at the ease she could take on Dr Rorke's authoritative tone.

"Margaret and I both think you should take a holiday. The North Italian lakes. Time to convalesce. Time for things to get back to normal." She made a point of studying the menu, amazed that at the age of fifty Alec still hadn't realised that most people ignore unsolicited advice. Especially from older brothers.

"Guess what? I heard today that Scotland's on the shortlist for Rubikon's new R&D centre. The Board are planning a visit in August. So definitely no time for a holiday."

"Margaret and I worry about you; in the papers all the time, courting controversy with everything you do. You don't think the problem with your face might have something to do with the stress of the job?"

"The antidote to stress, Alec, is not avoidance of pressure or going on holiday. It's making sure you're doing the things that give you energy and purpose," she said brightly.

"I suppose getting Scotland's economy back in good shape counts as having a purpose."

"I'm passionate about it, Alec. As a country I've

always felt Scotland has underachieved. So many of our talented people leave to build wealth elsewhere in the world. Including me for a while. But now I'm back I'm totally committed to building a culture where business can flourish, where people don't feel they have to leave to make their mark. This Rubikon project is only the start of what I'm planning to do," she said.

"All I'm saying is look after yourself. You might think you're invincible but you're flesh and blood just like the rest of us."

"OK big brother," she said, glad the topic was ending and they hadn't descended into a squabble.

The restaurant had the retro feel of a pre-war ocean liner; amber lighting, walnut panelling, a relief bias of floating tendrils of seaweed on the walls. She remembered Benjy talking about his project. *Porphyra haitanensis*. The way he had said it gave it a poetic sound.

"Do you remember Douglas McKinnon?"

"Wee Dougie McKinnon?" said Alec and they both laughed, remembering how much taller he was than anyone else they knew.

"His son Benjy was a finalist at the Young Entrepreneur Competition. I wasn't sure at the time it was him but I looked up the company online, and he was listed as a joint director of their oyster farm," she said, surprised to hear a hint of pleasure in her voice.

"Who'd have thought Dougie would have a son who was a dynamic business man? He must take after his mother, that's all I'll say," he added.

"Dougie wasn't lazy," she said, "he was a creative spirit, that's all."

"I liked him. Thought he was good for you. Softened your edges," said Alec, looking at her closely now and she felt herself flushing as she remembered the oceanic rush of love that had overwhelmed her during her last two years at university.

"Probably a fat old git by now," she said, laughing.

"Are you going to meet up?" asked Alec.

"Unlikely. Probably for the best."

"Bob Janes in the office met up with his childhood sweetheart at a school reunion three years ago. He left his wife for her, packed up his job and is happily shacked up in Shetland," said Alec.

"Dougie and I parted very badly if you remember," said Beth.

"Aren't you curious about him?" asked Alec.

"A little bit, yes, but I'm far too busy at the moment."

"There's never been anyone like him since, has there Beth?"

"It was too soon for me to settle down. It's the one thing I regret."

"Breaking it off with him?"

"No, the way I did it. I was too brutal, but maybe there's no nice way to break up," she said, leaning forward and sipping from her straw, shaking her head as if trying to rid herself of a regret.

"Oysters and Dougie McKinnon, a dangerous

combination," said Alec.

She laughed. "Anyhow, he's married. Her name's Sally and I'm happily married too: to my work."

"I like it when you laugh. Even if it's a bit lopsided these days. I think I'll call you Funny Face to encourage you to laugh more often."

"Funny Face? That's so insensitive," exclaimed Beth, but she was laughing.

"You see. It's working already. D'you think Dougie might be supplying the oysters here?"

"It's a possibility. I'll order us a dozen anyhow. It's the one thing that doesn't cause me too much hassle eating."

"I'm going outside for a quick smoke. Then I've got something that I want to talk you about." He was already searching in his pockets for his cigarettes with that edge of anxiety that is never far from an addict's eye.

He had barely left the table when Beth felt hot and cold needles jabbing at her scalp and chin, her headache building suddenly in intensity. She stood up but being vertical made her dizzy. She put her hand out to the back of the chair to steady herself. The room took on the swaying movement of a ship, the hum of conversations sounding like the drone of engines, the air waving in front of her. Saliva pooled in her mouth as the dizziness intensified. She reckoned she had a minute before the ravages of nerve pain would shred her face.

Then she saw him. He was tucked deep into one of the booths at the back of the restaurant. Seeing him had an immediate sobering effect. What was he doing here? This wasn't the sort of place she would expect Desmond, her Chief Financial Officer to come to. She took a better look at his companion: male, middle-aged, she didn't know him. They were deep in conversation and didn't see her as she slipped past them to the sanctuary of the ladies'.

The oysters had arrived by the time Beth returned to their table. Twelve fleshy patties glistened in their grey whorled nests on a platter of ice laced with lemon slices. The painkillers were already working; her face still felt like it was sliced in half but the pain no longer seemed relevant. She realised she was famished. She squeezed lemon juice over one of the oysters, watching the mollusc contract, then slipped it down the right side of her mouth, her serviette held around her chin to catch the juices. She wondered if Dougie's hand had touched this actual shell. She remembered his long thin fingers, the way he bit the skin round the nails.

Alec arrived, bringing a cloud of nicotine with him and reached over to the wine bucket and poured himself another glass of wine. She saw that the bottle was almost full. He must have ordered another without her noticing.

"Now what do you want to talk about?" she asked.

"I want to buy an oil company," he started. She wasn't surprised. Alec's ideas were never small. "All the big boys are moving out of Scotland now. The market has fragmented into smaller independents and there's a wee beauty that's ripe for plucking."

"How much?" asked Beth. She took a sip of water

through her straw. The waitress had given her one of those tiny cocktail ones and it was an effort for her lips to get enough suction.

"Five mill," said Alec.

"Pounds? Dollars? Euros?" asked Beth, as casually as if they were discussing the price of a second-hand car.

"Pounds," said Alec.

"Shame, if we were talking euros that would be different."

"Look, Beth. Don't patronise me. The numbers stack up."

"Good," replied Beth, "they'll need to if the banks are to lend you that sort of cash."

Alec took a swig from his glass. "The banks will never lend me that kind of money and you know it. I thought your Mr Tan might be interested. Maybe you could broker us a meeting."

"You want me to set up a meeting with the CEO of Rubikon? One of the most powerful businessmen in Singapore, on the basis of what exactly? A half-baked plan to buy an oil company with someone who has no experience or knowledge of the oil industry?"

"Businessmen are always interested in new opportunities. You should know that, you meet plenty of them every day."

"Businessmen and conmen can be difficult to tell apart, Alec. When will you realise there's no such thing as a bargain oil company? Stop dreaming, stop gambling, stop looking for the easy win."

"Didn't you say the Rubikon Board were all coming to Scotland? It wouldn't take much for you to set up a meeting with him surely?"

"Mr Tan didn't want anything to do with me when I first took the job in Singapore. It took years for me to build trust with him."

"But Beth, this is a dead cert."

"OK Alec, I'm not going to argue with you tonight. Send me the proposal and I'll take a look. I promise. Now, how's your real job with Hunters going?"

Alec made a face. "The housing market has perked up so sales are good. But Hunters is a building merchants, Beth. They're never going to set the heather on fire. And being the chief accountant and IT director, a.k.a. general dogsbody, is never going to make me rich."

"You've got Margaret and the boys. Those are the things that matter."

"Ha! So says the person who's married to their job! And don't think family life is a walk in the park. The school fees keep going up. I'm struggling with it all if I'm being honest. Look Beth, I hate to ask you," he said, his seal eyes pleading.

Beth dabbed her eye. "How much?"

"Five thousand. I'll be getting my bonus later this year. I'll pay you back then," he said.

"Look, Alec, it's not that I don't want to help but I'm wondering if all I'm doing is shoring you up against a lifestyle that you can't afford. Both Cameron and Callum are bright. They'd do fine at the local school," she said.

"What would you know about schools? It's been years since you've lived in this country. Education is not something that Margaret or I can compromise on. If you don't want to help, fine. Just say no."

"I'm not saying no, Alec, but..." she said.

"Come to dinner on Saturday night. Margaret would love to see you," he said, though they both knew that wasn't true. Alec drained his glass. "You know sometimes I envy your freedom, your independence. You've only got yourself to think about," he said, putting his knife and fork tidily together, the plate as clean as if it had been licked.

"And sometimes I envy men who have wives at home, looking after them, shopping, cooking food, picking up the dry cleaning," she replied.

"Hire a housekeeper. Much less hassle than a wife," said Alec.

"That's not a bad idea," said Beth.

Alec looked at his watch. "I need to be going."

"I'll get the bill. I'll call you later in the week about Saturday night."

Alec scraped his chair back and planted a meaty kiss against her good cheek. "It's great to have you back, Funny Face. It means a lot to me. To Margaret and the boys," and they exchanged a complicit look to settle on this fabrication. Perhaps if they believed it long enough it would become real.

The waitress came by to clear the table. She studiously avoided Beth's staring eye. "Dessert menu?" she asked.

"I already know what I want. Creamed rice

pudding." The waitress seemed surprised. Had her down as one of those ladies that starved themselves thin, thought Beth. "I can never resist it!" and the girl smiled back.

"Best headache cure I know," replied the waitress.

Beth smiled, remembering their earlier exchange. "Sorry about that. Customer service is one of my passions. I get irritated when I think the standards fall short."

"Are you ever off duty?" said a man's voice as he sat down opposite her where Alec had been. In the flattering light of the restaurant there was something about his gaunt features that could almost be attractive. He was wearing a suit and his white shirt glowed in the light.

"Hello Desmond. I saw you earlier with your friend but you were too cosy to be interrupted," she said.

"Malcolm Crawford from the *Daily Record*. This is his favourite restaurant. Can't stand the place myself. There's nothing on the menu that I can eat. The chef pushed the boat out and gave me a plate of boiled rice and veg. He obviously thinks vegan food is for invalids."

"It's not easy for some people to adapt is it, Desmond?"

"Adaptability? That's one of your favourite ideas isn't it, Beth?" he said, and she wondered if he was a little drunk, his eyes were glittering.

"And what's yours?"

"Integrity," he said.

"I imagine a journalist like Mr Crawford would

share that one too," she replied, but Desmond seemed distracted.

"You remember the Young Entrepreneur Competition? It turns out our winner Rachel Cunningham is not what she seems. Malcolm has just told me that the paper received a letter from a relative of the family. Turns out the software business that she touted as her own is really Daddy's and all we've done is gifted him twenty-five grand. Rachel Cunningham's an admin assistant, capable of writing emails but not computer code."

"We were both taken in with her. Have we given her the money yet?" asked Beth.

"No."

"One occasion where our inefficiency has been to our advantage at least."

"I've emailed her telling her we're launching a full investigation but if we're to assume that she's a cheat we still have the matter of who is the winner. I suppose the seaweed lad, McKelvin is the obvious choice."

"McKinnon," corrected Beth, "and will your pal from the *Daily Record* be prepared to do a feature on this? There's a positive angle if we're proactive. 'Agency weeds out cheat and gives the cash to a deserving winner'. It'll be a good story, a better story than a straight win."

"You are never off duty," said Desmond but he was smiling. "I hear congratulations are in order. Mr Tan and the Rubikon Board have confirmed their visit. I suppose you'll want me to ask Malcolm to mention that in the papers too?"

"No. It's too soon. If we look overconfident we'll scare them off. Tell him nothing for now."

The waitress arrived with her pudding; creamy bubbles of rice swimming in milky sweetness. Desmond could barely hide his disgust. "I'll leave you to it then," he said, "but let me know if I can help with the Rubikon visit. I've got a fair bit of experience with the big boys and you may not believe it Beth, but I really hope you pull this off." Beth nodded in acknowledgement and watched him leave, allowing herself a moment to imagine he might mean what he said.

She heard a sudden bust of laughter above the chatter of the restaurant and felt strangely happy. Painkillers and pudding had mixed pleasantly in her. Perhaps the job at The Agency would be a success after all. Perhaps she and Alec could become close like they had been as children. The runes of fate seemed to be mapping out a reunion with Dougie. She touched her cheek, perhaps this thing would have disappeared by the time she met him.

***

The rain had stopped and a mild westerly wind was blowing. She sauntered with a pleasant sense of wellbeing and was surprised to reach her flat so quickly. She wondered if she might extend her walk down to Glasgow Green when she saw the girl standing at the main door.

"I hear you've been looking for me," the girl said. The black tattoo on her neck moved as she spoke. Her knitted hat was pulled down, covering most of her face. Her hands were deep in the pockets of the large coat.

"Where are you sleeping tonight?" asked Beth, moving past her, already thinking that her prayers about hoping homeless people are warm and safe had in some way caused this to happen.

"Dunno," she replied.

"You'd better come in then," said Beth.

Chapter 6

Beth motioned for the girl to go in ahead of her. The lobby exuded confidence. The thick pile carpet muted their footfall, the radiators blasted out heat; the flowers on the sideboard perfumed the air. There was a deliberate quality to the girl's disinterest in her surroundings, an exaggeration in the way her shoulders hunched, her hat pulled down past her ears.

The security camera tucked up in the corner of the wall hummed as it swivelled towards them. Beth lifted her head and stared into its red eye. It dwelt on them longer than usual as they stood in awkward silence, waiting for the lift to arrive. It was like one of the games that she and Alec played as children. Who would break the silence first?

"What's your name?" asked Beth.

"Nine," said the girl.

"Nine? Spelt N I N E? Is that your real name?"

The girl looked at her then, a mixture of weariness and scorn. "Yes, it's my real name," she said.

"You mean your parents named you Nine?" repeated Beth, thinking she sounded like a lawyer drilling a witness in the stand.

"After eight children they had run out of ideas," she replied.

"My name's Beth Colquhoun."

"I know," said the girl.

"Did you know who I was when we first met in the doorway?" asked Beth.

"No. Afterwards. When I saw your photograph in the paper."

"I look a bit different from that picture now," said Beth, but the girl shrugged as if she neither cared nor properly noticed. The lift went noiselessly up to the top floor. Beth opened the door to her flat. The girl had the same empty expression.

"What do you think?" asked Beth.

"Smells like no one lives here." Beth went over to the window, closed the wooden shutters and switched on a couple of table lamps. She turned to the girl as if to say, 'You're wrong, I can make this place seem cosy,' but she had wandered into the kitchen and was leaning against the centre island, stroking the work surface as if it was the fur of an animal.

"Sorry, I don't think I've got much food in at the moment," said Beth, "I eat out most nights."

"Mind if I take my coat off? It's boiling in here," Nine asked. Beth could see under the large coat was an equally outsized sweater. She took it off in a swift movement, leaving her in a tee shirt, her clavicle bones standing proud, her arms as fragile as twigs. The neck of the tee shirt was loose fitting and the ugly stain of her throat tattoo stared out from her white neck.

"You don't look like someone who lives on the streets," said Beth, and Nine laughed, looking down at her tee shirt and pulling it wide, showing a myriad of moth holes.

"Yes," conceded Beth, "your clothes look shabby but something's not quite right about you." The girl shrugged and pulled off her hat; short blonde hair escaped, fizzing with static.

"Your hair's too clean for a start. So Nine, what's your story? Why are you here? What do you want?"

"My trolley's been nicked. You said you knew people who could help me," she replied.

"Sorry. Not convinced. If you don't give me a straight answer I'm going to ask you to leave," said Beth. They stood facing each other, arms crossed. Another competition of wills, thought Beth, only this time she would win.

"D'you want the short version or the long version?"

"The truthful version," replied Beth.

"OK, but can we eat first? There's a pizza place round the corner."

"I've already eaten and anyhow I don't eat pizza," said Beth.

"OK. I can see this was a mistake," replied Nine, turning to put her sweater back on.

"Look, take this and get whatever you want," said Beth, taking out her purse and handing her a twenty pound note. "I'll put a plate in the oven to warm."

The girl laughed. "Bloody Nora. You really don't

eat pizza do you?" she said as she let herself out of the flat.

***

Nine had fallen asleep on the sofa opposite Beth. The pizza box lay open, its insides resembling the carnage of roadkill, twists of dough and cheese snarled up amongst bloody clots of tomato. Nine had been right. It tasted better eaten out of the box. To Beth's surprise, between the two of them they had nearly finished it. She picked up the last slice, the limp triangle was weighed down by topping and she took a bite from the bottom as if it was a bunch of grapes. She luxuriated in its sweetness and the privacy of eating without anyone watching. She dabbed her mouth and chin with a napkin, then squeezed her dead cheek to move any trapped food over to the side that still had feeling.

She lifted her glass of wine; the straw lay at a jaunty angle and she had to chase it around the glass before she caught it. She remembered reading somewhere that drinking wine from a straw was the fastest way to get drunk. Something about the tongue absorbing alcohol faster than the gullet. The rich tannin of the wine cut through the numbness in her mouth as it flowed into her throat. She set down the glass, enjoying the thought of Dr Rorke's disapproval.

She watched Nine sleep. She could see the web of spidery veins beneath her eyelids. Her body was so small it barely made an impression beneath the blanket Beth had laid over her. Beth wasn't sure how much of her story she believed but it wouldn't take long to check it out. She picked up her laptop and typed 'Faslane' on the search engine.

A grainy photograph of protesters camping appeared. A banner floated above them – Faslane Peace Protest. There was a rough drawing of the peace symbol on the side of one of their tents. The text boasted that a Stop Trident campaign had been active for thirty years, and extended an invitation for people to join them at weekends, families welcome, assurances that there would be no drink, no drugs. The page hadn't been updated in years; it already had the look of something that had failed.

Beth knew that most Scots didn't like having a nuclear submarine base just outside Glasgow, but she couldn't remember any active resistance, it provided work for local people after all. Nine said she and her boyfriend George had dropped out of college in London to save the protest camp from this inertia but it wasn't long before they began to argue. Nine wanted to work with the people who were already there, George favoured a takeover and asked some of his pals from London to come up and join them.

It all came to a head when they had a massive argument during which he slapped her across the face. It wasn't hard enough to leave a bruise but it was the day love died, Nine said. She came to Glasgow, not knowing anyone but needing to get away. George hadn't followed her. Hadn't come looking for her to persuade her to return. She had slept rough for three weeks, but was running out of ideas about what to do next until Beth had come along with her offer of help.

"What about the tattoo on your neck?" Beth had asked.

"The original was two doves with George and

Nine written on them." She threw her head back and it stretched like a bloated snake. "It took a lot of ink to cover them. A fitting symbol for the big black nothingness that our relationship means to me now."

"It's the ugliest thing I've ever seen," said Beth, feeling dismay as powerfully as if she had been Nine's mother. "People must stare at it."

"It's normal for people to stare," she said. Beth thought Nine had the sort of confidence that you find in the young, not proud of her tattoo exactly but not ashamed of it either. She felt a tug of envy.

"I find it bad enough when one person looks at me like I'm an animal in a zoo, but when they get their pals to join in, that's the point when I think I might kill someone," said Beth. They had both laughed then, a moment of shared experience.

"Will your face get better?" asked Nine.

"The doctor says it only temporary, thank goodness."

Nine shifted in her sleep, dislodging the blanket. Beth leaned over and lifted her thin arm. She checked the underside for signs of needle tracks but the pale skin was clear. She pulled the blanket over her and tucked the weightless arm back under it. A small sigh came from her as if thanking her.

She must have dozed off herself because when she next woke, she knew it was late. The heating had gone off, the flat felt cold. Her staring eye raged as if full of hot grit. Nine was still asleep on the sofa, and hadn't stirred. Beth's computer had slipped off her lap and was lying on its side on the floor. She reached down to pick it up when a searing pain slashed her face. She sat there, stricken, her left eye feeling cauterised, the synapses inside her head firing ruthlessly. She was stunned into keeping as still as possible.

"Beth? You alright? You look weird." Nine had woken and was staring at her. "What can I get you?" she asked, throwing aside her blanket and coming towards her. She had a sleepy smell about her that reminded Beth of winceyette pyjamas.

"Pills," she whispered, "in my handbag."

"Man, you should not be taking these," said Nine as she scrutinised the label of the packet. "This is serious shit and not good for you."

Beth felt frustrated by her powerlessness. She turned her good eye to glare at Nine, immobilised by pain to do much more. The girl stared back, unnerved.

"I've got a much better idea," she said, putting the pills down on the coffee table. She dug into her jeans pocket and produced a packet of tobacco and some rolling papers. "Marijuana is used all over the world for medicinal purposes, you know. You can even get it on the NHS," she said.

Beth felt a flash of anger. "For God's sake," she managed to spit out before lunging forwards and grabbing the pills, "I don't smoke and I don't do drugs."

"What, you've never smoked dope before?" asked Nine, and Beth held her gaze as she pressed two pills into her palm and swallowed them. She waited a moment and like a powerful magic, the pain began to lessen.

"At university. A long time ago," she said. Nine smiled as if she had scored a point and Beth felt obliged to qualify her response. "A boyfriend led me astray."

"Ah," said Nine, "you're poisoning your system with those pills you're popping as well as that wine you suck down your throat," said Nine. "It's full of chemical crap." Beth thought her empty wine glass with its cocktail straw, sitting askew, looked a bit forlorn. The pain continued to subside. Relief, gratitude. It was almost overwhelming.

"Can you really get dope on the NHS?" she asked as she watched Nine's slim fingers rolling the paper and then licking the cigarette into shape.

"In a nasal spray. Doesn't give the same hit as smoking," said Nine as she solemnly handed the joint to her. She had one of those cheap flick lighters and the end of the joint gushed in a fiery flame as Beth inhaled. A blast of smoke filled her lungs but she didn't cough; unexpectedly, a rush of contentment flooded into her. Nine was up on her feet, plumping cushions behind her back. "Steady Beth. Just one or two small tokes to start with."

Beth dutifully returned the joint to her. They sat opposite each other, exchanging the joint as if on a cosmic seesaw. *Funny*, thought Beth, *I hate cigarettes, despise their smell, the neediness they evoke in people, yet here I am smoking*. She remembered her conversation with Desmond Davies earlier in the evening. Adaptability. A concept that she hadn't imagined would take the form it had this evening.

"So you were led astray by this boyfriend at university?"

"His name was Dougie."

"So how did it end?" asked Nine.

"One day he was the love of my life and the next day he wasn't."

"Sounds complicated." Nine had brought one of her best Wedgewood saucers from the kitchen to use as an ashtray but Beth didn't care; her mind was now capable of infinite adaptability. Who used bone china saucers these days anyhow?

"The first time I saw him was at the uni folk club. He played the fiddle. He looked like Clint Eastwood."

"So your eyes met across a crowded room?"

"No chance. He had a gorgeous girl hanging off his arm. No one else got a look in."

"So, how did you two get together?"

"I got my violin out. I hadn't played it for years but I had my Grade 8. I was the leader of the senior school orchestra you know."

"I'm not surprised," said Nine.

"It didn't take me long to get the hang of the folk style of playing. Bands were always on the lookout for a girl who can play."

"So you joined Dougie's band?"

"And from there it was a short distance to his bed. I don't remember much about the rest of that year. A frenzy of lust. By the time I was in my final year, I was beginning to feel unhinged by it; like we were soulmates and at the same time my future had been hijacked. I had to make a choice between me and us. And I chose me. I needed to find my own path, think my own thoughts, breath my own air."

"Play your own tune," said Nine, giggling at the naffness of her cliché, "and you've never seen him since? Never been in touch?" asked Nine.

"No but I did meet his son Benjy recently. He won the Young Entrepreneur of the Year Competition. He didn't actually win it first time round but that's a long story. Anyhow I'm going to Skye with Neil to present his prize. I expect Dougie will be there too," said Beth.

"Double wow," said Nine, "are you excited?"

"I don't know how I feel. A bit curious maybe but it was such a long time ago. He's married. To Sally. I hope he's happy. He deserves happiness."

"And this Neil you're going to Skye with? Is he your boyfriend?"

"He's single and we had an evening that went further than I'd planned but now I look like Gollum's sister, I won't be surprised if his ardour will cool."

"Fuckwit," said Nine.

Beth laughed. "I told my brother tonight that I was happily married to my work. I suppose some people would think that was sad."

"If you were a man no one would think having a stellar career was sad."

The joint was finished. Nine began to roll another.

"In my experience a lot of men are threatened by successful women," said Beth.

"We don't need men to make us happy, to define who we are," said Nine, handing the joint to Beth.

She marvelled at the neatness of the joint's construction. "You gave up your academic career, your family, for this George character. Sounds like he had quite a lot to do with defining your identity, your values, your decisions."

"Bullshit. I was a committed pacifist long before I met George. He followed me to Faslane, not the other way round," she said, taking the joint from Beth and inhaling deeply. The end glowed furiously.

"A committed pacifist? What does that mean exactly, Nine? Making a lot of noise? I come across that nonsense every day from critics, politicians, journalists. It's too easy. If you care about nuclear disarmament, get involved with an organisation that has ambitions to lead real change."

"Is that what you think you're doing with your life, Beth? Leading real change?" asked Nine, returning the joint.

Beth looked at her with suspicion. The dope was beginning to unravel her mind. "Of course it is. Creating economic growth in Scotland, not by relying on the UK government or the EU for handouts but by building a belief in people that they can achieve much more than they think they can," she said. Nine was squinting at her. She seemed unconvinced. "But to lead change, Nine, you have to get involved. Step up. Take responsibility."

"You mean not dick around on the sidelines?" said Nine.

Beth heard the sarcastic edge to her voice but was undeterred. "My first job was in the summer holidays at the Gas Board. I was fifteen. There must have been a hundred women working there. The office took up the entire length of the basement. We spent eight mind-numbing hours a day matching pieces of paper together. Invoices to payments. Credit notes to debit notes. Service callouts with service completes. All the bosses were men. Their offices were on the upper floors and we hardly ever saw them. Most of us were on temporary contracts and it was those bosses who decided who stayed and who got kicked out. They didn't know us. We were just numbers to them. Yet despite that, not one of those women, not one single one of them, wanted or believed they could be a boss, even though most of them were far too intelligent to be stuck in such dead-end jobs. I made my mind up there and then that I wanted to be a leader. Because then I could do something to help people like these women realise their full potential."

Beth slumped back in her chair. She was feeling suddenly lightheaded, as if she'd blown up too many balloons.

"So now you're a captain of industry with an office on the top floor. A role model for other women. An inspiration to all those who are prepared to step up and take responsibility." Nine's tone had retained a mild needling quality. She was in the kitchen filling a glass of water. She popped a straw in it and offered it to Beth.

"That's a good thing surely?" asked Beth, taking the glass from her and sipping on the straw. The water slid down her throat but she was struggling to keep her mind from floating away.

"But in the end, isn't it all just vanity?"

"Vanity? You think it's vanity that motivates me to want to make Scotland a better, more prosperous place? I've never heard anything so stupid." Her bad eye was ablaze. It was an effort not to rub it.

Nine was looking at her steadily. "I mean it's vanity for any human being to believe they can lead change, control the future, manipulate our environment. A bloody stupid vanity that builds bombs that could obliterate the human race and at the same time believe everything is under control."

Beth took another sip of water. She felt suddenly sober. A clarity descended. "If I have learned anything about life, it's the importance of having ambition; of having goals, of having a vision of the future and then the guts and determination to drive towards that vision. You may call that vanity but it's a vanity that I'm obstinately attached to."

Nine gave her an enigmatic smile.

"Now time for bed, I think," said Beth briskly.

***

She could hear Nine in the bathroom, the pipes gurgling, the hiss of the shower starting. Tomorrow was Saturday. She would sort out a room for her at The Beacon House. They would organise a job for her. Get her back on a stable footing. She was an intelligent girl, with potential. Beth had good instincts about her.

"There's a bed made up in the spare room," said Beth when Nine returned from the bathroom.

"I'll be fine kipping down here in the front room," said Nine. Beth noticed she was carrying her eye care bag; was looking inside it.

"Which ointment do you prefer?" asked Nine,

holding out two tubes.

"How do you know?" began Beth.

"I've worked in care homes before. Lots of strokes, facial paralysis."

Beth raised her face towards her and Nine put three drops into her eye, then massaged the ointment across the eyeball with the inside of her eyelid. When she stopped, the lid sprang open, clouding her vision, but the grittiness was soothed. Nine then gently shut her eyelid and laid two strips of tape to keep it closed, then placed the lint pad firmly over the eye. "Feels nice?" she asked.

Beth nodded. Nine's movements were as gentle as a fairy, as loving as a daughter.

"Are you doing any eye exercises?" asked Nine.

Beth shook her head.

"You could get a lot more movement in that eyelid if you did. Perhaps not fully closing it but more than you can do now," said Nine.

"Maybe you can show me in the morning," replied Beth, allowing herself to be guided back towards her bedroom. Nine pulled back the covers of her bed. Beth thought for a moment about undressing but lay down fully clothed. Drowsiness was rolling over her and she thought she heard Nine's voice whispering, "Sweet dreams Beth, sweet dreams about your lost love Dougie," but perhaps that was already part of her dream.

***

Beth woke to the sound of rain battering against the window. She prodded her face. Dead on the left.

Normal on the right. Low-level headache. Bearable. She got up, took off the eye patch and unpeeled the tape that held the eye pad in place. The final two strips came off almost on their own. The eye stared back. A little bloodshot but otherwise unchanged. She gazed out on to the sodden streets still half asleep when she remembered the girl. Nine.

The blanket had been folded on the edge of the sofa. She could see a solitary cup and her wine glass from last night. They had been washed and were sitting upended on the draining board. Perhaps there was a note, or some other evidence that Nine had been here but there was nothing, only a sweet smoky smell reminding her of their conversation and the joints from the night before.

She spotted her laptop on the side table. She felt both relief that the girl hadn't robbed her and oddly bereft; she would have liked her to have stayed longer. Had breakfast together. Debated more about the state of the modern world. She put on the kettle. There by the sugar bowl was a small joint, perfectly formed, and a pile of coins; the change from the pizza.

Chapter 7

It was in that moment of wakening, when the first pricks of awareness pepper the mind, that remorse slid over Dougie, as raw as a sea har. His parched throat and raging headache deepened in the gloom of his regret. He sat up. Gingerly. The other side of the bed was dishevelled, the covers twisted as if caught in a spin cycle. Fiona's perfume, lavender and musk, infused the air smelling like both an innocent girl and a seedy tart.

He fell back on the pillow and groaned. Snippets of memory, like pictures on a carousel slide projector flicked through his mind. The call from The Agency telling Benjy that he had won first prize after all; Mr Takashama smiling like an animated puppet, shaking Benjy's hand; Sally's freckled cheek squashed against Benjy's olive skin, her eyes lit up like a slot machine. Then off to the pub to celebrate. Benjy and Dougie's arms laced around each other singing, 'We are the Champions of the World.' Much later, the ten-minute stagger back to Fiona's cottage; her embrace, the beads of her necklace shining like precious stones in the light of the fire: the kisses and stroking; the tumbling into bed; the familiar routines of their lovemaking; and then sleep, drunken sleep, deep and disturbed with both abandon and regret.

He spotted Fiona's necklace on the bedside table and picked it up. The glass beads were smeary and cheap in the daylight. He needed to tell Fiona that it had been a mistake.

He got to his feet, feeling surprisingly steady, though his skull felt as thin as skin. He wet his hands and smoothed down his hair and beard, but it all sprang back, untamed. He pulled on his jeans and jumper from last night. The smell of woodsmoke from the pub fire had infused the fibres and smelt sour.

He walked into the kitchen, drawn by the nutty smell of toast and bacon. Fiona was sitting at the kitchen table with her hands round a mug of tea. She was dressed for the shop, wearing an apron pulled tight around her waist. She turned round on hearing him come in, the Oyster Shack logo on the chest of the apron stretched over her breasts.

"Plenty of tea in the pot," she said happily. He held up his arm, half in greeting, half in refusal.

"No thanks," he said, going back into the bedroom, sitting down on the bed, trying to work out how to escape. He felt the bed sag with her weight as she sat beside him. She found his hand and entwined her fingers through his.

"I'm glad about last night," she said. He looked at her hand and the way her fingers had found their way to tangle with his.

"Are you?" he asked.

"Everything's fine Dougie," she said. He thought that was usually his line and it struck him how empty and hopeless it sounded. "Don't look so worried," she said, squeezing his fingers, "last night doesn't mean we're back together again."

He felt a swell of relief but couldn't look at her.

"You're welcome in my bed any time. I'm not asking for more," she said.

"You should. You're worth more," said Dougie sadly.

"Let me be the judge of that," she said firmly, "what you need is a good breakfast after all that drinking last night." She got to her feet. "One egg or two?" she called out.

So that was it, he thought, things settled between them as easily as how many eggs he wanted. He felt a wave of panic, of feeling more trapped than ever by her generosity. It was too much, there was nothing for him to push against or complain about.

"C'mon," she cried, "you'll be late for the meeting with Mr Takashama."

"What's he still doing here? I thought at first he had his eye on you Fiona," he said, ambling into the kitchen.

"Benjy tells me he has a wife and grown up daughter in Singapore," said Fiona.

"There's something about him that I don't like. Can't work out what his real motives are."

"He's only been here two weeks, Dougie. It takes time for someone like him to open up. Benjy thinks that reading between the lines, he and his wife aren't a strong couple."

Dougie thought for moment what it might mean to be a strong couple. Perhaps it was an accumulation of all the small things of everyday living: the odd laugh; the odd cuddle; the odd sharp word; one egg or two; making allowances for your drunken behaviour the night before.

"Now Benjy has won the money, perhaps he'll show his hand," said Dougie, squeezing Fiona's waist. She laughed like a girl being tickled and he didn't move his hand away.

It had only been a week since Dougie had been in the office Portakabin and the changes seemed radical. The desks were cleared of paper, the filing cabinet drawers were shut, the Christmas decorations that had become a year-long feature had gone. It looked as if they had either just moved in or were just about to move out.

Benjy and Mr Takashama were standing together at the far side of the conference table. Benjy had his jeans on as usual but was wearing a jacket. Mr Takashama was immaculate in his dark suit and Dougie wondered who was doing his laundry for him. He knew he must look like he'd slept in his clothes but at least his hair was freshly washed and combed, flowing over his shoulders in a snowy wave. Sally was handing Mr Takashama a coffee in a small espresso cup. Dougie was mystified, he didn't know they owned a coffee machine let alone such silly wee cups.

"How's Sally today?" asked Dougie. Sally grinned. She was wearing a dress he hadn't seen before. It was made of fine wool and clung to her body, showing the outline of her underwear, in unflattering pulls and lumps.

"Very excited," she said breathlessly.

"Good," replied Dougie, trying to match her mood but failing. He sat down at the conference table, his hangover settling on him; that familiar mix of low-level paranoia and thirst.

Benjy bustled over and slapped him on the back. "OK Dad?" Dougie nodded enthusiastically, not wanting to give Benjy any cause to take the moral high ground.

"Right. We're all here so let's get started," began Benjy. "With the very welcome news that we're £25,000 richer, courtesy of The Agency, it's time to move things forward."

Dougie felt he was listening to a formalised version of his son; a version he showed to other people. Mr Takashama was looking on benevolently. Dougie had the unpleasant notion that if a stranger came into the room, they would mistake Mr Takashama for Benjy's father. He felt his hangover intensifying.

"As agreed we're going to concentrate our production on fine seaweed for the sushi and miso markets. We will need a seeding shed and racks and nets to go out in the loch. Sally and I will need to put together some financials to present to The Agency team when they visit."

Dougie's attention had begun to drift. He had a sudden impulse to row out into the loch and check on the native oysters. Then remembering the high bacteria levels of last week, he wondered if the latest lab report had come back. He spotted a pile of mail stacked up neatly on his desk and it took an effort of will not to reach over and look for it.

"The challenge we've got, Dad," said Benjy, bringing Dougie's attention back to the meeting, "is that harvested seaweed needs to be dried and rolled as close to production as possible. I've asked Mr Takashama to take us through a packaging proposal," said Benjy, sitting down.

There was a silence and Dougie found himself looking towards Mr Takashama, who was getting to his feet. The last time he had seen Mr Takashama stand up in front of people, was when he had sang in the pub at Benjy's birthday party. He could see he was preparing himself in a similar way, standing still with a look of contained concentration, looking down at the floor almost in a bow.

"Benjy is right. Packaging must take place close to the source of production. There are two possible avenues for funding. The first is to apply for an additional grant from The Agency, the second is of course, the banks."

"No banks," said Dougie, "I vowed we would never use them. D'you not think this is getting too big, Benjy? Growing the seaweed is one thing but now you're talking about building a packaging plant?"

Benjy seemed pleased at Dougie's question. "In Japan, growing seaweed is done in small family farms like us, but they work as a collective to run the packaging plant. Although we'll be the first commercial seaweed farm in Scotland, the plan eventually is to get others to join us."

"By being the first, we'll be taking all the risk," said Dougie.

"Mr McKinnon," said Mr Takashama, "I agree banks are seldom a good idea. The Agency offer several grants for this type of enterprise but timing is against us. It will take months to endure the torture of their bureaucracy. I therefore propose that my company will put up the money for the packaging plant as well as the cutting and drying equipment. We can apply for grants retrospectively."

"Oh aye. And what's your price?"

"A full partnership in the new seaweed company. This would be a separate entity from the Oyster Farm."

Silence. Dougie was grateful for it. He was struggling to take it all in. He could see the seaweed plan had gone too far to stop it, but it felt more than just a losing battle. It was like he was losing his son altogether. That Benjy was gaining a new father.

"Please say yes, Dad," said Benjy.

"But what do we know about this man?" asked Dougie, pointing at Mr Takashama, which he knew flouted all boundaries of politeness. "He appeared in our lives a few days ago and now we're starting up a new business with him."

"You could ask him the same question, what does he know about us? He's putting his own money into this, Dad. The risks are even," said Benjy back.

"That's just it, Benjy. Too many bloody risks. And what do we know about seaweed? We eat black pudding and oysters. It's all too foreign. Too different. I don't like it, Benjy. We're doing fine just as we are."

"I respect caution, Mr McKinnon," said Mr Takashama, and at that moment Dougie thought he might hit him. "Dr Colquhoun and her team from The Agency have confirmed they're coming here in a month's time." Dougie noticed that Mr Takashama's normally flawless BBC accent faltered at Colquhoun. He pronounced it like a Chinese surname, Ka-Hone with the emphasis on each syllable. "Please honour me with this time to convince you of my good intentions," he said, and finished with a slight inclination of his head. Dougie felt his politeness was a slimy thing you couldn't get to grips with.

"Dad, I want to build on what we've got here, not destroy it. Please give us a chance to convince you," said Benjy. Dougie remembered that voice when Benjy wanted to see *Jurassic Park* for the third time.

"You don't need my approval, son. You've got everything nicely tied up without me," said Dougie, standing up, "and I don't need time to be convinced. I'm not interested in this and never will be, but I would never stand in your way, Benjy. Go ahead but leave me out of it. Now I'm off back to the house to change into my work clothes and then I'm going to check on the oysters and harvest the crop for the weekend orders. As far as I'm concerned it's business as usual."

He walked down the path behind the Portakabin that led towards his cottage. So much for being in the estuary of life, he thought ruefully. Beth Colquhoun was going to visit. A new company was going to be formed. Thousands were going to be spent on equipment and a packaging plant. It felt more like an imminent deluge. He remembered seeing the flooding in the Thames Estuary on the TV and the shock on the faces of people who had never experienced it before: 'How could such a thing happen in their well-ordered lives?' He had a similar feeling now. All these people, plans, ideas would cause one hell of a mess and he didn't know who to blame for it.

His cottage sat behind the sand dunes, screened from the wind by a line of silver birch trees. He let himself in the front door. It was never locked. The small windows made the kitchen seem gloomy even on a bright spring morning like this. He switched on the kitchen light and poured himself a whisky.

He sat on his regular chair. It was dark red leather, cracked with age around the buttonholes and cold to the touch. There was a smell of damp in the room that would only disappear if he lit a fire. The walls half rendered, half stone added to the chilly feel. He faced Benjy's chair and tried to remember the last time they had sat opposite each other of an evening, chatting, playing cards. Benjy preferred staying at Sally's place these days and it was only a matter of time before he would be gone for good. The dank air hung around him; it was the smell of absence; an absence so profound it was as if no one had lived here for a long time.

He remembered the pile of mail he had picked up on his way out of the office. He got up, refilling his glass as he leafed through the letters. There it was. The most recent lab report on the water quality. It was two pages long. Not good news but not a catastrophe either. The water was still deteriorating, but only slightly. It was now borderline. He knew what Benjy would say. Trash the lot. Never take a risk that the crop would cause food poisoning. Dougie took a swallow of the whisky. As long as it was borderline there was hope, he thought. He would test the water again today. If the results were still poor, then he would mention it to Benjy. Meanwhile he would tell no one. It was only then he realised the irony of that thought. He was the only person interested in oysters now. There was really no one else to tell.

Chapter 8

Beth watched Margaret, her sister-in-law, as she busied herself with the canapés. She was like a woman in those fat lady paintings with huge bloated bodies and tiny hands, surprisingly dainty on their feet.

"Smoked mackerel and horseradish," she said, holding out a tray of pastries. "C'mon now, eat up, you need building up." Her voice had a nasal whine, common amongst the refined accents of Glasgow.

Beth smiled. "You were always a great cook," she said, taking one.

"Silly me. What was I thinking of? Offering you one like this. Alec told me you can only eat and drink with a straw these days. I'll mash these up for you."

"No need," protested Beth, but Margaret was already pulling the liquidiser from the cupboard.

"You don't have to be a doctor to see your face is not getting any better," she stated. Beth thought unhappiness spilled out of Margaret's big body and was manifested in these small cruel insensitivities. The buzz of the liquidiser began and she had a sudden longing for one of Nine's joints.

"I'm finding talking easier," she said brightly.

Margaret turned, pity oozing from her.

"I mean I know I look like one of those Shari Lewis hand puppets, you know the ones that speak from the side of their mouth, but at least people can understand what I'm saying."

"Alec and I think you should have a second opinion. It's been going on too long."

Beth wondered what would happen if she shared her innermost fears with Margaret. That she thought it had gone on too long, that it might never get better, but it was an idle thought, her vulnerability was too tender to be exposed.

"Compared to some people's problems, this Palsy is inconvenient but not serious. I mean some people have health problems that are potentially life threatening," said Beth. Margaret looked perplexed, as if she knew that Beth's comment was directed at her but couldn't work out the connection.

Beth watched as Margaret posted mouthfuls of food into the red yawn of her mouth. It was the eating action of a famished hamster, thought Beth, though Margaret was looking more like a hippo than a hamster these days. Her wrists were braceletted with fat, forcing her watch to be fastened further up her arm. Beth couldn't remember seeing the watch before. She hoped it wasn't new. She had believed Alec when he said there was no money for school fees for their two boys.

Margaret flicked her hair away from her face; it was blonde, glossy, and expensively highlighted. It reminded her of the lovely girl his brother had married twenty years ago. Her hair was the last thing to be neglected whilst the rest of her had grown and grown, then melted, like wax from a large candle.

"You look exhausted," said Margaret, "and no wonder. You're in the papers all the time. They never say anything nice about you. Always finding something to criticise. It must wear you down."

She had the sudden impulse to reply that she had had plenty of practice fielding Margaret's snipes over the years but she smiled instead. "Did you read the article about Dougie's son winning the Young Entrepreneur Competition after the original winner was caught cheating?"

"Alec thought that was a clever bit of PR to show people you had a softer side," she said, scooping a spoonful of pale cream sludge into a bowl. "So you're going to meet Dougie McKinnon after all these years."

"I'm going to Skye to meet his son, Benjy McKinnon."

"I never thought you and Dougie were suited," said Margaret. "He had no drive or ambition, he'd have been a weight round your neck," she said authoritatively, in the way something who is used to carrying a lot of weight would.

"Alec and I have some business to discuss," she said, and Margaret's eyes brightened; she knew the business would be the school fees. "I think we should do that before dinner, don't you?"

"He'll be in his office down the garden I expect. Having a smoke." Her face contorted, a pantomime of disgust. "I'll bring down your canapés."

"Thanks, and remember that straw!" she said,

attempting a note of lightness but Margaret returned it with another look of pity.

***

"So Alec, how are things in the world of oil company bargains?" Beth asked, settling into a chair opposite him in his log cabin in the garden. Pieces of grass and mud had stuck to the soles of her shoes where she had stumbled off the path in the dark.

He peered at her through a cloud of smoke. "You'll be getting the proposal shortly."

She reached over to take one of his cigarettes, but Alec moved them out of her reach.

"How does Margaret seem to you Beth? The doctor's put her on some new pills to help with her nerves but they're slowing down the metabolism. She's putting on more weight."

"Margaret needs tranquilisers because she's miserable. She's miserable because she's fat. She's fat because she eats too much and does too little exercise. The solution is self-evident."

"That's harsh," he said, and this time she caught him off guard and grabbed the cigarette packet. He gave her one of his older brother's looks of disapproval as she took one out and lit it.

"Harsh but true, Alec. It's denial, blaming her weight problems on depression, rather than her lack of willpower and laziness. She's inside that house as we speak, stuffing canapés into herself."

He was just about to reply when the door of the cabin creaked open and Margaret appeared with a tray. She was flushed from the effort of walking. Beth watched her backside spread as she put the tray on the table.

"Main course will be ready in fifteen minutes. Beef Wellington. Dauphinoise potatoes. Your favourite," she announced.

"Thank you dear," replied Alec.

"I'll leave you to it then," she said as she turned and left.

"D'you think she heard us talking about her?" hissed Alec.

"I hope so. Might give her a kick up that generous backside of hers," said Beth.

"Honestly Beth, you haven't mellowed with age have you?" said Alec.

"Margaret's heading for serious health problems if she doesn't do something about her weight. I think some plain speaking is needed."

"You've always been good at that. Even as kids."

"I had nothing to lose did I? You were the one they poured all their love and expectations into. That private school that you hated, you never wanted any of it did you?"

"I used to envy you, Beth. It all came so easily, the school work, the violin."

"Only they didn't notice."

"You weren't frightened to answer back. Remember that time when you told Mum and Dad you were leaving the Girl Guides? I thought they would explode."

"You tried too hard to please, Alec, and here you are, aged fifty, still trying to please Margaret by keeping the boys at a school you can't really afford."

"This isn't about me trying to please anyone. It's about doing the best for my kids. I need a loan of five thousand for the summer and autumn school fees. That's all I'm asking."

"I'm not going to lend you money, Alec," said Beth.

"Honestly Beth. You're loaded. You wouldn't miss fifty grand and all I'm asking is for five. I'll pay you back in full. With interest if you want. "

"I'm not going to lend you the money, I'm going to it give to you. I'll transfer two and a half thousand to your bank account tonight. That'll pay the fees up till the end of the summer term. It'll give you time to make other arrangements for the autumn term, an advance on your bonus perhaps, or a loan from the bank, or even to make arrangements for the boys to go to another school."

"Better than a snotter up my nose I suppose."

"Thank you for that display of gratitude. However, there's a condition," she said.

"You surprise me," he said sarcastically.

"I never want you to ask me to lend you money again."

"Favourite son must fund his own way in future, is that what you're saying?"

"Something like that," she replied, reaching for her bowl, realising that Margaret had forgotten a straw. "This damn Palsy," she said, taking a deep breath and blowing smoke out the side of her mouth.

"Is that why you're smoking?" he said.

"I've taken to having the odd spliff in the evening. It helps with the headaches," she said, "purely for medicinal purposes you understand."

"D'you not think it makes more sense to go to a doctor and get a second opinion rather self-medicate with illegal drugs?" said Alec, sounding exasperated. "And what about our conversation at dinner the other week? About getting some help? A housekeeper? Have you done anything about that?"

"Don't despair, Alec. I have a plan."

"I worry about you being on your own in that big flat of yours."

"Being alone is not the same as being lonely. I've plenty of friends, a wonderful job; doing something important for the country I love. At times my life can be so frantic, time to myself is a real luxury."

"I know what you mean. I often escape to my log cabin to get away from Margaret and the boys. Have a smoke without being nagged. But my family are the most important thing I have. I would hate it if I didn't have one."

"But I've got a family," she said. "You."

He leaned forward to stub out his cigarette out. They both avoided eye contact, both avoiding the reality that they were finding their relationship hard work. She was about to say this when there was a sudden crash and a cry outside. She thought it was a cat overturning a bin but Alec had leapt to his feet.

"Put the outside light on!" he shouted as he rushed

out the door. There, illuminated on the pathway, was the fallen shape of Margaret. Alec was leaning over her. Beth stood in the doorway, watching as he tried to turn her over. Another drama, another avoidable drama.

"Help me get her to her feet."

"D'you think it's wise to move her, Alec? She may have broken something. Let me call an ambulance."

"Are you alright dear?" asked Alec, moving strands of hair away from her eyes.

"Leg hurts," said Margaret in a small voice.

Beth told the 999 operator that Margaret was a large lady.

"How heavy?" They had asked. She hadn't known. She guessed twenty stone.

The two paramedics who turned up found it hard to disguise their delight. "We've got the first bariatric ambulance in Scotland. We haven't had a chance to try it out on the sort of patient it was designed for. It can take up to fifty-five stone you know," he said, lowering the hydraulic ramp to the pavement and a pushing out a wide trolley with side bars.

"Margaret isn't fifty-five stone," said Alec, looking dazed as they wheeled the trolley through the house to the back garden.

They placed an arc light on the path. It had begun to drizzle, raindrops illuminated like a shower of pearls in the white light. Their mission statement might be to treat obese patients with respect and safety but Beth wondered if that was actually possible. The heaving and pushing, the instructions yelled over the body of Margaret who lay rigid, eyes squeezed tight as if wishing herself away from this scene. It took an hour to manoeuvre her into the ambulance.

Beth stood in the kitchen surrounded by the detritus of the dinner party preparations, a cup of coffee in her hand. She had found a pack of straws in the cupboard and stood smoking one of Alec cigarettes and sipping on her straw. The boys were due back shortly. She should stay and make sure they were OK, tidy up the place for when Alec and Margaret got back from the hospital but she stubbed her cigarette out on one of the plates, picked up her coat and quietly closed the door behind her.

***

The Beacon House was the last building at the end of a line of tenement flats in a part of town that had avoided the gentrification creep of the west end. Beth had accepted the invitation to chair the Board of Trustees without hesitation. A charity dedicated to rebuilding the lives of homeless and vulnerable young women was a cause dear to her heart.

She parked outside the house and sat in her car, the night sounds of the city distant and sporadic. She could see lights on in the hallway and in the upper bedrooms. She waited for ten minutes but no one came or went. She got out of the car, rang the bell and waited on the stone step.

"Hello Nine," she said. Nine stood with her arms wrapped round her. She was wearing a polo neck jumper, her blonde hair tousled in a spikey cut that suited her elfin features. She had begun to shiver.

"How are you?" asked Beth.

Nine seemed preoccupied, as if she had asked a difficult question. "Come in," she said finally.

The house smelt of curry, sweet and musty at the same time. Nine led her down to the kitchen at the end of the corridor. It was a large room. The Formica surfaces were scrubbed clean; a large table in the corner had mismatched chairs pushed under it. The light from the neon strip was harsh, washing all colour from Nine's complexion.

"Most of the girls go to bed before ten on Saturdays," said Nine, filling up the kettle. The pipes creaked, the gas stove hissed. "We all work weekends. Sunday's our busiest day." Beth nodded and sat down at the kitchen table.

"I'm stacking shelves at Bargain Basement. I'll get promoted to the till if I don't screw up. Something to aim for," said Nine, putting a cup of black coffee in front of her. "Sorry, no milk. No straws either I'm afraid," she added.

"I'm glad you're settling in," said Beth, warming her hands on the mug but not making any effort to drink it. "No sign of George then?" she asked. Nine looked up, startled, as if she had forgotten that Beth knew about him.

"I'm sure you didn't turn up here for an update on my love life." She pulled the neck of her jumper down in an involuntary act of tension. Beth could see the black hole of her tattoo peeping out and wondered if she needed to wear a scarf to cover the tattoo for work.

"I've been thinking about you these past weeks. Wondering how you're getting on."

"Have you been doing your eye exercises?" asked Nine.

"Not as much as I should have. I'm going back to the doctor next week. She's going to arrange more tests. See if anything more nasty is going on," she said, surprised by how much easier it was to confide in Nine than her sister-in-law.

"Your body has all the resources to heal itself without doctors but you've got to listen to it. Work with it," she said.

"I want to ask you something."

Nine relaxed, then took a sip from her cup and waited for Beth to speak.

"Do you know anything about Excel spreadsheets?" asked Beth.

"What? Reading them? Creating them? Transferring data onto them?"

"What about social media? I had a look at the Faslane Site. It was as antiquated as The Agency's."

"Those folks at Faslane were technology dinosaurs but anyone with half a brain knows that social media is the future of communicating with your supporters. But why all the questions?"

"How would you feel about doing some light domestic duties? No heavy cleaning but shopping, a bit of cooking maybe," added Beth.

"Are you offering me a job?"

"I need help, Nine. Domestic stuff but also some administration. I'm organising a big visit for businessmen in the summer and frankly the staff at

The Agency are too stretched to cope. I'd pay a good salary," she added.

"Living in your flat? With you?" asked Nine.

"Yes," added Beth. She could see Nine was trying to hide her surprise.

"Just till the end of the summer until the deal is finished. Till this Palsy clears up," added Beth, shocked that she was playing the sympathy card.

"I'll have to think about it," said Nine, recovering her normal nonchalance.

Beth put down her coffee. "I imagine you'll have plenty of time to do that at Bargain Basement."

Chapter 9

Dougie and Benjy had transferred the mature oysters from the trestles in the bay into the holding area where the low tide would expose them to air twice a day. Opening and closing their shells would make them stronger and prepare them for a life outside water. They worked in silence which was their usual way, though Dougie could tell there was an edge to it today. Benjy was frowning, his mouth tight, his eyes down. He remembered the same expression when he was at school and had fallen out with Allie McCallum. The air was thick with dampness as if it too was brooding about something. Dougie hauled the last of the nets into the holding bay.

"Get the tractor, Benjy, and we'll start packing the ones from last week. They'll be well hardened off by now. I reckon we've got enough for the extra order from the Four Sisters as well as the Glasgow shipment."

"Did you get the results of the latest water test, Dad?" asked Benjy. "Sally told me she sent off another sample."

"The levels are back to normal. Just natural variation," replied Dougie. The lie had slipped out of him as if it had a will of its own. The latest report had shown the bacteria levels had worsened and were now at dangerous level. Even the most optimistic farmer would have stopped harvesting by now. Dougie thought he was about to say something but he nodded and walked off towards the tractor parked on the sand dunes.

Dougie watched him, the sound of his waders schlepping in the shallows merging with the soft breeze, and wondered why he had lied to Benjy. He had never done that before.

Benjy returned with the tractor and they began to pack the oysters in wooden crates, lightly taping each shell to retain a bit of water, keeping them fresh for longer. It was gentle, loving work and it never failed to soothe Dougie. He noticed Benjy was working fast, with a roughness in his movement,

"Not too tight with the tape," he said quietly.

Benjy stopped working. "Dad. Please say you'll stay for the prize-giving weekend. The Agency folks have invited us all for dinner at the Four Sisters."

"I've told you before. I've no intention of turning up."

"C'mon Dad. You're my secret weapon. You'll charm the pants off Beth Colquhoun and Neil Phillips. Look how you handled Mr Takashama when he first arrived. He was all for going home but you and Fiona made him want to stay. He even sang that weird song. People like you, Dad, they open up to you."

"I'll drive the oyster shipment down to Glasgow as usual on Friday night and stay over with Malcolm Crawford on Saturday night. They'll be long gone by the time I'm back."

"So what do I say to people when they ask me where you are?" he asked.

"The truth, of course. I'm in Glasgow on a delivery. Someone's got to keep the business going," said Dougie.

Benjy stared at him then, a mixture of hurt and pride. Dougie knew he wouldn't ask again. Benjy marched back to the tractor, carrying a stack of pallets as easily as if they were empty. He hadn't told Benjy that he knew Beth; that she had broken his heart, that he couldn't face meeting her again. It wasn't a lie as such, he reasoned, but he knew an omission that big was even worse than a lie. He felt as heavy as one of the loaded palettes but like Benjy, had no intention of showing it.

Six hours later and Dougie had arrived in Glasgow and finished all his deliveries. He pushed open the door and a rush of pub air escaped to greet him. The polished wood of the bar, the golden glow of the light behind the optics drew him forwards. He took a bar menu that was slotted in a stainless steel holder on the bar; there was a picture of a sombrero with 'Mexican Specials' written below it. He decided on a chicken burrito.

After twenty-five years there were bound to be changes. A fruit machine in the corner where the dartboard used to be; the bar stools reupholstered in black plastic that felt sticky to the touch; but as he took it all in, he realised the pub was much as he remembered it from all those years ago. He could swear it was the same carpet, dark blue with a small geometric pattern in cream. He thought, *My feet have walked across this carpet many times before. Perhaps microfibres of my clothing, skin particles are still here, ingrained in the fabric of the place.*

One or two solitary men sat around nursing their pints. He could hear the faint twang of guitar chords from country and western music being piped in to fill the silence. It was Friday night and in his day the place would have been heaving. Since the university had been relocated across town, the pub had become stranded from its old clientele, making it feel both neglected and preserved at the same time.

He ordered a pint and his food, staring at the gassy froth of the beer as the barman put it down in front of him. He thought about telling him that this was the pub where he asked Beth to marry him, where she had said yes. Where he had taken the ring pull from a can of lager and placed it on her wedding ring finger. He had a sudden feeling that he might have invented the bit about the ring pull; maybe he'd seen it in a movie somewhere, but as he thought about it more, he was sure. He hadn't made it up.

"Penny for them?" asked Malcolm as he sat down beside him.

"Cost you a lot more than that," replied Dougie.

"God I haven't been in this pub since I first came to Glasgow and that was over twenty years ago. Now I know why. I would've preferred a plate of your oysters and a glass of champagne at Pier 42," said Malcolm, "it's what I would have expected a prize-winning oyster farmer would have suggested."

"I'll get the drinks seeing as I've dragged you here. It was a lovely piece you wrote about Benjy by the way."

"Glad you liked it."

"Thanks for keeping my name and picture out of it. Benjy's the one to take the credit."

"I've known you long enough, Dougie, to know you like to keep a low profile. Though that son of yours is going to make it hard for you. He's a star in the making."

"I'm worried about him, Malkie. He's about to get into a business partnership with a Singapore businessman. Mr Takashama. There's something about the man I don't trust. I was hoping you could use your contacts to find out more about him."

"Dougie, I'm flattered you think I could but it doesn't work like that. These people are smart. They only make available the information they want you to read. I'm unlikely to find out anything more than you could find if you Googled him. You do know how to use a search engine, don't you?"

"I don't have a computer and the only engines I know about are those in my tractor and my boat. This Mr Takashama sings Japanese folk songs. Apparently it takes a lifetime to learn the technique. Maybe that's an angle."

"I'll have a look but don't hold your breath. And talking of folk singing, how is the lovely Fiona?"

"It was all getting a bit heavy."

"Poor Fiona. Has anyone told her she'd be better off without you?"

"She's excited about the prize-giving ceremony next weekend. Everybody's excited about it. I'm surprised that a busy woman like Beth Colquhoun is coming," said Dougie.

"She's smart with a nose for positive PR. I know Desmond Davies from The Agency. He spends most of the time complaining about her. He's as useless as a chocolate teapot, but she'll need to be careful."

"Why?"

"Spends too much time looking Eastwards with this Rubikon brigade. She's neglected the distilleries and oilmen closer to home. My editor's always looking for an excuse to discredit her, misogynist bastard that he is. But you'll get a chance to meet her. Make up your own mind."

"That's what I wanted to talk to you about, Malkie. I'm not going. I'm doing my normal run down here and after I've made the deliveries, I was hoping you could put me up."

"I would have thought you would have wanted to be there, that Benjy would have wanted it too. Big celebration and all that."

"Can you keep a secret?"

"You're asking a journalist if he can keep a secret?"

"I'm asking one of my oldest friends if he'll keep something to himself," said Dougie.

"I'm all ears," replied Malcolm, ordering them another two pints.

Dougie waited for the barman to put the two glasses in front of them and move out of earshot.

"I was engaged to Beth Colquhoun when we were at university. In our final year. I proposed to her in this pub."

"Bloody hell, Dougie. Beth Colquhoun?"

"One day we were going to get married, the next she was gone. It nearly broke me." Dougie stared at his pint morosely. "I've learned over the years to put it at the back of my mind. To pretend it never happened. I can't face the thought of seeing her, of stirring up the past again."

"Does Benjy know?"

"No, and I don't want him to know."

"I'm surprised."

"That I don't want to tell him?"

"Not that, no but Beth's behaviour's odd. She's a pro. She's made no declaration of interest."

"What are you talking about?"

"When you're judging something that involves giving away public money like this Young Entrepreneur Competition, you must declare any connection with any of the competitors. Beth's made no such declaration that I know of. My editor would be all over me if she had. If it was found out that she was an ex-fiancée of yours, Benjy's win could be invalid. You know how people these days are paranoid about public service employees being dishonest with public money."

"That's ridiculous Malcolm. She hasn't made a formal notice that she knows me because she doesn't know me. All this happened over twenty years ago. We haven't spoken since."

"There's definitely something smelly about this, Dougie. There was all that palaver about the first choice lass being a cheat and now the second choice turns out to be the son of an old fiancée. It all makes a cracking story, Dougie. My editor would fucking love it," he said, draining his glass.

"But you're not going to tell him are you Malkie? You and me are going to have a nice bevvy next weekend whilst Benjy gets his prize and then all this will blow over."

"I'll keep my word to you Dougie because I care about Benjy and it's been a while since I was out on a bevvy with Dougie McKinnon, famous for his bird pulling. We could start off at the new bar at the top of Byers Road and then go on to The Swing in Sauchiehall Street."

"Sounds bloody awful but if you're buying, fine."

"I'm not sure about the double denim and donkey jacket look Dougie. It makes you stand out as a bit of a chuechter. And that pony tail. Have you thought about getting your hair cut?"

Dougie looked at the shiny pate of Malcolm Crawford and let out a roar of laughter.

"You're just a jealous guy," he said, but Malcolm was serious.

"Actually Dougie you're not far off the mark with that. You've a wonderful son that any father would be proud of. Don't screw up his life because you're too much of a coward to face up to your past. If I were you I'd see Beth this week and tell her to make a formal declaration of interest before it's too late. The presentation can go ahead as planned with you at Benjy's side. That's where you should be and you know it."

"And if she doesn't make this declaration?"

"If she doesn't, and this story gets out, it could be the firing squad for all of you."

"And how do you suggest I get to see her? And even if I did, would she listen to what I've got to say?"

"If you care about Benjy you'll figure that out, Dougie."

Chapter 10

"Just the usual trim?" asked Jamie. Dougie thought he sounded absentminded, as if he didn't expect a reply. He could see black pockmarks peppering the edge of the mirror where the silvering had worn. He had been coming here for fifteen years and had never noticed before that the place was growing old in small incremental examples of wear and tear, just like him. Jamie undid the elastic band that held Dougie's ponytail, fanning the hair over his shoulders where it hung unappetisingly around his face.

"My pal Malcolm thinks long hair's a bit naff," said Dougie.

"I've been telling you that for years," said Jamie.

"Most men my age are bald," said Dougie, but as he watched Jamie lifting a swag and let it fall on his shoulders, he could see that some people might think it was neglect, not pride that had stopped him from cutting it before.

"Aye OK then, cut it all off," he said, enjoying Jamie's look of surprise.

"It'll cost you more than your usual tenner you know," said Jamie, laughing, "and how much d'you want off? A number two all over? Very on trend."

"Just a tidy cut above the ears but enough on top to put a comb through. That's plenty change for now," he said.

Jamie towelled his wet hair, then sprayed something on it and raked it into slick furrows. Jamie winked as he picked up the scissors. It was as if he was picking up a knife and fork and was about to tuck into a big plate of food. It was the speed of it that most shocked Dougie. His hair had been long for twenty-six years, the same number of seconds it was taking Jamie to cut it off. Dougie watched as hanks of hair fell from him, littering the floor, causing him mild feelings of panic.

"So what's brought this on? Is there a new lass on the scene?" asked Jamie as he began to chop further into his hairline, fluffy tufts of white hair landing in his lap like thistledown.

"No lassies but change is in the air. Benjy's engaged. No doubt they'll set a date soon. And he wants to expand the business."

"Nice picture of him in the paper winning that competition. Sea urchins or something was it? You must be very proud," and Dougie realised with a small start of guilt that he was feeling more burdened than proud. He wouldn't be gearing himself up to meet Beth Colquhoun if Benjy hadn't won that competition. He couldn't explain it in rational terms but having his hair cut felt like a way to get some control back in his life.

"A wee beard tidy too? Finish things off nicely," said Jamie, not waiting for an objection before switching on the trimmer and moving in around his chin and cheeks in deft movements. "No extra charge," he said, smiling. "There. All done," he said, fluffing the back of his neck and shoulders with a brush. It felt like a pesky mosquito and Dougie shooed it away. He looked at his reflection like a prisoner posing for a mug shot. "Don't look so miserable," said Jamie cheerily, "if there isn't a new lass on the scene there soon will be. You look the business," and he took the cloak from his shoulders with a flourish, like a matador working his cape.

"The big bosses are coming to Skye to present his prize. I don't want him to be ashamed of how his old dad looks," he said, slipping off the chair and putting on his donkey jacket. He saw Jamie look at it despairingly.

The wind felt cold on his neck and Dougie turned up the collar of his jacket. He had never understood why men wore scarves till now. He walked towards the town centre, catching his profile on the shop windows as he walked past, surprising himself a little less on each occasion so by the time he reached George Square he had become familiar with his new look. He had even begun to enjoy the way the wind whipped his hair around his face and then settled back on itself in a messy way, with a bit of curl to it. The clock on the Town Hall told him there was no time for a quick bolster, and the thought of meeting Beth sober added to the impression that this was happening to someone other than himself.

There was a queue outside the exhibition centre. He never queued normally and this one would have put him off, no question. However, he was already getting used to idea of doing strange things as he joined the back of it.

A banner had been strung up outside. 'Have your say about the BIG PLAN for Glasgow'. He marvelled that so many people didn't have better things to do on a Saturday afternoon. A couple of ladies in their early sixties stood in front of him. They were discussing the fact that vegetables didn't taste of anything these days: "Carrots," said one of them, "soft as butter." Dougie didn't think this sounded like the conversation of political activists; maybe they had confused this queue for the bingo next door but as they got to the entrance, they hurried inside with the eagerness of bargain hunters.

The Centre was filled with cream-coloured light from a plastic roof and smelt of damp wool carpet mixed with cleaning fluid. Rows of metal seats had been arranged in lecture style in front of a stage and around the perimeter were various display boards. One said 'BIG PLANS FOR GLASGOW'S FUTURE' and beneath it was a picture of the old electronics factory on the Edinburgh Road with an artist's impression of a renovated building, thin people walking purposefully on a wide boulevard against a modern skyline. The sky was blue with fluffy clouds, a dead giveaway that whoever had drawn it had never actually been to Glasgow, let alone the old electronics factory on the Edinburgh Road.

Dougie chose a seat at the end of a row, near to the front. He picked up the programme and pretended to read it. His palms had begun to sweat, his heartbeat was raised. The waiting was always the worst bit, he told himself. Worrying that it would all go wrong. He studied at the programme. Beth's welcome was scheduled to be first. His plan was to go up to her after she came off the stage and give her a note. He had written down his number and a message, 'Please call, it's important.' He had swithered about whether she would recognise him so he wrote his name at the bottom. Now he'd had his hair cut off he thought that was a sensible precaution. The whole thing would be over in a second and then he could escape.

The place was filling up and he felt glad that Beth had attracted a good crowd. He imagined it would be a dispiriting experience to talk to an empty room, especially one this big. The stage was dominated by a long table that had been covered in a tartan cloth with vases of thistles placed at regular intervals along its length. The thistles were like colourless weeds against the dark cloth. *You can take nationalistic sensibilities too far,* he thought. They would have been better choosing something more showy: chrysanthemums or roses.

A girl had come on to the stage. She had long, heavy hair that made Dougie remember the loss of his own. He recalled Benjy talking about Beth's secretary and thought this might be the same girl. The hair and heavy make-up gave her an unhappy look. She bustled over to the table and was laying sheaves of papers and place names against each of the table settings. *Crikey,* thought Dougie, what if Beth didn't come off the stage after her bit but went back to sit at the table? That would mean he would have to sit through all the presentations and try and catch her at the end. Then there would be a risk he would miss her in the midst of all the others leaving the stage at the same time.

He was so preoccupied with figuring out what he

would do in that eventuality that he didn't notice the first of the presenters filing onto the stage. A smatter of applause started. Dougie found himself clapping too although he didn't remember making a decision to participate in the proceedings.

Beth was the last person to come onto the stage. She was wearing a dark red jacket and black skirt, her flesh-coloured tights had a silky sheen. Her hair was like an auburn curtain that fell over to the side; he craned his neck but couldn't see her face properly. She was carrying a folder under her right arm and compared to the four men in front of her she seemed tiny. He had a sudden impulse to leap to his feet and help her up the steps to the stage. To his amazement he felt tears fill his eyes at the sight of her. She seemed so familiar and precious. He knew in that instant he couldn't face her. He saw the witch girl dawdling at the side. He half-walked, half-ran up to her and pushed the note into her hands. She looked at him and blinked, her eyelashes so laden with mascara, it was like she was blinking in slow motion.

"Give this to Beth Colquhoun," he said, and as if remembering his manners added, "please. It's important."

The girl appraised him coldly for a second and shrugged her shoulders in the way he had seen Benjy's Sally doing when it was one of her moody days. He turned and hurried out of the hall without looking back.

***

It had been seven years since the smoking ban but the walls in the old Doublet pub still gave off a stale smell of nicotine. A whiff from the toilets hung in the air like disappointment. The afternoon crowd were all men, middle-aged and sullen. Dougie put his phone on the bar in front of him but apart from Benjy calling and asking when he'd be home, the thing remained silent. Maybe the devil lassie hadn't given Beth the note. Or maybe she had and Beth didn't fancy calling him. Whatever the reason, it was useless to speculate and he ordered another pint to ease the waiting.

The afternoon drifted by in a daze; a TV had been switched on in the corner and a game of snooker was making its slow progress to the climax. The volume had been switched off and Dougie missed the click and clack of balls hitting each other. It was a lovely sound, snooker balls kissing. He went to the toilet, realising only when he was washing his hands that he had left his phone on the bar. Fuck. He wouldn't blame any of the poor buggers in the pub if they had taken it. "That'll learn me," he said to himself ruefully.

His pint, half-finished, was waiting for him when he returned and there beside it was his phone. He didn't know what was more surprising, the fact that the phone hadn't been stolen or that there was a text message from Beth. 'Got your note. 3 Bell Street, Merchant city, 8pm.' He finished off the pint and pocketed his phone. The bartender lifted his glass to refill it but Dougie shook his head; he already felt queasy with nerves.

He was early getting to Bell Street. There was a low wall adjacent to Beth's apartment and he decided to sit there and pass the time by watching the Saturday evening crowd. The Merchant City was full of pretentious pubs, as unlike the Doublet as you could imagine. The clientele were mostly young, well-heeled men and women wearing tight clothes that seemed to be designed to restrict movement and promote discomfort. It had begun to rain and the girls were skittering along under hastily put up umbrellas, tottering on high heels and being saved from falling by their friends. It was like someone had put them all on a skating rink and sped up the film.

Dougie was beginning to feel odd, as if he had been lifted outside his body and was observing the business of life looking down from the sky. He felt light-headed as if he hadn't eaten for hours, though he had wolfed down a pie supper from the chip shop next door to the Doublet. Queasiness settled on him, his insides feeling like they had been coated in grease. He turned up the collar of his jacket, the rain trickled down his forehead and neck; it felt cooling, soothing. He wondered if he was developing a temperature.

He had rehearsed the meeting with Beth so that it was ingrained in his mind, able to withstand any onslaught of nerves that might hit him. He would accept a cup of coffee, have a wee chit-chat about what they had been up to in the lifetime since they had last met; maybe have a laugh about how things had turned out for the best after all. Then when things had warmed up between them, he would mention the conversation with Malcolm Crawford and suggest she tells the authorities that she had known him at university so there would be no problem with Benjy and his prize. Then a quick cheerio and see you in Skye.

A girl was hurrying across the road towards him. She was a skinny slip of a thing wearing a huge coat that flapped about her like black wings.

"Dougie McKinnon?" she asked. "I've been watching you for the last twenty minutes from Beth's flat. She's on the phone just now but you'd better come up before you get soaked."

Dougie was dazzled by the possibility of who this girl might be. She was in her early twenties, and a mad thought came to him that she was the right age to be their daughter. He could see a black tattoo on her neck. Crikey, what was Beth thinking of to allow her to mutilate herself like that? He stared at her like a dumb animal.

"Chill. It's just a tattoo. C'mon, I'm getting wet," she said impatiently, and he levered himself off the small wall and followed her. It was only as he got moving did the dizziness hit him. *It must be nerves*, he told himself. He was never sick with drink, especially not after only two pints.

The flat was one of those corporate places that oozed money and loneliness at the same time, as if no one enjoyed living in it, just enjoyed the business of owning something expensive. The girl took away his jacket. He watched it dripping, leaving dark marks on the blond-coloured carpet. He sat down gingerly on the sofa. It had deep cushions that pulled you under, the sort of furniture that was the height of luxury in photographs but was uncomfortable to sit on.

"What's your name?" he asked the girl as she came back into the living room offering him a glass of water. *I must look like I need one*, he thought, and took it gratefully from her. Chucking up over Beth's expensive carpet was definitely not part of his plan.

"Nine," she said. Dougie wondered if he had heard her correctly. He was about to ask her to repeat it when she said. "You're exactly as I expected you to look." Dougie nodded, although he had no idea what she was talking about. "Beth said you looked like Clint Eastwood when she first met you."

Dougie smiled. "Unfortunately I don't have his money," he said, loosening the top button of his shirt; the place was like a furnace. He got up from the couch and walked round the room. Nine's gaze followed him. He picked up a jade dragon that had been placed on an occasional table. He remembered buying one for Mei when they set up home in Thailand when she was expecting Benjy. This one was heavy, probably genuine. "And where d'you fit into this?" he asked.

"I'm Beth's business manager. I organise her social diary, supervise the domestic side of her life, do some admin for her non-exec work outside The Agency. As you can imagine she's very busy," she said. Dougie took a moment to digest this information; unlikely then that this was their daughter.

"Does she always work weekends?" asked Dougie.

"Beth doesn't understand the concept of weekends," replied Nine.

"Not much fun for you then?" asked Dougie.

"I'm not complaining," she said.

"And you live here with her? Just the two of you?" he asked. She appraised him in the measured way women do when they've rumbled you.

"No husband if that's what you're asking," said

Nine. The black tattoo expanded like a snake as she spoke. "But she's got a boyfriend. Neil Phillips."

"The professor guy on the telly?" asked Dougie, remembering that he was the sort of vacuous smoothie that Sally and Fiona liked. "Benjy mentioned he was one of the judges," he said, realising with a jolt that a weekend away together was probably the main reason for the pair of them agreeing to present the prize. His head began to thump and his face was burning with the uncomfortable sensation that things were turning out to be more complicated than his plan could cope with.

"And how is she? I mean…"

"What aspect of her welfare are you particularly interested in?"

Dougie was warming to her prickliness. "My son Benjy mentioned she'd had a stroke or something."

"Well Beth being Beth will say she's fine. But well…"

"Well what?" asked Dougie.

"Well I shouldn't be talking about her to strangers."

He liked that Nine was challenging him to convince her of his trustworthiness. He took another swallow of water and was about to sit down when he spotted a fiddle case.

"Does she still play?" asked Dougie. "We first met when she played in my band. She was classically trained you know. I had a bit of work to loosen her up."

"I'm sure you did. Have you kept it up?" asked Nine, and for a moment the innuendo hung between them like a plum, ripe for picking. They both burst out laughing when suddenly he felt a wave of nausea rolling towards him and he wasn't sure he could dodge out of its path. "Where's the bathroom?" he asked. He was rocking on his feet and his only focus was to get there on time. The girl, as if sensing his urgency, guided him quickly and wordlessly to the bathroom door.

The lock slid back expensively and he took three steps towards the toilet. He lifted the lid but before he had time to lift the toilet seat, the first retch came, a dribble of bile hitting the pristine porcelain, just catching the edge of a plastic basket holding a block of toilet bleach. There was a moment of hiatus; a brief pause before the main action started; just time for Dougie to lift the seat and hunker down so that his head was fully over the bowl. He did his best to relax, as his stomach clenched and the next few retches propelled the contents of his stomach down the toilet. He slumped down, feeling the cold enamel of the toilet bowl cool against his cheek and thought, *I bet no one's chundered down this toilet before.*

Chapter 11

It is the nature of conference calls, thought Beth, *that the more you want one to finish, the longer they are likely to go on.* Rubikon's Head of Research was reading out their requirements for their visit. It was the same list they had already sent her and Beth felt a rush of impatience at the pointlessness of repeating what everybody already knew. His voice had a peevish tone that made listening to him difficult.

She turned down the volume and listened to the low rumble of a man's voice from the lounge. She had heard Nine leave the flat and then return a few minutes later. She guessed it was Dougie although if it was, he was early, and in all the time she'd known him, the only thing he had ever been early for was opening time at the pub. She scooted back on her chair and pushed the office door ajar but couldn't see into the lounge or hear their conversation any more clearly.

"So Beth," said Peter Tan, drawing her attention back to the call, "can we confirm our visit for early August?"

"Yes. You'll have a draft itinerary next week. We're looking forward to welcoming you," she said, hoping that sounded like a suitable closing comment.

"You haven't asked how our visit here in Mexico is going," said Peter Tan.

Beth winced, it was a beginner's mistake to rush the man, let alone have the temerity to attempt to end the call.

"And how are our Mexican friends shaping up?"

"Let's just say they're full of surprises," he replied.

"Pleasant surprises?" she asked, gritting her teeth.

"Yes."

"I intend to make your visit here full of pleasant surprises too, perhaps even better than pleasant," she replied. She knew she was sounding over anxious to please. Focus. Focus. She scribbled on the notepad beside the phone. Mexico City; transportation and infrastructure; labour availability; rates of pay; cost of living index.

"It's a beautiful afternoon here, very little humidity and in the mid-twenties," he said. She added climate per month and pollution levels to her list. She looked out at the gloom of a rainy evening in Glasgow,

"It's a beautiful evening here too," she replied.

"Pleasurable though it is to chat with you Beth, we need to wrap up the call now. Our hosts in the Industry department have arranged a trip to the pyramids at Teotihuacan. I admit to being very excited."

"Sounds great," she replied, suddenly at a loss as to what she could arrange for them in Scotland that would match a visit to the birthplace of the Gods.

"Adios Beth," he said, which provoked a flurry of

muted farewells from the rest of the Board.

"Enjoy your afternoon gentlemen," she said, stabbing the off button and watching the green LED light snuff out. She let her head fall on her hands and felt a flicker of defeat. She knew it was part of the game to keep all the prospective bidders on their toes, but she had forgotten the first rule of competitive tendering was not to get distracted by what the competition has to offer and to focus instead on your strengths and advantages.

She sucked the end of her pen and added a couple of notes to her list – personal hobbies and interests of Peter Tan and the rest of the Rubikon Board. Royal Family visiting Scotland in August? She was aware of a tightening around her temples, her nostrils sizzling with pins and needles, a deep ache in her gums and teeth radiating downwards and sideways. The pain was with her all the time these days in various degrees. It would leech the life force out of her if she let it.

She went into her bedroom and sat at the dressing table. Dougie was in her flat. In the next few minutes she would meet him for the first time in twenty-three years. *Not quite true*, she thought. She had spotted him in the audience at the afternoon presentation but when she stood at the lectern to start her introduction, he had gone.

It took Flora the whole afternoon to remember he had given her a note. She guessed he wanted to break the ice between them before her visit to Skye. It was a good idea, she thought, and wondered why she hadn't thought of it herself. An anticipatory frisson ruffled her.

Sainsbury's
Chesham

VAT Reg No 660 4548 36

TICKET

TICKET NUMBER: 171185
EXPIRY TIME:
16:31
05/02/16

AMOUNT: £ 1.00

05/02/16 15:31 01n0

PLACE THIS TICKET
ON YOUR DASHBOARD

Singapry's
Cheapest
Two Boy not too Sweet

TICKET

1Sct TIGER POWDER

18:31
9T'20'90
E 1.00

Her face was flushed and lively on one side, pallid and lifeless on the other. She hated looking like this, absolutely loathed it. She swallowed a couple of painkillers and waited for them to give her the strength to tidy away her anger in the 'let it go' compartment in her brain. She brushed her hair until it shone, then tilted her head to put in her earrings. The gold twists reflected prettily in the light. She took out her lipstick and had a moment of longing before putting it back in the drawer.

She pinched both her cheeks, smiled her crooked smile and let a small wave of despair pass over and disappear. There was no possibility to recapture the way she had looked when she knew Dougie before and the sheer hopelessness of it made it easier to accept. He was extending the hand of friendship. That was all.

Nine was sitting on a bar stool in the kitchen texting. She inclined her head towards the bathroom in response to Beth's expectant look.

"He's been in there for a while," said Nine.

"Is he OK?"

Nine shrugged, "I'm off to meet some of the girls from The Beacon. Call me if you need rescuing." Beth had the impression that she was like a child making herself scarce before her parents had an argument.

Beth sat on the kitchen stool feeling her heart slow down in her chest. She hadn't realised it was pounding until she sat down. She crisscrossed her legs and pulled a lock of hair behind her ear and then loosened it and let it fall over her face. She listened for sounds coming from the bathroom.

She remembered a time he had kept her waiting

before; standing outside Frasers in Sauchihall Street. It was a cool evening and her jacket wasn't warm enough. She stood fidgeting and shivering, thinking that the whole world knew she was waiting for someone, feeling as exposed as if she was standing on a window ledge on the top floor. She remembered the moment she saw him coming towards her, his long hair flowing behind him, that saunter of a walk. He was smiling and it warmed the air around him. He had hugged her with abandon and she felt so proud and happy that the whole world could see this beautiful man was with her. She smiled at the memory of herself as that young nervous girl. How much of that girl remained within her today, she wondered. She had shrunk to a miniature size over the years, but oddly could feel her grow and take up space as she waited. It wasn't entirely unpleasant.

She picked up her phone, idly scrolling through her emails. Neil was asking if she wanted a drink tomorrow night. She texted back. OK. She was pleased at her pithiness. What had Nine called him? A fuckwit. She had small chuckle to herself. Ten minutes later, the balm of fond reminiscing and catching up on emails had worn through to irritation. She marched towards the bathroom and knocked sharply, "Dougie. Are you in there?"

There was silence and then the sound of shuffling. "Who else were you expecting to be in here?"

She glared at the shut door and watched as it slowly opened. If a door opening could be described as sheepish, then it opened sheepishly. Dougie's head was down; he wiped the back of his mouth with a wad of toilet paper; she could smell vomit and alcohol.

"Must have been something I ate," he mumbled. Beth appraised him coldly which she felt was more eloquent than words. He had the miserable and guilty look of a boy caught shoplifting. She felt a fresh surge of irritation that a grown man in his forties could get himself into such a state.

"Black coffee?" she asked but he shook his head. "Water then," she said, going over to the sink and filling a glass. She handed it to him and he accepted it without resistance. They sat opposite each other on the kitchen stools, irritation leaking out of Beth, contrition pooling around Dougie.

His face was glassy with perspiration but she had to admit he was still a handsome man; he had a decent haircut; his white hair thick and curling attractively at the collar line; his beard fashionably trimmed. She noticed his fingers as he picked up his glass of water, could see the familiar bitten down nails and cuticles and felt herself soften. She didn't want to look into his eyes, could predict that the softening might progress into something more alarming, so she concentrated instead on a small dusting of dandruff on his shoulder. He was wearing a denim shirt caught in an eighties time warp. She welcomed a rise of exasperation that his wife would allow him to look so scruffy. Her bad eye was watering. She dabbed it automatically.

"Does that hurt?" asked Dougie.

"No," she said quickly.

"Of course not," he said, smiling, and a brief moment of familiarity passed between them.

"How's the family? How's Sally?" she asked.

Always ask about the wife first.

"Sally?" he repeated, looking as surprised as if she'd asked him about a little-known acquaintance. "Fine I suppose, though I haven't spoken to her for a few days." Beth made a mental note to do a little more probing about his relationship with his wife. Not speaking for several days was usually a sign of trouble in her experience. He had begun to chew a hangnail on his left thumb and she wanted to ask him if he still used that liquid to stop biting your nails.

"I like Nine. She's got a mind of her own. I like that in a lassie," he said. This time he looked up from his fingers and she was caught by an old surprise that his eyes could be so pale yet so blue.

"Young people get too much criticism these days," said Beth. "I like Benjy too. Talented, enthusiastic, ambitious." She could see Dougie relaxing.

"I'm here because of Benjy," he said.

"Of course," said Beth, "we're both here because of Benjy."

"Malcolm thought it would be a good idea to speak to you," began Dougie.

"Malcolm?" she asked.

"Malcolm Crawford. An old friend. He's a journalist at *The Record*," said Dougie. "He told me to tell you that you need to say you knew me or Benjy's prize may not count."

Beth rocked back in her seat. Of all the things she had expected Dougie to say this was not one of them.

"And here was me thinking you wanted to break the ice between us before I meet your family in Skye," she said, but Dougie had lowered his head and was shaking it quietly side to side.

"I just didn't want..."

"Didn't want what, Dougie? Didn't want to have a conversation? About what happened all those years ago between us?"

"Beth," he started, "I think it best..."

"Best if we forgot all about it? That's how you've always handled things isn't it Dougie? By pretending things didn't happen. If you ignore things long enough they'll just go away."

His eyes were cloudy with bewilderment.

"I just want everything to go smoothly for Benjy. Malcolm said you needed to make a declaration of interest."

She felt fury rise within her. "So you've come here to tell me how to do my job? Is that what this is about, Dougie? That I need to be reminded of the very protocols that I introduced?"

Dougie had that hounded, wounded look that she remembered so well. He got his feet. "I didn't come here to upset you, Beth," he said.

"I've got an even better idea, Dougie. Let's pretend that we never knew each other. Or if we did it was such a brief fling that neither of us can remember it. Less hassle than a lot of form filling."

He was putting on his jacket. A navy donkey style, it was ancient, shiny at the elbows; she thought it might even be the same jacket he had worn when they were students. He turned to face her. He looked as if he had aged ten years in ten minutes. His face was pallid, his eyes sunken. He was working his mouth as if there was too much saliva in it.

"I've often wished over the years that I had never known you Beth, so that'll suit me fine," he said walking to the door.

She wanted to call out to him, to apologise for being unreasonable, to explain she was under a lot of pressure; to say, 'Take off your jacket, come back, let's start again,' but she said nothing. She heard him leave, the soft click of the latch on the front door. She continued to sit on the kitchen stool, gazing into mid-space, feeling as spent as a used firework.

Chapter 12

The Four Sisters restaurant had been converted from a row of cottages. Local folklore claimed four spinsters who spurned all suitors in preference to the independent life of crofting and fishing had lived in them. The historical evidence for this was non-existent. Dougie thought it more likely they were four widows whose husbands had died from the hard grind of subsistence farming or tuberculosis, but historical fact was an inconvenient thing when coming up with a name for a Michelin starred restaurant. Even Dougie, who didn't have a feel for these things, could see that calling the place The Four Poor Souls wouldn't have the same welcoming ring to it.

Dougie swung the crate of seaweed from the back of the truck and carried it up to the back door. Johnny the sous chef came down the path to greet him, cooing over the algae, holding up the strings to the light as if they were jewels. He was telling Dougie about the menu they were putting on for The Agency visitors, showcasing the variations of seaweed that Benjy planned to grow. Dougie snorted and ducked his head under the low mantel of the back door and put the crate on the kitchen table. It drew the rest of the kitchen staff into an excited huddle and no one noticed him slipping out of the kitchen to the dining room beyond.

Benjy was tucked into the far alcove of the main dining room, his laptop opened in front of him. Dust motes danced in the weak light from the small windows, giving the room a melancholy ambiance as if the ghosts of the spinsters were still present, troubled by the changes that had been made to their houses. Dougie knew by the time evening came, the candles would transform the mood to cosy intimacy but he liked the brooding atmosphere, it was more in keeping with his mood.

"Where's everyone?" asked Dougie.

Benjy didn't lift his eyes from the screen. "Mr Takashama's upstairs in his room. Said I'd give him a call when you arrived. Sally's not coming. She's caught a bug. Been sick most of the day."

Dougie sat down digesting this information. "Shame," he said, "sure it's only a bug she's caught?"

Benjy laughed good-naturedly. "She'll be fine in the morning. At least I bloody well hope so. I'd be panicking if I had to do this presentation on my own."

"I'll be there," said Dougie, although he knew he wouldn't be much help when it came to presenting the business plan.

"I'm glad you changed your mind, Dad, and got Billy to drive the oyster shipment to Glasgow tonight," he said.

Dougie smiled though he didn't feel happy. Beth's plan to pretend they were vaguely remembered acquaintances from university seemed straightforward enough, but misgivings hung about him, as persistent as the mist down at the waterside.

"I was being a stubborn old bugger. Sorry son."

"Less of the old. That new haircut's taken years off you."

"I don't know why I didn't do it before. It's easy to get stuck in your ways," said Dougie, running his fingers through the sides of his hair. He found himself doing that a lot these days, as if reminding himself what he'd done to himself.

"I like the new gear too. You should listen to Fiona more often," he added. Dougie looked down at his shirt and jeans. An updated look rather than a transformation, he thought, surprised that people noticed.

"Where is Fiona?" asked Dougie.

Benjy went back to his laptop. "Haven't seen her."

"You finish what you're doing. I'll give her a ring."

Dougie walked down to the water and sat on a rocky outcrop overlooking the widest part of the inlet. Waves ruffled the water and a creamy spume bubbled at the edge. There was a trembling in the air, and although the clouds looked benign, he could smell rain.

Fiona picked up after a couple of rings, her voice weak. She had been sick all afternoon. "Don't worry about the dinner," he said, the important thing was to get better, keep hydrated. He tried Sally's number next but there was no reply. Sally and Fiona both sick. Coincidence? He had seen them both at the Long Inn last night. They had both seemed perfectly normal.

Then he remembered his own bout of sickness at Beth's flat a week ago; he had eaten oysters the day before and had felt fine at the time, but twenty-four hours later the nausea had come from nowhere and poleaxed him.

The wind was building, the waves getting choppier; the mist starting to gather and swirl. Doubts gathered in his mind like the clouds above him. The last water report had said the bacteria levels were at danger level yet he had told Benjy they were fine. Common sense should have told him to stop the harvest, yet he had carried on delivering as usual. Sally and Fiona were excited about the dinner tonight. They had both bought new outfits to wear yet were too ill to even contemplate it.

Banks of squally clouds were moving towards him, the wind building in blustery gusts. He had to make a decision. Fast. Billy would be on the outskirts of Glasgow by now. His first delivery was due in half an hour. He felt the first drops of rain as he dialled Billy's number.

"Billy? Dougie here. Can you hear me?" There was a crackle on the line; he could hear rock music blaring out of the radio.

"What's up Dougie lad?" shouted Billy over the music.

"You need to turn back Billy. Don't make the delivery!" shouted Dougie back.

"What d'you mean?" asked Billy.

"Turn back. I'll tell you what it's about when I see you," repeated Dougie.

"You want me to turn back after I've delivered?" asked Billy. The line was now a crackling mass of noise. The rain had begun to fall in earnest.

"Turn back NOW. Do not deliver ANYTHING. D'you understand?" but the line had gone dead. Dougie looked in desperation at the mobile as the rain drove into him.

When he got back to the restaurant, Benjy was sitting with another man. They were leaning into the computer, their heads almost touching.

"Dad, this is Dr Neil Phillips, one of the judges from the competition," said Benjy, looking up.

"Dougie McKinnon. Pleased to meet you," he said, stepping forward to shake his hand. The man shook it back, not seeming to mind the rain that was dripping off Dougie's cuff. So this was Beth's boyfriend, thought Dougie. He recognised him from the telly and the newspapers of course, but close up, he looked older and seedier.

"Excuse me Dr Phillips but I need a quick word with Benjy. In private," added Dougie.

Benjy gave him an exasperated look. "Dr Phillips has offered to look over the presentation."

"Call me Neil," said Dr Phillips, "after all we're both alumni of Glasgow University," he said, giving Dougie one his TV smiles.

"Alumni?" repeated Dougie, thinking he must sound a bit simple.

"Yes. It turns out you and Beth were at Glasgow University at the same time. I came a few years later but unlike you two, never left."

"I didn't know you and Beth Colquhoun were at uni together, Dad," said Benjy.

Dougie's mind was darting and skittering. Both Benjy and Neil were looking at him expectedly. "We probably met. I don't really remember," said Dougie, hoping this would put them off asking anything more.

"I can see you two have business to discuss. The offer to look over the presentation still stands if you want to email it to me, Benjy. See you at dinner tonight. Plenty of time to reminisce about student days then," said Neil pleasantly.

"Smarmy chancer," said Dougie under his breath when he was out of earshot. Benjy gave him an expression Dougie felt parents reserve for children on the edge of misbehaving. "Sorry Benjy, I wasn't much of a secret weapon with Neil but something's come up. I think we may have a problem."

"Problem? What problem?" asked Mr Takashama, walking briskly towards them. Gone was the business suit and in its place was a full dress kilt. The red, white, and black of the tartan overwhelmed his small frame. The dress jacket was cut so loose he looked like a child dressing up in grown up's clothes. Dougie noticed he had a small dirk tucked into his socks. Amethysts were set into the handle. It must have cost a fortune.

Benjy let out a whoop of delight. "Bloody fantastic," he said in wonderment.

Mr Takashama grinned. "Made to measure. Chisholm's of Inverness. Kilt maker to the queen," he said, lifting his sporran and inviting Benjy to feel the seal fur.

"For goodness' sake," spluttered Dougie.

"I have offended you, Dougie," said Mr Takashama looking crestfallen. "I was assured this was the correct tartan but perhaps I've been misinformed," he said.

"Don't pay any attention to him. You look grand," said Benjy, walking up to Mr Takashama and hugging his shoulder. "Welcome to the McKinnon Clan. I'll ask Sally's mum to bring my kilt over and I'll wear it tonight too," said Benjy.

"You have the same kilt?" asked Mr Takashama hopefully.

"No. I got mine off eBay for a mate's wedding but it'll do the job," replied Benjy. "What about you, Dad?"

"No thanks," said Dougie, making no attempt to hide his sulkiness.

"Please yourself. So what's this problem you were talking about, Dad?" asked Benjy.

"Fiona's ill. She won't be coming tonight. We were hoping she'd give our guests a song," explained Dougie to Mr Takashama.

"That's no problem!" said Mr Takashama beaming broadly. "It's an opportunity. I can take her place."

Across the other side of the island, Beth leant against the window and watched the rain skid across the glass, her cheek inert, immune to the chill. The cottage was tucked under a high bluff that sheltered it from the wind and it had an uninterrupted view of the inlet that meandered out to the sea. Seabirds wheeled and cried, the marshy foreground a patchwork of amber, gold and ochre, and beyond it were craggy hills that the rain had softened to a peaty blur. It was the sort of location that the holiday brochure described as idyllic but its wild beauty struck her as bleak. She put down her pen and re-read her journal entry.

Intermittent paralysis now evident on lower right side. Seems worse when tired. Left side, no improvement. I have entered a dark place. Sleep very disturbed. Even work can't keep gloomy thoughts away. Only the pills and Nine's joints seem to help. Not good. Seeing Dougie tonight. Dreading it.

She shivered and pulled her shawl round her shoulders. Nine was trying to light the wood burner stove; smoke was belching out into the room. She was humming the Sky Boat Song and didn't seem disheartened by her lack of success with the fire.

Speed bonny boat like a bird on the wing, over the sea to Skye,

Carry the lad that's born to be king over the sea to Skye.

Beth joined in under her breath but she couldn't remember the words and her voice petered out. Nine kept singing, substituting forgotten words with la la la's.

Beth thought through every carefully choreographed detail of what lay ahead. The dinner tonight at The Four Sisters with Dougie and his family; the business presentation tomorrow morning; the prize-giving in the afternoon; the tour of the oyster farm on Sunday. It was a long list of tedious duties. She felt the familiar squeezing of her headache. She dabbed her watering eye.

Nine was moving about the kitchen, opening and shutting drawers, tutting and letting out small exclamations of surprise at what she found. Beth wanted to tell her to be quiet but instead, waited for the irritation to pass, waves of pain pulsing behind her eyelids. She wondered if Nine would think it odd if she suggested they have their evening joint early.

"Two hours to party time," said Nine cheerily. "I suppose you'll want to catch up on the backlog from yesterday. I've made an agenda."

Beth walked to the kitchen table with the enthusiasm of a zombie as Nine rustled in her briefcase and pulled out folders and sheaves of papers.

"Item one. Oil Company proposal from your brother Alec." Beth sighed, she had hoped that would have died a quiet death by now. Nine produced a file; it landed on the table with a discouraging thud. "He brought this round last night when you were at the theatre. I think he wanted to check me out as he didn't seem bothered that you weren't at home," said Nine. "I offered him a spliff and a blow job. He declined both."

Beth found herself smiling, a small pinhole of light in her mood. "I suppose I'll have to take a look at it. Book us a table at Pier 42 in two weeks' time."

"You'll not need two weeks to make up your mind about it," said Nine.

"Since when have you become an expert on oil companies?" asked Beth.

Nine looked at her scornfully. "It's crap," she said. "By the way 'crap' is a scholarly term meaning 'low likelihood of ever delivering a return on investment'."

"Do you ever think about going back to college? You'd do great in business," said Beth.

"Woah Beth. It's bad enough I've agreed to work for you for the summer but I've no intention of defecting to the capitalist camp on a permanent basis."

"Admit it, Nine. You're enjoying yourself," said Beth.

"I'll admit I'm surprised how much I like you, Beth, considering our philosophical differences. I can see we're both warriors, albeit for different causes. And your flat is heaven compared to sleeping rough, but once the summer's over I'm off. You'll have landed the Rubikon deal by then. Your Palsy will be better. You won't need me. "

"D'you think so?" she said. "Sometimes I wonder. It scares me to think that this is how I'll be forever."

Nine looked up surprised, her eyes narrowed. "I'd be scared too if it happened to me."

"So… best not to dwell on it eh? Next item on the agenda."

"If you want to talk about it," offered Nine.

Beth shook her head. "Don't be kind. It'll only make it worse. Now what's next?"

"Sister-in-law update. Alec said the flowers were lovely. Margaret's leg is out of plaster in two weeks' time. Will need physio for the next three months. He was moaning about waiting times for the NHS."

"I've told him weeks ago that the bank of Beth is closed," answered Beth. "She would never stick to the exercises anyhow. Send her a card wishing her a speedy recovery."

As Nine made a note of this, Beth reached over and read the next item on the agenda. "Rubikon Board visit. Have you read my recommendation?" Beth asked, shrugging off her shawl. The room felt warmer, she could feel her lassitude lifting.

"I can tell you're pleased with it," replied Nine.

"There's one thing that will transform our chances of Rubikon choosing Scotland over Mexico," said Beth, looking out to the wet barren view. "I'll give you a clue. It's not the weather."

"Could it be... let me think... golf?" replied Nine.

Beth poked her in the ribs. "So you have read it! How lucky was that? Six out of the seven Board members are obsessed with golf and five of the world's top ten courses are here in Scotland. I've asked Ainslie to help. He's a member of the Royal and Ancient. I've also suggested we invite some of the old boys from the Scottish trade association. Building bridges and all that. It'll be the golf junket of the century."

"You said six out of seven of the Rubikon Board like golf. What about the one who doesn't?" asked Nine.

"That's Mike Ho, the Director of Operations. He's into birdwatching," replied Beth.

"One of the biggest puffin colonies in the world is on the Isle of May, just off the coast at St Andrews.

Meant to be amazing," said Nine.

Beth sighed. "Not that kind of bird watching. Ainslie has contacts. He'll do the organising."

"Fuck, Beth. The whole thing's disgusting: elitist sport; old boy network; prostitution. I mean what sort of person calls women 'birds' these days? Don't you despair of having to work with such wankers?"

"It scunners me as much as you. But if I fought it head on it would be like going into a boxing ring with a bunch of heavyweights. I'd get knocked out by the first blow. So my way of fighting is to go along with it, absorb their energy, and wait for my chance to turn any weakness to my advantage."

"That's just a clever way of justifying your collusion with them," said Nine.

"Life's not a simple case of baddies and goodies," replied Beth, "it's easy to vilify men but I've worked with women-only teams before and believe me, that's no picnic either."

"What you're saying is that the end justifies the means. Hardly a moral standpoint is it?" she asked.

"If the Rubikon deal is signed it'll be a massive injection of jobs for the Scottish people and cash for the Scottish economy. Surely that's a legacy that we can both agree is worthwhile," she said. Beth expected her to agree in principle but an odd blankness had descended on Nine's face as if she was suddenly absent, severing their connection as cleanly as a guillotine separates a head from body. Beth felt a frisson of fear, as if she didn't know who Nine was or what she was capable of.

"Anyhow, Ainslie will be the figurehead for the visit. We'll be in the background," she said.

"Brilliant. Let Ainslie take all the credit whilst we do all the work," scoffed Nine and Beth knew she was back, their usual banter resumed.

"Rule number one in organisational life, always make your boss look good. Anyhow while they're busy whacking golf balls, drinking whisky, and womanising, I'll be watching, planning my next move."

"There's only one person I've liked in all the people I've met since working for you," said Nine.

"Let me guess," replied Beth wearily.

"And you threw him out your flat."

"The facts of the evening were that after being sick in my toilet, Dougie left of his own accord."

"I don't think he was drunk, Beth," said Nine.

"I don't give a toss what he was. Our job this weekend is to be pleasant to everyone and then leave. Dougie and I have agreed to behave as if we didn't know each other before and I'm asking you to go along with that story."

"Don't be angry with me," said Nine. Beth felt her heart drop. "I've been doing some research. You're always telling me about the importance of preparation, of having all the facts to hand," she said.

There was an awkward silence. Beth sighed. "OK. You've got two minutes," she said, making a point of looking at her watch.

"Dougie's not married. Never has been. Is a bit of

a ladies man on the island but by all accounts but he's a devoted dad to Benjy. Benjy's mother Mei, was from Japan. She met Dougie when he was travelling in Thailand and died shortly after giving birth. Septicaemia."

"How did you find this out?" asked Beth.

"Sally. Benjy's fiancée. I asked her for a bit of background info on the family."

"Sally is Benjy's fiancée? I thought she was Dougie's wife."

"Sally's the sort of girl that once she starts talking she doesn't stop. She's nice though. Hoping that winning might persuade Benjy to set a date for their wedding."

"Did she tell you that?"

"No. Educated guess."

"Benjy's love life may be of interest to you but not to me."

"No? But this may be. A Mr Takashama showed up a few weeks ago with an offer to set up a packaging plant and to control the Asian distribution of the seaweed from his Singapore hub. Sally says Dougie doesn't trust him but Benjy plans to sign a deal with him, offering him a half share in the new business. I've been doing a little digging and Mr Takashama's not all that he seems. His company has posted losses for the past three years. Last year it was for..." and at this point Nine rummaged in her sheaf of papers, "yeah, here it is. Three million Singapore dollars."

Plenty of companies post losses. Could be the company's in trouble or a con to avoid tax," said Beth.

"Shouldn't we tell Dougie and Benjy what we've found out?" she asked.

"Mr Takashama's company accounts are public knowledge," said Beth.

"Don't you think it's a bit ambitious for Benjy to go from a small production start up to a full blown packaging and distribution capability?" asked Nine.

"I would say it's typical of him. He's ambitious. It's what I like about him."

"Ambition can oe'r reach itself."

"You're full of surprises aren't you Nine? Quoting *Macbeth* was not something I expected when I first saw you sleeping rough in that doorway," said Beth, "but you know my views about ambition. Most people have far too little of it. Desmond will meet with Benjy regularly to make sure his plans are properly thought through. Anyhow you're way over your two minutes. I think we're done here."

"One last thing. This came for you this morning. Thought you would want to open it yourself."

Beth had a prescient feeling of dread at the sight of the Edinburgh postmark.

"Good news?" asked Nine.

"Dr Rorke confirming my appointment at hospital next Wednesday. She says I should be prepared to spend the whole day. Take a look if you want."

"She's thorough. Scans, ultrasound, hearing and sight tests. I suppose it's good to check out that nothing nasty is going on," said Nine.

"Yes," said Beth brightly.

"D'you want me to drive you there? Stay with you?"

"Good God no. Just reschedule my appointments to another day. Now what should I wear tonight? Something to impress Neil?"

"Who cares about that twat?" she said. "I think you should wear something that impresses you," offered Nine.

Beth felt a punch of unfairness as real as if Nine had actually landed a blow in her midriff. "Very little impresses me about how I look these days," she said. Nine was wearing black as usual, jeans and black polo-necked jumper. Her pixie mop had flashes of purple streaked through it. Her white skin was perfect.

"Beth..." said Nine, reaching out to touch her.

Beth recoiled. "I know a lot of women my age are locked in a battle to hang on to their looks for as long as they can. I wasn't one of them you know. I thought I was reconciled to ageing. But this. This," she said, poking her cheek. "I hate it and I can't accept it. I don't want a new improved version of my face. I just want the old one back."

"Beth, I'm sorry..."

"No need to apologise Nine. I'm fine. Absolutely fine."

Chapter 13

Nine was locked in concentration, hunched over the driving wheel, uncharacteristically silent. Beth checked her phone but it had been without signal for the last twenty minutes. She tried switching the navigation system on and off but the screen remained blank. She felt the first prickle of worry. They were already late; the gloaming had darkened to a funereal blackness. The road had petered out into a single track. Beth suspected Nine was thinking the same thing. No Michelin starred restaurant could be this far off the beaten track.

She was on the point of suggesting going back to the last village when they were momentarily blinded by a set of headlamps heading at speed towards them. Both cars dipped their lights at the same time, as if they were doffing their caps at each other. The other car slipped into a passing place and Nine waved her hand in acknowledgement. Beth felt heartened that they had come across another car and, in five minutes, a string of houses came into view. A road sign reared out of the darkness. 'Four Sisters, half a mile.' It had a painting of a long white cottage and an arrow pointing in the direction they were heading.

"I know it's meant to be a destination restaurant

but this is fucking ridiculous," said Nine, sounding cross and relieved at the same time.

The restaurant sat a hundred metres back from the road, floodlit and surreal against the starless night. A dozen cars were parked at drunken angles, half on the verge and half on the road. After all those miles of solitary driving coming upon this amount of human life felt almost intoxicating.

"C'mon Cinderella, we're late for the ball," said Nine, reaching over to the back seat for her coat and bag. Beth smiled wanly, finding it difficult to summon the effort to move. "Pop a couple of your little helpers. You'll be fine," said Nine cheerfully.

The door of the restaurant opened onto a cramped hallway suffused with the smell of garlic and roasted meat. Nine screwed up her face in distaste but Beth knew that Desmond would have arranged a vegan option. A waiter helped Beth off with her coat. Her silk dress was creased and exhausted from sitting so long in the car.

Nine was struggling out of her coat, having declined the offer of help. Beth could see she had changed out of her usual head-to-toe black, and into a bright blue blouse. Her throat tattoo blared out from her creamy skin. Beth thought it took a certain talent to both conform to a dress code and rebel against it. They walked past a lounge area, packed with diners drinking aperitifs, anticipation and excitement spilling out into the corridor. The waiter motioned them to continue walking towards the main dining room.

Beth could see Neil and Desmond talking to Benjy and a Japanese man that she guessed was Mr

Takashama. Both he and Benjy were wearing kilts. Mr Takashama's had a bold scarlet and black plaid, the fullness of the pleating exaggerating the thinness of his calves. He stood with his legs planted wide, giving the impression that he was trying to make himself look bigger than he was. She restrained an impulse to laugh.

Benjy's kilt was frayed round the hem and even in the soft light she could see it needed a good press, but there was something in the easy way it sat on his hips that was effortlessly attractive. Dougie had his back against the dining room, looking out into the dark night beyond. She felt a lump in her throat, nerves, dread, a frisson of something else that she didn't want to dwell on. He was wearing a check shirt and black jeans. He too had made a special effort.

Neil came forward and grasping both shoulders, kissed her on each cheek. She knew the others were watching this display of proprietorial affection but found herself not caring about that, allowing herself to linger in his protective aura.

"Beth. Thank goodness. We were beginning to worry," he said jovially. *That was for the benefit of others,* she thought. Neil never worried about anything for long.

"You remember my business manager Nine," said Beth, and Nine nodded towards him.

"Of course, of course," he said, hardly glancing at Nine. "Now let me introduce you to everyone," he said, keeping hold of her elbow as he guided her towards the others. A small man with a large camera darted in between them. She guessed it was the photographer from the *Daily Record*. As Neil introduced her to each person, the photographer insisted that they pose in front of him, their handshake and smile frozen in time while he clicked and fussed. Dougie was the last to be introduced to her.

"Dougie, this is Beth Colquhoun," said Neil with a flourish. Dougie turned round as he spoke. "I was telling Dougie earlier that you two were at Glasgow University at the same time," said Neil. Dougie gave Beth a look of mild bewilderment and began to chew a hangnail on his right thumb. Beth had to admire his acting skills; he was coming across as someone so distracted by other matters that he barely registered her presence.

"Pleased to meet you," she said and stepped forward to shake his hand. "I don't think we've met before, have we?" she said, but Dougie continued to look as if he was having difficulty following the thread of the conversation.

"I thought not," said Neil. "Dougie pretended he might have met you but I think he was just being polite."

The photographer appeared and asked them to repeat the handshake for the camera. Beth offered her hand and smiled. "Pleased to meet you," she repeated. Dougie looked at her then and she saw a flicker of recognition. He took her hand but instead of a normal handshake, he folded his middle finger and stroked her palm. It was like the tickle of a feather and so unexpected that a small yelp escaped her. Dougie kept a magnificently straight face. "Pleased to meet you too." They both laughed. The flash went off, momentarily blinding her and when she recovered from the glare, her eye began to water. She was searching up the sleeve of her dress for a tissue when she felt Dougie press his handkerchief into her hand.

"Thanks. I had forgotten about your silly handshakes," she whispered.

"Still makes you laugh," he whispered back. His breath felt hot against her neck. She could feel herself blushing.

"Well!" said Neil brightly. "I can see we're all going to get on famously tonight."

"We certainly are," agreed Dougie, matching his hearty tone and turned to look at Beth. It was the most extraordinary experience. The years between them were disappearing. She was back at the folk club, the night she auditioned for his band. He had done that funny handshake thing to her then too. She knew it was a trick of the mind, the painkillers jumbling memories of the past and the present into a sentimental soup. She looked into Dougie's blue eyes and despite herself, hoped he was remembering too.

A line of young waiters appeared from the kitchen carrying trays of drinks. They circled the party and offered everyone a choice of champagne or sparkling water. "For the toast," they murmured, then traipsed back to the kitchen door and lined up on either side of it as if they were a guard of honour.

Eyes were drawn to the door as it opened and a small man dressed in chef's whites appeared. Beth had met Scott Smith at the Taste of Scotland Awards dinner two months ago and was reminded of his irrepressible energy as he jogged towards them. He made a beeline for her and gave her a hearty hug as if they were old pals.

"Welcome Beth and to all our guests tonight," he said. Beth inclined her head in acknowledgement. "Tonight we're celebrating Benjy winning the Young Entrepreneur of Scotland competition." He paused for a smattering of applause. "We've always drawn our inspiration from local food and Dougie and Benjy have been working in partnership with us for many years." This time the applause was louder and more sustained. "We've prepared a very special menu for you tonight, featuring Benjy's seaweed in a variety of dishes. We'll start with razor clams with samphire and foraged leaves in a light seaweed dressing. The dish will be finished with Tallisker crumb and Dulse. We hope you enjoy eating it as much as we have enjoyed preparing it for you. And now please join me in a toast. To Benjy."

"To Benjy!" they all cried.

Scott jogged back to the kitchen, the young waiters scurrying after him like courtiers after their king. The rest of the diners were being ushered from the lounge into the restaurant and like an audience settling into their seats before the start of a performance, there was a bustle of activity; scraping of chairs; glasses clinking; the hubbub of conversation rising. Beth noticed an elderly couple being seated at the next table. Their voices were strident, a tone above everyone else, an American or perhaps Canadian twang. They were drinking champagne. It was a special night for everyone.

She found herself sitting between Neil and Dougie and for a moment was unsure who to give her attention to. She fiddled with the serviette in her lap, trying to cover the worst of the creases in her dress. Neil began discussing the wine list with Desmond, making a joke about Agency expenses guidelines and asking if a special exception could be made to order the Bordeaux. It was a conversation intended to entertain the whole table. Beth could see Desmond was both pained and gratified at being given his place.

Nine was sitting directly opposite her, between Mr Takashama and Benjy. She was turning her head from one side to the other as she spoke to each of them. In the ambient light her blue blouse and her blonde and purple hair flashed and flamed as prettily as an exotic bird.

"She's a bonnie girl," said Dougie, as if reading her thoughts.

"I keep thinking how much better she would look without that horrible tattoo but I don't think Benjy's noticed," said Beth in wonderment.

"Beth, about that time in your flat, I'm sorry..."

"Look, as we're pretending this is the first time we've met, let's forget about that shall we?" she said, lifting her glass to his.

"To starting over," he said, and they clinked their glasses.

She could feel her face flushing. "It must be a wonderful to see Benjy making such a success of things," she said, hoping that talking would calm her heart rate.

"What could possibly go wrong?" he said, and she was surprised by the edge to his voice. For a moment she thought he would say more, confide his troubles to her, but the moment was broken by a shout of dismay at the other side of the table. Mr Takashama was standing looking down at his kilt, spreading the skirt wide. Nine was leaning over him, dabbing it with her napkin.

"Mr Takashama's kilt's had its first Scottish bath. A bottle of the Four Sisters' Bordeaux," said Benjy loudly. Beth wondered if Benjy might be a bit drunk. Nine's complexion was also heightened. Mr Takashama's small face darkened, he was struggling to see the funny side. A waiter sidled up to him. "We'll get that cleaned, sir, right away," he said, leading him away.

Benjy and Nine resumed their conversation as if there had been no interruption. Beth made a mental note to ask Dougie where Sally, the fiancée, was tonight. A waiter offered her a choice of four types of roll, placing one on her plate with a pair of oversized tongs. The bread had a yeasty breath with a rich buttery note. Her mouth filled with saliva and she dabbed her lips to check no dribble had escaped. Dougie's handkerchief felt soft against her lips.

There was a hiatus in the conversation as they all stared at their bread with a similar sense of hunger. The conversation levels had dropped in the restaurant; there was a general shifting in seats; the first signs of impatience. A small knot of waiters was clustered outside the kitchen door, whispering and conferring together.

"Let me check how the food's coming along," said Dougie quietly, placing his hand on the back of her chair to steady himself. She felt the lightest of pressure from his fingers through the silk of her dress.

"It's going well isn't it?" breathed Neil in her ear and she was about to reply when the kitchen door swung open. Scott Smith stood framing the doorway with Dougie at his shoulder. Something was wrong. Behind them were two men in suits. An absurd thought came into her mind. Detectives? The conversation in the room slowed and Scott raised his arms until it came to a complete stop. Everyone was drawn to his direction.

"I am devastated to announce that the restaurant will not be serving food tonight."

The announcement was met with an incredulous silence. Scott's usual bravado had become a hoarse whisper. "Last night we had a wedding reception. The groom has just informed us that several of the party have come down with food poisoning during the day. The family contacted the health and safety department and these two gentlemen have arrived to carry out an investigation. I will of course cooperate fully with them. The restaurant will close until tests can be carried out and the source of the outbreak established. I am so very sorry," he said.

Beth could see Scott was broken and she realised with a shock that Dougie had a similar look to him. A noise like a communal wail rose up from the diners. Scott silenced them for a second time.

"We've explained the situation to the Long Inn at Astinch and we can offer you all a complimentary meal there. Of course this doesn't in any way compensate for the disappointment but in the circumstances it's the best I can do."

The photographer from the *Daily Record* came to

life at that moment and began snapping pictures as if they were all stars on the red carpet. The flash was heartless, illuminating the disappointment and shock on the diners' faces. The couple at the next table had got to their feet. The man was supporting his wife as she stumbled towards the door, her face a study of grief. He was talking out loud to no one in particular. "It's our golden wedding anniversary today. We've come all the way from Toronto."

Neil was the first to speak. "Shellfish is the usual culprit," he said with his polymath authority.

"Shut up," Nine hissed. Neil had an expression that was both blank and blameless.

"This isn't the time to speculate," Beth said calmly, and an uneasy silence settled on them.

Benjy got to his feet. "I don't know what to say," he started, but Dougie had come alongside him and said gently, "I think it best if we went back to the office, Benjy. The health inspectors have told me that they'll be round to check us out too."

"D'you need any help?" asked Nine.

Beth was surprised her offer wasn't discounted immediately. "I'm sure Benjy and Dougie can manage, Nine. There's Sally isn't there?" she asked.

"Actually I think we could use some help couldn't we Dad? Especially if you have any ideas about dealing with the media," said Benjy. Nine was already on her feet. "I'm your girl when it comes to media communications. Isn't that right Beth?" she said. It wasn't a question, more a statement of fact.

"I'll drive Beth to The Long Inn," offered Neil,

and before she could say more, Benjy, Dougie, and Nine were walking out of the restaurant together. She could see Desmond and Neil were watching them and she wondered if they too had noticed the conspiratorial chemistry between them.

"What about the presentation and prize giving tomorrow?" asked Desmond.

"We'll meet as planned tomorrow morning at 10 o'clock at their office," said Beth, "take it from there."

"If it's discovered that their oysters are implicated does this invalidate his prize?" asked Desmond.

"I don't see why. Oysters have nothing to do with Benjy's proposal," reasoned Neil.

"It might if the oysters are contaminated in the same waters where the seaweed is grown," said Desmond, warming to his subject. "No one would blame us for bailing out before our reputation gets tainted," said Desmond.

"It's not our reputation that we should be worried about," said Beth, surveying the empty dining room. "I wonder if this place will ever recover. The business must be on a knife edge at the best of times."

Desmond shrugged his shoulders. "If you both want to go ahead with the presentation, I'll go along with it, but let's keep it short and low key. Now I'm going back to my bed and breakfast. I took the precaution of preparing extra sandwiches at lunchtime. I often find myself hungrier after a meal at these places than before. Goodnight."

Desmond joined the last of the stragglers, their demeanour and posture like survivors from some disaster. Neil settled back into his seat beside her. The place had an eerie silence, as if they were sitting in a stranger's front room when everybody else had gone to bed.

"You look nice tonight, Beth," said Neil, pouring her another glass of champagne.

"Candlelight helps. A lot. Also you're sitting on my best side."

"This Palsy is only temporary. You said so yourself. Nothing to be worried about."

"Next you'll be telling me beauty comes from within," she said, attempting a lighter tone but suspecting it came out as bitter.

"Sorry, I'm not saying the right thing," he said.

"It helps if you don't bullshit me. I'd rather you said nothing than telling me it's no big deal."

"One good thing has come out of tonight," said Neil, putting his hand over hers, "we've got a night off together and there's a fish and chip shop near my hotel. Can I tempt you?"

There was a beguiling mix of lust and loneliness in his expression. She remembered his competent touch, considerate and measured. There was a comfort in that, almost a safety, so different from the dangerous passion she remembered with Dougie.

"You might," she said, allowing him to lean over towards her. They were about to kiss when she saw over his shoulder the bewildered expression on Mr Takashama's face. He had changed out of his kilt and was small and sober in a dark suit.

"What's happened? Where is everyone?" he asked.

They jerked apart. "The restaurant's closed. They've all gone to The Long Inn," said Neil.

"The Long Inn? The place next to the oyster farm? But why?"

"There aren't many other places to eat round here," replied Neil.

"C'mon Mr Takashama," said Beth, "Neil and I will give you a lift. We'll tell you all about it on the way," and as she stood up, she saw Dougie's handkerchief lying on the floor. She thought for a moment she might to leave it there, but only for a moment, before scooping it up and tucking it in her sleeve.

Chapter 14

Dougie sat in his usual chair in the office, staring into mid-space, his mind suspended. The whine of the strip lighting, the patter of the rain against the windows, the whirring of the fan heater seemed to intensify the silence in the room. Benjy and Nine were pouring over the water quality reports, heads down, blue-black alongside blonde streaked with purple. Nine's pretty face was puzzled. Benjy stared into his lap as if he didn't trust himself to look at him directly. "Why didn't you tell me, Dad?"

Dougie was expecting anger. This quiet disappointment seemed much harsher. "I hoped the water would get better on its own I suppose," he said lamely. He knew it wasn't a good reason but it was all he had.

"But you could see it was getting worse. The last report especially. Look," said Benjy, jabbing his finger at the report, "it clearly states the bacteria was at danger level. I asked you about it when we were hardening off the oysters last week. I just don't get it," he said sadly.

"We don't know if our oysters are responsible for the food poisoning," said Dougie quietly.

"Dad..."

"You were so busy with the seaweed..." he said, his voice tailing off.

"That's no excuse and you know it," said Benjy, raising his voice.

"Look," said Nine, her voice sounding sharp and soft at the same time, "there'll be time later to figure out how this happened but now we need to focus on the here and now. Get our act together," she said.

"What d'you mean?" asked Benjy.

"We need to agree on a story and then communicate it."

Dougie looked at the girl with interest. On one level she was just a skinny lassie with an alternative look about her but those eyes had a calculating type of energy that he hadn't noticed before. "Oh aye, and what d'you suggest?"

"I've learned a lot from Beth. The important thing is to communicate your message before the media communicates it for you."

"I've got media contacts, you know. Malcolm Crawford is one of my oldest friends. He's a journalist at *The Record*," said Dougie, although as he spoke be didn't know what actual use Malcolm could be to them.

"The train's already left the station, Dougie," said Nine, "those photos the guy took tonight could now be online. Journalists might already have left Glasgow and be on their way. If we're really unlucky, there'll be TV crews too. Then there's all the diners. Many of them will have Facebook and Twitter accounts as well as texts and emails. They'll be telling everyone about what's happened. Even as we speak the story may have gone viral. Have you ever dealt with anything like this before? Either of you?"

"But we haven't been found guilty of anything yet," argued Dougie.

"It might seem like a good idea to do nothing until you're forced to, but believe me, it is far better to think of the worst case scenario and be proactive."

"Yes, Dad, we need to be proactive," agreed Benjy. Dougie thought he was behaving like a lap dog.

"You need to tell all your customers what's happened at The Four Sisters tonight. Be clear the causes haven't been identified but that you're taking the precautionary step of recalling all your oysters. Emphasise that your first priority is the health and wellbeing of your clients and their customers."

"We can get started on that right away," said Benjy, "it's only 9 o'clock. Some of them will still be up."

"You'll also need to offer full refunds," added Nine.

"Wait a minute," protested Dougie.

"If we're telling them they can't sell our oysters we can hardly expect them to pay for them," reasoned Benjy.

Dougie was aghast. "I don't understand why we would admit blame before we've been found guilty. Let's at least wait for the results of the Health and Safety Inspector's tests."

"We've got to be honest with our customers, Dad. If it turns out we're blameless, then they'll remember what we did. And if it turns out we're the problem, they'll be glad we told them as soon as we could."

"We're wasting time arguing about this," said Nine. Dougie glared at her and was about to say something when the door banged open, the wind making it bounce off the wall. A bedraggled figure struggled through the door. It took Dougie a moment to recognise him. "Billy?" he asked. Squally gusts blew into the Portakabin. The man shook off his hood and stood in front of them. "Aye it's me. I've a vanload of undelivered oysters here. What d'you want me to do with them?" he asked.

"You have?" asked Benjy.

"I don't know what's going on but Dougie called me hours ago and told me to turn back."

Dougie could see Benjy and Nine directing the same accusatory look towards him but Billy seemed oblivious to the atmosphere.

"I'm off to the pub for a pint and a pie. Any of youse joining me?" he asked.

"Later maybe," said Dougie, seeing Billy to the door. "Thanks for coming back."

He turned to face them, like a defendant before two judges. "OK. I admit when I heard both Sally and Fiona were ill this afternoon I was worried. I had a bout of sickness myself last week. At the time I thought it was just a bug and for all we know it may still be a bug but... I did try to tell you Benjy but... I'm sorry son, I've fucked up."

Benjy was crestfallen. Dougie could feel his disappointment as tangibly as if he had been hit over the head with it.

"At least you had the sense to do something," said Nine. He thought she was trying to sound encouraging but she only succeeded in making him feel even more inadequate.

"Tell me what you want me to do," he said quietly. Dougie felt a change in the atmosphere then, as if blame, anger, and disappointment had gone and like a team of medical staff in the emergency room, had been replaced with calmness and order.

"Dad, you make a list of everyone that's had a delivery of oysters in the past week with telephone numbers and email addresses. Nine and I will draft an announcement," said Benjy.

"Not just last week. All your customer base," added Nine.

"Right," said Dougie, "anything else?"

"Plenty. We'll need to look at your website, Facebook and whatever else you've got that makes contact with the outside world. We'll know by the morning if the story is trending," she added.

"Morning?" repeated Benjy. "I'd forgotten all about the morning. The presentation and all that. D'you think it'll go ahead?

"No one would blame them if it didn't," said Dougie, "where there's mud, it sticks."

"Beth's not like that," said Nine, "you of all people should know that, Dougie." Benjy turned to her in surprise. "Dad doesn't know Beth Colquhoun. He met her for the first time tonight. Didn't you Dad?"

Dougie sat down wearily. "I'll get started on that

customer list," he said.

Benjy was looking at him incredulously. "Once this is over, Dad, I want you to tell me everything. D'you hear me? Everything," said Benjy, firing up his computer, stabbing at the keys grimly.

Dougie took down the lever arch files where they kept all the invoices and began to make a list of the customers. After a few minutes Benjy handed him a piece of paper. "Your script for the calls," he said. Nine was sitting in Sally's chair opposite him. She was behaving as if she belonged.

The Four Sisters Restaurant has been temporarily closed tonight due to a suspected Norovirus outbreak. As a supplier to the restaurant we wanted to inform you of this unfortunate episode as soon as possible and to advise you to remove from sale any oysters we have supplied you. We would emphasise that this is a precautionary measure but because we put the health and safety of our customers as our top priority, we feel it is a sensible course of action. Tests are being carried out by Health and Safety Inspectors and we expect their results in the next 24 to 72 hours. We are cooperating fully with them and will keep you informed of events as they unfold. All paid invoices will be refunded in full.

Privately he thought it a bit formal. He had known all his customers for years, they were more like friends than clients. However, he wasn't going to argue with Benjy and Nine. He cleared his throat and waited for the line to connect. He stared out into the darkness of the wild night and wondered where it would all lead to.

He worked through the calls steadily, making a note where there was no answer. It reminded him of the time his old mum died and he had to go through her address book and tell everyone. He worried he would need to deal with grief and despair but whilst everyone was sorry to hear the news, most were straightforward about it; wanted to trade bits of news and gossip, to admonish him for not being in touch more often. It was the same here. His customers seemed to take the news in their stride, an inconvenience rather than tragedy, ending the calls with an agreement to meet up for a drink. It made him wonder why he hadn't been in touch more regularly. By the time he had got to the end of the list he was feeling surprisingly upbeat.

Benjy and Nine were at the far end of the Portakabin in the kitchen area. At first he thought they were arguing but as he got nearer he could hear the tone was good natured. Nine was firing questions at Benjy. "Why didn't you act on the first report? Why did you stop the shipment going to Glasgow but not inform the restaurant? How many times have you had naturally occurring bacteria problems in the past? How will customers be able to trust you again?"

The questions were horrible, but he could see that having an answer prepared was better than being caught short. He realised that despite the calamity of the situation the two of them seemed to be enjoying themselves.

"I've finished the calls and I've put a list of emails that need to go out on your desk," said Dougie, "it wasn't as bad as I expected."

"Good," said Benjy.

"I think I'll go back to the house. You coming?" asked Dougie.

'I'll not be long. Beth's coming over to go back with Nine back to their cottage. We've got a bit of website stuff to finish off before she arrives," said Benjy. Dougie thought Nine was pleased at the thought of being left alone together. Neither of them seemed tired.

The sky was clear, studded with a million stars. The moon hung like a silver disk, its outline as sharp as if someone had cut it out of silver paper and stuck it on black paper. The air was cool but dry, the storm spent, and in its place was a granite clarity. High pressure was dominating; it would mean a glorious day tomorrow and despite the potential for disaster, he felt cheered by the thought of vast clear skies.

She was lying on the couch. He wasn't sure if she awake or not. The moonlight shafted in from the window, highlighting her russet hair. The fallen side of her face was pushed up against the back of the cushion so that it lifted a little. She was like a young girl again. A small fire struggled in the grate, the embers grey and on the verge of going out.

"Oh hi there," she said, shifting in her seat and sitting up. "Neil's taken Mr Takashama back to his room at The Four Sisters. I texted Nine and said I'd come over to the office and get a lift back with her but as I passed the house, something drew me in. I hope you don't mind," she said.

Dougie shook his head. "The door's never locked."

"Any sign of the inspectors?" she asked.

He shook his head again, and bent down to add a

couple of logs to the fire. The flames rose satisfyingly and illuminated both their faces. The fallen side of her face looked unbearably sad.

"Hopefully they'll hold off making an appearance till after the presentation."

"I wasn't sure if that would still go ahead," said Dougie.

"If it turns out your oysters are implicated in the food poisoning, we'll need assurances that the same problem won't happen with the seaweed. But that's something you would do anyway isn't it?" she said.

He thought she sounded businesslike but kind. "I suppose so," he said.

"Neil's been boring the backside off us all about the phenomena of naturally occurring bacteria. If it turns out your oysters are dodgy, he thinks you've been unlucky. Nothing you could do about it." Dougie remained silent, enjoying his temporary innocence and the matter of fact way Beth had of dealing with things. He suspected she did this a lot, seeing disaster as just another problem to be solved.

"Drink?" he asked, realising that he was craving a glass of whisky.

"I prefer this," she replied, bringing out a small joint. His eyes widened but then she always had the capability to surprise him. She lit the joint, inhaling a couple of deep breaths before offering it to him. He sat down in the chair opposite the sofa, took a lungful of smoke, experiencing a rushing in his head as it swirled and eddied. He handed it back, feeling like the smoke was weaving a web between them. "I didn't expect you still to be smoking this stuff," he said.

"It helps with the headaches. Helps me relax," she said. Dougie watched her breathe out the smoke, trails of vapour curling in the air.

"You give the impression that you're always relaxed," he said.

She let out a rueful laugh. "Last night I woke at 3am convinced I've got a brain tumour. And even though I know it's unlikely, I got the laptop out and researched symptoms, tumour types, treatment options, survival rates. I can't stop myself. I have to know the worst case scenario so that I can prepare, plan contingencies. I must have fallen asleep because the alarm woke me at 6am. I felt worn out, like I've survived some ordeal," she said.

"I'm knackered just listening to you," said Dougie, taking the joint from her.

"I know. I can't seem to stop myself. Always thinking ahead, having a plan of action," said Beth.

"But don't you ever ask yourself what's the point of trying to control things?"

"Nine says it's vanity that makes us think we can control things. But I don't agree. We always have an option to act. We don't have to accept everything that life throws at us."

"And this tumour?" said Dougie. "Is there any chance you could have one?"

"The doctors say no. Brain tumour symptoms tend to creep up on people. Seizures and stuff. But I've persuaded them to do more tests."

"Tests. We've got that in common," said Dougie.

"We've got a whole history in common, Dougie.

The past. Tonight. Just now. It's like it's all merging into one."

"Memories. They're really just stories we tell ourselves aren't they? Not accurate accounts of the past, just how we've chosen to remember things. That night in the pub when I asked you to marry me? I remember ordering a can of IPA. I pulled off the ring pull and you laughed when I slid it on your finger. It was way too big for you. I asked you to marry me. Right away, you said yes. We kissed. You were smiling but I saw fear in your eyes. I think it was the first time you hadn't told me the truth about your feelings. It's as clear to me now as it was then but perhaps you remember it differently."

"I loved you but I wasn't ready to settle down. I should never have accepted your proposal. That was selfish. Cruel. I wish I had been kinder."

"I don't think it's possible to break up in a kind way. I'm not sure I would have let you be kind."

"And after the break up? How did you meet Benjy's mum?"

"In Thailand when I was travelling. The baby wasn't planned. Nothing in my life was planned then, but as soon as I saw my beautiful son I knew that everything was going to be fine. Love, happiness, the whole shaboodle was possible again."

"I'm glad, Dougie," she said.

"I play the safe game, Beth. Drift along, keeping Benjy close."

"But things are changing aren't they?"

"This oyster scare, the new business, Benjy getting

married one of these days. I feel like I'm losing him and there is nothing I can do about it."

"There's always something you can do. Every day I wake up hoping my face is better and every day I feel shattered that it's not. But I'm not giving up hope. Trying to find an answer, a cure." Her eye was watering, partly the smoky atmosphere but mostly tears. Dougie got up then and sat down beside her, bringing a woollen blanket with him. He covered them both and put his arm round her. "You haven't changed a bit you know."

"Why is it when people who meet up after long time say that to each other? It's obvious to anyone looking on, they sure as hell have," said Beth.

"Oh I don't know. Maybe we forgive our aging. Or maybe we choose only to see the things that haven't changed; your snaggletooth, the small scar on your lip; your fighting talk and the vulnerable person underneath. All still there. Just as I remember them."

"I should go. Nine will be expecting me," said Beth.

"She might be expecting you but I don't think either Benjy or Nine will be pleased to see you."

"Won't that cause trouble with Sally?"

"Beth we're in so much trouble that I don't think a bit more will make much difference. There comes a point where the only thing that matters is."

"Is what?"

"This," he said simply.

Chapter 15

Dougie was the last to arrive and the tension in the room was as thick as Fiona's barley soup. Scott was standing at the back. Dougie could see a knot of tension on his neck, his cocky grin fixed. Benjy and Sally were sitting next to each other with a telling space between them. Mr Takashama sat a little apart from everyone, as inscrutable as ever. Dougie wondered who had invited him. The same reporter from the *West Highland Gazette* who attended the prize-giving ceremony was there with his notebook at the ready, looking more nervous than anyone else. Dougie supposed the announcement of the Health and Safety Inspectors' results was a major scoop in the world of a provincial newspaper.

The two boys from the Health Inspectorate were standing at the front of the dining room. They were wearing polo shirts and slacks as if they had just come in from a round of golf. He had got to know them quite well over the past couple of days as they poked around the oyster farm; jobbing council workers with an interest in thoroughness and making sure their backs were covered. The older of the two got to his feet as soon as Dougie sat down. He was holding a sheet of paper. Dougie could see there was a slight trembling in his hands.

"A report will be submitted to the Scottish department of Health and Safety regarding the recent outbreak of food poisoning at The Four Sisters Restaurant in the next two days. I'm here to give you a summary of our preliminary findings." He cleared his throat. Dougie could see the reporter had begun scribbling. He wondered what he had found to write about.

"The good news is that we've been able to reach a conclusion after analysing the samples taken from the restaurant and their suppliers. I say good news because it's not uncommon in these investigations for it to take several weeks for us to get to the bottom of things." He paused, perhaps expecting there to be smiles, but the audience was stony faced. "I can confirm that norovirus was responsible for the food poisoning outbreak at The Four Sister Restaurant and that the source of that virus was razor clams served as part of the wedding supper on the Friday night. We have tested the supplier, McKenzie fisheries in Morar and found significant infestation. The McKenzie fisheries have been closed until further notice and there is an ongoing investigation at that establishment which I'm not at liberty to discuss further here."

Benjy let out a whoop of delight and it took a frown from the safety man and a prod in the ribs from Sally to quieten him.

"To date we know that seventy people have been affected as a result of eating razor clams at the restaurant. Forty-five attended the wedding party and a further twenty-five have been identified as a result of following up with diners on previous days. We cannot discount that more people will come forward, but it is our belief that the outbreak has been contained. The numbers would have been much higher if Mr McCaulley, the groom of the wedding party, had not contacted both the restaurant and the health authorities resulting in the prompt closure of the restaurant itself. We have made a special note in our report complimenting the speed and transparency with which Mr Scott and his team have responded to events. However, we did observe some examples of poor food handling practice in the kitchen of The Four Sisters Restaurant and will be sending Mr Smith recommendations for further training. We are pleased to announce that The Four Sisters Restaurant can reopen immediately."

There was an outbreak of applause from the audience. Dougie thought it was more from relief than celebration. Scott's face had reddened, a mixture of delight and irritation at being told to do further training. One or two of the staff got up and made for the door but the safety man's sidekick guided them back to their seats. They hadn't finished.

"We also tested the McKinnon oysters, both here in the restaurant and in situ. We found low-level traces of norovirus in forty percent of the oyster samples but as the majority of British oysters carry the virus we do not deem them responsible for this outbreak. However, we will be making recommendations in a separate report to the McKinnon family about additional measures they should take to ensure the quality of their product. We are also pleased to authorise the reopening of the McKinnon oyster farm."

There was a louder round of applause, this time

led by Benjy. The health inspector surveyed the audience and asked, "Are there any questions before we go?" but the crowd was dispersing and no one paid any attention to him. The reporter from the *Gazette* had shut his notebook and seemed fed up. Dougie supposed he would have preferred bad news. Scott Smith gave each of the inspectors a quick handshake before ushering them out.

"Bloody hell," he said after they had gone, "this has been the worst three days of my life. Thank fuck it's over."

Dougie put an arm round his shoulders. "It could have been worse."

"I suppose so, though I'm going to be hit by claims for compensation from seventy people. Maybe more if they can work out how to jump on the bandwagon. My insurers are talking about a major incident and a posse of them are coming up later this week. Not to mention the impact on the business and our reputation."

"I don't know about you but I'm looking forward to getting back to work. All this hanging about and waiting for results was driving me crazy," said Dougie, rubbing his hands together.

Scott said in a small voice, "I'm sorry Dougie. I won't be serving oysters for a while. Not yours. Not anyone's. Sorry mate."

Dougie felt pained but didn't know what to say. He could hardly blame the man.

"Isn't it great, Dad?" said Benjy, coming up him. "I'll send out a press release to all our customers right away."

"You do that," said Dougie thoughtfully.

Dougie glanced over to where Sally and Mr Takashama were standing. Sally looked ill, her skin pasty and wan.

"Sally OK?" asked Dougie.

"Not really. The doctor thinks it's gastric flu," said Benjy, although Dougie didn't hear much sympathy in his tone. "Have you seen today's *Gazette*?" asked Benjy.

"No," said Dougie, "is there something about the prize-giving ceremony?"

"We've made the headlines but not in the way we thought we would," he said, pushing the newspaper in Dougie's direction.

"Lovers Reunited," said Dougie out loud. There was a photograph of Beth and Dougie shaking hands in the restaurant. Beth had her head back and was laughing. That silly handshake had set her off. The photographer had caught her good side.

"Bloody hell," said Dougie, reading on further. "'Dougie McKinnon meets up with his ex-fiancée after twenty-two years.' How did they find out about this?"

"I told Sally about you two. I asked her to keep it quiet but you know Sally. She thought it was romantic, would make a good story. We've had words about it this morning. I've told her I'm very unhappy that she's turned the prize-giving ceremony into a bloody soap opera."

"I hope this doesn't make trouble for anyone," said Dougie, his mind already weaving dark scenarios.

"I don't think anyone's going to be interested in your old love life, Dad. It's just a shame we didn't get coverage about the seaweed business," he said.

Mr Takashama had sidled up to his shoulder. "You make a handsome couple," he said.

"So Mr Takashama, what are your plans?" asked Dougie.

Mr Takashama looked at him coldly. "I am considering all my options at the moment," he said.

"I bet you are," snorted Dougie.

Mr Takashama ignored the derision in his voice. "Forgive me for not staying longer to discuss this but I've urgent business in London to attend to."

Dougie and Benjy watched him go.

"I always knew he'd be a fair weather friend," said Dougie.

Dougie found Fiona in the back of the shop sorting out biscuits. She was putting on sale stickers and then placing them in a basket that had been lined with a tartan cloth. She had the *Gazette* spread out in front of her.

"It's a good photo," said Fiona, peering at the paper.

"It's a lot of crap," Dougie said, picking up her mug of coffee and taking a swallow. She had dunked one of the biscuits in it and the coffee had become an over-sweetened sludge. "No wonder Benjy's angry with Sally for telling the paper about it."

"Sally told me she's had a stroke and it's affected her face. It was nice of the photographer to pick her good side," said Fiona.

"Never mind about her, how are you? Feeling better? Benjy tells me Sally's got gastric flu."

"It must be terrible to be disfigured when you were once beautiful," said Fiona, lifting up the basket of biscuits and taking it into the shop.

"For God's sake Fiona," said Dougie, exasperated.

"Don't 'for God's sake' me," retorted Fiona, "you've been like a lovesick puppy ever since Saturday night."

"That's ridiculous and you know it," said Dougie.

"What I know, Dougie McKinnon, is that you're still carrying a candle for this woman. How else do you explain why you've never told me, or Benjy, or anyone else for that matter that you were once engaged to her? You only keep that sort of secret when someone's still important to you."

"Romantic nonsense, Fiona. It happened over twenty years ago. It's ancient history."

"Not so ancient now," she said.

"Why d'you think Sally told the press about it? She wasn't even there that night. What could she have to gain from it?"

"It's a nice love story isn't it? Maybe that's all she thought," said Fiona.

"Benjy's furious with her. My best shucking knife couldn't cut the atmosphere between them."

"You're so naïve aren't you Dougie? You can't see what's staring you in the face," she said.

"Obviously because I've no idea what you're talking about."

"It's not you and your old flame that's causing trouble between Benjy and Sally. It's that assistant of hers."

Dougie knew better than to ask how Fiona had so much information about the events of the evening. The island was a leaky old boat when it came to holding secrets.

"Beth and Nine have gone back to Glasgow. In a couple of weeks it'll all be forgotten about."

"No doubt," said Fiona pleasantly, untying the ties of her apron and folding it neatly on the side. "I'm off now, Dougie. I'll see you Friday."

Dougie could see she was wearing a new dress, her hair was washed and she had applied her makeup a bit more carefully than usual.

"Off somewhere nice?" he asked.

She smiled at him then, a mix of affection and disdain. "None of your business," she said. He noticed a small suitcase in the corner of the room.

"Tell him from me he's a lucky man," said Dougie, laughing, but she stared at him as if he'd insulted her. She took her coat from the counter and carefully folded it over her arm. She tugged the suitcase out from the corner and dragged it along behind her at a brisk pace. He went to the window to see if there was someone waiting for her but all he could see was her picking her way over the rough ground in her high heels; pulling the suitcase behind her, bumping and skittering over the cobbles like a tipsy chicken.

The wind had died down by the time Dougie

rowed out to the oyster rails. The water was still and silky. A watery sun struggled behind cement-coloured clouds, a humid day that would encourage the first of the season's midges although they hadn't travelled this far from shore yet. He planned to move the rails over to the far side of the loch where the current was stronger. Moving the rail sites more frequently had been one of the inspector's recommendations and Dougie had to agree it was a good one.

The great castellated ridge of the Cuillins, with their slabby cliffs and buttresses, dominated the skyline. He expected to find comfort in their unchanging grandeur, expected their permanence to give him peace of mind that life was predictable and return his mind to a pleasant state of vacuity, but he felt more stirred up than ever.

Was Fiona right? Was he still holding a candle for Beth? She often seemed to know him better than he knew himself. He was finding it hard to forget Beth's beguiling mix of strength and vulnerability. She was at the hospital today for her tests. He closed his eyes and for the first time in a long time, prayed to a God he didn't know, but knew of no other to try, and asked him to protect her from harm.

He opened his eyes. The sea sparkled, shifting with an imperceptible movement. Hardly waves at all, just a gentle disturbance of the surface. Waders pecked and danced at the shoreline, running in and out of the surf like excited children trying to avoid getting their feet wet. Then from behind the clouds a glorious burst of sunshine. He thought it was a sign. Beth would be fine.

He heard the buzz of a motorboat making its way

towards him and saw Benjy at the helm. They hadn't spoken much since Beth and Nine had gone back to Glasgow but he could feel the same troubling current around him too. He was finding fault with Sally too easily. Perhaps her leaking the story was a way of seeking attention from Benjy, even if it was the irritating kind. He watched as he came closer. He was wearing sunglasses and was standing up so that in some fancier boat he might look like a rich man. He cut the engine and Dougie reached out to pull him alongside.

"You OK Dad? You've been out a long time," he said.

"Just thinking about how many of the rails to move over to the new site and how many to move to the hardening pens for the Glasgow shipment for the weekend," he said.

"Pier 42 has been on the phone, Dad. It's not good news," he said.

"They've pulled out too?" said Dougie.

"I thought I'd go to Glasgow. See if I can talk some sense into them," said Benjy. He was speaking quickly. Too quickly, thought Dougie. Pier 42 wasn't the reason he wanted to go to Glasgow.

"No harm in trying," agreed Dougie.

"I've plenty of pals I could stay over with," he said. He looked away. *He would make a terrible poker player*, thought Dougie.

"Mr Takashama's gone away for a few days so nothing much will happen here," said Dougie.

"Did you know he's taken Fiona with him?" said

Benjy. "Sally thinks Fiona's doing it to make you jealous."

"Does she now?" said Dougie.

Benjy seemed worried. "Best not tell Sally about the Glasgow trip. She'll only put two and two together and…"

"…Get the right answer," finished Dougie. "Give Nine my best and if you see Beth, tell her I hope it went well at the hospital today."

"I love you, Dad," said Benjy.

Chapter 16

The nurse greeted Beth warmly. She was wearing lipstick in an optimistic shade of pink, her hair sprayed into a tidy nest. Beth had to pay attention to keep up with her pace. The hospital smelt of coffee and freesias and had the reassuring look of a bank, carpeted in dark blue with matching chairs. They reached a waiting area at the end of a corridor and she gestured for Beth to take a seat.

There was only one other person in the room, an elderly lady who was standing by a drinks machine. She waved a pouch forlornly in the air and the nurse went over to her and pressed it into the right slot in the machine. The nurse smiled back, confident in her helping ability.

"They'll be along for you shortly," the nurse said, and gave Beth the same reassuring smile.

A tidy pile of *Scottish Field* magazines lay on a coffee table. Beth hadn't seen one since she last visited her mother in the hospice over fifteen years ago but they had a timeless quality to them: a portrayal of Scotland that relied on heathered hills and stags in defiant poses. Her eye was drawn to a headline. 'Award-winning restaurateur, Scott Smith, shares family secrets about living with four sisters.'

Scott was smiling, ruddy and plump-cheeked, holding up a bunch of leeks. They had clods of earth on their roots, as if freshly pulled from the ground and he admired them proudly as if they were a trophy. Beth felt a stab of sadness at the turn of events since this picture had been taken. The Health Inspectorate was still investigating the food poisoning incident and she imagined Scott was caught in an unhappy hiatus, hoping for the best and dreading the worst.

She returned the magazine to the top of the pile and took the newspaper from her briefcase. She carefully scanned each page, expecting to see a headline about the closing of the restaurant. Nothing. Nine trawled the internet daily but apart from the odd Facebook and Twitter comment it was quiet. There had been a murder in Glasgow over the weekend involving a mother and her twin daughters that was taking up a lot of column inches in the press. Perhaps that explained the silence.

Beth took a deep breath and allowed Dougie to come to the forefront of her mind. He had been lurking in the shadows of her mind ever since the weekend. They had parted with no conversation about what would happen next. The more she thought about it, the more confused she became about what she wanted, how she felt about him. She guessed Nine was thinking about Benjy too although they had an unspoken agreement not to talk about what had happened or hadn't happened between them. It was like they were all caught in in a kind of waiting, an uncertain hiatus.

A man was hurrying along the corridor, his gait unmistakable. She got to her feet, the newspaper falling off her lap and she called after him, "Alec?" He continued to walk and she had to run to catch up with him, "Alec," she said as she came alongside him, "I knew it was you."

"Beth?" he said, looking surprised.

"Did Nine tell you I was coming here today?" asked Beth, feeling both irritated and pleased.

"No."

There was an awkward silence, quickly recovered. "You're here visiting someone else?" she asked, looking around. She followed his gaze toward the main reception. Margaret was wearing a dress consisting of layers of linen that flowed over her body, her plastered leg stuck out at right angles taking up two extra seats.

It took an effort of will for Beth to smile and walk towards her. "What brings you here?" she asked, bending down to kiss her floury cheek. "A problem with the leg?"

Margaret sighed dramatically and pursed her lips. "So Alec hasn't told you?"

Alec responded with his small-boy guilty look. It was a trademark expression he had honed over the years. She had a sudden recollection of the time their mother had made pancakes as a special treat for tea. They had been stacked under a tea towel to keep them warm, their smell irresistible. When their mother left the room Beth grabbed two and ate them quickly, too quickly to be enjoyed. Alec, in his greater wisdom, took a bite out of each one and then placed them back under the tea towel so the missing bits were hidden. When this was discovered (inevitably said Beth at the time) Alec had given his mother this very same look but rather than inflaming the situation, it seemed to charm her and all he got was a playful cuff around the head. Beth, on admitting she ate two whole ones, was sent to bed without tea. The unfairness still rankled.

"I'm here for a consultation about a gastric band," said Margaret, bringing Beth back to the present. "The NHS won't consider one unless I lose two stone. How can I do that with this stookie on my leg? And even if I did manage it, they've told me there's a waiting list. Mr Frost said he would do it privately. Right away."

"So you see it was an opportunity," added Alec.

"Of course," said Beth, already guessing that the money she had given for school fees was not going towards school fees after all.

"So, why are you here, Beth?" asked Margaret, scrutinising her more closely.

"Some tests for this Palsy," replied Beth lightly.

"I'm so glad," said Margaret, "we were talking about you the other night, weren't we Alec? Thinking that more needed to be done." Alec shifted his weight from one foot to the other.

"I hope it goes well for us both. Better get back," said Beth, turning to leave, surprised to find tears pricking her eyes, a bubble of self-pity swelling in her throat. It felt as solid as a goitre. She speeded up her step and was almost back at the waiting area when Alec caught up with her.

"Beth, if you'd told me you were coming to

hospital... I had no idea," he said, breathing heavily, his forehead perspiring.

"Why would you? I didn't want anyone to know," she said.

"I'm going to use your money for Margaret's op," said Alec.

Beth nodded. "It's not my money anymore, it's yours."

"The school have given me a moratorium on fees for a term you see."

"Really Alec, you don't have to explain, it's no business of mine."

"I just wanted to say, good luck." He hugged her then. The suddenness of his movement felt awkward. She found herself responding half-heartedly to the embrace. She could feel a slight dampness on his shirt. He glanced back to where Margaret was waiting.

"I'll be fine. Off you go," she said briskly. The nurse had reappeared in the waiting area and had picked up Beth's dropped newspaper. She held it out to her. "They're ready for you now," she said.

She was taken to a room, asked to undress and to put on a gown that tied at the back. She was grateful they allowed her to keep her knickers on. All her clothes and possessions, including her phone, were put in a small bag and taken away.

She sat on the edge of the bed and waited. Minutes passed. Five minutes had gone by but it felt like fifteen. She thought about putting the TV on but couldn't face the fiddle of finding out how to work it and then only to watch junk.

Her mind drifted back to the meeting with Alec. There was a part of her that would have liked him to be here with her but if she had to choose anyone, it would be Dougie. She imagined his patience and humour would be a godsend. Yet she understood why some people kept their illness a secret. Family and friends can be a comfort but in the end they're more of a drain; managing their anxiety and needs can be harder than managing your own. Life's a solo act, she reminded herself, and there was relief in that truth. Focusing on yourself is clearer, easier to control. She summoned her usual mantras. *The likelihood of anything being seriously wrong with me is statistically low. Whatever happens I have the resources to cope. Worse things happen to people. Every day.*

A new nurse appeared. She was wearing blue theatre scrubs and was carrying a clipboard. Beth felt both glad the waiting was over and worried about what lay ahead. She explained that the first test would be an EMG, which measures electrical activity and assesses nerve damage. Painless, she added reassuringly. In the last few days Beth's teeth had become unbearably sensitive, as if they'd been stripped of their enamel. Hopefully the test would measure what was going on. And anything that could be measured could be managed. She felt a flicker of gratitude for her capacity for rational thought.

The day turned out to be like the interview she had for her first job after graduating. A day-long ordeal for the foreign office with a lot of hanging about interspersed with occasional meetings and tests. The test measuring nerve activity had been long and boring. She had focused on being stoic and patient, the machine producing an impressive amount of graph paper that the doctors seemed pleased with.

The eye and hearing tests involved pressing buttons at dots of light and sounds. She put her full effort into it and privately thought she had done rather well. She had been surprised they needed to fill seven different phials of blood, but the nurse had said she had splendid veins and although she knew it was illogical, she felt pleased her body was so accommodating.

Beth had seen MRI machines on television but close up this one was like a space age coffin, the opening impossibly narrow for an adult to fit into. The nurse was explaining the procedure but Beth was barely listening, fixated on trying to imagine herself being inserted into that tiny tunnel.

"It will last twenty minutes. It's very important that you mustn't move. There's a panic button but if you press it, we'll have to start again, so please do everything you can to avoid that."

"Is this the point you ask me about my choice of music?" asked Beth, hoping the nurse would be fooled by the lightness of her tone.

"Not with this machine I'm afraid. You'll just have to lie back, think nice thoughts and keep completely still."

Panic like a slow wave worked up through her body. Her claustrophobia came mainly in dreams, being buried alive, her mouth full of dirt, an unbearable sense of suffocating. The nightmares had started when she was a child. She and Alec would play a game where she would dive under the bedcovers pretending she was swimming underwater. Alec had leapt on top of the bed and wrapped her tightly in the sheet shouting, "Caught you."

Her lungs felt clogged up with cotton. "I can't breathe! I can't breathe!" she yelled, but that had only spurred him to wrap her tighter and tighter till she kicked and screamed with the abandonment of sheer terror.

He had laughed his cruel tormentor laugh, saying that she was obviously breathing because she was shouting, but the air through the thin sheet had not been enough and afterwards she lay gasping, terrified, grateful for the release. The nurse was looking at her clipboard, checking her watch. She wanted to shout, "I can't do this. I CAN'T DO THIS!"

She knew the only way to avoid pressing the panic button was to close her eyes for the duration of the test. *Closing your eyes for twenty minutes can't be that hard,* she reasoned. Yet she knew she would only have one shot at it. If she opened her eyes before the test was finished, the terror of being buried alive in this great white coffin would overwhelm her. She asked the nurse for an eye patch, explaining that she couldn't close her eye. Her voice sounded perfectly controlled.

"I'll see what I can do," said the nurse. It didn't sound promising. A small tsk of disapproval escaped from the nurse's lips. "I don't know what the hold-up is. Let me go and check," she said.

Beth blew out a breath. *Take as long as you like,* she thought. *I need time to practice.* She looked at the clock. Five past three. Then she closed her eyes. The left eyelid remained half open. She closed it with her finger but it lifted, letting in a shaft of light. It would have to do.

At first thoughts flew in and out of her head like vapour trails in the sky. She thought about Dougie and where that might lead to or not lead to; Nine and Benjy and what his fiancée Sally was feeling; Scott Smith and his restaurant; the Rubikon deal, she must remember to confirm Gleneagles; Margaret and her gastric band, what she would look like thin; Alec and the pancakes; suffocating in the sheet.

Stop. Stop. Stop. Her eyes flickered. It was a monumental effort to keep them shut. *Concentrate on breathing. In through the nostrils; out through the mouth. Imagine the nicest place on earth.* A Scottish seaside; marram grass; a warm wind; Dougie beside her; those beautiful eyes; hands holding. The sting of salt on her skin. Dougie licking it off. Her fingers through his hair. His laugh. His touch. Her eyes snapped open. She looked at the clock. Ten past three. Seven minutes. Bloody hell.

"Ready for you now!" said the nurse cheerfully. A porter was with her. Beth thought he had the demeanour of an executioner. There was no sign of an eye patch.

The doctor had a moustache and a full ginger beard that tapered down to the top of his breastbone. He was like a cross between Big Ears and a Scots warrior at Bannockburn. Beth wondered if so much facial hair was hygienic, but decided to focus on his kind eyes. They were green, flecked with brown.

"It's been a long day for you," said the doctor. Beth wondered if he knew she'd needed three attempts and a tablet of Valium to complete the MRI scan. She must still be woozy from its effects because she found herself not caring if he knew or not.

"The next stage is for us to analyse the results and send them to Dr Rorke. They should be with her in a week's time," he said, "so any questions before you go?"

She could feel confusion gathering. "So that's it? No preliminary findings to report?"

"Our protocol is..."

"Of course," interrupted Beth, wondering why she wasn't asking him who he thought the customer was, but the sedatives and the power of protocols made complaining seem like a lost cause.

"Would you like me to call you a taxi?" offered the nurse.

"No," said Beth. She got to her feet and shook the hands of both the doctor and the nurse, thanking them. It was a formalised appreciation that meant nothing to any of them.

The roar of the traffic on the Great Western Road assailed her as she left the hospital. It felt too loud. She turned into Kelvingrove Gardens and the traffic noise receded immediately. She walked up the gentle incline of the main boulevard. The early evening had released a complex perfumery from the plants and trees: floral, bark, and the sweetness of manure. She sat on a bench feeling dislocated from life.

It was six o'clock, a good time to go back to the office where there would be peace to catch up. Work, after all, was her usual saviour. A place where she could be useful, get things done. She switched on her phone and scrolled through the emails. There was a dizzying number. She leaned back and inhaled the fragrant air. She decided to stay here for a while longer when her phone rang.

It was Nine. "So, how was it?"

"We'll know all the grisly details in a week's time," replied Beth.

"You going to the office or coming home?" she asked.

Beth squinted up at the cloudy sky, the glare of sun trying to find a way. "Not sure. Anything happen today that I should know about?" she asked. There was pause; a telling pause.

"The *West Highland Gazette* is running a story today entitled 'Lovers Reunited'."

"Don't tell me…" said Beth.

"'Romance was in the air last Saturday night as Beth Colquhoun, head of The Agency came to Skye to meet with her ex-fiancée Dougie McKinnon whose son had just won…'"

"Who the hell leaked this?"

"Benjy told me it was Sally. Apparently she thought it was a nice love story," said Nine.

"Very nice. We've just given £25,000 of public money to my ex-fiancé's son. I'm already pilloried as an overpaid public servant. Now we can add corruption too," said Beth.

"We'll make sure that's not the angle the press takes up," said Nine, laughing.

"Do Ainslie and Desmond know about this?"

"Don't think so."

"Good. We've got some time to prepare a response then."

"Come home, Beth. You sound tired," said Nine. "We can work out a plan of action. Anyhow I've got a nice surprise for you."

Chapter 17

The smell of cooking and chatter greeted Beth as she opened her front door. She stood for a moment in the hallway, taking in the unfamiliar experience of coming home to people in her flat: a baritone voice, the colour of burnt umber, then Nine's, higher and brighter, a light violet. She popped her head round the kitchen door. Benjy was wearing an apron and standing by the cooker as if commanding it. Nine was washing lettuce in the sink. They were both dressed in black as if they were a matching pair; a couple engaged in happy domesticity, and it was Beth who was the visitor.

Benjy smiled in that open carefree way of his and bounded forward to hug her. She wasn't sure it was wholly appropriate but she let him anyway, smelling his aftershave, feeling the strength of his back.

"Amazing kitchen, Beth," he enthused.

"And it smells delicious, whatever it is," said Beth. "I haven't eaten all day."

"Poor thing," said Nine, taking her briefcase and putting it in the living room with a showy flourish. "Benjy's brought oysters! Isn't that great?"

"The Health and Safety Inspectors have cleared

you?" asked Beth.

Benjy nodded. "Razor clams were the culprit, not us."

There was a pause. She was waiting for one of them to explain why he was here in her flat with Nine and not back at the farm, catching up on past orders, taking his fiancée out for a celebration meal.

"We've lost our Pier 42 contract. Dad thought it would be a good idea if I came down to Glasgow to speak to them."

"And I said he could stay here with us. I didn't think you'd mind," said Nine carelessly. Beth could see she was wearing a trace of lipstick and mascara. Her alabaster skin flushed, the colour of rosé wine.

"Of course," said Beth, smiling inwardly. It was a tactic she had perfected herself over the years. Ask for forgiveness, not permission. "Nine can make up a bed on the sofa for you Benjy."

Nine's smile was enigmatic. "I've told Benjy about the foodie market at Glasgow Green. It might be a potential channel to market," said Nine. "I thought we could go down tomorrow and take a look. What d'you think?" They were both facing her now, standing side by side, their hands almost touching.

"Good idea," said Beth, debating whether she should spoil the mood by asking about the fiancée in Skye, but the moment passed and Benjy turned his attention back to the meal.

"I'm going to cook your oysters tonight," he said, "nothing to do with the food poisoning scare but because they're delicious lightly pan fried in butter with herbs and breadcrumbs." His black hair had flopped over one eye.

"Your dad must be relieved about the test results," said Beth.

"Of course but it'll take a while to get back to normal. It's not only Pier 42 that's pulled out. Scotty at The Four Sisters says he's taking oysters and all other shellfish off the menu. Permanently."

"It's good you've got the seaweed project to fall back on," said Nine. There was a hint of pride in her voice, thought Beth.

"And what about your Japanese friend Mr Takashama? Has he been put off backing you?"

"Dad thinks we can't rely on him. We'll have to scale back if he pulls out."

"I've done a bit of alternative business modelling if you're interested," said Nine casually. Benjy stopped chopping herbs and looked up in surprise. "If you concentrated on drying your seaweed, then milling it into a condiment, you wouldn't need a big packaging plant. Just a few polytunnels for drying and some grinding equipment. It would be a simpler, cheaper option but potentially with greater margins and a wider global market."

"I know The Four Sisters dried and smoked our seaweed to flake over their salads but d'you really think there's a demand for it?" asked Benjy.

"It's healthier than salt. It's the new Superfood," said Nine authoritatively.

"Skye Superfoods," suggested Beth, "it's got a ring to it."

"You two are amazing," said Benjy, but Beth could see he was only looking at Nine. His eyes were shining, and then he seemed to check himself, rubbing the back of his neck. "I'll have to talk to Dad though."

"Parents are a drag," said Nine, "it's time for you to fly solo." She said this casually, as if it was a well-known fact, but Benjy was aghast at the suggestion. "Dad and I make all the big decisions together." Nine shrugged her thin shoulders.

"Talking of your dad, I hear we're in the paper today?" said Beth, picking up the *West Highland Gazette* that was lying on the table. She opened it as if disinterested. The photograph of her and Dougie was shocking. How happy they both looked; as if they were sharing some private joke, and then she remembered the silly handshake and realised that they were.

"I imagine we're the talk of the steamie," said Beth, picking the paper up and taking a closer look. The photographer had got her good side; a bittersweet reminder of what she had lost.

"People are more interested in you guys than me winning the Young Entrepreneur prize," said Benjy. "Oh by the way, he asked me to tell you he hoped the hospital tests went OK."

"Tell him I'll give him a call when I get the results. But what about your dad's girlfriend? I bet she's not happy with this," said Beth.

"You mean Fiona? Poor Fiona. She's gone off for the weekend with Mr Takashama in the hope that Dad will be jealous but there's zero chance of that," said

Benjy. He was taking off the beardy bit of an oyster with a beautiful knife with the speed and confidence of someone who had done this many times.

"Poor Fiona indeed," said Beth, "and poor me if my bosses see this and jump to the wrong conclusion. Can I borrow Nine for a few minutes Benjy? We need to discuss how we handle this situation."

"Take as much time as you need," he said cheerfully, "I'll only need three minutes to get this meal to the table."

Nine walked silently to the office and Beth shut the door behind them. There was a sullenness in the way she fired up her laptop, her head tilted to the side. When their eyes met it was hard to tell who was the more defiant.

"Don't even start," said Nine.

"What are you doing? You know he's engaged."

"I don't know what you're talking about. We haven't done anything," she said.

"For God's sake Nine," replied Beth.

"I like him Beth. I really like him. And he likes me too."

"He's already taken," said Beth gently.

"Surely if someone realises he's making a mistake, it's better he does something about it before getting married?"

"Look, Nine. If it's true that Sally is a mistake, then Benjy needs to tell her and break it off properly."

"I'm not going to lie to you, Beth. I'm not going to wait till he does that."

"How do you know he's not just using you? A wee fling before he settles down. You could be making a fool of yourself. Falling all over him like this."

"And what about you and Dougie? I saw the look on your face when Benjy mentioned Fiona. Poor Fiona. You loved that bit didn't you?"

"You're playing a dangerous game, Nine. Be careful. Be very careful."

"You're a bloody hypocrite, Beth. Since when have you been careful about anything?" said Nine, leaving the room.

Beth felt too tired to go after her. She longed to sleep but her headache had drifted down into her left jaw and was as persistent as a jabbing stick. She heard the muffled laughter of Benjy and Nine and suddenly it seemed as if happiness was a complicated thing.

Chapter 18

"Board Meetings are well named," said Ainslie, "I was deeply bored. The presentations were tedious, no one wanted to make a decision, all people did was play out their petty jealousies that I was expected to facilitate into a useful conversation."

Beth made a soothing sound. "Did you want to speak to me about something in particular?" she asked. She was looking forward to getting home. Nine had been particularly pleasant since their spat about Benjy. She was cooking her favourite supper. Lemon linguini.

"Take a seat, Beth," said Ainslie. It seemed like he was in pain, his features strained. She noticed a small stain on his silk tie and wanted to sponge it off. She sat down slowly. Something bad was about to happen; she knew it with same certainty that when the sky darkens, you know a storm is coming.

"Beth," he began and then paused.

"Oh for God's sake, get on with it. I can see it's serious," she said.

He looked even more tense. "It's come to my attention... your affair with McKinnon."

"I'm not having an affair with Mr McKinnon,

Ainslie," said Beth, affecting a tone of wearied boredom though her heart was clattering, her mind racing.

"What do you call this then?" he said, moving *The West Highland Gazette* across his desk towards her. There was the photo of her and Dougie laughing and although she knew her situation was perilous she wanted to smile at the sight of them together. "Desmond tells me the Glasgow papers are going to run the story tomorrow with an altogether more unflattering commentary. He thinks the nationals might follow. Sex and corruption will always sell newspapers."

"That's a vicious piece of slander Ainslie."

"I agree. In fact I would be taking a leaf out of your book and wondering how we might use the exposure to our benefit but the thing I'm struggling with… the point at which your judgement may be questioned is…"

"I know," said Beth quietly, "I didn't submit a declaration of interest."

"And its absence, I'm afraid, is a problem."

Beth could never hear the word problem without an extraordinary instinct kicking in that shifted her mind into finding solutions. She felt preternaturally calm.

"I'm surprised I need to explain to you why I didn't tell you. I didn't want to run the danger that a minor excursion of my youth would cause The Agency further embarrassment. We were already looking pretty stupid after our first choice turned out to be a cheat."

"The paper says he was your fiancé. A little more than a minor excursion, Beth," said Ainslie.

"We were never officially engaged," replied Beth.

"You look pleased to see each other."

"That was the first time I'd met Dougie in over twenty years." She bit her lip then. That was a lie, though she doubted anyone had seen Dougie when he visited her flat.

"There are some people that can be very tenacious when it comes to following the rules," sighed Ainslie.

"Let me lay out the facts. As both Neil and Desmond will testify my vote wasn't for Benjy McKinnon but for Rachel Cunningham. When it was found out that she cheated it was Desmond who suggested Benjy McKinnon be given the prize. At that point I didn't even know he was the son of a very old boyfriend whom I hadn't seen in over twenty years."

"Nonetheless it doesn't explain why you didn't make it known when you became aware of who he was. You of all people know the sensitivity of these things."

"You could always tell people that you and I discussed it and thought on balance we would bring further unwanted to attention to The Agency if we raised it."

"I could, but we didn't have that conversation did we Beth?" said Ainslie, but Beth could see his face had become alert, the possibility of an escape brightening his features.

"I think if you remember hard enough Ainslie it'll come back to you," said Beth slowly. Ainslie nodded deliberately. "Good," said Beth, "I'll speak to the legal department. Fire off a broadside to the press lawyers threatening libel if they print. Even if that doesn't work for tomorrow's edition of the Scottish papers, it might scare off the nationals. Cause everyone to take a step back. Check their facts."

"Raking up the past is never a good idea in my experience," said Ainslie in a world weary voice that gave Beth the impression that he was well-versed in the wisdom of shoring up the murkier aspects of his past against public scrutiny.

"I knew you'd understand," said Beth, feeling a fleeting reflux of disgust that she had descended into the same moral territory as Ainslie. "Now is not the time for The Agency to get side tracked by tabloid gossip. Not with the Rubikon visit coming up so soon."

"Beth," said Ainslie, "it's vital that we pull off this Rubikon deal. The Agency needs a public success. You need a public success."

"I'm fully aware that my reputation, probably even my job, depends on us winning the Rubikon bid. But I'm quietly confident. The feedback on our written submission was excellent. I've been told, unofficially of course, that we're in a final shortlist of two. Mexico versus Scotland."

"How do we compare?"

"We have a clear lead in terms of political stability, education, infrastructure, transport, and pool of experienced professionals. In terms of straight cash and tax incentives, the Mexican government is throwing everything at them. We can't match them.

Running costs and basic labour are also cheaper. However the R&D centre will need highly qualified people and we have a massive advantage there."

"And the visit itself? I'm assuming my pals at the Royal and Ancient have been helpful with the golf arrangements?"

"Outstanding, thank you. St Andrews, Gleneagles, Carnoustie, and Muirfield all booked."

"Good. I'll take the lead on the evening activities as agreed. No need for you to get involved," said Ainslie. Beth thought he failed to disguise a leery edge to his smile.

"It's going to be a big success, Ainslie," assured Beth. Ainslie seemed as satisfied as if he'd eaten a large, expensive meal.

She walked back towards her office thinking she had sidestepped a landmine but had yet to fully disarm it. She was in debt to Ainslie for the covering lie and that was never a good position to be in for long. She would need to find something about him she could use to hedge the risk. Shouldn't be difficult. There were plenty of corners in his life to explore.

She thought for a moment about the lemon linguini waiting for her, the hot bath afterwards, but knew she would have to forgo both. She would text Neil inviting him to dinner, book the new Thai restaurant in George Street and arrange the PR department to have a photographer on hand, an insurance in case the Lovers Reunited Story broke tomorrow.

As she approached her office, two girls from the account's office were sitting on Flora's desk, perched on either side of her, too preoccupied to hear her approach.

"Wow, he's not bad looking. She's done well to pull him," said one.

"He's probably sorry for her. A face like that is enough to frighten small children."

"Even without the face, she's an all-round scary lady."

"The son's drop dead gorgeous," said Flora, "he asked me for my number when he was here for the competition but I said, 'Nah, my boyfriend wouldn't like it.'"

The two girls laughed at this show of bravado. Flora held Beth's gaze, pulling her fingers through her hair and slowly uncrossing her legs before making a show of folding the newspaper. The other two girls scattered away as fast as if running from a fire.

"Any messages?" asked Beth neutrally.

"On your desk," said Flora, equally neutrally.

"Thank you," said Beth. "No interruptions please," she added, shutting the office door behind her.

Of course it was upsetting to hear the girls talk about her like that but for all its unpleasantness, having a thick skin was a prerequisite of the job and knowing what the staff really thought was far more useful than superficial politeness. She emailed Desmond requesting a short meeting. Not an official complaint. Just to make him aware that two of his staff were gossiping about the Chief Executive in unflattering terms. It would rankle against his precious values of integrity and perhaps more telling, he wouldn't like Beth having anything that could be used against him.

Flora needed a different approach. A rebuke would only incite more rebellion. She would send her a bouquet of flowers instead. It would be unexpected, perhaps even destabilise her enough for Beth to make another move to sustain the upper hand.

She had a fleeting moment of disquiet that the honest, decent person at her centre was becoming smaller and smaller by this scheming and dissembling. Nine was always berating the toxic culture of organisations, the dog-eat-dog competiveness of capitalist values, the long-term interest of people and the planet sacrificed at the altar of short-term profit and greed. She defended herself as one of the good guys in this, working to improve the lives of people in Scotland by attracting more jobs, more wealth. Yet she knew, if pressed, she couldn't deny the sweet sense of satisfaction she gained from being several moves ahead of everyone else.

She texted Neil inviting him to dinner and invited the PR photographer to drop by. She glanced at her emails. One hundred and twenty had arrived in the last two hours. *Time to buckle down and get on with them*, she thought. She spotted Desmond's email immediately.

I noticed this article on the Reuters link today. No doubt you know about it already. Rubikon's Paris Headquarters targeted by animal rights activists - French police make four arrests.

She clicked on the link and read the article quickly. There were some photographs of primates in cages but frustratingly little detail. A Rubikon representative had given an official statement saying animals were used for their cancer drug research in China and that there was no animal testing in Europe nor any plans to introduce it. She would forward the link to Nine, asking her to get the names of those who were arrested and find out what organisations they represented. She felt suddenly weakened, as if the air had been knocked out of her. Why had Nine missed this? She was normally so reliable. The answer was obvious. Benjy was distracting her and this was no time to get distracted.

Her phone vibrated. She expected it to be a text from Neil agreeing to meet for dinner but it was from Dr Rorke. "Can you come in to see me tomorrow? Results are in."

Chapter 19

The wind whipped round the headland. Dougie thought it must be cutting right through Malcolm's cagoule, a thin orange affair, probably one of his freebies. Dougie grinned at his discomfort and offered him the oars. "This'll warm you up." But Malcolm shook his head and sunk lower in the boat, curling into a foetal position as if he was naked. Dougie continued rowing till they cleared the headland and glided into the bay beyond. The wind dropped and the temperature rose several degrees. Malcolm was visibly relieved.

"This is where the new seaweed beds will be sited," said Dougie, waving the oar in a wide arc in front of him. "The tides are a bit more active here, they'll help keep the sea free from algae and other bacterial nasties."

"Dougie," said Malcolm, "I'm not here to report on your new seaweed venture. My editor's unhappy. The Agency's lawyers are threatening libel if we print the story that appeared in the *West Highland Gazette* about you and Beth. As I confirmed the story with my editor, he's holding me personally responsible for sorting out the mess, getting to the truth."

Dougie laughed. "The truth? That'll be something

new for you. Serves you right anyhow. I asked you to keep it a secret about Beth and me, remember?"

"Now wait a minute. Someone had already told the *Gazette*. I only confirmed it when my editor asked me about it."

"Don't act the innocent with me, Malkie Crawford. That piece in the *West Highland Gazette* was a bit of light-hearted local nonsense. I'm guessing that editor of yours saw it as a chance to get Beth in trouble. You should know by now she's far too clever for that. Bound to make you look like a bunch of numpties."

"I don't know what I'm going to do, Dougie. I'm in a tricky position."

"Relax. Have a holiday. I'm sure you'll think of another story to keep him happy. Only it won't be about me and Beth. Got that?"

Malcolm shuffled in his seat looking as fed up as a schoolboy who hadn't been picked for the team. "What about writing a story about The Four Sisters?" suggested Dougie. "They were closed for four days you know. Over seventy people poisoned, though Scottie tells me that bookings for the restaurant have bounced right back. Even busier in fact."

"No one's interested in good news. Especially not my editor," said Malcolm, looking morose.

"Scottie's taken oysters off his menu so it's not all good news. We've had no option but to focus on the seaweed."

"Dougie, I've told you I'm not interested in your seaweed business. Well not as a story for the paper anyhow."

"Come to the pub tonight with me. Drown your sorrows. I'm on my tod at the moment."

"Where's everybody?"

"Benjy's in Glasgow trying to talk sense into the Pier 42 boys and Fiona's in London with Mr Takashama. Trade dinner. Purely platonic."

"Purely platonic? That'll be right. I didn't see that one coming. Did you?" asked Malcolm.

"She's a free agent," said Dougie, realising as he said it that apart from a small bruise of hurt pride, he felt happy for her, hoped she was having a good time. "I don't think Mr Takashama will be going into partnership with Benjy though. Between you and me, it'll be better for everyone in the long run."

Dougie rowed into the shoreline. Malcolm stood up in the boat, causing it to wobble, and missed his footing as he got out. He fell into the shallows, yelping like a small dog. Dougie laughed as he took his arm and guided him to the shore, then vaulted out of the boat and pulled it up onto the beach. Malcolm had taken off his shoes and socks and was wringing out the bottom of his trousers. He gazed out across the bay. "It's bloody beautiful here, even if it freezes the balls off you," said Malcolm.

"Come and meet Sally," said Dougie. Malcolm walked gingerly in his bare feet, hopping and skipping from stone to stone as if they were hot. Dougie could see Sally at the far side of the shoreline. She stood up, shielding her eyes as they got near. Her orange waders came up to her armpits and she was wearing black rubber gloves that came as high as her elbows. As they got closer she pulled her gloves off. Underneath the waders she was wearing a tee shirt made of fine cotton. Dougie could see the swell of her breasts above the bib of her waders. Small rings of sweat had formed under her arms. Malcolm was looking at her admiringly.

"Hello there," she said, smiling.

"Hello to you too," breathed Malcolm.

"Malcolm's a journalist from *The Record*," explained Dougie.

"Oh great. Have you come to do a piece on the seaweed project?" she said, schlepping towards them.

"I'm definitely thinking about it," said Malcolm.

"These are trial beds and we've got the first of our polytunnels over on the shore side," she said, pointing in the distance. Malcolm dutifully followed her pointed finger to two rows of plastic tunnels. "That's where we'll dry the seaweed before grinding it into flakes."

"Fascinating," said Malcolm.

"And that's just the start. Benjy's got even bigger ideas but he's not here at the moment. He's in Glasgow. He'll be sorry he missed you."

She had stopped smiling. Dougie imagined it was the mention of Benjy that had brought on the thoughtfulness.

"D'you need a hand with these baskets, Sally?" asked Dougie, walking over to baskets filled with seaweed.

"Thanks Dougie," she replied, "the trailer's on the dunes over there."

Dougie turned to Malcolm but he held his hands up in protest. "Sorry, can't help, no shoes," he said, looking down at his bare feet. Dougie shrugged and picked up a basket under each arm. Sally did the same and they walked side by side towards the tractor.

"Have you heard from him?" asked Sally as soon as they were out of earshot of Malcolm. "I've called him, left texts, but nothing." Her face was pinched with worry. "He was so angry with me about telling the *Gazette* about you and Beth. I said I was sorry but he left in a right mood."

Her walking was getting faster, so that Dougie had to lengthen his stride to keep up.

"I don't know what to do, Dougie. I just keep working. Working hard so everything is in good shape when he gets back. So he can see we're still part of a team," she said, "but I don't think he cares about me, not anymore."

They had reached the tractor and she slung her baskets on the back as if she was angry with them.

"He's only been away a couple of days, Sally. He's been trying to persuade Pier 42 to give us back our order. Then he's had meetings at The Agency. There's an awful lot going on. It's because he trusts you to keep things going here that he doesn't feel the need to keep in contact all the time," he said, thinking as he spoke that it had a faint edge of credibility.

"But surely if you love someone you reply to their texts and calls, tell them what you're doing. Maybe even ask them to join you?" she said.

There was a telling silence as Dougie could think of no rejoinder to this sad truth.

"Mum told me that Jeanie Briggs, who works as a waitress at The Four Sisters, said that Benjy was flirting with Beth's assistant the night the place was closed down. Is that true Dougie?" He put his baskets next to hers and faced her. Her eyes were blazing. In all the time he had known her, he had never seen her look so fierce.

"It's true that Nine helped us out that night. We needed all the help we could get."

"So, when I was in bed with gastric flu Benjy was making out with another girl and you went right along with it. I can't believe it. Or maybe I can. You've never thought me good enough for your precious son," she said.

He let the outburst settle. She was crying now.

"I know you love him, Sally. And if Benjy loves you I'm very happy for you both. But I think you're right, his head's been turned by this other girl."

"What's she got that I haven't?"

Dougie felt genuinely bewildered by the question. They were so different that he was truly stumped how Benjy could like them both. He could see Malcolm was walking along the waterline, hobbling and fussing, holding his shoes out at the end of each arm for balance.

"You'll have to ask Benjy that, not me," he said quietly. "I've no idea what he sees in her. All I know is that if you want him, you're going to have to fight for him, Sally."

"Dougie," said Sally. Her voice was quieter now, the wind carrying the sound towards him. She was standing backlit by the sun, looking like a warrior in her working clothes. Strands of hair had escaped from her ponytail and streaked across her face. Her cheeks were reddened by the wind and crying; her eyes were narrowed but bright. He felt for the first time that he was seeing her, seeing her properly. The wind gusted, she moved the hair out of her eyes. "Thank you."

Later that evening, Dougie made his way to the Long Inn to wait for Malkie. Fiona was polishing glasses with her back to him and as it was quiet there was no easy way for Dougie to slip in unnoticed. Her laugh was louder than normal. She took a moment before turning to face him. "Dougie darling," she enthused. Her hair was cut into layers and coloured with different shades of gold and copper. It was an expensive-looking haircut, thought Dougie, but too severe to flatter.

"Like the new hairdo?" she asked coquettishly. He could tell her mood was brittle. There was only one possible answer.

"Very nice," he said.

She began to pull him a pint. "Did you miss me then?" she replied, looking at him candidly now, her hand on hip, eyes flashing.

"Of course I did. C'mon, and tell me all about it," he offered, motioning her to join him at the small booth by the door. She sat down heavily, fiddling with the bow tied at the front of her blouse.

"It's at a time like this that I wished I smoked," she said, staring listlessly out to space. "The mad thing is, Dougie, I never fancied him in the first place but that doesn't make it any easier does it?"

"I don't suppose it does."

"He gave me money to get my hair done, buy a dress. I felt like fucking Julia Roberts."

Dougie didn't know who Julia Roberts was but didn't interrupt the flow by asking.

"I waited and waited for him in the hotel room. Dressed up like a turkey. I think I knew all along he wasn't coming. Reception called eventually and told me that unfortunately Mr Takashama had been called away on urgent business and wouldn't be returning. He had ordered dinner and champagne to be sent to the room. It arrived with a note saying 'sorry'. It wasn't even signed by him. Just something the hotel had put together."

"I suppose that was…"

"…Was bloody criminal of him. I felt so humiliated. But the worst thing, Dougie, I felt cheap. Sitting amongst all that expensive food and drink I felt cheap."

"I can see that," said Dougie, though in all honesty he was struggling to understand any of it. "And did he eventually turn up? You've been away two days."

"I spoke to him on the phone the next day. He was in Norway and didn't know when he would be back. I told him that was just an excuse and he should at least be man enough to admit he'd got cold feet at the last minute. D'you know what he said then? He had too much respect for me. Respect? Bullshit. I told him I wanted to stay for another night in the hotel. He agreed right away. The only thing I regret now is…"

"Going in the first place?"

"That I didn't say I was staying for a week. I think he would have agreed to anything as long as I didn't tell his wife."

"What a tosser," said Dougie.

"The biggest tosser I've ever known," agreed Fiona.

Dougie could see she had cheered up, was pleased to see her old spirit returning.

"If it's any consolation Fiona, I didn't think you two were right for one another."

Fiona's look was pure poison. "Correction. You, Dougie McKinnon, are the biggest tosser I've ever known," she said, getting up and moving back to the bar. He knew he had said the wrong thing but the conversation had been like playing one of those buzzwire games where you had to guide a loop through a maze of wire without touching; it was inevitable that he would set her off.

He was glad to see Malcolm coming through the door. "Hi mate. Another pint?" he asked. Dougie nodded. "Fiona's back. The trip wasn't a success. Tread carefully," he whispered.

Malcolm smiled. "I'll be like twinkle toes," he said, and Dougie watched with admiration as he fussed over her. Demanded a kiss. No, a proper one. Not one of those namby-pamby ones that don't touch flesh. Right on the smacker, thank you very much. Dougie saw her blush as she kissed him, calling him an old letch. He felt a sisterly love towards her, and hoped she'd find someone one day who didn't leave her on her own with a fancy hairdo and expensive food. Only it wasn't going to be him.

"So, Fiona's kicked Mr T into touch," said Malcolm, sitting down opposite him.

"I don't think we'll be seeing him here again," said Dougie.

"I felt bad that I hadn't followed up on my promise to do some digging about him so I asked the news desk this afternoon if they'd heard anything. They told me he popped up in Oslo as the main guest for the Sustainable Food Cooperative last night. Made a speech backing the country's commitment to new initiatives in their fisheries industry and announced a one million euro backing to the setting up of new seaweed businesses on the proviso that the Norwegian Government matches his offer."

"They're welcome to him. Benjy's already got plans to concentrate on the seaweed flakes. He doesn't need him."

"I think our Mr Takashama might be a bit of a conman. Persuade the Norwegian Government to give him development funding and then bugger off. Life's funny isn't it Dougie? This morning I thought I was in deep shit with my editor but now he's asking me to go to Oslo to see what I can find out about our singing seaweed man. One door closes. Another opens."

Dougie nodded. "I never thought of you as a philosopher, Malkie, but you're right. When one door closes it often means it was never meant to open in the first place."

Chapter 20

"Are you ready?"

Nine's voice brought Beth back to the present. Her thoughts had drifted to dark corners in her mind. Four thousand three hundred people diagnosed with benign brain tumours in the UK each year. The majority were low-grade gliomas. Most common symptoms were severe persistent headaches.

"We're going to be late," said Nine.

Beth had been awake for hours wondering if this is what the doctor would tell her this morning. Her headache had been unrelenting. Definitely severe. Definitely persistent.

"Coming," replied Beth cheerily.

Nine took the motorway from Glasgow to Edinburgh and filled the worried silence by reading out the overhead gantry messages.

'Don't drink and drive!'

'Wear your seat belt!'

'Watch your speed!'

Then substituting them for some of her own:

'Use three sheets to wipe your bottom.'

'Clean knickers every day.'

Beth smiled, appreciating her effort to lift the mood but after a few miles, her commentary ran dry. Bursts of sun alternated with chilly spells and Nine kept busy by adjusting the temperature of the car, never quite satisfied with it.

"Flora's scheduled three meetings in Glasgow this afternoon for you," said Nine, "she must think I'm taking you to Edinburgh and back by helicopter."

"I told her I was attending a short business meeting in Edinburgh and would be back by the afternoon," said Beth.

Nine scowled. "Still, three meetings. It's ridiculous."

"It'll be fine," replied Beth.

"I don't know why you sent her those flowers. Thank you for all your hard work. It's shite. That girl wouldn't know hard work if it went up to her and said, 'Good morning Flora, my name is Mr Hard Work.'"

"Are you going to tell me what's wrong?"

"I'm worried about what the doctor's going to tell you."

"That makes two of us," said Beth, looking out of the window.

"And... Benjy's gone back to Skye, back to his fiancée," she said, changing gears, crunching the clutch. "I expect you approve."

"It was always going to be difficult wasn't it?" she said gently.

"I told him to go back. That I didn't want to be

responsible for the break-up of his engagement, but the truth is Beth, I care about him so much that I don't give a damn about his fiancée."

"And he went. Just like that?"

"I don't know what's more devastating; that he's gone without a backward glance or that I was an idiot to tell him to go."

Beth didn't know what to say. She could only think in terms of clichés, plenty more fish in the sea, better to know now than be dumped later.

"So, I'm reconciling myself to serving my time with you till the end of the summer. I think I'll have enough saved to go travelling. Asia I think. I've heard there are parts of Malaysia that are amazing," said Nine, "maybe you have some ideas?"

"You make working for me sound like serving a jail sentence," said Beth.

"Well... now you say it," replied Nine, giving her a rueful smile.

"Benjy will be in Glasgow plenty of times over the summer, you know. Desmond's set up meetings with him every two weeks to help launch Skye Superfoods." Beth said this casually but the information had the power of a hand grenade. She saw Nine's fingers tighten round the driving wheel. "But Nine, please don't get distracted. We're in excellent shape with the preparations for the Rubikon visit but we still must be vigilant."

"Since when have I ever been distracted?" asked Nine with an edge of tetchiness.

"OK, I was going to wait till later to speak to you

about it but there was an animal rights demo at Rubikon's European Headquarters in Paris," said Beth quietly. "Desmond told me about it."

"Really? That's strange. The only place Rubikon test animals is in Wuhan. Chemo drugs. They've no animal testing in Europe that I know about," said Nine.

"And no plans to do any if they come to Scotland either, thank goodness. Nevertheless I would have expected you to pick it up," said Beth, trying to maintain a gentle tone but Nine looked stricken and she wondered if she'd been too harsh. "Four people were arrested. One of them British. You can redeem yourself by finding out the names and anything else you can about their organisation."

"Sure," said Nine, her face set in a frozen expression.

Beth couldn't decide whether she was sulking or taking her mistake seriously. "Look, I'm not mad at you. Just get me the information as soon you can."

"Will do," said Nine, but Beth felt the atmosphere between them had sullied. Nine put on the radio, turning up the volume so that music filled the car and she suspected they were both relieved it eliminated the need for further conversation.

***

"D'you want me to come in with you?" asked Nine as she slowed up outside the doctor's surgery.

"I'll meet you in Anderson's coffee shop round the corner. I don't imagine I'll be long," said Beth. As she walked round the car Nine rolled down her window and called her back. "Beth," she said. "Good luck."

"Thanks," said Beth, putting her hand over hers.

The waiting room was just as she remembered it, large with a smell of furniture polish and antiseptic. The pamphlets for facial disfigurement were on the table as before. The toothy teenage boy with his face crumpled in burns scars grinned at her. She sat down, took off her sunglasses, dabbed her eye and breathed deeply, trying to empty her mind.

"Ms Colquhoun," said Dr Rorke, coming forward to meet her, "come in."

The doctor was wearing a gingham dress with puffed sleeves, the kind Beth wore for the summer term at school. Her sandy hair was caught in a tortoiseshell barrette by the side of her head. Beth remembered she used to wear a barrette. It had been plastic with blue flowers.

"I imagine you want to get to this right away," the doctor said, settling herself behind the desk. Beth stared across the oak expanse and realised she didn't want to get to anything right away. All she wanted to do was to sit and look at the doctor's barrette and remember when she was at school, sixteen, on a hot summer day.

"Do I have a brain tumour?" asked Beth. It came out of her unbidden.

"No, you don't have a brain tumour," the doctor replied evenly.

Beth said nothing. The information hadn't quite sunk in.

"Normal hearing and sight tests, nothing untoward in the bloods or MRI. The EMG test that measures nerve activity shows what we would expect it to, an almost total paralysis on the left side of your face."

"So, apart from the Palsy, I'm in the clear?" said Beth.

The short silence that followed was ominous. "Yes, although I would have hoped for some improvement by now. However as I explained to you, it can take a year for facial nerves to recover."

"A year?" repeated Beth.

"And in a small number of cases the damage is permanent and there's no improvement," added the doctor.

"So this is good news isn't it?" said Beth. She could hear the pitch in her voice rising, "nothing to worry about except how I look, and worrying about that is frankly trivial in the big scheme of things."

"I realise living with facial disfigurement is difficult," said the doctor, her voice lowering and softening, I understand the importance society attributes to the way we look."

Beth looked at her incredulously. "You may think you understand, doctor, but I doubt it. People staring, pointing, avoiding sitting beside you, that's bad enough. But I put up with it because all the time I thought it was temporary. Now you're telling me it may not be. I'm not sure I can accept looking like this for ever. I look in the mirror and I hate the ugly old woman who stares back at me."

"There's a facial unit in the NHS that I'd like you to consider. It offers physiotherapy, dietary advice to accelerate healing of nerve damage and any psychological support that's required."

"Psychological support?" asked Beth, feeling a

gruff energy coming back to her.

"Their philosophy is to harness the natural healing energy of the body as well as the mind."

Beth felt overcome with a deep weariness. "So all you can suggest is a few exercises and a shrink? You don't know what causes Bell's Palsy. You have no cure for it and it seems to me, no interest to find one. Your lack of ambition is frankly, staggering."

The doctor looked as though Beth had slapped her. "I don't think that's entirely…"

"…Fair? Probably not. But neither is having to suffer this Palsy."

"I wish there was something I could offer that would reassure you but…" Her voice trailed away.

"There's a doctor in Texas who has pioneered a new surgical technique that takes healthy nerves from other parts of the body and transplants them into the face."

"I really wouldn't advise…"

"I've arranged to have a consultation with him. Initially over Skype but I'm prepared to go to Texas if I need to."

Dr Rorke seemed shocked. "Of course that's your prerogative but these are invasive, risky procedures."

"Maybe, but sitting around waiting for your natural resources to kick in doesn't sound like much of an option either," said Beth. She could see the doctor was doing her best to control her irritation, her sympathetic face had reappeared like a mask. Beth didn't trust herself to say another word and they parted, bad-tempered and wordless.

Outside the sun sparkled on the New Town cobbles. There had been a recent shower and the air was rinsed with freshness. Beth walked towards the garden in the centre of the grand circular terrace in front of her. She sat on a bench in the shade of a monkey puzzle tree. It reminded her of the Botanic Gardens in Singapore and she felt a sudden burst of homesickness. Without thinking about what she was doing, she picked up her phone and dialled.

"Hello?" said a voice. Male. Tentative.

"Dougie?" asked Beth.

"Speaking...?" the voice replied. Still tentative.

"Dougie, it's Beth," she said. To her surprise she found she had to blink back tears.

"Beth," his voice now sounding more like himself, "how are you?"

"So-so. How are you?" she said, finding a hankie in her bag.

"Are you calling because of that photo of us in the *Gazette*? Did it cause you trouble at work? I don't think Sally meant…"

"The photo? No. No real trouble. Storm in a teacup," she said. There was a pause then.

"That's good to hear."

"I was happy to hear your oysters were cleared."

"Aye but it'll take a while to get back to normal."

"Benjy told me about Pier 42 cancelling their order."

"He's come back from Glasgow in a foul mood. I

told him not to worry. They'll come round in time."

"Of course they will."

"I meant to call to ask you about the hospital tests."

"You must be busy."

"Everything OK?"

"Yes. Fine. Another storm in a teacup thank goodness." There was another pause. This time longer.

"Is it Benjy you wanted to speak to?"

"Just a quick word. If he's about."

"He's not here. He and Sally have gone to see the minister. They've set a date for the wedding. End of July."

"Gosh. Not long. Only a few weeks away," said Beth.

"Why wait?" said Dougie

"You never know what's round the corner do you?" agreed Beth.

Tears were falling in a silent stream. She wiped her face as a wild idea came to her. She would get on train and go to Skye. This afternoon. The silence between them lengthened. She hoped he might read her mind and suggest she visits but as the moments passed, that hope faded.

"D'you want Benjy's mobile number?" he asked.

"No, don't bother, I can get it later," said Beth, "I've got to go now," she said, clearing her throat.

"I'll tell Benjy you called," he said.

"Thanks," she said, her throat so tight that she

suspected the next thing to come out of her mouth would be a sob.

"Bye for now then lass. I'm glad you're OK."

She sat looking at the phone in her lap. A hammer drummed in her head, her gums felt as raw as if they had been burned. She could hear the sound of a jackhammer in the distance, the rumble of traffic. Her mind calmed and common sense regained the upper hand. Getting involved with Dougie would be madness. Disappointment and heartache guaranteed. Thank God she hadn't suggested visiting. At best a mistake, at worst a humiliation if the old girlfriend was still on the scene. She would call Dr Rorke, apologise for her rudeness, arrange an appointment with the facial unit. She would ask them if they had some new suggestions, more avenues to explore. She got to her feet, the ground felt solid beneath her.

She pushed open the door of the coffee shop. Nine was looking skywards, her phone pressed to her ear. Her concentration gave her an aura that separated her from everyone else in the cafe. Her spikey haircut, the sharply tailored jacket, the hellish hole in her gullet. It gave her a distinctive look, aggressive yet feminine at the same time. She was writing something down, holding the pen between her middle and ring finger in that distinctive, awkward way that seemed so natural to her. As Beth approached she could see someone was sitting opposite her and felt a flash of irritation that Nine hadn't managed to keep the table to herself. She had already resolved to ask the person to leave when she realised it wasn't a stranger, but Neil Phillips.

"Hello there. I wasn't expecting to see you," she

said, allowing him to kiss her on both cheeks.

"I bullied Nine into telling me when your appointment was," said Neil, looking pleased with himself. Nine had finished her call and shrugged her shoulders as if she was helpless.

"Well," said Beth, sitting next to Neil, "it saves me a phone call. I can tell you both the good news at the same time."

"You're OK then?" asked Nine, looking genuinely pleased. Neil, embarrassingly had taken her hand.

"All I've got is a stubborn case of Bell's Palsy," said Beth.

"That's good," said Neil in a tone that sounded heartfelt.

"Terrific. Wonderful. Fantastic," agreed Beth. "I've got something where there's no treatment, no cure, and no guarantee it'll get better on its own," said Beth.

"Now Beth, you mustn't talk like that. Seventy-eight percent of Bell's Palsy cases have a full or partial recovery," said Neil.

Beth glared at him and then turned to Nine. "The doctor had a fit when I suggested going to see a surgeon in the US who transplants facial nerves," said Beth.

"You're not seriously considering that are you?" asked Nine.

"No. Not really. She wants to refer me to a facial unit that harnesses the natural resources of mind and body or some such nonsense."

"Sounds good," said Nine.

"I agree," joined in Neil, "it's incredibly important to keep positive." He was still holding Beth's hand.

"For Christ sake will you both give it a rest?" said Beth, looking at her watch. "I can't stand any more of this tea and sympathy. I've got to get back to work."

She saw Neil and Nine trade a look between them.

"Look," said Neil, "both Nine and I think working this hard isn't helping. We think you should take the weekend off."

"Impossible."

"You keep telling me there's no such word as impossible," said Nine.

"And don't tell me that the Chief Executive of The Agency can't manage her diary to go away for a weekend if she wants to," added Neil.

"We're up to date with everything for the Rubikon visit. I'd call you if anything comes up," said Nine.

"Emergency calls only," said Neil sternly to her.

Neil was stroking her hand as if she was ill.

"I'll need to check the diary first," she said cautiously.

"Good," said Neil, with the look of someone who knew it was a foregone conclusion.

Nine lifted her glass of water in salute towards her. "Cheers. It'll be just what the doctor ordered."

Beth looked at their smiling faces. It would take the gentlest of prods for her to burst this bubble of joy: if Nine knew about Benjy's wedding date; if Neil understood the transiency of her feelings towards him. Happiness was fragile, sometimes no more than a fleeting breath. A waitress approached their table. She was wearing a tee shirt. CARPE THAT DIEM was emblazoned on her chest. Beth turned to Nine and Neil and raised her glass. "As the lady with the tee shirt advises us, let's carpe that diem," she replied, clinking her glass with theirs.

Chapter 21

The sky was high and vast, streaked with cirrus clouds, the sun already warm. It was going to be another lovely day. The whole of July had been the same and Dougie had got to the point of expecting it. The port was quiet, the fishing fleet had left hours ago. The tourists would soon be jamming the streets of the town but few ventured to the industrial part of the harbour. The lifeboat had been winched out of the water and two volunteers were inspecting the hull. A small dog barked and nipped around their feet.

Two storage tanks dominated the far end of the quayside, painted dark green and studded with ladders and walkways between them. A fuel tanker had backed up alongside them and the driver was dragging a hose to the fuel inlet valve. He had left the door of his cab open and Dougie had to squeeze by.

He walked onto the pier, past the shed where the MacBride brothers ran their fishing and boat tour business. The sign, 'Hand Dived Highland Shellfish', had faded to near illegibility by the weather and wind. A poster advertising Sea Eagle Wildlife Trips had a picture of a boat filled with tourists but that too had an air of neglect about it. The departure times were dated last year. The MacBride brothers had gradually lost interest since their dad had passed away two years ago, preferring to spend their time and inheritance in the Long Inn. *Easy done in a place like this*, thought Dougie.

The warehouse at the end of pier had its doors wide open. Dougie stepped into the gloom and shouted, "Donny!" His voice echoed and reverberated in the space.

"Dougie," said Donny, appearing from a mysterious place at the back, "you'll be here for the tunnels." He was small, sprightly, and spoke with an asthmatic breathiness.

"Aye," said Dougie, "Sally will be along with the trailer soon. She's at the hairdressers."

"Come and have a cup of tea whilst you're waiting. I expect you'll be glad to get away from all the fuss," he said. Dougie wiped his brow, already sweating in the dusty heat. He didn't understand why people would want hot drinks in weather like this, but having a cup of tea with Donny wasn't an option, it was a requirement.

"Sally's more excited about the polytunnels than what hairdo she's having for the wedding," replied Dougie.

"She was always different from the other lassies wasn't she? And this seaweed business, it's taken off hasn't it?"

"There seems to be plenty of call for it."

"You couldn't make it up," said Donny, shaking his head in wonderment. "Who would have thought people would pay good money to eat ground up seaweed?"

"Tastes like salt only healthier for you. Benjy and Sally are getting orders from all over the world."

"I suppose the seaweed's easier to grow than the oysters."

"Aye but it'll be a while yet before we know if we'll make any money out of it. The oysters are still paying the wages."

"It's been hard for you after all that business at The Four Sisters," said Donny.

"People will always love oysters, Donny, and I'll always love growing them. I could never feel the same way about kelp."

"You're an old romantic, Dougie McKinnon. And what about you and Fiona? There's a bit of gossip in the town about the pair of you."

"I wouldn't want to spoil anyone's enjoyment of a bit of gossip by telling you the truth," said Dougie, draining his cup and putting it one side. "Now let's get these polytunnels ready for loading."

Sally reversed the trailer up the side of the harbour and jumped down from the cabin. She was wearing her work dungarees and Dougie could see that outdoor working had toned her arms. She had lost weight and the blistering summer had given her a tan. Her hair was piled up on the top of her head in an elaborate style. It sat awkwardly as if it might topple off at any moment. Dougie thought it best if he made no comment. They loaded the polytunnels onto the flatbed in companionable silence. By the time they had finished, loose bits of hair had fallen out from the bun at the back of her head. Dougie thought it was an improvement.

"Stop staring at me Dougie,' she moaned as she swung herself up into the driver's seat, "I know I look ridiculous. I told Mum I didn't want anything this fancy but she wouldn't listen," she said.

"I suppose the point of a trial hairdo is to see if you like it," said Dougie, but he could see she was still troubled.

She put the tractor in gear and hauled off the handbrake. "I can't wait for this wedding to be over so we can get back to normal. Is that a terrible thing to say? Mum and Dad are so excited about it," she said.

"They've got their heart set on a big occasion. The kindest thing to do is to go along with it and try to enjoy it."

"You don't mind wearing one of those stupid kilts?" she asked.

"Kilts? They're not kilts. They're grey skirts with a buckle. But no, I don't mind though I might think differently if I was paying for it."

"The whole thing's costing a fortune. I keep thinking how much equipment we could buy with the money," she said, her brow creasing. "At least they've agreed to a simple reception. No speeches, no top tables. If we're lucky with the weather it'll be like a big picnic in the grounds of the Long Inn with a ceilidh at night."

"How many are coming?" asked Dougie.

"The whole island," she said, laughing. "Has Benjy told you he's invited Desmond and Beth from The Agency? He thought it would be a nice way to say thank you for all the help they've given him over the summer."

"I don't suppose it'll harm any future applications for grants either," added Dougie.

"And you don't mind?" asked Sally.

"Why should I?"

"I thought after that business between you and Beth."

"There was no business between us, Sally. That was all in your romantic imagination."

"She's been in the gossip magazines recently with that Dr Neil fellow. The one from the telly."

"I've met him. A wet fish. I doubt he'll last long," said Dougie, feeling a stab of jealousy and then immediately discounting it as worthy of a thought at all.

"It's a shame about her face isn't it? She was once very attractive."

"She wouldn't welcome you feeling sorry for her," said Dougie and felt another stab of guilt. He knew Beth had been crying when she called him after getting her test results; silent tears that neither of them could acknowledge. He could have been a better friend.

"Benjy and I would like you and Beth to play your famous fiddle duet at the ceilidh in the evening."

"The Glasgow Reel? You can ask but I doubt whether it'll happen."

"Because you've forgotten how to play it?"

"I'll be able to find my way round that piece on my death bed. But Beth? I doubt she's played it in over twenty years. She'll be too busy to practice and she would never want to play unless it was perfect."

"Anyhow I don't think she'll come," said Sally, "her diary's likely to be booked months ahead. Film premieres in Cannes, opera festivals in Europe."

"I take it Benjy's not invited the assistant then?" asked Dougie.

"Definitely not," said Sally with an edge in her voice.

"Good for you. There aren't many things you need to put your foot down at this wedding but ex-girlfriends are one of them," said Dougie.

"She was never a girlfriend," said Sally quietly. Dougie could hear the warning note in her voice and knew better than to say more.

They jostled along in the cab, both preoccupied with their own thoughts. Dougie agreed with Sally about wedding days. They shouldn't be the biggest day in anyone's life. It was the everyday memories that he reckoned were most important, the ordinary days that when put together, amounted to something extraordinary.

He remembered the first time he played The Glasgow Reel with Beth. It was a wet Saturday afternoon. They were walking down Sauchihall Street and popped into their favourite shop, Browns Music. Neither of them had any money, but Fraser Brown didn't mind them playing the instruments. They had gone to the back shop where he kept the sheet music and found a book of fiddle reels. They chose The Glasgow Reel because Beth liked the title. At first, they played it straight, sight-reading as they went, then after they got to know it, began to fool around a bit, the tune skittering away into the stratosphere. The customers in the shop had stopped to hear them play. Gave them a nice round of applause at the end. Since then they had played it hundreds of times but it was that first time, on an ordinary wet afternoon in Glasgow, that he remembered as something special. *Memories,* he mused, remembering the conversation with Beth in his cottage. *They are just stories we tell ourselves.* Nevertheless he made a mental note to get out his fiddle and do a bit of practice in the unlikely event she would come to the wedding and agree to play.

Sally shut off the engine as they drew up outside the office. She pulled down the driver's visor to examine her hair. Dougie turned in his seat to look at her. He could see that the back of her head was a mass of twists and knots and that the bits that had come loose at the front were framing her face into a soft angularity now that she was slimmer. The glasses were gone, replaced by contact lenses and her eyes were a bonny shade of green that he felt he was seeing for the first time. She was wetting a piece of hair and winding it round her finger to make a tendril.

"Oh I'm not sure about this hair. Not sure at all," she said, and turned in her seat to face him. "Tell me honestly Dougie, what do you think?"

He could feel his emotions building. "You'll look beautiful whatever hairstyle you have," he said, realising he had tears in his eyes. "Absolutely beautiful."

"Dougie, that's lovely of you but no help at all. I'm going to tell Mum that I'm having it long and loose. I expect I'll have a battle on my hands to persuade her. Tell Benjy I'll be back as soon as I can and we can unload the tunnels together."

Benjy was buzzing about the Portakabin in a way that Dougie knew was building to something dramatic. It was like watching him being ratcheted up on a roller coaster, getting higher and higher and all the time you knew there would be a drop; a great whooshing downwards.

"Dad, we have to make a decision about the packaging in order for the prototypes to be made up in time."

"It seems mad to prepare for a trade show and your wedding at the same time," said Dougie, picking up the various drums that had been laid out on the table.

"Sally and her mum are doing all the wedding stuff. The more I stay out of it the better," said Benjy.

"I think Sally needs your support. Her mum could easily dominate."

"Nah. All women love planning weddings," said Benjy breezily, "they moan about it but underneath they're having a ball. I've told her I'll go along with anything she wants." He picked up one of the drums and handed it to Dougie. "What d'you think of this one?"

The cylinder had an outline of the Cuillin mountains in the background and said in bold letters **'Skye Superfoods'**. Underneath in smaller letters, *'from the seas of Skye, dried, flaked seaweed – a natural alternative to salt.'*

"I like it," said Dougie.

"The marketing people at The Agency designed it," said Benjy.

"So these meetings you go to every fortnight in Glasgow. Do Beth and Desmond turn up?"

"Sometimes Desmond pops his head round the door. I've not seen Beth since that time at her flat with Nine," he said.

"So you've not seen either Beth or Nine all summer?" Dougie thought he had done well to affect an innocent tone but there was a stony silence.

"Are you asking me if I'm carrying on with another lassie when I'm getting married in two weeks' time?" said Benjy.

"I've always thought it a good idea to play the field before you settle down. Marriage is a serious commitment you know."

"What would you know about marriage? About serious commitment?" joked Benjy and then turned serious. "Sally's forgiven that one weekend I had with Nine. I think it best if we all forgot about it too."

Chapter 22

One bonus of this long hot summer, thought Beth, was that she could wear sunglasses with impunity without being considered visually impaired or pretentious. She had chosen a designer brand with large lenses that covered most of the upper half of her face and she sat in pleasant anonymity at the back of a taxi. The driver had dropped her off at the entrance of the hospital with no curiosity about whether she was a visitor or a patient.

The hospital consisted of a number of buildings spread over an untidy-looking campus. There was a large sign welcoming her and below a list of departments with arrows in different directions. She scanned the list but couldn't see a sign for the Facial Unit. *The NHS need to get their shit together*, she decided. *This place is a physical metaphor for inefficiency and confusion.* She found the arrow pointing to the main reception and decided to head for that.

She walked down a covered walkway lined with folded wheelchairs and through a set of double doors that opened into large area with a low ceiling and poor lighting. Hundreds of people milled about. In the dingy gloom it was like a waiting room in Hell. There was a long queue at the reception window, moving very slowly.

She wandered down a corridor off the main waiting area and was rewarded by an overhead sign for Facial Therapy Unit. She turned right, then left, then through two sets of double doors until the signs petered out and the trail went cold. It was like being in a surreal labyrinth, she thought. She had become so disorientated that retracing her steps to where she had last seen a sign seemed more difficult than going blindly onwards. She found herself in a small, unmanned reception area with a bell on the counter. She pressed it, not expecting anyone to respond, so was surprised when a women in theatre scrubs appeared. *Goodness,* she thought, *I've stumbled into an operating theatre by mistake.* But the woman took off her mask, smiled and asked if she could help.

"Facial therapy unit? You'll need to go out through this door, turn left, go down the alleyway and you'll come to a Portakabin down the side of the main building. There's a bell on the side of the door."

"Thank you," said Beth, thinking the NHS must be doing something right after all to have such helpful staff.

She found the Portakabin easily enough. It had a large sign on the door saying 'FIRE DOOR KEEP SHUT'. There was a small sign at the side that said 'Dictation'. *This can't be the place,* she thought, but hopefully there would be more kind and accommodating people to help her.

"Well done! You found us," said a nurse, opening the door and ushering her inside. She was small and squat. Beth could see her face was shining with perspiration.

"It says Dictation on the sign outside."

"We took over from them four years ago. It was only meant to be temporary. We were promised a new building but what with all the cuts, it hasn't happened yet," she replied with a stoic cheerfulness.

Four years on and they still hadn't changed the sign? These people are lovely but they wouldn't last a minute in business, thought Beth.

"We like to keep the old sign there. It's what Joseph calls passive resistance. You'll meet him soon," she said. Beth didn't know who Joseph was but she liked his thinking.

The place reminded her of Benjy and Dougie's office. There was a jumble of mismatched desks and chairs, grey filing cabinets and piles of paper waiting to be filed. No *Scottish Field* magazines, just an old *Radio Times* on a low table. She pulled a hanky out of her bag, patted her face and neck, dabbed her eye and wandered over to the open window.

"The heating's jammed on and we can't open the door because it's a fire door," said the nurse. "At least the windows open."

"I suppose you have to do the best with what you've got," said Beth.

"That could be the motto for our patients too," she said briskly, "now, how about a cup of tea?"

Beth couldn't see a drinks machine.

"I've got a kettle out in the back. It's against health and safety but if you don't tell, then neither will I," she said, disappearing into a large cupboard.

"Where's everyone?" asked Beth. "I was expecting

there to be a queue. The reception area was mobbed."

"We've had a few cancellations. People are struggling to get about in this heat," said the nurse, and Beth again felt awkward that she sounded so critical when she was being met by unfailing pragmatism.

"Straw?" asked the nurse, as if it was as normal as asking if someone takes sugar. Beth nodded and for reasons she couldn't explain, felt her defences crumbling. She looked at the mug of tea, the white straw bobbing in the centre and began to cry. And once she began, it was hard to stop.

The nurse guided her to a chair and waited till her crying stopped. "Now, let me take a wee look at you," said the nurse.

"I've got Bell's Palsy," said Beth.

"You have indeed," said the nurse, "but you've come to the right place. Joseph's the best. He's a hard task master, mind."

"I like the sound of him," said Beth, drying her eyes.

"Oh I think the two of you will get on just fine," said the nurse.

***

Beth woke early the next morning. Heat was powering though the flat despite the windows having been opened all night. She unlatched the wooden shutters to another dazzling day and then quietly closed them, worried that the light and noise might wake him. She took out the homework sheet Joseph had given her and studied it carefully.

First the warm up: sniffle, wrinkle nose, flare

nostrils. Repeat three times. Rest. Repeat. Then the puckering: compress lips, pucker up, pull the corners of lips in towards the centre. Repeat three times. Rest. Repeat. Slowly move the lips into a smile, going only as far as there is equal movement from both sides. Her attention, as focused as a laser, was willing the left side of her mouth to move upwards. No movement. She tried again. And again. And again. Rest. Repeat. Still nothing. Joseph had told her the biggest predicator of success was the amount of patience and persistence people had. She had told him she had plenty of both, her vanity was of the obstinate variety, but she wondered now if she had underestimated the resolve this needed.

She went back to the instructions. Eye exercises. Gently wink with good eye, then bad one. See how far you can go. Joseph had warned her against trying to do too much. Don't push it, he said. *No chance*, thought Beth, as the left eye stared back at her unwilling to even try. Like her mouth it had taken the huff and was not playing the game. Forehead massage. Place three fingertips on the eyebrow and rotate gently to hairline. Two minutes. Rest. Repeat. She was about to repeat the movement when she saw in the mirror that Neil was awake and watching her. She turned round to see him sitting up in bed.

"This type of exercise will help prevent synkineses."

"I'm not going to humour you by asking what synkineses is," replied Beth, "it sounds revolting."

"D'you think this will work?" asked Neil.

"I don't know but I haven't got a better idea. That place in Texas where they transplant nerves from other parts of the body to your face wasn't an option. Most of the people looked worse after their op than before."

She turned back to the mirror, looking despairingly at her fallen face. "This is going to be one hell of a long road. I've only done ten minutes and I'm worn out already." She got up from her dressing table. "It's so hot. D'you want something cold to drink?" He caught her as she passed by the bed and she allowed him to pull her back in beside him. He pulled up the hem of her nightshirt and began to stroke her between her legs. Always so measured, so competent, already an expert at the rhythms of her body.

"Wait," she said, putting her hand over his, "too much."

"Let me," he whispered in her hair, and because she could think of no reason not to, she let him. Afterwards, they lay sticky with sweat, too drugged by heat and sex to move. He stroked her arm idly, she could see a downy covering of sandy hair covering his freckles.

"What did this Joseph guy say about the headaches?"

"Reckons they're mostly tension. Not happy that I'm taking painkillers. Seemed OK about the occasional spliff though. I've to do two sessions of meditation a day. Mindfulness. Breathing. Relaxation exercises."

"I think you should add sex to that list of therapies," he said, nuzzling into her shoulder, "and taking every weekend off. All work and no play makes Beth..." he said, moving his hand towards her breast. She covered his fingers to stop him from going further.

"Nine and I have taken the last three weekends off. She's got a new boyfriend you know."

"Do you approve?"

"I haven't met him. She'll tell me when she's ready. Anyhow I can't object at what she does with her time. Everything's ready for the Rubikon visit," said Beth.

"Does she know you're going to Benjy's wedding?"

"I haven't told her. Benjy is a topic that is off limits. She knows he comes in to The Agency for meetings but she's probably more interested in her new man these days. At least I hope she is."

"Benjy and Nine were never serious about each other were they?"

"I think Nine was but it was just a fling on Benjy's part before settling down."

"And the seaweed project, it's going well?"

"Shaping up to be one of The Agency's big successes. Desmond's keen to give Benjy more funding. We've got a meeting next week to discuss it."

"Smart move. Keep your enemies close and all that," said Neil.

"Desmond and I get on fine these days. Certainly all that nonsense about me and Dougie in the paper has been forgotten."

"I'm feeling jealous at the prospect of you and Dougie at the wedding."

She laughed. "Desmond's going to be my chaperone. Actually, I'm beginning to regret accepting the invitation myself."

"I can imagine, being stuck with him all day," said Neil.

"It's not that. Benjy and Sally have asked Dougie and me to play our old party piece on the fiddles at the evening ceilidh. I didn't know how to say no. I've even been practising although I think it's unlikely we'll actually play it on the night."

"Why's that?"

"Dougie won't have done any practising, that's for sure, and he's likely to be pissed by the evening. Still, it's been fun to get the fiddle out again."

"I demand to hear a performance," said Neil, sitting bolt upright.

"I don't think so..." said Beth.

"Won't leave this bed until you do."

"Well..." said Beth, "seeing as you've been so nice to me this morning," and she kissed him before slipping out of bed. The heat in the bedroom was as thick as a blanket. She tucked the fiddle under her chin and plucked the strings. They were in tune but it wouldn't last in this heat. She could see Neil had put on his glasses and was touched by the seriousness he was taking this. She drew herself up to her full height and straightened her night shirt.

"OK, this is called *The Glasgow Reel*. One of the fiddles starts with the melody whilst the other plays the chords. Then after thirty seconds the other violin takes up the melody but this time a little faster, then each fiddle eggs the other to go faster and faster. So you'll only get half the effect with me on my own," she said. Neil nodded solemnly.

She laid the bow across the strings and the plaintive melody of the Celtic tune filled the room. Her fingers felt slippery across the strings, a couple of notes slid away from her but she adjusted her pressure and was soon immersed in the speed and birl of it, her foot tapping to keep the beat. She could hear the other violin in her head as it joined her, both competing and in perfect harmony. She played faster and faster till she felt the music had overtaken her, and her body had become a conduit for it to pass through her. She ended the final chord with a flourish of her bow, suddenly exhausted, her body streaming, her hair stuck to her forehead.

"That was terrific," said Neil, "and so very sexy. Come here," he said, laughing and lunging for her.

She dodged out of his grasp. "Showtime's over. Time for you to get going, young man. You'll be late for the studio and I have to go to my brother's for Sunday lunch."

He became serious. "I'd like to come for Sunday lunch, meet your family," he said.

"That would be difficult seeing as you have a live TV programme to host every Sunday," she said, keeping her tone playful.

"You know what I mean, Beth. It doesn't have to be Sunday lunch."

She wanted to say it was too soon. Part of her knew it would always be too soon.

"I don't think…" she started, but he interrupted.

"I know not to chance my luck. I'll ask another time," he said pleasantly.

She watched him as he got out of bed. His body toned, his tousled head of hair attractively ruffled. She heard him in the shower and tried to imagine a future life together; a detached villa in the fancier suburbs or perhaps a small country estate in Perthshire. An article in *Scottish Field* about the restoration project of their house. She couldn't think of anything she wanted less.

She wandered down the corridor, hesitating outside Nine's room. She tried the handle, it was normally locked, but to her surprise, the door opened. She half expected to see Nine sitting on her bed, bent over her laptop but the room was empty. She hadn't been here since Friday morning and already the room felt airless and stuffy. She could smell the citrus from Nine's perfume and the sweet overtone of hash.

She opened her wardrobe and ran her hands through her clothes, stopping at the cornflower blue silk blouse, remembering the night at The Four Sisters when she first met Benjy. How lovely she had been that night. How happy they had looked together. She fingered the soft collar of the blouse, noticing black streaks had soiled the inner facings. She examined the marks more closely. Eye liner or mascara probably. She thought about popping it in the washing machine but didn't want Nine to know she had been poking about in her room.

Neil was out of the shower. She could hear him moving about in the bedroom next door. She put the blouse back on its hanger, slipped out of Nine's room and went to the kitchen. She put on the coffee machine and set out two cups on the kitchen island. She was glad Nine had found someone new, yet she wondered why she was being so secretive about him. Perhaps it was the old boyfriend George from the Faslane Peace Camp who had reappeared. No sooner had she thought that, when another darker thought appeared. Perhaps the new boyfriend was Benjy. He was in Glasgow every other Friday for meetings at The Agency. It would certainly explain the secrecy. Ridiculous. Benjy was getting married in two weeks' time. She poured out the coffee, a rich smell permeated the room and like her suspicion about Nine and Benjy, seemed to fill every corner of the apartment.

The country was struggling to cope with the heatwave. The weather had gone from being lovely to a liability. The taxi had no air conditioning and was so hot Beth wondered if it might be illegal to carry passengers in it. She slid from side to side in the roomy back seat, as the driver swung round corners, perspiration greasing the seat.

Seeing the old family home in Bearsden always gave her a moment of dislocation, as if time had shifted and she was a schoolgirl again. Margaret had changed the interior of the house beyond all recognition but the outside was persistently old fashioned, sitting on its plot halfway down the hillside, unchanged for fifty years. Sprinklers from the neighbour's garden arced droplets of water onto the drive, reflecting prettily in the light. Alec hadn't given the same attention to his lawn and the grass was yellowed and bare.

Alec greeted her at the front door, nut brown and full of smiles. He was wearing Hawaii printed shorts that fell below his knees, making his calves look spindly, his belly more rounded. They had been on holiday. An all-inclusive luxury hotel in Dubai, he enthused. Beth thought it ironic that they had travelled all that way when it had been hotter here in Bearsden. Alec said it had done wonders for Margaret. She didn't ask how he had afforded it.

They sat in the garden in the shade, looking out to the expanse of dead-looking grass. Alec handed her some lemonade in a tall glass with a blue and stripy straw in it. She laid the straw down. "Cause for celebration, I don't need straws anymore thanks to all the puckering practice I'm doing. I reckon I'm puckering over thirty times a day," she said, but Alec didn't seem to find this as funny as she intended. She took a careful swallow, conscious that he was watching her. She dabbed the edge of her mouth with her hanky. Dry.

"It's unbelievable that the doctors can't do more for you than come up with few exercises," said Alec, "but you're an inspiration. A lot of people would be broken by this you know," he said.

"Nonsense. Most people would just get on with it. How's Margaret doing with her gastric band?"

"It's been a struggle and this heat doesn't help," he said despondently, "but Dubai was brilliant. All that air conditioning."

"But the operation's been a success?"

"Yes and no. She lost weight at the beginning but felt terrible. Couldn't hold anything down. Said it was worse than the morning sickness she had with the boys. The only thing that doesn't make her sick is chocolate. We melt it down for her. Her weight's creeping back up as a result."

"I can see that might happen," said Beth tactfully.

"It was better when she was heavy. She's talking about having it reversed but that's even more expensive than the original operation."

Beth was saved from having to talk about money by Margaret's arrival. She was wearing a sleeveless dress, her arms puckered and dimpled with cellulite. Her face was as pale as if it was the middle of winter, and she walked slowly with a stiffness in her gait.

"Goodness, come and have a sit down in the shade," said Beth, getting up and offering her seat.

"Lunch is ready whenever you are," she said. "Nothing fancy. Cold meat and some salad. Beth, I've pureed ours though I doubt I'll be eating any. Has Alec told you that I'm sick all the time? I spend most of the days lying in front of the telly with a basin in my lap."

"Poor you," said Beth.

"People don't understand do they Beth? How pureed food takes the joy out of eating and that's before it makes you feel sick to your stomach."

"Yes," soothed Beth, resolving to remain pleasant.

"Have you told her, Alec?" asked Margaret.

"Told me what?" asked Beth.

Margaret gave Alec her usual exasperated expression. "He's leaving Hunters. Handed in his notice last week. They took it without a by-your-leave or thank you. No mention of the annual bonus either."

"Margaret..." implored Alec, as if Margaret had already told Beth too much.

"Leaving? Gosh? Where to?" asked Beth.

"We're going to Dubai," said Margaret. Beth could see the telling of their news had rejuvenated her, her eyes were shining. "You might think it's hot in the desert but the air conditioning's lovely."

"Dubai? That's a surprise," said Beth.

"You remember that oil company proposal I showed you?" said Alec. She could see defensiveness had come into his expression. "The one that you thought was too ambitious? I've got the funding from an Emirates company. They didn't end up backing the plan but they could see it had potential. Offered me a business development job instead," said Alec.

"And housing, school fees, private medical cover, the lot," chipped in Margaret.

"That sounds wonderful, Alec. Congratulations. Congratulations to you both," she said.

Margaret heaved herself to her feet. "I'll go and set the table. I'll call you when it's ready."

"That's the answer to a lot of your problems isn't it?" said Beth. "I'm delighted for you."

"Well the thing is Beth, Margaret may not have quite understood the conditions of the offer. I'm expected to put a fair bit of equity into the new company. So I'll be selling this house."

"That's OK isn't it? Mum's will said that you could live here as long as you wanted but if you sold up, the proceeds of the sale would be split between us," said Beth.

"The problem is, the valuation the estate agent has given me isn't enough if I have to split it fifty-fifty with you."

"So you resigned your job, accepted this, whatever you call it, this business arrangement, assuming I would give you my share?"

He looked at her with a half smiling, half-rueful expression.

"For God's sake don't think looking like a small boy who's taken a bite out of every pancake is going to get round me," said Beth.

"C'mon. You've not reckoned on getting any money from this house have you? As far as you're concerned I was going to live here till they carried me out feet first." He lit a cigarette and drew on it heavily, avoiding eye contact.

"You know the saddest thing about this Alec? If you have talked to me before you handed in your notice I would have given you my share."

Alec snorted. "You say that now but the last time we spoke about money you told me never to ask for a loan again. I was hardly going to come cap in hand."

"And if I don't agree to giving you my share? Have you thought about that?"

"I could rent the house and use the income to fund a loan. It would still leave me short but I might be able to negotiate further borrowing."

"More debt, Alec? That's not a good idea is it?"

"No but if you force my hand, it's my only option."

Beth sighed. She didn't understand how this had suddenly become her problem.

"Do you remember when we were kids, Alec, and were both given a chocolate bar. You always ate yours right away."

"And you would eat one square at a time and save some till the next day to taunt me with."

"We haven't changed that much since then, have we?" she said.

"I suppose not," he said, stubbing out his cigarette.

"Sell the house. Take my share. Start your new life in Dubai," she said.

He seemed relieved but not surprised. "And what will you do with your life, Beth? Stay here? Marry Neil Phillips? He'd be quite a catch."

She felt stunned by how little he knew her. "I've no plans to marry anyone," she replied.

Margaret was calling them to the table. Alec got up as if pulled by an invisible string. He had expected her to give him her share all along. He hadn't even said thank you. She could see it all clearly now; Alec would go to Dubai and their relationship would fade out into the odd Christmas card, the occasional family gathering until over time, it would hardly be there at all.

Chapter 23

The church was full, a flurry of colour and finery, hats, sporrans, the odd flash of a skean dhu tucked in a sock. Beth was sitting in the back pew, a perfect vantage point to watch others and not be watched in return. The stone walls held in the heat, swelling and filling in the ancient space, intensifying the mustiness so that the air hung thickly.

The lady beside her wiped her forehead, cheeks, chin and neck then flapped her hankie in front of her. Others were using their order of service leaflets as fans and the congregation looked like a flock of fluttering wings. Beth thought there must have been a collective agreement for the men to take off their jackets; white shirts peppered every pew.

Benjy was standing at the altar, looking straight ahead, his arms crossed in front of him. She could tell from the line of his shoulders that he was relaxed, might even be enjoying the waiting. His best man stood beside him, dressed in identical clothes, white shirt, plain grey kilt, purple socks. He was smaller and slighter with a shock of blond hair that hadn't been combed. In contrast to the stillness of Benjy, he was shifting his weight from foot to foot, pulling down the cuffs of his shirt, checking his pockets and looking behind him. Benjy leant over and said something in his ear that seemed to calm him.

She glanced along each of the rows, methodically checking, but she was sure Dougie hadn't arrived. He was leaving it to the last minute as usual. There was commotion at the entrance of the church and a portly lady barrelled past her. Beth guessed it was Sally's mum. Her outfit had probably seemed like a good choice when she bought it months ago, but was a disaster for a boiling day in July. The purple dress was made of heavy silk wrapped like a bandage, tight around her curves. The matching bolero jacket was already stained with perspiration. Her hat had an enormous flower that looked like she had bumped into something and had knocked it off centre. The enormous brim hid most of her face, only a chin, a shiny cheek, and half of a dazzling smile peeped out from under it.

She took her time walking up the aisle, stopping to hug, kiss, and have a quiet word with the guests, enjoying the attention of the entire congregation. When she got to the front, she tapped Benjy on the shoulder and as he turned she took him into her arms and planted a kiss on the lips. Her dress rucked up, exposing fatty cuffs of flesh above her knees but the irrepressibility of her happiness seemed to ignite the mood and there was a spontaneous round of applause from the congregation.

The guests settled back into anticipation of the bride's entrance. Beth worried that if Dougie didn't turn up soon, he was going to miss it. She heard the crunch of gravel outside and turned to see a car slide up to the church door and two bridesmaids step out.

Both were willowy and slim, moving like flamingos, gliding over the rough stones despite wearing the highest stiletto heels Beth had ever seen. They were dressed in sleeveless pink-coloured dresses, made of a light fabric that ruffled prettily in the light breeze. One reached up and did some minor adjustments to the other's hair, which was long, and held back with wild flowers. *How lovely they are*, thought Beth, *so unaware of their beauty.*

A second car arrived. This time it was Sally and her dad. Dougie was going to be late. *How difficult is it to be on time for your son's wedding?* she thought, and then shook her head quietly as if ridding herself of an irritation that didn't belong to her. The two bridesmaids clustered around Sally helping her with her dress, and when they stood aside, Beth could see her standing in the church doorway, backlit by the sun.

All thoughts about Dougie's whereabouts disappeared as she stared transfixed by the image. She was wearing the same dress as her bridesmaids but hers was full length and cream in colour. It draped over her shapely figure, skimming the ground, shimmering in the light wind. Her long blonde hair had been loosely curled and threaded with wild flowers, her bouquet a simple arrangement of thistles florets and white roses that managed to look both dramatic and low key. Her dad was stocky, shorter than her by several inches. Sally bent down and gave him a quick hug round his shoulders. One of the bridesmaids offered him a hanky but he batted it away.

All brides should look like this on their wedding day, thought Beth, feeling both joy and regret. How would she feel if it was Nine standing there and not Sally? It was hard to imagine. Where Sally was tall and rounded, Nine was small and angular. Sally's hair was a tumble of soft curls, Nine's was spikey and streaked in unnatural colours. Sally exuded sweetness whereas Nine's energy was altogether edgier, and then there was the business of her neck tattoo. *No*, thought Beth. This moment, this dress, this day, this groom belonged to Sally and no one else.

They made their way down the aisle to the opening chords of a solo fiddle. She guessed the fiddler was upstairs in the organ gallery, hidden from the congregation. The playing was controlled yet free and the soaring melody had that particular Celtic character that manages to be both melancholic and uplifting. The fanning of programmes seemed to still, as everybody was caught by the magic and romance of the music. When they reached the altar, Sally's dad reluctantly let go of the hand of his beautiful daughter to another man.

"Ha, ha. Bet you thought I hadn't been practising," whispered Dougie as he slipped in beside her. He was carrying his fiddle.

"Was that you playing? And here was me thinking you were late," she whispered back. He looked outrageously pleased with himself and Beth found herself inflating with pleasure.

He took her hand. "And they ain't heard nothing yet have they?" he said, patting the back of her hand and craning his neck to catch a better view of the couple who were now standing side by side, listening to the minister. He turned to her expecting a reply. He hadn't seemed to notice that he was still holding her hand. She pointed towards her feet where her fiddle case was propped up.

"Good lass. I'll take that back to the hotel for you. Benjy and Sally want it to be a surprise," he said, getting to his feet. The first hymn was about to start and she was sorry that he had dropped her hand to hold the order of service.

The wedding had taken over the hotel grounds and given it the atmosphere of a village fete. Tables with parasols dotted the lawn, each covered in the same cream chiffon as Sally's dress. Posies of thistles and wild flowers were placed in birdcages whose ironwork had been painted cream. A long trestle table at the front had, at one end, a forest of bottles and a huge bowl of punch stuffed with fruit and torn mint floating on top. An untidy queue was forming as guests filled their glasses. A procession of waiters was carrying trays of food and placing them at the other end of the table; platters of langoustine, oysters, sandwiches and fresh strawberries; the colours, the smells of summer, thought Beth.

Desmond had found their table and they took their seats. Beth didn't mind that Dougie had been seated elsewhere because she already felt connected to him by their conspiracy to perform later on. She took off her hat but kept her sunglasses on. They were sitting with a group of friends from Benjy and Sally's schooldays. They were talking about marriage and romance, animated about the pros and cons of the latest in internet dating and phone apps, bemoaning the lack of G coverage on the island that rendered their phones unreliable, their connection patchy.

"So how did you two meet then?" asked one of the boys. Desmond had flushed. The boy had mistaken them for a couple, thought Beth.

"We met on a scuba diving holiday," she said, "sixty feet down in tropical waters. Exploring a coral reef when a shark decided to join us."

"What? A real shark?"

"Yup," said Beth, "I didn't see it but Desmond did and he swam in front of me and gave me the, 'not OK' signal." She laid her hand out flat and rotated it side by side. "He then gave me the thumbs up signal which meant we needed to get the hell out of there."

"That was quite a first meeting," said the boy.

Beth nodded. "And he's been watching my back for sharks ever since, haven't you Desmond?"

Desmond looked stricken and for a moment she thought he was going to spoil the fun but he relaxed and smiled. "And there are plenty of sharks to watch for," he said.

"She's having you on," said one of the girls, "you're Beth Colquhoun aren't you? There was a picture of you and Neil Phillips in the paper attending some gala dinner at the opera. My mum really fancies him," she added.

Beth felt momentarily discomforted by the truth of her social life being exposed but was saved from having to respond by Benjy passing their table. "Thanks for coming," he said, placing a hand on each of their shoulders.

"Congratulations," said Desmond, getting up to shake his hand.

"The whole team send their congratulations Benjy," added Beth. He seemed distracted, as if he was in a rush to get away from them.

"He's a good kid," said Desmond as Benjy moved on to greet more guests, "it's one of the reasons I get such a buzz from our work. Helping young people like him. We should do more of it. A lot more."

"Couldn't agree more," said Beth equably.

There was a lull between the end of the picnic and the start of the evening party. The girls had left to change; Desmond and the boys had gone to the bar. Beth watched a small dog snuffling under the tables, gorging himself on leftovers. The sun had gone behind some thin clouds and the air had lost the brutal heat of the afternoon. She pulled her shawl around her shoulders, feeling a shiver of anticipation about the prospect of playing with Dougie. She hadn't seen him for a while and part of her hoped he had got himself quietly plastered and the whole thing would be forgotten.

"I hope fizzy water's OK," said Desmond, sitting down beside her.

"Sensible choice," she replied, although having kept off the alcohol all afternoon she had a sudden impulse to have a couple of stiff drinks to bolster her for what lay ahead.

"Apparently they're not having speeches. Pity. I always look forward to bad jokes and embarrassing revelations."

"It's been a lovely day, don't you think?" she asked.

"I nearly didn't come you know," said Desmond, "if I'm being honest, Beth, I didn't think being in your company for a whole day would be that enjoyable." She let the remark sink in. "Sorry," he said, "I didn't mean it to come out like that."

"Best to be honest, Desmond. Integrity and all that," she said. She wanted to bite back the sarcastic edge to her voice.

"What I'm learning about you, Beth, is that you don't mind not being liked."

"I think that's putting it too harshly," she said.

"I mean you can detach yourself from your emotions."

"I've had to grow a thick skin if that's what you mean," said Beth, "but you're wrong if you think it doesn't hurt me when I hear people say horrible things about me."

"It must do. But you never show it so people assume you don't feel it. But there's something different about you here. You're funny, easy going. If people at The Agency could see this side of you, I think you'd find it easier."

"Thanks for the advice, Desmond," she said frostily, yet she could see the man was trying to help. She looked at him steadily. "Really. I mean that. Thank you," she said, putting her hand on his arm but she couldn't decide if his smile was real or placatory.

"Ladies and gentleman, lads and lassies. The ceilidh is about to begin!" shouted the Master of Ceremony.

"Wish me luck," she said, but Desmond hadn't heard her, he was already walking towards the open door of the hotel, leaving her wondering if she was destined to always spoil things between them.

Later that evening, she found herself walking arm in arm with Dougie. He was leading her to the edge of the garden.

"Tell me that again," said Beth, throwing back her head and laughing.

"You were A-MAZ-ING," said Dougie, swigging from the bottle of champagne.

"You're not just saying that?" asked Beth, taking the bottle from him and taking a swig herself. It was too ambitious a move and most of it dribbled out her bad side but Dougie didn't notice and she didn't care. "It could have gone either way you know. A disaster or a triumph," said Beth.

"No way. We were always going to be the dog's bollocks," he said, taking back the bottle.

"The dog's bollocks, the cat's pyjamas, the bee's knees," said Beth.

"Ah that and a bag of chips," laughed Dougie, "and that wee fella from The Agency. He couldn't take his eyes off you."

"Desmond Davies? I don't think so," said Beth.

"C'mon," said Dougie, taking her hand. "I've got a pressie for you."

They walked hand in hand towards the shoreline, and sat down on the rocks. The rocky beach was deserted, the water as still as glass. The evening air was fragrant with clover, wild blueberries and broom, still radiating warmth. She could hear the muted sound of pipes and drums and the distant thudding of dancing feet. Dougie reached into the pocket of his shirt and took out a joint. "For my fellow partner in crime," he said, fishing in his pocket for a lighter, "as wicked a team as ever we were."

He was sitting so close that Beth wasn't sure if their bodies were touching or not. She could see her dress was ruined with grass stains and water marks. He took off his socks and shoes, exposing his bony knees, the kilt rucking up, a flash of white thigh. She felt the warmth of his body, the beauty of the setting and the world stopped and gave her a moment of the purest happiness.

"Thank you kind sir," she said, taking the joint from him.

"You and Nine still quietly toking away?" he asked.

"Not so much these days," said Beth.

"You know I thought there might have been something going on between Benjy and Nine over the summer. I asked him about it but he swore he hasn't seen her."

Beth felt herself start and didn't want to admit she'd had the same doubts. "Sally's a lovely girl, they were really happy today," said Beth, handing him back the joint. He took it from her and put his arm round her and she let herself relax, her bones melting into his.

"That time you called. After the test results. You were crying," he said.

"I had spent the morning holding all my emotions in and in that moment I heard your voice, heard myself telling you that I didn't have a life-threatening condition, it all came out of me. Anger, relief, hope, frustration. Sorry if I didn't make much sense."

"I'm not a big fan of always having to making sense. You can talk to me anytime, Beth. About anything."

"I know, Dougie."

"Now there's only one thing left to do to make this perfect day even more perfect," he said. He got to his feet and was tearing off his shirt, unwrapping his kilt. "Last one in's a cissy," he shouted, stepping out of his underwear and running towards the sea. Beth let out a cry as she stood up and watched his naked body gleaming in the grainy light running towards the sea. She hesitated for a second before she slipped off her dress, unclipped her bra and stepping out of her panties, ran into the dark waters after him.

Chapter 24

The sea was cold at first but as Dougie swam it became viscous, coating his body with a tepid warmth. A haze of midges zig-zagged crazily above the surface as he lay on his back looking up at the gloaming sky still streaked with high pale threads of clouds. In the half-light he could see a full moon had risen. It felt mystical to Dougie, as if unusual things could happen. He turned on his front and saw Beth swimming towards him. He had never thought she would come to the wedding, let alone agree to play, yet it seemed the most natural thing in the world for her to be swimming towards him now.

He treaded water watching her, her face slowly coming into focus as she got nearer. There was a quality to it that he never tired of. Her auburn hair and olive skin were like shades from the same palette and although in the fading light he couldn't see her eyes, he knew they were the colour of rich loam. She bobbed up beside him, her hair slicked back from her face.

"The water feels amazing, not nearly as cold as I expected," she said. *Small talk,* thought Dougie, to cover her shyness perhaps. He found himself drawn towards the side of her face that had fallen. It had a power, a fascination, a beauty of its own.

"When was the last time you went skinny dipping?" he asked, thinking it best to keep the small talk going.

"With you. When we climbed Ben Lui on that hot day in June. D'you remember?" The memory caught him like a hook. She swam closer towards him, their faces almost touching. He did nothing then but allow her to kiss him. Her mouth felt cold and warm at the same time, hot and moist, a tang of salt, either the sea or sweat, perhaps a bit of both and twenty years of longing flowed from his mouth to hers. He lifted her weightless body around his, her legs circling his waist.

"Let's go back, to my place," he said.

"What about our clothes?" she asked, "and I'm going to need my eye stuff. The water's already making it sting," she said.

He remembered then how often her sensible side had blended with his spontaneity. "We'll swim round the headland to my house then I can swim back to the hotel beach. It'll only take me a few minutes."

"Will you be alright swimming back on your own? It's not very safe, especially when you've been drinking" she added.

Dougie remembered that sometimes her sensible side could go too far. "Don't worry about me. Where's your room key?" he asked.

"In the pocket of my dress. The eye stuff's on the dressing table in my room," said Beth.

She kissed him again, the pressure more urgent and together they kicked out to beyond the headland and round. He watched her stumble out of the water.

She turned and waved. He waved back.

A fire had been lit on the rocky beach and several of the wedding guests were huddled round it, drinking, smoking, the first of many drunken embraces. There were hoots of laughter as Dougie emerged naked from the water. He laughed back good-naturedly and put on his shirt, wrapping his kilt around himself. The clothes felt cold and sticky. He could see Beth's dress nearby in a tidy bundle hidden behind a large stone. He felt for the key in the pocket. Still there. The dress, a wisp of linen, folded easily into his shirt. Her underwear and sandals lay on the rocks but he had no place to hide them.

"Come and join us Dougie. Give us a tune!" shouted one of the girls. She got to her feet and staggered towards him, locking him in a tipsy embrace. Dougie gently entangled himself from her. "Aye OK then," he said, "I'll go and get my fiddle," he said, figuring that they'd soon forget about him, were already satiated with the combination of alcohol, heat, and the feel of their bodies close together.

Fiona was behind the bar polishing glasses, chatting to a few of the guests who had taken a rest from the dancing. *She was meant to be a guest herself but I suppose old habits are hard to break,* thought Dougie. He could hear the band playing in the function room beyond the bar. A Gay Gordons was in full swing accompanied by a lot of banshee cries. He crept past, hoping she wouldn't see him.

"Dougie McKinnon," she called out. Her voice was soft but directed at him in a way he couldn't ignore. "You look like you're in need of a dram," she said.

Dougie ran his hand through his wet hair. "Aye, a spot of ill-advised night swimming," he explained, "off to the gents' to dry off."

"You come straight back here when you're finished," she said. He could tell she had been drinking. She had a glassy-eyed, available look about her. He looked down and could see Beth's dress was poking out above the buttons of his shirt. His heart dropped a beat, "OK," he said. She nodded and went back to drying her glasses.

He waited in the corridor for a few seconds to check that she hadn't followed him. He could hear the band had gone up a gear, the stamping of feet and cries were getting louder, the battle cries from the dancers more bloodthirsty. He crept up the stairs and let himself into Beth's room. He stood with his back against the door, his heart thudding. No one had seen him.

He switched the light on. The room was tidy, her nightdress folded on her pillow. He picked it up, smelling her perfume. Lily of the Valley. He buried his head in its softness and thought about the pleasures that lay ahead then shook himself as if to sober up. "Best not to think about this too closely, Dougie mate," he said to himself.

He went to the dressing table and found a wash bag by the mirror. In it was a tube of cream, eye drops, eye pads, tape and a mask. He couldn't decide whether it was just the eye drops she needed or whether he should bring the whole bag. He spotted a small duffle bag at the side of the table and emptied it out onto the floor. A cagoule, water bottle and an Ordinance Survey map spilled out. He shoved her dress and wash bag in it and as a final thought opened one of the drawers and put in some fresh underwear in it.

He was looking around to see if there was anything else he should bring when her phone rang. The ring tone was of birds singing, the warbling as loud as if they had flown into the room. He followed the singing to the bedside table on the far side. The phone said Neil calling. The photo showed him smiling his smarmy smile. For a moment he felt taken aback by this reminder of her life in Glasgow and then smiled. "Tough luck pal. Tonight she's mine," he said to the phone, before putting it back on the table and letting it go to voicemail.

He closed the door softly and crept down the corridor, thinking he'd take the back door through the kitchen to avoid bumping into Fiona or anybody else. His damp feet rubbed in his shoes but he barely registered the discomfort. The back stairs were narrow and he had to stoop, standing sideways to get down them. The back door was open, the hum of the air conditioning unit blasting heat out into the back yard. He walked to the edge of the car park, thinking he had already escaped when he heard his name. Quietly called but unmistakable.

"Dougie? Where are you going?" she asked.

Her dress was dishevelled, her hair was tumbled as if she and Benjy had already been to bed.

"You OK Sally?" he asked.

"What's in the bag?" She asked, walking toward him. He could see she was barefoot and had a dreamy air about her.

"You look beautiful," said Dougie, kissing her on the cheek. Her skin smelt of vanilla, her breath of alcohol. He realised she was paralytic.

"You told me to fight for him Dougie, d'you remember? And that's what I've done. Lost weight, worked hard and today I've landed my fish." She hung her head as if her neck had snapped and then slowly looked up. Her eyes were enormous, smudged with mascara. "But Dougie, I think he's wriggled off the hook and is swimming away."

"What d'you mean?"

"He can't bear to be near me."

"Weddings are like that. Benjy just wants to make sure everyone having a good time."

"Especially that wee bitch, Nine."

"Now. Now. You're not still worrying about her are you?" said Dougie, putting his arm round her.

"No. Yes. I don't know. Maybe I've had too much to drink," she said.

Dougie led her over to the log pile at the back of the car park and sat her down. He didn't want to leave her but time was ticking by. Beth was waiting. Sally was staring at her feet. "I just want Benjy," she wailed.

"Right," said Dougie, "let me go and find him," but she pulled him back by his arm.

"Don't. It'll only give him an excuse to be angry with me. You go wherever you're going. I'll be fine," she said. Her arms had dropped by her side, her head as loose as rag doll.

"If you're sure," he said, and she waved her arms at him as if to shoo him away.

"Go. Go," she said.

Dougie picked up the duffle bag and walked towards the woods. He had walked twenty yards into the path before realising he couldn't leave her. He turned back towards the car park. She was still there. Her head had dropped in her lap. She was about to keel over. He got to her just in time to wrap her arms round his neck and lift her to a standing position. Her feet dragged along the ground as he pulled her back to the bar. Fiona, seeing Dougie struggle, took the other arm and they folded Sally into one of the chairs in the corner.

"You go find the bridesmaids," said Fiona, "I'll stay with her."

Dougie went outside catching two flashes of pink dress about to disappear down to the waterside. He ran after them and brought them back to the bar.

"I think she's going to be sick," said Fiona, "it'll be the best thing if she was."

"We'll take it from here," said one of the bridesmaids and Dougie watched as they walked towards the toilet, their soft dresses swaying and merging together.

"You took your time. All nice and dry then?" asked Fiona, her coquettish tone slurring. She slipped her hand into his shirt, he could feel it snaking toward his waistband.

"Not here," said Dougie, gently removing it.

"Come here you gorgeous man," she said, pulling him close and kissing him soundly. Dougie emerged from the kiss breathless, a slow dawning that getting away from her was going to be more difficult than he imagined.

"Let's go to your house. It's only two minutes away," she said.

"No. Your place will be better. Less chance of us being interrupted. It's only a ten-minute walk. You go first. I'll just check with the girls that Sally's OK and I'll follow on."

He thought for a moment she might object but drink had dulled her. "Ten minutes then. I'll be counting," she said in a pretend warning voice. He patted her on her bottom as she sashayed off.

It had been over an hour since he had parted from Beth. Hopelessness settled on him like a hangover. He slugged back a whisky that had been left on the table, then got up and knocked quietly on the ladies door. "Everything OK in there?" he asked. There was no reply. He breathed a sigh of relief and quietly left by the back door.

His front door gave a small creak as he opened it and then was silent. In the glow from the moon he could see the kitchen table was covered in stems, stalks, thistle florets and sheaves of grasses; the happy detritus of the wedding preparations when Sally and the bridesmaids had made up their bouquets earlier that day. Dishes were piled in the sink. Not in a fit state for visitors he thought. That is if he still had a visitor.

He took off his shoes and tiptoed into the bedroom, stumbling against the chest of drawers that had mysteriously shifted a foot from its usual position. Beth had lit some candles; most of them had gone out but the one or two that still guttered gave the room a forgiving glow. He walked round to her side. She was sleeping, the fallen side of her face squashed upwards, matching the other side. From this angle she was perfect. He brought one of the candles over to the bedside. Her left eye was half open and for a moment he thought she was awake but her breathing was deep and steady.

He shook her gently. "Beth, it's Dougie."

She opened both her eyes. "So it is," she said sleepily. She half sat up. The covers slipped and he saw the swell of her breast. It was hard to take his eyes away from it.

"Sorry it took longer than I expected," he said.

"You're here now," she replied, and she leaned forward and unbuttoned his shirt. The bed cover had fallen away completely and he could see both breasts in the candlelight. He stood up and took off his shirt, unzipping his trousers. His movements felt sluggish though he was going as fast as he could.

"Do you want the eye cream?" he asked.

"Later," she murmured as he slipped in beside her, pulling him towards him. She took his hand and guided it to her breast. Her body felt both familiar and new, hot against his coldness. His hands wanted to sculpt and explore every curve and cranny of her, to remember and discover her at the same time.

***

The morning light streamed through the window. Sounds of dishes clattering in the kitchen finished the job of waking Dougie up.

"I didn't mean you to clear up," said Dougie. Beth was wearing his shirt. It barely covered her bottom. She had found a pair of rubber gloves and was working her way through a sink full of dirty dishes.

"I wanted to make you a cup of tea but couldn't find a clean cup and once I got started, I thought I would finish," she said, reaching over and laying a soapy plate on the draining board. He was captivated by her body and by the way it moved beneath his shirt. "You could help you know," she added.

"I could," he said, coming up behind her, wrapping his arms around her and kissing her ear. She leant back against him, laughing.

"Maybe later," she said turning to face him. She was still wearing her eye patch. Her hair tumbled about it, giving her the look of a beautiful pirate. Dougie swept aside the flowers and stalks from the kitchen table. A jam jar fell on the floor, smashing against the tiles. The noise made them both start then laugh. He hoisted Beth on top of the table, her legs gripping him as he moved inside her, two bodies fitting together.

"Don't stop," she breathed, but as soon as she said it, he lost himself inside her. He fell on top of her, breathing heavily.

"Sorry…" he began, but she pressed her fingers to his mouth and kissed him.

"You're forgiven," she whispered.

They sat side by side on kitchen chairs outside the back door; the Cuillin ridge shrouded in a heat haze, sharp pinnacles pushing above the clouds as the midday sun began to break through. Beth had made some scrambled eggs but Dougie wasn't hungry, he only wanted to sit beside her, to smell, touch, taste her. She hooked one of her legs over his. He stroked the firm tendons of her hamstrings behind her knees.

"This is so beautiful Dougie. It's literally breathtaking," she said.

"Are you talking about the mountains or what my hand is doing?" he said.

"Both," she laughed, "it's lovely to be away from Glasgow and the hassle of the place."

"How's that brother of yours doing?"

"Not so good. I'm not sure if I can be bothered to make any more effort," said Beth.

"You should be bothered. Family's important," said Dougie.

"Maybe you're right, I should try harder."

"Trying hard is your speciality, Beth."

"I'll see him when I get back. Give it another go," she said.

"Good," he said.

"Why is it when I'm with you that everything seems so straightforward?" she asked.

"It's not me. It's this place," said Dougie. "There's space and freedom here, a chance for your soul to expand, time to think. Reflect on what's important."

"I wonder sometimes what I'm doing with my life. The job's going well but I spend most of my time playing games. I'm good at them but sometimes I wonder if the person who is really me is getting smaller and smaller. Like one those old valve tellies that has been switched off and I'm watching the white dot of me gradually disappear."

"What about the boyfriend? Is he part of a game too?" As soon as he said it Dougie thought she would think it a crass attempt at fishing for information, but she answered with a lack of guile.

"I suppose he is," she said, and looked so sad he wanted to take her in his arms and squeeze all the unhappiness out of her. She reached over to get her wash bag. She balanced a small mirror precariously on her lap.

"Let me hold that for you," he offered.

"I can't believe you don't have a bathroom mirror. In fact you don't have a mirror in the whole house," she said in wonderment.

"The mountains don't care what I look like, so neither do I," replied Dougie, positioning the mirror at the level of her sightline. She examined her reflection carefully before dropping eye drops into her left eye, using the eyelid to massage.

"This doesn't disgust you?" she asked.

"No," he said.

She winked her good eye. He could see she was trying to wink the bad one.

"Could you see that? I think it winked a little didn't it?" she asked.

Dougie laughed. "I think it did."

"This Palsy doesn't belong to me you know. I've been invaded by some alien."

"Better than having a brain tumour surely," replied Dougie.

"I suppose so. I do these exercises hoping for some improvement but it's very slow. But as you say, trying hard is my speciality. I'm hardwired to keep going. Even if there's just a tiny sliver of a chance, I'll go for it."

"It's what I love about you," said Dougie. The word slipped out and lay there like a physical object, something that could be touched and wondered over.

"Oh Dougie," said Beth, "it would never work between us. I mean if I were to come and live here, I would end up getting restless, bored, and if you came to Glasgow to live with me, you would feel the same before long."

"I'm not sure I can let you go again," said Dougie.

"You don't have to. At least not right away. I don't have to be in Glasgow till tonight. That gives us six hours left of today," said Beth.

"You can fit a lifetime into six hours," said Dougie, taking her hand, stroking her strong fingers. They embraced. He could feel himself getting aroused and was about to suggest they move back inside when Beth jerked back from him, the eye cream and wash bag falling from her lap.

"You've got a visitor," she hissed in his ear.

Dougie looked up to see Fiona standing in the path. She was carrying a Tupperware box. Her face, a familiar mix of stoicism and heartache.

Chapter 25

"Beth, I'm not asking for a lifelong commitment, just lunch."

"I'm sorry Neil. I've got to be at The Westwood for a final briefing with Ainslie in less than an hour. Nine and I need to run through some last-minute details," she said, opening her briefcase and giving Nine a stack of folders.

"You've been back from Skye for nearly a week, we haven't been out once since then."

"Neil, please," she said, with a note of finality that she hoped would be enough. Nine was laying out the folders on the dining room table. She went over to look at them.

"It's all got to be on your terms hasn't it Beth?"

"Neil, this isn't the right time..."

"Oh and when you say it's not the right time, that's the end of the discussion."

She stared at him, hands on hips. "Finished?" she flared.

"I haven't even started," he said. His voice had dropped to an ominous whisper.

"I don't know what's got into you Neil," she said,

exasperated.

"I'll tell you what's got into me Beth. You have. I've tried to fit my life around yours, I've done my best to be supportive but being brushed aside like a piece of lint off your well-tailored shoulder is very hard to bear."

"I don't have the time to discuss this now," said Beth.

"This may come as news to you but neither do I. You know where to reach me if you ever find time in your busy schedule," he said, turning and leaving. She stared at the door. It was always the way, she thought, these emotional storms come out of nowhere and at the least convenient time.

"I really don't need this hassle at the moment," said Beth to Nine.

"You can't blame him."

"What d'you mean?" asked Beth, stung by her reply.

"I don't think we should be defined by men but treating them like a piece of shit isn't smart either," she replied.

"I don't have time to argue with you either," said Beth tartly, "let's stick to the matter in hand shall we?" She sat down at the table, opening the top folder.

"Where's the report on the Animal Rights activists who were arrested in Paris?"

"It's somewhere here," said Nine, shuffling the papers in front of her, "or maybe I left it in your signing folder at The Agency. I'll pick it up this afternoon."

"Nine, I need it now."

"I said I'll pick it up later."

They stood staring at each other. An impasse.

"I think you're obsessing over detail," said Nine, "everything's fine. Chill."

"Next you'll be telling me all I need is a good fuck," said Beth, spitting her words at her.

Nine smiled. "…Not a bad suggestion. You've been foul since the wedding."

"Don't talk to me about being foul," warned Beth.

"What's that supposed to mean?" said Nine, her eyes flashing.

"I don't know what you've been up to these past weekends or who the mystery man is, but your work has gone downhill and your attitude with it."

Nine leaned across at her. "You can't treat me like one of your pansy boyfriends you know."

"Why the big secret about this new guy? I think you're hiding something."

"Like what?"

"Like Benjy McKinnon. That's what."

"Fuck off."

"No, you can fuck off," replied Beth.

"With pleasure."

The door when it banged shut seemed louder and more final than Beth imagined a door could sound. She was stunned at the maelstrom of antagonism that she had managed to generate. She looked at her watch.

Twenty minutes before her meeting with Ainslie. She bundled the folders into her briefcase. One fell to the floor. She bent down and stuffed it back in. A slice of pain shot through the left side of her head. *No. No. No. Not now.* She went to the bathroom, her fingers trembling as she pressed out the painkillers into her palm. One, two. She hesitated before pressing out a third. She caught herself in the mirror. An ugly, sour old face stared back. She winked the good eye then tried again with the bad. Nothing. Not a slightest twitch. *Fuck Joseph. Fuck his useless exercises.*

The weather had broken, the long hot summer an unlikely memory. The wind was whipping up, the sky glowering. She lowered her head into the wind and marched against it as if powering her way through the vicissitudes of life. She stopped at the doorway where she had first met Nine. There was a drift of newspapers; a discarded wrapper from a sandwich bar, a faint smell of ammonia. *She'll be back by the evening,* she thought, *she wouldn't want to sleep in this passageway again.*

The function room at The Westwood was described in the hotel brochure as grandiose, but as Beth surveyed its scale, she thought its size only exaggerated the absence of style. She remembered the magnificent hotels in Singapore, their exuberant light-filled spaces, their steel and glass sculptures. This place seemed dark and tawdry by comparison. She imagined seeing it through the eyes of the Rubikon Board. It might be the best Glasgow could offer but it wouldn't impress.

Flora was waiting for her by the top table. She was wearing her worried expression. Beth took a deep breath, making a promise to herself that she would not upset another person today.

"We've got a problem with the flowers," Flora blurted out, "the price has gone through the roof since our original quotation. The dry summer you see."

Beth took a look at Flora's clipboard. "Our original budget was for £3,000. That seems a reasonable amount although this place will need as much help as it can get to cheer itself up."

"That was for table bouquets, a centre piece, wall dressings and some trellising at the back. They're now saying they could only do the table bouquets and the centre piece for the same money."

"You can tell them right back that you expect them to provide the flowers as per their original contract."

Flora blinked at Beth. She wasn't wearing her usual layer of foundation; a rash of small tender pimples had spread around her chin.

"And what if they say they can't? What will I do then?" she asked. She seemed to be on the point of tears.

"I was at a wedding in Skye at the weekend. The flowers were lovely, wild flowers, thistles and stuff. Probably picked for nothing. Tell the florist you expect them to do some creative thinking and provide us with some alternative ideas." Beth intended her tone to be encouraging but Flora acted as if she'd been abandoned. "Some florists might regard this as an opportunity rather than a problem," added Beth, but Flora slouched off, her shoulders bent in a discouraging line.

Beth surveyed the ballroom, imagining it filled with tables and chairs, flower arrangements, glassware sparkling, but the vision failed to lift her. There was a smell of mildew and coffee, a sense that the space had hosted a thousand functions that had gone through the motions in a desultory fashion. Ainslie came through the double doors, nodding to Flora as she passed him on her way out and seeing Beth raised his hand in greeting. "Everything OK?" he asked.

"It will be," she replied.

"Flora doesn't look happy," said Ainslie.

"She's learning the importance of thinking creatively when you have problems," said Beth.

"She's looking for a transfer you know," said Ainslie, planting himself at the centre of the top table. "Well, not officially. She's had a word with my PA. Asked if she knew about any vacancies coming up."

"Did she say why?"

"Something about lack of chemistry," he said.

"Maybe it's for the best," said Beth, although she was surprised to feel that Flora's defection seemed like a blow.

Ainslie picked up a brochure from a cardboard box that had been put on the table. "So this is the programme?"

"We wanted it to look like an edition of *Scottish Field* magazine. Highland Cattle, golf courses, beautiful food, happy people drinking whisky," said Beth.

"You've done an outstanding job. This programme's a winner. After the opening reception, four rounds of golf at the world's finest courses. And then of course there's the ornithologist outings," said Ainslie.

Beth swallowed her distaste. "We've also arranged tours of industrial estates so they can get an idea of locations. I think they'll like the technology park just outside Muirfield. However it's this opening reception when we present our case that's critical. That's when they'll make their decision. The rest of the trip will be negotiating the detail."

"So, run me through what's going to happen."

"You'll be introduced to all the Rubikon board members at the reception before dinner. Then the Strathclyde Police Band will pipe us into the main banqueting room. Our meal has been prepared by Scott Smith from the Four Sisters in Skye and when they're nicely watered and fed, we'll hit them with our case. You'll start with an opening welcome. I'll go through a short presentation outlining the strengths of our bid. Then I'll invite three of our current life science companies to come up and give short testimonials of their experience."

"Of their positive experience."

"Naturally. I've also invited some of their staff to the dinner so they can talk informally with the Rubikon people."

"Won't that be a risk? What if they say something that might put them off?"

"It's a risk worth taking. Their testimony will be more believable, more powerful than if it was scripted."

"Anything else?" asked Ainslie.

"One thing. Recently, there was a demonstration at

Rubikon's offices in Paris. An animal rights group protesting about the testing of primates in their China facility. It got a bit ugly and four people were arrested. Rubikon aren't planning to test animals here in Scotland, but it's something to be aware of."

"How active is the animal rights movement in Scotland?"

"Hard to tell. I've done as much digging as my limited resources will allow but nothing's come up."

"The protesters will have been too busy getting stoned at summer pop festivals to worry about this."

"Just thought I'd mention it," said Beth.

"Beth, you've done a great job here. I can't see how Mexico can compete with this."

"Your support has been incredibly important," said Beth. It was a sycophantic reflex that also had an uncomfortable element of truth.

***

It was late when she returned to her flat. She was full of a restless mixture of exhaustion and exhilaration. The banqueting hall had eventually managed a transformation of sorts, the audiovisuals had worked first time, the sound checks had been fine. Flora had returned with the florist and a plan. She had reached that point where she needed to allow others to get on with their jobs and turn her attention to preparing herself. Being calm. Focused. Positive.

She stood outside Nine's room. She knew the flat was empty but she still felt disappointed at the sight of her deserted room. She sat down on her bed and dialled Nine's number but it went to voicemail, as it had all day. Something was different from this morning. Her pile of paperbacks had gone. She got up and opened the wardrobe. *Thank God*, she thought as she saw her clothes still hanging there. She ran her hands through them, the bright blue cornflower blouse standing out, when a slow realisation hit her. These were only her work clothes. She slid out each drawer from the chest of drawers. All empty. The tatty great coat that had hung on the back of the door all summer had gone. She looked around for her laptop but couldn't see it. She opened the drawer of the bedside table. There was her mobile phone; the screen was blank, long since run out of battery. She knew if she powered it up she would see all her missed calls.

She went back into the kitchen half expecting to find a note but there was nothing. Nine had left without a word. Beth had expected a better, kinder ending. The solitude of the flat closed in on her; she longed to hear a friendly voice, someone to wish her luck, to tell her that everything was going to be alright, but Nine had buggered off, Neil was in a huff, Alec and she were barely speaking. There was only Dougie. Her darling Dougie, but the memory of a distraught Fiona at his back door and their hasty farewell had left all that in an unresolved tangle.

She spotted her fiddle case on the sofa. She tucked the instrument under her chin, tuned the strings and played *The Glasgow Reel*. It was only half a song without Dougie but she could hear him playing in her head as clearly as if he'd been in the room. "I am sending you a message of love," she said. She hoped he had heard it.

She sat at the mirror in her bedroom and began the familiar routine. Sniffle, wrinkle nose, flare nostrils. Repeat three times. Rest. Repeat. Rather than calming her, she became aware of doubt creeping up on her, deepening into a sense of misgiving until it became a certain knowledge that something terrible had happened. The thought became so visceral it was like a heavy weight pressing down on her. She struggled to breathe, her heart squeezed inside her chest. She rested her head on the dressing table, gripping the sides.

Her phone rang. It was two metres away on the other side of her bed. It seemed almost out of her grasp but she got there just in time to see a photo of Alec grinning. Alec calling. A rush of love inflated her. She had misjudged him, he was calling to wish her luck.

"Beth," said a woman. Not Alec then. "Beth it's me, Margaret."

"Margaret?" repeated Beth. "Is everything alright?"

"Alec's been arrested."

"What?" asked Beth, but Margaret was crying like an animal caught in trap. "OK Margaret, try to breathe. That's it. Big breath in through the nose, out in through the mouth." The wailing reduced, then a stuttering cough, great lungfuls of breath. "He was arrested at Hunters this evening. They say he's embezzled millions," she said.

"OK Margaret," said Beth, her voice had become controlled, focused. "I'm going to call Angelo Forsyth. He's a lawyer."

"But what if it's true, Beth?" The jag of crying started again.

"I'm going to call the lawyer now and then I'm going to call you right back and tell you what to do next. OK?"

"OK," said Margaret weakly.

Chapter 26

It had been a week since the wedding but already Dougie felt that Benjy had become a visitor. He knocked before coming into the house and sat at a different seat than his usual one. There was an air of unkemptness to him, bristle sprouted unevenly across his face and neck. "I'm looking forward to the Trade Fair. Getting away for a few days," he said.

"Mmm, things that bad?" asked Dougie.

"I wish you could come with me, Dad."

"Someone's got to look after the shop now Fiona's gone," said Dougie.

"I don't know why Fiona's so mad at you. It was her that went off with Mr Takashama."

"Women can be difficult to understand sometimes," replied Dougie.

"I suppose she heard about you and Beth at the wedding and I'm not just talking about the fiddle playing."

"Aye that was a bit unfortunate but it doesn't mean what Fiona thinks it means. Beth and I will always be friends but we want different things from life," said Dougie, though no matter how often he said that to himself, he still felt a poke of sorrow.

"I'm wondering if me and Sally want different things too. We've done nothing but argue since the wedding. I keep thinking, is this it for the rest of my life? It scares the shit out of me."

"Things will settle. Give it time," said Dougie.

"I lie awake for hours at night thinking I'm slowly dying. She's got it into her head that I don't want to be married. That I went along with it because I didn't want to disappoint everyone. The more I tell her that's not true, the more she seems to believe it."

"What about asking her to come to Glasgow with you? Maybe some time alone together would help?"

Benjy shook his head. "I've thought about it but this trade fair's too important. We're very close to landing a couple of big orders. I don't want any distractions."

"Then you'll just have to keep reassuring her."

Benjy seemed helpless. "God knows I'm trying, Dad, but she's eaten up with jealousy."

"What's she got to be jealous about?"

"That wee drift off course earlier in the summer with Nine? She says she's forgiven me but she sure as hell hasn't forgotten. She's grilling me about the trade show. Asking if I'll be seeing her."

"And will you be seeing Nine when you're in Glasgow?"

"Don't you start, Dad. You're as bad as she is," he said. "I'll see you later."

"You haven't drunk your tea," said Dougie, but

Benjy had gone.

He took the untouched cup to the sink and washed it out. *He's overtired from the build up to the wedding and the trade show*, thought Dougie. *Sally probably feels the same. They could both do with a holiday. A honeymoon.* He could book something as a surprise. He dried the cups and put them back in the cupboard and seeing the whisky, poured himself a large measure into one of the empty mugs and knocked it back in one gulp. It warmed its way down and coupled with his plan to get Benjy and Sally on a better footing, he began to feel better. He put on his Oyster Shack apron and left the house, hoping the customers wouldn't smell whisky on his breath this early in the morning.

Mharie, Sally's mum, was his first customer. Her broad face was shining with anxiety. "Dougie. I'm glad I've got you on your own," she said. Dougie could sense hassle was coming his way and knew there was no way to avoid it.

"I'm worried about Sally," she said, "she's got it into her head that Benjy still fancies that assistant of Beth Colquhoun's."

"I know. He doesn't know what he can say or do to reassure her."

"So you believe him? That there's nothing between him and this girl?" she asked. Her stare was as hard as granite.

"Of course I do," said Dougie, sounding as incredulous as he could muster.

"Give me that apron," she demanded.

"What?"

"Give me that apron. I'll look after the shop for a couple of days. You go down to Glasgow and keep an eye on him."

"I don't think that'll be necessary."

"I'd go myself if my arthritis wasn't so bad and John wasn't on nights this week," she said, tying on the apron.

"Benjy said he wished I could come with him. He'd hardly have said that if he was off to meet a lassie would he?"

"Just go, Dougie. I'll take care of things here. Call me when you see him."

The shop bell rang and three Japanese girls came in. They were as sleek as otters, with glossy hair and bright black eyes. They were wearing mini dresses that showed off their slim thighs. Handbags were slung over their bony shoulders and the gold straps sparkled. *Who dresses up like that to go shopping for fish?* thought Dougie.

Mharie shouted over to them cheerily. "Now girls, what can I do for you?"

One of them handed her camera over to her, shyly.

"Give that to my friend Dougie over here, he'll take a nice snap of us all before he goes, won't you Dougie?"

***

It was after nine o'clock when Dougie arrived in Glasgow. He took the bus from Portree to Inverness and then the train to Glasgow. Ten hours later and he felt as if he'd been wearing the same clothes for a week. He swithered about whether he should call

Benjy and tell him he was here. He was staying with an old school friend and there would probably be a spare sofa for him, but there was also a part of him, he was loath to admit, that didn't want to call just in case his worst fears about him and Nine were confirmed. Malkie Crawford was a safer bet but Dougie wasn't in the mood for his journalistic curiosity.

He wandered into a pub to think through his options and realised with a start it was The Doublet, the same dive he had been in before going to Beth's flat for the first time. There was a different barman but apart from that, things were the same: a scattering of solo men nursing their pints, the unsavoury combination of the smells of piss and whisky. He sat at the bar, comforted in the knowledge that no one would bother him. He ordered a pint and a whisky chaser. He told himself the whisky was the only way to make the beer drinkable but he knew it would help give him the courage to execute the plan that was forming in his mind. Getting into Beth's bed.

The merchant city was buzzing. The weather had turned chilly but it didn't stop clusters of youngsters drinking outside. He found himself searching through the faces for Benjy and Nine, looking and dreading at the same time.

The light on Beth's top floor window was on. He thought he caught a shadow of someone crossing the room but couldn't be sure. He knew it was a bad idea to turn up at her door out of the blue. The boyfriend may be there. The thought stuck in his throat like a fishbone. Still, there was only one way to find out, he thought as he dialled her number. He waited for her to answer but the dial tone came back engaged. He sat on the same wall he had waited at before, looking up at her lighted window. He would give it another five minutes before trying again. His heart louped in his chest when his phone started ringing.

"Dougie. Is that you? It's Mharie." His heart dipped. "Have you seen Benjy?" she asked.

"Not yet. I've just arrived," replied Dougie.

"Call me as soon as you've seen him."

"I will," said Dougie wearily.

"I sold those Japanese girls three bottles of whisky cream liqueur. They were a wee bit past their sell-by date so I gave them a discount. Hope that's OK."

"If you're looking for a permanent job, let me know," he said. He was only half joking but he realised as he said it that it wasn't a bad idea.

"I'll think about it," she said magnanimously, and hung up. He looked up to Beth's window. The light had gone out. He stared at the black window and the courage to go up to the door and press her buzzer leaked out of him.

He wandered down to the Clyde towpath. In the past ten years the city had taken off its industrial coat and put on something smarter. The dry docks and cranes were gone, replaced by an exhibition campus. Three large buildings sat in landscaped grounds; swathes of newly planted trees ringed the edges, looking weak and spindly. The central hall was like an outsized armadillo, its silver scales backlit by hundreds of lamps in acres of empty car parking space. A string of lampposts fringed the perimeter road. Banners like sails fluttered with alternating images of red and green apples with 'Naked Food Fair' written up the side. Dougie gazed at them a while, finding some comfort in them. At least the trade fair part of Benjy's story had been true.

There was a budget hotel opposite and he walked into the reception area. It had the same deserted look as the car park, as if everyone had gone to bed. He shouted out "Hello?" a couple of times and was on the point of leaving when a girl appeared. She glared at him as if he was an intruder.

"What d'you want?" she asked rudely.

"A room?" asked Dougie pleasantly.

The girl looked at him as if he was either stupid or drunk. "We're fully booked. There's a trade show on next door you know."

"I know. I'm here to help my son with our stand. Skye Superfoods. Me coming down was a last-minute thing," said Dougie. "Can you check you're really full? Maybe someone hasn't showed up?"

She sighed theatrically and went round the other side of the desk, shaking her head as she stared at the computer screen. "Oh, wait a minute," she said. She clicked her mouse, "Room 104 hasn't checked in yet." She glanced behind her at the clock. "It's after ten. If someone hasn't showed up by then, technically I can give the room away."

"There you go!" said Dougie heartily and didn't argue when she asked for a scandalous amount of money for what turned out to be a room barely big enough for a bed and a minibar. There wasn't even a wardrobe, just a small rail with four hangers on it. He took off his jacket, and hung it up on one of them, threw down his overnight bag and lay on his expensive bed, spreading his legs out to the edges of it, wishing he had brought his own whisky with him. The price of the minibar miniatures was too painful to contemplate. The phone rang again. That Mharie woman was going to be a pain in the arse he thought as he picked it up.

"Dougie?" It was Beth. Her voice sounded smoky.

"Beth."

"I saw there had been a missed call from you."

"I'm in Glasgow. At the Naked Food Trade Fair."

"Is that what you called to tell me?"

"That and to ask how you are."

"Not good. Nine's gone."

"What d'you mean gone?"

"We had a row this morning. I accused her of seeing Benjy. She's taken all her things. Didn't even say goodbye."

"We all say things in the heat of the moment that we don't mean," said Dougie, but his misgivings about Benjy and Nine deepened.

"I don't know what got into me. Must be the stress of this Rubikon deal. It's so important I pull it off."

"Maybe we could meet up?" There was a pause. He sat up on the bed, nibbling the hangnail on his thumb.

"The big presentation is tomorrow."

"Ah, so you're busy then."

"They're here for the next four days."

"That's a pity."

"I've got a bad feeling about it, Dougie."

"About the presentation? You'll be the dog's bollocks, Beth."

"I know, the cat's pyjamas, the bee's knees."

"Ah that and a bag of chips," finished Dougie.

"It's good to hear your voice, Dougie."

"Good to hear yours, too," he replied. There was a silence then, the sort to luxuriate in.

"The bad news doesn't stop there I'm afraid. Alec's been arrested. Charged with embezzling money at Hunters, the company he used to work for."

"Shit."

"I've spoken to a lawyer. He thinks he'll get bail."

"That's something I suppose."

"You said family's important, Dougie. I just wish mine wasn't so screwed up."

"Most families are," said Dougie, "is there anything I can do to help?" he asked, feeling a stab of selfishness at the hope that she might suggest he comes round and provide some comfort in her bed.

"I don't think so."

"I'm here if you need me," he said.

"I know."

"Everything will be alright," he said. That sounded lame even to him.

"I know. Thanks Dougie." Her voice was almost a whisper.

He held the phone to his ear, reluctant to hang up. He could hear her soft breathing over the crackle of the connection and hoped she could hear his breathing too. He lay down on his bed and imagined they were lying beside each other.

"I have to go now. Bye then," she said finally.

"Bye bye," he whispered. She hung up and the dial tone replaced the rhythm of her breathing. He wasn't ready to let her go though and continued to hold the phone against his ear until his eyes closed and he slipped into sleep.

Chapter 27

The rain was unequivocal, drenching the pavements. Beth tried to avoid the puddles but soon the hem of her dress was damp from where her coat had flapped open. She barely noticed it. Her fighting spirit was turned up to maximum. "Go ahead, throw whatever weather you like at me," she wanted to shout out. "You won't break me."

She had been awake most of the night compartmentalising the various crises into three separate plans. Plan one. Alec. Angelo Forsyth the lawyer had called and confirmed that the bail hearing was scheduled for later that day. He didn't anticipate a problem as long as Beth had the funds. She had. They agreed to speak after the hearing. She would call Margaret and update her.

Plan two. Rubikon visit. The weather was forecast to worsen. She fast forwarded to four days of rain-blasted fairways and steamed-up coach windows. Not ideal but this too could be turned around. She would set it up as one of the most challenging golf experiences they were ever going to have. Offer prizes. Ensure plenty of whisky flasks. Commission a video.

Plan three. Nine. Her disappearance sent a pulse of sadness through her. There was nothing she could do but wait and hope she'd come back. Let Nine go. It was the only plan she could think of.

The doorman at The Westwood nodded as she arrived. He seemed as miserable as the weather. "No long faces today," she said cheerfully, her curt undertone unmistakeable. He looked at her as if working out who she was. "Beth Colquhoun, Chief Executive of The Agency," she informed him brusquely. "We've important visitors this afternoon. Sunny faces required at all times."

The man stared at her as if she had come directly from the asylum. She registered his stare, that particular mix of curiosity, alarm and pity, and it bounced off her as if she had a force field around her. She pulled out her phone and called the hotel general manager, leaving a message with his PA that left no one in doubt what she expected of the hotel staff that day.

She opened the door to the banqueting hall. It looked like an earthquake had hit it. The tables were pushed to the far side of the room and the top table had been dismantled into three smaller tables. A dozen vases, the flowers, straggly and wilted, had been placed in a corner on the floor.

"What's going on here?" she cried out. Two bellboys in purple and gold brocade were moving the tables back into position, their heads down with no intention of lifting them to face her. She punched the general manager's number on her phone but before it had connected she saw him marching towards her.

"What on earth has happened here?" she asked. "The meeting's due to begin in less than three hours."

"Dr Colquhoun," said the general manager, sounding both concerned and confident, "good morning. A coffee please for Dr Colquhoun," he said to one of the bellboys.

"I don't want a coffee, I want an explanation and then I want a solution," she said. It was an effort to hang on to her composure.

"There's been a misunderstanding. The staff were told that the room was to be cleared. It'll take us no time to get it back to how it was last night."

"The flowers look like someone's stamped on them," said Beth.

"Another unfortunate…"

"…Misunderstanding," said Beth. "I'll return in an hour and I expect everything to be perfect. Tables, chairs, flowers, the lot. And if it isn't exactly to my requirements, there'll be hell to pay."

The general manager seemed unfazed. "I assure you everything will be to your satisfaction," he replied. She fixed him with a steely gaze, his face remained impassive but she could see his fingers were pressed tight at the edge of his clipboard.

She found a quiet corner in reception and wondered fleetingly if that coffee she refused might materialise. She opened her briefcase and took out her phone. So much to do.

"Margaret. How are you?"

"I'm going to the police station this morning. Mr Forsyth arranged for me to see him."

"Good."

"I just can't believe this is happening, Beth. Alec's such a loyal, trustworthy person. We were so excited about Dubai. Our dream's turning into a nightmare."

"Try not to think too far ahead," coaxed Beth.

"I haven't told the boys."

"Best to wait till after the bail hearing."

"I've told them Dad's gone away on business for a few days." She began to cry. "I'm not like you, Beth. I'm not used to lying and deceit."

"Well," said Beth, thinking the call had gone surprisingly smoothly up to that point, "it's important we all put on a brave face. For Alec's sake." Margaret took a gulp of air and said she'd try. When Beth hung up, she could still hear an echo of Margaret's whimpering.

OK, she thought, blowing out a breath, *that's Alec dealt with for the time being.* Next on the list was Rubikon and sorting out this useless hotel. She gazed onto the street. The hotel was on one of Glasgow's biggest shopping streets and despite the sleeting rain it seemed to be remarkably busy for a Friday lunchtime. There was something about the movement of the shoppers that troubled her. Not the usual flow of people going up and down, but a milling and swirling as if there was a blockage somewhere. The doorman came inside, his uniform dripping. He was looking wildly from left and right.

"What's the matter?" she asked.

"I need to speak to Mr Masters," he said.

"The general manager? I can call him for you," said Beth, dialling his number and going to the front door. People were circling round the entrance. Some were wearing orange cagoules, others black hoodies. Most of them hadn't put their hoods up. Their drenched look added to her disquiet. Her phone connected and she heard the smooth tones of Mr Masters. "Dr Colquhoun. We're very nearly ready if you could just give us…"

"Get down here," said Beth as it began to dawn on her what was happening. "Get down here right away."

Chapter 28

Dougie was surprised at the size of the crowd but enjoyed being carried along by its momentum. A poster at the side of the entrance said 'The Naked Food Show: An unrivalled opportunity to see, taste and experience the latest in natural food.' He shuffled up to one of the entrance booths. The lad asked for thirty pounds. Dougie gave him a 'you must be joking' look, but he remained impassive. He looked back towards the crush of people behind him and peeled off three tenners from his wallet. The boy handed him a wad of brochures and a floor plan as if it was a fair exchange.

He walked into the vast interior and took a moment to take it in. The cavernous space was divided into blocks for the exhibitor stands; each a massive metal framed box, with broad boulevards between them. It was like a cross between a giant supermarket and a warehouse. Dougie scoured his map but the writing was too small and the map too complicated to understand. He dumped it in the nearest bin and decided instead to have a wander about, get a feel for the place. Let Skye Superfoods find him.

Two young girls, as slim as whippets, were standing behind a counter. The banner above them said 'Food Kitchen – Live Demos'. Dougie stopped to watch as they pulled on rubber gloves and began spraying the surface with disinfectant. They were wearing matching tee shirts with 'food kitchen' written across them and their breasts danced as they wiped. He felt a pull of disappointment when they both decided to put on aprons.

"First demo in an hour," said one of them. A curl of hair had fallen attractively across her cheek.

"Very good," replied Dougie, smiling.

"It's called 'Putting the wow into wheat berries'," added the other.

Dougie managed to keep a straight face. "I wouldn't want to miss that one."

The Pukka Café was situated in the central boulevard and Dougie was one of its first customers. A middle-aged man with sideburns and two sleeves of tattoos told him he'd take his order in a couple of minutes after he had flushed through the coffee machine, an aluminium contraception that hissed and steamed like a dragon. Dougie said a cup of instant would be fine but the man seemed as offended as if he'd sworn at him. Dougie found a seat and watched the steady tide of people as they passed by. He expected everybody to be slim and fit-looking but it looked like the usual crowd you would find shopping in Glasgow on a Saturday afternoon. His eye seemed drawn to the overweight and infirm. Perhaps they had come to help them change their ways.

There was a group of student types setting up their stall next door to the café. An excellent spot to attract passing trade, thought Dougie as he watched them shifting around tables, opening up boxes of materials. They were wearing black tee shirts and jeans as if it was a uniform. One of the young men was tall with stringy Rasta hair that went down his back. Dougie admired his long knots and tangles with nostalgia. He'd had his hair cut twice since that first time and each time he felt a small sense of betrayal towards his former self. He was finding it hard to remember the feel of it down his back, the weight of it on his head. A squabble was developing between the tall lad and one of the girls about what poster to put where. They had unfurled a photograph of a monkey spread-eagled on a rack, his head lolling to one side, his tongue hanging out of its mouth.

"That's horrible," said Dougie, louder than he had intended.

The girl smiled. "You can lend us a hand if you like," she said.

Dougie sauntered over and tried to hide his shock as he saw the pamphlets that were emerging from the cardboard boxes. More pictures of dead and dying animals in varying scenarios of torture and abuse.

"You're against cruelty to animals then?" asked Dougie. "I would have thought you were preaching to the converted with this crowd."

The girl laughed. She had small pearly teeth that glinted and it took a moment for Dougie to realise she had small gems drilled into the enamel. "We're here to raise money from people who share our values. You can set up a direct debit if you like."

"After being fleeced thirty quid to get in, I'm afraid I can't help you there."

"There's a demo in Buchanan Street today. You should go. Show your support for the cause."

"Buchanan Street? Don't tell me, Marks and Spencer are selling donkey jackets."

The girl laughed. Dougie laughed back, enjoying seeing his patter appreciated.

"It's outside the Westwood Hotel. Against Rubikon."

"Rubikon?" said Dougie, thinking the name sounded familiar.

"They're the big bad wolves of life sciences. They torture animals. They say it's to test cancer drugs but that's just a con. It's really for sun tan lotion and mascara."

A flurry of thoughts, like snow in a glass jar, was swirling in his head. The name Rubikon was definitely familiar but he had got to that age where he knew the harder you try to remember something, the more elusive it becomes. "I'll think about it," he said to the girl.

He walked down the main boulevard and there in front of him was the Cuillin Ridge. Three large photographs had been pasted onto separate panels creating a majestic vista. He could see two tiny figures near to the summit of the Inaccessible Peak. He imagined the climbers' bursting lungs, legs like boulders, but feeling as light as birds with the certainty that they were going to make it to the top. Skye Superfoods was written across the lower slopes in bright red lettering. Benjy had done a good job, thought Dougie, the photographs alone were enough to stop all passing traffic in its tracks.

Benjy had his back to him, talking to someone, and Dougie enjoyed a moment unseen to watch him. He was leaning forwards, giving the other person his full attention. They laughed, he could hear a lighter note, a woman he supposed and shifted his position to get a better look. Benjy leaned even further forwards as if to embrace her. Dougie had a sudden desire to walk away but was rooted to the spot, destined to witness what would come next. The girl, for surely it was a girl, threaded her arms around his neck and they kissed. Dougie was assailed with dismay and an odd sense of relief that no more detective work would be required of him. He had stumbled upon Benjy's secret.

They broke off and Dougie caught sight of the girl as she walked away. She had short brown hair that for a moment confused him, but the purposefulness of her step, the way she dug her hands deep in her pockets was all too familiar. There was writing on the back of her jacket. 'Justice for Animals'.

Dougie watched as Benjy turned his attention back to the stand, constructing small pyramids of drums of seaweed flakes, standing back to admire his work, rubbing his hands in happy anticipation of the day ahead, thought Dougie sadly. He then saw him pulling out his phone. Dougie thought he was probably texting some loving message even though she had only been gone a minute but it was his phone that buzzed in his pocket. He read the text. 'Wish me luck Dad. XX'. Dougie walked towards him, the phone still in his hands.

"Dad. I can't believe it. I've just texted you," said Benjy. Dougie tried to smile back but his face was immobile. His brain had cleared. The connection between Rubikon and Beth, Nine, and Cruelty to Animals had become as bright and as painful as the blade of his shucking knife.

"We need to talk, son."

Chapter 29

Beth watched as the group of protesters swelled in numbers. It was hard to work out who was part of the original group and who were passers-by who had got caught up in it. Those at the front were holding placards: 'Justice for Animals'. 'Liberate the Innocents'. Pictures of monkeys stretched on torture racks, rabbits with wires in their ears, pink eyed and terrified. A woman had taken her position to face the crowd and was speaking into a microphone. "This is a fight against oppression and injustice. When people hurt animals, they hurt nature. What is beautiful in this world is resistance. To have the courage to say enough is enough."

The crowd repeated, "Enough is enough. Enough is enough."

A paralysis had begun to creep over Beth's body. All she could do was stand, watch and listen. Horrified. A man had taken the microphone from the woman and had begun talking. He had an educated accent. English. Home Counties. "Rubikon have over seventy thousand animals in their R&D centre in China. An animal dies there every two minutes. Seven hundred and twenty animals die needlessly. Every day. Poisoned by household products, food colouring and chemicals. Do we want this here in Scotland? Do we need these people in our country?"

The crowd responded, "Enough is enough. Enough is enough."

Mr Masters, the general manager appeared beside her.

"Get rid of these people. Now," hissed Beth.

"I'm afraid..." he said.

"I'm not interested in what you're afraid of. Get rid of them now."

"I can't. This is a public street."

"If you don't get rid of them, then I will," said Beth, pushing past him. The rain drove into her and for a moment her vision was blurred. She could feel her dress getting wet but it was too late to go back inside for a coat. "Please. You've made your point. Please leave," she said to the man who was holding the microphone. He glanced at her and turned his back on her. A fresh burst of indignity flooded her. How dare he fuck up her big day? He lifted the microphone to his lips and was about to speak. "Please. Please stop!" cried Beth, trying to grab the microphone from his hands. He turned round and shrugged her off, sending her flying backwards. She staggered against the plate glass of the hotel window.

She could see three mounted policeman in full riot gear wheeling and circling at the back of the crowd like modern-day jousters. A policeman was coming towards her. He took out his truncheon and for a wild moment Beth thought he was going to hit her but he turned to face the crowd, waving his truncheon and shouting, "Move back. Move back!" The people at the front tried to step backwards but there were more people arriving all the time and those in the middle were getting squeezed. "Move back," he said as six or seven more policemen joined him, all dressed in black padded clothes, helmets, and wielding Perspex shields.

Fear gripped Beth as the air filled with sirens, shouting, pelting rain. The man was still speaking into his megaphone but Beth couldn't hear the words, only his clipped tone. For a few minutes things seemed to calm down as the crowd shuffled back and more policemen arrived setting up a line of barriers at the front. Then a surge of people pushed forward from the back. A scuffle broke out to the left.

She could see Peter Tan trying to find his way through the crowd. *Oh God no*, she thought as she saw him, head down, trying to make progress as people pressed around him. Two policemen materialised at his side and each took an arm, pushing him towards the hotel entrance. One of the protesters appeared to realise who he was and was shouting at him. Then she saw an arm raised and an egg flying towards him. It landed on his face. Even in all the noise and chaos Beth couldn't help admire the accuracy of the aim.

Peter Tan looked around him in bewilderment to see who had hit him. There was untidy scuffle between a policeman and a girl who was trying to push him away. Another policeman joined him and they both tried to pull the girl away. She was fighting like a polecat, the hood of her coat coming off in the struggle until she was finally caught. Beth had a good view of her. Her hair had been dyed brown, but her face was unmistakeable.

Peter Tan struggled towards the entrance of the hotel, shaking off his police bodyguards as if they were a nuisance. His suit was drenched, egg white and yolk dripped down his face and jacket. He was standing less than a metre from Beth, wiping his cheek with angry strokes. The photographers' flashbulbs lit up his face as he stared at Beth, his expression murderous.

Beth pushed her way through the crowd to where the two policemen were marching Nine off. By the time she had caught up with them, they had broken away from the main demonstration and were making their way towards Stewart Street.

"D'you know what you've done?" she yelled. She knew she must look like a crazy women. Her dress stuck to her body, her hair drenched. Nine said nothing. Her eyes were dulled, her expression blank as if she was slightly bored. They had been here before, thought Beth, shouting in the street at each other.

"You haven't even the balls to speak to me," said Beth. Nine lifted her chin but said nothing. Rain was rolling down her face and neck. Her brown hair was matted, the rain sitting like sparkles on the surface.

"Is that a bloody wig you're wearing?" said Beth, and lurched forward to pull it off but Nine weaved out of her reach.

"Steady on there," said one of the policeman as they regained control of Nine. "We're taking her to Stewart Street Police Station. You can wait for her there."

The other policeman looked at his colleague with a

kindly expression. "Give her a minute, Jock. It's obviously the girl's mother."

"You've ruined everything. Was that the plan all along?" said Beth. She could feel her fury evaporate, a numb pointlessness settling in its place.

"She's not my mother," said Nine to the two policeman.

Her hoodie had come undone at the neck and Beth could see her tattoo. It was like a pale bruise, the colour of rose wine, as if the rain was washing it off. Beth's disorientation deepened to distraction. "What's going on, Nine?"

"She'll be charged with a breach of the peace and likely released before having to appear in court," said the policeman kindly, "come to the station later."

"Nine. Please. Say something," pleaded Beth, but the three of them had walked off and Beth watched as Nine was led away, flanked by policeman, looking no more dangerous than a defenceless child.

Chapter 30

"How long has this thing between you and Nine been going on?" asked Dougie. They were back at the Pukka Café. The coffee machine was working and the place was nearly full. They were lucky to get a seat.

"What d'you mean 'this thing'?" asked Benjy.

"For God's sake, I think I've known all summer. Mharie's suspicious, too. She sent me down here to check up you. Even Beth's convinced you've been seeing each other."

"The whole world thinks there's something going on between us and the daft thing is, you're all wrong."

"I saw you kissing just five minutes ago."

Benjy put his head in his hands. "I fell in love with Nine that night at the Four Sisters. Working on those press releases together. I knew I'd found my soulmate and I didn't know what to do about it. I thought that maybe she was a passing infatuation, a panic reaction to settling down with Sally, so I stopped seeing her after that first time at Beth's flat. I thought if I concentrated on the seaweed business, set a date for the wedding, everything would go back to how it was before. But that's not what happens when you fall in love is it Dad?"

"I suppose not," conceded Dougie.

"We texted a few times over the summer. That's all. I promise you. But she was in my head all the time. I knew that getting married to Sally was wrong but I didn't know what to do about it. You, Sally, Sally's family, the whole of the Isle of Skye was in a parallel universe. Everyone was so excited about the wedding. I didn't want to let anyone down. It was like being on a sledge going downhill, it had started sliding and there was no way I could stop it. I don't know if I can make you understand what a nightmare this has been for me."

"I knew you were unhappy, Benjy. I just didn't know how unhappy. I wished you could have spoken to me about it."

"I didn't know how to, Dad."

"I always thought you could tell me anything. That there would never be any lies between us."

"D'you remember when you lied about the bacteria levels? Lied about knowing Beth at university? We all lie at times. Not because we're bad people. We lie because we don't want to hurt each other."

"I should have made it easier for you to talk about it. Maybe I was a wee bit distracted myself."

"After the wedding things got worse. Sally was convinced I was having an affair. There came a point where I thought, why I am resisting this? I'm being accused of it anyhow. I'm twenty-two with my whole life ahead of me and I'm with the wrong person. So I called Nine two nights ago and I told her I loved her and she said she felt the same about me. She said that Beth had accused her of seeing me and that she'd left her flat. It felt like our destiny was already decided. I was going to tell you, Dad. Honestly I was."

"So Nine's gone to this demo on Buchanan Street? Does Beth know about that?"

"No. I didn't know about it either till the other night. Nine's been working undercover all summer planning this demo against Rubikon."

"We need to go there. Warn Beth," said Dougie. Benjy's phone buzzed. "Who's that from?"

"I don't recognise the name. One of Nine's friends I think," said Benjy.

"C'mon, we need to get going otherwise everything Beth's worked for will be finished."

"It's too late, Dad," said Benjy, looking up from his phone. "We're too late."

Chapter 31

"Tea?" asked Ainslie.

"No thank you," replied Beth politely. It felt like a small but significant gesture of defiance, though Ainslie ignored it and placed a cup and saucer in front of her. The china was fine porcelain with an elaborate pattern of pink peony flowers and a delicate butterfly painted on the inside lip. She felt her situation was not unlike that of the butterfly, destined to be burned alive.

She looked around the ballroom. The hotel had surpassed her expectations. The floral centrepiece was magnificent, yellow chrysanthemums, white lilies and blue hydrangeas. Flora was skulking about in the background, not sure if she was expected to be there or not. "You managed to get in touch with everybody?" asked Beth.

Flora nodded. "The Rubikon board were all staying here at the hotel so it was easy to tell them it was cancelled. We got hold of the rest of the guests bar one or two. They've probably heard it on the news by now though."

"Thank you," she said quietly and turned to Ainslie. "How many arrests were made in the end?" It was as if she was asking how many holes of golf he had played that morning.

"Six, including your business manager."

"My ex-business manager," she corrected.

"No injuries. Just a couple of walking wounded," added Ainslie.

"That's something at least," said Beth.

"Flora," said Ainslie, his voice lowering, "perhaps you could…"

"Of course," said Flora walking towards the door. "I'll see you back in the office later," she said. Neither Beth nor Ainslie replied.

"There's still a possibility of having the presentation at Gleneagles or the Old Course hotel in St Andrews. It would be lower key but it could still have a certain charm," said Beth. Her voice sounded breathy, her icy calmness was thawing into something more unstable.

"Beth," said Ainslie, his voice growly, deep like a distant stampede.

"Contingency thinking, Ainslie. A hard habit to break. Admitting defeat is even harder." She sipped her tea. It was scalding hot. Some of it spilled out the side of her mouth. She took the linen napkin that had been folded beside her cup and dabbed her mouth dry. She looked at Ainslie. He had trouble returning her gaze.

"It's over," he said.

She nodded slowly, taking in the finality of it. "I knew that as soon as I saw the protesters."

He sipped his tea, a delicate gesture, his mouth pursing prettily. He placed the cup in its saucer.

Chink, chink. It sounded like bells calling time.

"I'm assuming you would prefer a resignation?" said Beth.

Ainslie nodded.

"When would you like to announce it?" she asked, although in truth she had no interest in the reply. Asking questions, showing interest, was just another old habit that was hard to break.

"Desmond will be here shortly. We'll discuss the detail with him."

"Desmond was always good at the detail," she replied mildly as she saw him standing in front of her. She thought he had the good grace to appear stunned at the turn of events though Beth knew he would have spoken with Ainslie already, prepared their approach, agreed their respective roles.

"I've scheduled a press conference at 5 o'clock," he began importantly. Beth wanted to hit him but sat as obediently as a schoolgirl at the front of the classroom. "Ainslie will announce Beth's resignation. No mention of the girl. I've had a word with my contact in *The Record* and they've agreed to keep her out of the story."

"That was good of them," said Beth.

Desmond continued as if she hadn't spoken. "We'll position Beth as a Chief Executive who's had the integrity to take responsibility for her failure rather than someone who actively harboured animal rights activists."

"Desmond," said Ainslie gently, "I think we have the picture."

"Of course, Nine may decide to speak to the papers herself. If she does you're on your own, Beth, but at least The Agency will be in the clear."

She wanted to say that she had known all along that she was on her own but managed a forced smile. "Will you be announcing my successor at the press conference?" asked Beth. "You know how people hate a void."

"Desmond will take over as a temporary measure," replied Ainslie. Beth marvelled at the sweet timbre in his voice.

"Congratulations," she murmured. "So all that's left to discuss are the conditions in which I'll go quietly?" She let the remark brew for a moment. "I think it reasonable if you honoured my contractual obligations. Two years' salary and a final bonus of £750,000," she said, feeling pleased to have matched Ainslie's saccharin tone.

Desmond and Ainslie exchanged a knowing look. Desmond spoke first. "We expected a conversation about a settlement of course. But you're talking about a package of £1.12 million."

"I know," said Beth, "a reasonable amount, wouldn't you agree?"

Ainslie wouldn't argue, thought Beth. They both knew the costs of a court case for unfair dismissal and the damage of unwelcome publicity would be higher.

"Desmond will instruct the lawyers to draw up the settlement. We'll include a gagging clause of course," said Ainslie.

"Of course," replied Beth, "but there's one thing

I'd like to say." She paused, thinking she sounded like Anne Boleyn at her execution grasping for the last vestiges of dignity before she got the chop. She wanted to say that everything she had done had been in the service of others, that although history may judge her harshly, her only motivation was to attract jobs and prosperity for the people of Scotland. Ainslie and Desmond were both waiting for her to speak.

"I'm sorry it ended this way," she said finally.

She saw them both visibly relax. Desmond seemed thoughtful. "I wish you well, Beth." For a moment she believed him.

"Beth… if there is anything I can do…" said Ainslie.

"I think not," she replied, getting up, the sensation of behaving like Anne Boleyn never quite leaving her.

Chapter 32

Dougie and Benjy walked in silence as they left the Exhibition Centre. Benjy's mobile buzzed periodically, punctuating their progress as he stopped to read and reply to texts. Dougie guessed there were updates from the Animal Rights people on what had happened after Nine's arrest but he didn't ask for details.

"Nine's back at the house now. I told her we'd be there in fifteen minutes," said Benjy. Dougie thought he sounded relieved, as if he'd lost a dog and it had been found.

"Whose house are we going to?"

"George's. He's the head of Animals Against Cruelty but he was arrested in Paris last month. Nine's been living there at weekends recently. Looking after the place for him."

"And you say that Nine's been working as an undercover agent for this organisation, planning all summer to scupper Beth's plans?"

"Well, planning to stop Rubikon's plans to set up a R&D centre. Nine knew that Beth was a patron of The Beacon House that supports vulnerable young women so posing as a homeless girl was a way to get close to her."

"I always thought there was something about that girl was... well... more than she seemed," said Dougie, but stopped himself saying more. He could see Benjy's expression had clouded at any hint of criticism.

They arrived at an estate of modern flats just off the Maryhill Road. The buildings were four stories high, clad in red brick and concrete with glazed stairwells. Dougie thought they looked more like offices than homes. Benjy opened a door on the ground floor and they went into an open-plan living area, kitchen, dining area, and lounge.

The place was furnished with flat-pack furniture that didn't look like it had been out the box for long. There was a bookcase in the lounge but it was empty, not even one or two paperbacks to fill the lonely shelves. Nine was sitting on a sofa fiddling with her fingers. She got up on seeing them come in, shifting uneasily from foot to foot. It was as if no one knew how to greet each other.

"I nearly didn't recognise you," said Dougie. She raked her fingers through her brown hair. "You look awfully peely wally."

"He means you look tired," said Benjy, going over and giving her a reassuring hug. They sat down on the couch together, Benjy's arms remaining round her shoulders in a protective embrace.

Dougie's eyes were drawn to Nine's neck. "And what happened to the tattoo? It looks as though you've rubbed it off."

"It wasn't a proper tattoo. Only henna. Fades on its own after a week or two," said Nine, touching her throat.

Dougie could see purple bruises of tiredness beneath her eyes and shook his head. "Nothing about you is quite as it seems is it, Nine? Benjy tells me you were the mastermind behind this demo. You must be pleased with yourself. Mission accomplished and all that."

"Dad," started Benjy, "Nine's just been released from the police station. I think she's been through enough without you giving her the third degree."

Nine shrugged. "I don't care what you think of me, Dougie, or what punishment I receive. Seeing Peter Tan's face covered in egg was worth it." Dougie could see Benjy's admiring glance had deepened. "You know Rubikon manufacture chemicals and enzymes that are added to chicken feed to make egg yolks more yellow. People think the yellower the yolk the healthier the egg, when in fact they're being stuffed full of chemical shit," she added.

"I don't suppose you'll get locked up for throwing an egg, even one with a chemical yolk," conceded Dougie, "but you must have known this would be a disaster for Beth."

Nine seemed confused and for the first time Dougie sensed her uncertainty. "I've never seen Beth so angry, so out of control. She was yelling at me in the street. I didn't know what to say."

"I suppose 'sorry' didn't come to mind did it?" suggested Dougie.

"I'm sorry it had to be this way, Dougie, but she was keeping dangerous company. Rubikon are evil bastards. I'm not sorry about letting the world know that."

"Beth seems tough but this will hit her hard," said Dougie.

"Beth taught me how to fight. She told me to watch and wait for your chance to use your enemy's weakness against them. I knew that first night I helped her with her eye that I had a chance to get really close to her."

"You met her at a time when her defences were down. The caring nurse routine was very clever, it would be a sucker punch for anyone," said Dougie. Nine squirmed in her seat. Dougie couldn't work out whether it was through embarrassment or because she was cold. The heating was off, rain lashed against the window.

"Dad... please..." said Benjy. They were sitting so close together on the sofa that there was no space between them. "Of course we're concerned about Beth. We both are. Will you see her? Make sure she's OK?" asked Benjy.

Dougie could see they were holding hands. "Of course I'll see her."

"I don't think she'll ever speak to me again," said Nine.

"She was very fond of you, Nine."

"And I was very fond of her, Dougie. I don't expect you to understand but if you see her, I'd like you to tell her that I'll always respect her. That I'll remember our time working together with great affection."

"Bullshit, Nine. You don't do this to someone you respect."

"Dad. Stop," said Benjy. His eyes had become alight. He was making his boundary known.

"I've said my piece. I'll leave it at that. So what about you two?"

"This has all happened so quickly," said Nine, "we haven't had a chance to talk it through have we Benjy?" She touched his face. It was the smallest of gestures, thought Dougie, yet it showed the magnitude of their feelings for each other.

"Norway," said Benjy. "What d'you think of that idea, Nine? We could set up a seaweed farm there." Nine looked at him, a small startle of shock, her face glowing.

"Norway? Norway's so far away," said Dougie. He could hear his voice breaking.

"We can hardly go back to Skye can we Dad? I expect Sally will take me to the cleaners. She's got every right to. I'll give her my share of Skye Superfoods. Give her whatever she wants."

"But why Norway?"

"Mr Takashama's idea," said Benjy. Dougie thought he had the good grace to look embarrassed.

"That wee blighter? He's back on the scene, is he?"

"He never left it, Dad. I've been in touch with him all summer. He thinks the waters around the West Coast of Scotland are too unpredictable. He recommended a site near Tromso long before... well long before this happened between Nine and me."

"Malkie Crawford thinks he's a conman," said Dougie.

"We wouldn't make any commitments until we're sure of him," said Benjy. He had regained his usual confidence. How easily the words 'we' came out his mouth, wrapping them together, thought Dougie. Keeping him out.

"I'm struggling, son. Struggling to take it in," admitted Dougie.

"You could always come with us," said Benjy, "we could start again together." Dougie thought he saw a small nod of agreement from Nine. He could see their happy hopeful faces and felt overwhelmed with grief. "Skye's my home. I don't want to leave it. I don't want you to leave it either," said Dougie, feeling his throat close.

"Nothing's been decided, Dad. These are just ideas," said Benjy.

"I'll make a cup of tea," suggested Nine.

"You're bloody joking aren't you?" replied Dougie. "I'm off to the pub."

"I'll come with you," said Benjy, getting to his feet.

Dougie could see his anxious face, so eager to make amends. "I'd rather be on my own, son. Looks like I need to get used to that from now on."

The air was leaden with failing light. The nearest pub was the sort Dougie normally avoided, modern but faked to look old. Wooden floorboards that had been deliberately distressed, air vents wrapped in aluminium foil hanging from the ceiling like Christmas decorations, plaintive music about loss and the cruelty of life piped into the room a little too loudly.

Fakery and bullshit were everywhere, he thought, as he ordered a pint and double whisky chaser, finishing them both quickly, waiting for the alcohol to dull the pain. Bad enough that Nine had betrayed Beth and that Benjy had left Sally, but Benjy thinking of leaving him for Norway was so much worse. The bond with his son, once so strong had become as fragile as a spider's web on a misty morning. He held out his whisky glass for a refill. The barman topped it up without using the optics. Dougie smiled at him gratefully. He took out his phone and texted Beth. "I need to see you. I know where Benjy and Nine are."

Chapter 33

Beth opened the wooden shutters and the bright glare of a cloudy day lit up the living room. She gazed down at the street below, the odd person drifted along with the gait and demeanour of the seriously hungover. She gazed at the Sunday paper headline, 'Agency Boss Resigns after Rubikon Fiasco.' Underneath was the picture of Peter Tan, an arm of a policeman across his face failing to hide his startled eyes and the egg on his face. Beth must have seen it a dozen times already but it still made her smile.

Her external life may have exploded, changed beyond imagination, but here in her flat everything seemed normal, unchanged, from the slight indentation on the cushion where she had been sitting last night to the half-drunk cup of coffee on the table. She had disabled the telephone and intercom, her mobile was off, the only sound was of the fridge humming in the background.

She switched on the radio. Radio Three's Sunday lunchtime concert from The Wigmore Hall – a violin sonata. Mozart. She stood for a moment, listening. Her violin case by the side of the window caught her eye. *Plenty of time to practise that now*, she thought.

She opened her laptop. There was a long and

eclectic mix of messages of support, requests for interviews and abusive emails. It was like letting the outside world into her inner world, polluting the atmosphere, clouding the clarity of the next steps of her plan. Deleting her email, Twitter, Facebook, and Instagram accounts was quick and easy. It felt as cathartic as if she had spent all day cleaning the house. A life. A history. A world. Obliterated in seconds.

She called her phone and internet provider to set up new phone and email accounts, making arrangements to allow only Dougie and Angelo's calls, texts, and messages to be forwarded. Her phone pinged immediately. A text from Dougie. *I need to see you. I know where Benjy and Nine are.* She suggested meeting him at lunchtime.

Neil's programme was due to begin shortly but she had time to tackle the new exercises Joseph had given her. He said they were only for his 'longtimers', an unhappy promotion. She picked up the radio and sat in front of her bedroom mirror. The heading read 'designed to minimise hypertonic muscles' which was medical speak for involuntary twitches and spasms. Just when she thought paralysis was bad enough, the alien Palsy god had more horrors in store.

Put thumb inside cheek, grasping the outside and pull up and out. Hold for minimum ten seconds. *Ouch, that hurt.* Joseph said it might. Shift position towards the centre. Repeat stretch. Apply and hold pressure for ten seconds. *Double ouch.* Repeat stretches four times. The last set turned out to be less painful than the first, which she decided to regard as a good sign. Next exercise. Snarl. *Easy*, she thought, images of Desmond and Ainslie floating into her mind.

Match movement on both sides. *A little more movement on left side today*, she thought. Repeat snarl four times more. She could hear Joseph's coaxing in her head saying to be patient. To give it time. She had plenty of that now.

She returned to the lounge and turned on the television. There was a swirl of anodyne music and then the camera panned in on Neil's face. He looked younger, his features sharper, his hair spikier than in the flesh. He sat on a wide-armed leather chair, a script in one hand, his smile beckoning his unseen audience towards him. Beth shifted forwards in her seat and watched him with the same attention a cat might give a fledgling.

"Good afternoon," he said, fixing the audience with his hallmark grin. "Today we're discussing boss's pay. British bosses are paid a hundred and thirty times more than their average employee. Is it that our bosses are getting better at their jobs or is it simply because they can get away with it? Today in the studio, discussing this with me is Sir Ainslie McFarlane, Chairman of The Agency and by video link, Jean NcMonnies from UNITED, Scotland's biggest trade union. Perhaps we can start with you, Ainslie." The camera panned to Ainslie who was sitting on a matching leather chair. He had one arm across the back of his chair, his shirt stretched unflatteringly over his paunch. He seemed half asleep, thought Beth, and he could do with a haircut.

"Good morning Neil," said Ainslie, firing back a smile that tried to match Neil's for charm but failed to look anything other than sleazy.

"Ainslie. Yesterday we saw the departure of Beth

Colquhoun, CEO of The Agency. Her salary was more than the Prime Minister's yet it's rumoured she received a severance payment of over two million pounds. How can you justify such an amount?"

Beth assumed Neil's producer had guessed the severance payment and had gone for a high number to goad Ainslie into correcting him. Standard tactics, she thought, but Ainslie appeared winded by the question. *He hasn't been properly briefed*, she thought, shaking her head in wonderment. Ainslie shifted in his seat, his mouth working but no sound came out. "I can't comment on individual cases," he said eventually, pausing for breath, but before he could continue was interrupted by Jean McMonnies on the video link.

"Dead right you can't!" she shouted. She was a small woman, in her mid-fifties with thinning hair and the animated energy of a young terrier. "Because there is no justification. Beth Colquhoun sacked hundreds of workers last year. None of them got so much as a penny in severance pay before they were tossed on the scrap heap."

Neil looked politely towards Ainslie, who seemed to have woken up. "Beth Colquhoun streamlined the management layers in the organisation to improve productivity. I can assure you everyone who was affected was treated fairly."

Beth groaned. Ainslie would have to do better than offer a bit of bluster about fairness. Neil leaned forward, loosening the back of his shirt collar as if the studio was too warm; Beth guessed his producer would be talking to him through his earpiece urging him to move in for the kill.

"Nevertheless Ainslie," said Neil, "giving two million pounds of public money to an executive who was clearly incompetent. It beggars belief. The public deserve an explanation."

That producer was good, thought Beth. *It was unlikely Neil would have come up with that on his own. Neil's face flushed, he hooked his finger at the back of his collar and loosened it more vigorously than before. He must know there was no way back for them, after this,* she thought. She took the remote control and shut the TV off. "Fuckwit," she said quietly to the blank screen.

She checked her new email account. There was one message from Angelo. She paused for a moment to savour the uniqueness of having only one email to look at. She opened each of the attachments, making calculations as she went. Alec had found ways to borrow money with impressive creativity. Unfortunately his creativity in finding ways to lose money was also impressive. She estimated he was £2.5 million in debt and had embezzled nearly the same amount from Hunters. Angelo had included a table from the Scottish Department of Justice with a guideline on prison tariffs. Alec was looking at four to six years. Even with a reduction of fifty per cent for good behaviour, it would be two to three years in prison. Not good.

She spent the next couple of hours calculating her own assets. Including the properties in Singapore, her portfolio of investments and her settlement from The Agency, she could raise five to six million. If Alec's creditors could be paid off, the court would look more favourably on him. The idea of emptying her bank account might seem more dramatic than deleting her online accounts but she found it gave her a similar clarity of purpose, of clearing out the old to make way for the new. She replied to Angelo, setting up a meeting with him on Monday morning.

She tried another snarl at the hall mirror. Hold for ten seconds. *Definitely better*, she thought. She pulled back her hair in a ponytail and threaded it through a baseball cap and put on her sunglasses. Her tracksuit bottoms and white tee shirt felt as comfortable as pyjamas and so ubiquitous on a Sunday morning, that she might as well have been invisible.

She pulled on her hoodie and skipped down the stairs to the fire exit at the back of the building. Tentatively she opened the door. She could see the bins were stacked neatly to one side and slowly edged open the door. Most of the journalists were camped out at the front but there might be one or two more enterprising than the others. The door opened fully. The courtyard was empty. *Lazy buggers*, she thought dismissively.

The city was in the process of coming to. Coffee smells wafted as she strode past pavement cafes, the buttery smell of croissants and pastries, a crumbly sweetness that she could almost taste. She felt untethered, as if she could lift off the ground like a hot air balloon. Letting go of trying to save the country from the economic doldrums was turning out to be a delightful sensation. Her public life was over, but being a nobody meant no expectations, no commitments; a chance to start over again, a sort of freedom.

Dougie was sitting on a park bench wearing his old donkey jacket, his shoulders hunched. As she got closer, she could see he hadn't shaved, his pale eyes rheumy and hungover.

"Beth, lass," he said, "nearly didn't recognise you. You OK?"

She didn't answer but hugged him instead. He responded to her pressure by trying to squeeze the breath out of her. It felt as if every passing second was healing her. When they sat down, it was as if they couldn't bear to be fully separated, his arm tightened round her.

"I can't believe you're still wearing that old jacket," she breathed quietly to him.

"Am I?" said Dougie, looking surprised that it was on his back.

"Some things don't change when everything else does," she said, and kissed him.

He stroked her hair, looking at her quizzically. "I thought you'd be raging."

"Raging? No. Not anymore. At this moment sitting here with you I'm very happy and I'm glad you know where Nine is because I want to see her."

He seemed pained then. "Beth I hate to tell you this but she's no friend of yours. Her mission was to befriend you and then betray you."

"I know. I ran out after her in the street and yelled at her like a mad woman at the demo but I've had time to calm down since then. I've been able to think things through. Getting sacked has made everything very clear to me."

"It's clear she's ruined your career."

"Nine didn't ruin my career. I did that all by myself."

"She told me that you taught her how to fight, to watch and wait for the moment to exploit the other person's vulnerability."

"She was a natural."

"She says she's very fond of you but she's not sorry about what she did."

"I wouldn't expect her to be. She's very principled."

"And what about the performance your boyfriend and your boss gave on the telly this morning?" he added. "You must be mad with them?"

"My ex-boyfriend and my ex-boss. There are better way of dealing with them than getting mad."

"I wish I could be so forgiving. I'm furious with Benjy and Nine. They've done so much damage."

"What'll happen to Sally? To Skye Superfoods?"

"Benjy knows he's done wrong by Sally. He'll give her anything she wants, including the business, though I'm not sure she'll want it. They're talking of going to Norway to start a new seaweed company. Even our old pal Mr Takashama knows more about it than me," he said. "They were up all last night making plans. They've asked me to come with them. I don't want to live in that frozen wasteland but I don't know if I could live my life with Benjy so far away."

"Being far away doesn't mean you're apart. Not these days," said Beth.

"You mean using video phones and computers? That's not for me. I need to have someone close to me, like with you are now," he said, squeezing her and kissing her briefly on the side of her head.

"You can learn if you want to."

"You can't teach an old dog new tricks. You should know that about me by now."

"Sometimes things happen, Dougie, and you have no option but to adapt. Sometimes it's not as bad or as hard as you think."

"I can't see me staying in Skye on my own without him."

"There's always Fiona."

Dougie laughed. "After her last visit to the house when she saw us together? I don't think so."

"When one chapter finishes, Dougie, another starts. It's in your power to write what you want that chapter to be, you know."

"I don't know about that. I can't think too far ahead. Now are you sure you want to see Nine or do you fancy going back to your place?"

***

Beth thought the new blocks of flats were like toy houses against the rows of grey roughcast council houses behind them. She was surprised that George, with all his revolutionary tendencies, would live somewhere so conventional.

"Nine has been looking after the place whilst George has been spending his summer holidays as a guest of the French gendarme," explained Dougie.

"I'm feeling a bit nervous," admitted Beth. A low thump had begun in her temples.

"Benjy's waiting for me round the corner in the pub. Give me call when you want us to come back," he said, letting her in.

Nine seemed younger, smaller. She was wearing her familiar look of indifference, although Beth could see tension around her eyes. She felt a swell of emotion that she realised was mostly relief. Thank God she was safe. She sat down opposite her, fascinated by the physical changes in her; the brown hair, the fading shape of the tattoo on her throat. "I always hated that tattoo. I wanted to rub it off and here it is – disappearing on its own." Beth felt she was talking too quickly, trying too hard.

"It was part of my undercover disguise. I didn't think I would end up living with you. It was a pain being lumbered with touching it up every day with mascara and eyeliner."

"If I had the option of rubbing off a facial disfigurement I would definitely take it," said Beth. Nine looked confused and a silence fell between them.

"I admired the way you handled yourself," said Nine. "You showed me that there's power in having a disfigurement. Most people don't know what to say, how to react. I saw you take advantage of that, take control of situations."

"Yes, but we both know it's always an act," said Beth, "and if you admit how much you hate the way you look, how unfair it feels, how frustratingly slow and inadequate the treatments are, it can destabilise you, make you vulnerable."

"I took advantage of that vulnerability in you."

"I knew it was a risk to let you into my life. Maybe I should have done more checking. Maybe I didn't want to find a reason not to work together. You were great company, we were a great team."

"Look Beth, I'd rather you be angry with me. I'm not sure I can take you being so nice and reasonable about this."

"OK I think you're a heartless, manipulative bitch who shafted the one person who showed you kindness and trust. Does that make you feel better?"

"No," said Nine and they both laughed.

"Why did they have to sack you? Couldn't they give you a final warning or something? I'm probably going to get a suspended sentence, why couldn't you be given a second chance too?"

"Different world. Different rules. Anyhow this isn't finished," said Beth.

"It's not?" asked Nine.

"Do you remember the number one rule of organisational life?"

"To always make your boss look good."

"Correct. And do you know the number two rule? If you can't make your boss look good, make sure you look good. At the moment I'm famous for incompetence, greed, and self-interest. I have to change that before I can say this is finished. But I need your help. It would be a way of making it up to me."

"Go on," said Nine, looking interested.

"Do you remember the bird-watching element of the Rubikon junket?" asked Beth.

"You mean the prostitutes," said Nine, grimacing.

"I have every detail of it from Ainslie's personal

computer."

"How the hell did you get that?"

"Flora. As you kept telling me she was crap. She actually had post-it notes on her desk with everyone's personal password on it. Including Ainslie's. It was easy to slip in and copy files when his secretary was at lunch. I've got locations, names, appearances of the girls and the preferences of each of the board members, and I'm not just talking about hair colour. Ainslie was in email contact with all the Rubikon Board as well as some whisky and oil executives."

"And he kept a record of all that? Not just Flora that was useless then."

"Not completely useless. They use alias names. Different email addresses."

"They probably didn't change their server addresses though. It should be possible to trace them back to the original accounts."

"He also sent a sizeable deposit using a separate expenses account."

"In his name?"

"No in The Agency's name but not through Desmond's department."

"Desmond won't be pleased."

"You know how important rules are to him."

"What do you want me to do?" asked Nine.

"A pincer movement. On the left flank, send an anonymous letter with the accounts data to Desmond. On the right flank, email the bird-watching files to Jean McMonnies. She's from UNITED,

Scotland's biggest trade union."

"I know who Jean McMonnies is. She's active in animal welfare too," said Nine.

"Then you know she'll be won't like this. She'll make sure the public know all about it."

"Their careers could be ruined," said Nine.

"Yes," said Beth.

"Marriages blown apart," added Nine.

"That's a possibility," agreed Beth. "The trail tracing this back to me must be cold. Jean will give you protection as an anonymous whistleblower, but you'll need to take additional measures. We're not the only people who know how to play this game and we're taking on some big players here."

"I've several connections with other protest groups. I can weave a web so complicated they could spend a very long time trying to unravel it."

"Good," said Beth.

"One question," said Nine, "why bother? You've got your pay-off. A tidy amount if Neil's programme this morning is to be believed. Why not wash your hands of the whole dirty lot of them?"

"It's not about money. It's about how people will remember me. Ainslie and the rest of them are doing a great job making me a scapegoat for a host of shoddy values associated with business. It's only right the public know the full story."

"They'll deny it of course," said Nine, "try and wriggle out of it."

"I hope they do. Denials, rebuttals, personal

attacks usually result in extending the time they're in the public eye, digging a bigger hole for themselves."

"Our last project together," said Nine.

Beth got up and gave her a hug. Nine felt as tiny as a bird, her bones as strong as iron. "One thing is clear to me. I've no intention of ever working for a big company again."

"Really?"

"You once told me I was being poisoned by a toxic culture and you were right. I was becoming a stranger to myself."

"You know me, Beth. Always happy to assist with your existential journey," said Nine.

"At first I thought I'll have to leave Scotland to escape all this bad press. But if our plan works, others will be in the headlines. Scotland's my home. My brother needs me. I'm going to pay off as many of his debts as I can and use what's left to fund a new business that will help young people realise their dream of working for themselves. Where better to do that than here."

"Benjy would love to stay in Skye but we can't go back there," said Nine.

"Not in the short-term perhaps, but the dust will settle eventually."

"How can you be sure?"

"Because life must continue. However much Sally loves Benjy now, she'll realise that being married to someone who loves someone else is hell. She's young, she's beautiful, she'll be financially secure."

"We've asked Dougie to come with us to Norway," said Nine.

"Is that what you want?" asked Beth.

"It's what Benjy wants," replied Nine.

The door opened then and Dougie and Benjy came in. Benjy was carrying a stack of pizzas. The cheesy smell floated out of the cardboard boxes and filled the small flat.

"Nine told me pizza's your favourite, Beth," said Benjy.

Beth smiled at Nine. "I hope that's the only secret you've told him."

"Seventeen quid for a bit of dough and cheese?" said Dougie incredulously, putting the boxes on George's small dining table.

"We got a good deal Dad, four for the price of three," said Benjy.

"If you ever get tired of seaweed, Benjy, this is the business to be in," said Dougie, going to the kitchen and bringing back four bottles of beer.

"Beth's going to stay in Scotland," announced Nine, "she's going to set up a new business helping young entrepreneurs."

"Perhaps you might like to run your Norwegian plan past me? I'm going to need a good project to get started."

"I'd be delighted," said Benjy, "I've learned a lot since that day I first pitched an idea to you."

"Where will you live, Beth?" interrupted Dougie. "Here in Glasgow?"

There was a pause. A silence as the three of them looked at her. She chewed a mouthful of pizza. "It depends if I get a better offer."

Chapter 34

"Glad you found us, Alec," said Dougie. "So, how are you doing?"

Alec remained standing and seemed perplexed, as if he was being asked a trick question. "Beth knows I'm coming doesn't she?" he asked.

"She runs a young entrepreneur club at the college on Thursdays. I was expecting her half an hour ago but she often runs late," replied Dougie, guiding Alec to the kitchen table.

"I can't wait for long," he replied.

"How's the family?" asked Dougie.

"It's been a tough on them. Me being in prison for two years. We had to take the boys out of their old school. There was a bit of bullying at the new one."

The mention of prison fell like a stone in water. Dougie could feel the ripples of disturbance spread out between them.

"Beth tells me Margaret went back to teaching," said Dougie, but Alec had the same distracted look he'd had since he arrived and he wasn't sure he was listening.

"D'you think she'll be long? Only I said I wouldn't

be late," said Alec, looking around the kitchen as if Dougie was hiding her somewhere. There was the sound of a car on gravel outside. "That'll be her now," said Dougie.

Beth came into the kitchen and exchanged a knowing look with Dougie. "Alec," she said gently, taking his hand. His fingers were still plump and soft, one part of him that was still familiar but so little else was. He had become muscled, his shaved head was like a bullet, his bright button eyes filmed over with defeat.

"I'll leave you two in peace. Don't leave without saying goodbye, Alec," said Dougie, closing the kitchen door behind him.

Beth put her arm round him. He felt as solid as a wall. "Have you been working out?"

"Not much else to do inside. You look happy," he said, and reached out to touch her frozen cheek; it felt both tender and numb. "It's good to see you, Funny Face."

"Yeah well, I'm reconciled to my face always looking funny."

"Has that been hard to accept?"

"At first yes, but I've come to terms with it now. Time helps. Dougie helps. Living here in Skye helps."

"I never thought you'd settle in a place like this," he said, looking out of the window to the sweep of the dunes beyond.

"I suppose life has taken unexpected turns for both of us."

"I've come to say thank you, Beth. Thank you for everything."

"It was only money, Alec. And as you never tired of reminding me, I had plenty of it," said Beth. He smiled and she felt her heart lift, life had come back into his eye.

"It was a helluva lot of money, Beth. Even for you. I'll never be able to pay you back you know."

"Of course you will. By making a go of your life. It's all I'll ever ask of you."

"I said to Margaret that as soon as I got out I had to see you. To say thank you."

"Well now you've said it you can bugger off," she replied, and again that smile of his came back, perhaps a little brighter.

"You're packed in as tight as anchovies in prison yet I've never felt so alone. Your letters were important. You never gave up on me. I know how much you helped Margaret. She would never have had the confidence to go back to teacher training if you hadn't encouraged her."

"She surprised everyone. Including me. The teacher training was just the start. She got rid of that gastric band, started her Nordic walking, lost a bit of weight. She's strong, Alec. You should be proud of her."

"You must have enjoyed seeing that old boss of yours get caught fiddling his expenses. For a while, I thought he might be joining me in Barlinnie."

"He got a two-year suspended sentence but the real punishment was the publicity."

"He made you look like a saint," said Alec.

"I'm no saint. The world of business makes it hard

for anyone to be that. But I'm glad people know the full story and I think my reputation is more or less restored by now."

"My career, my reputation will never be restored. I'm ignored, avoided by people I thought were my friends."

"That must be the hardest thing," said Beth.

"Listen to me. I didn't come here to have a moan. Least of all to you."

"C'mon, let's go for a walk," she suggested.

"I'm desperate for a smoke," said Alec.

The wind was blowing in off the bay, though it was mild for autumn. Beth could smell a hint of decay and hear leaves rasping in the wind. Alec was struggling to walk on the uneven sand.

"Take your socks and shoes off," she suggested, stopping to slip off her plimsolls, but he kept walking with a determination that struck her as more stubborn then sensible.

He had his head bent down and was shuffling into the wind. "I don't know if I'll be able to start a new life like you have. I miss my old life so much. It's like a pain that won't go away. I don't know who I am. What the point of me is. Margaret and the boys are at school all day. The boys have got clubs after school. Even when they don't, they make up excuses to avoid me. Margret has taken on extra responsibilities too. She says it's so we can afford a holiday but I think she just wants out of the house. And I can't complain to anyone because I'm meant to be so fucking grateful. D'you know what her favourite saying is?"

"Tell me," said Beth.

"No one has died. Like that's the worst thing that can happen. Well Beth I'm not so sure."

"Now Alec. I'm going to draw the line at having a conversation about suicide, at least not until you've heard my proposal."

"What proposal?"

"I run a Young Entrepreneur Club at the college here," she said. Alec sat down on the sand and began to remove his shoes and socks. He took a cigarette from a packet and offered her one. She shook her head but felt pleased by the invitation.

"I want to connect my young entrepreneurs here in Skye with other entrepreneurs."

"In Scotland only or…"

"I want to connect them to the world. To create a network that will unleash the collective energy of 16-18 year olds globally."

Alec blew out a lungful of smoke, looking at her fondly. "Never do anything by halves do you Beth?"

"What would make this different from other online groups is that the network would be run like a business. Members would get cheap start-up capital, mentoring support and business planning and when their businesses took off, they would pay a percentage of their profits back into the network. I've spent the last two years working this out. Planning every detail."

"The challenge will be to find enough start-up cash to get the first businesses up and running before revenue flows back in, assuming it ever does," said Alec.

"I have enough cash to get us started but you're right, we'll need to pick the first business ideas carefully so that the cash doesn't disappear too quickly. If fifty per cent of the first fifty businesses pay something back in, the cash will grow exponentially. That way the network will be able to sustain itself even if we hit a bumpy spell later on. I've even thought of a name for it. Kandoo. One word spelt with a K and double O."

"What does this have to do with me?"

"I need someone to design the computer infrastructure, the technical platform, the interfaces."

"Beth I can't…"

"I know you can't be a director till after your bankruptcy sentence is served and you can never be a finance director but you could easily do an IT job like this. I need someone I can trust."

Alec threw back his head at that point and laughed. He laughed so hard she moved from feeling pleased to being irritated.

"You're the only person I know who could apply the word 'trust' to a convicted embezzler," he said eventually.

"I'm applying the word 'trust' to my brother," she said quietly. "I want to launch in three months' time. Are you interested or shall we go back and talk about suicide?"

"I don't know, Beth. I'll have to think about it."

"I understand the only ways to guarantee death are jumping off a tall building or a gun to the head. All other methods have too great a margin for error.

Which of those two options appeals more to you?"

He said nothing but she could see he was smiling. They got up and walked to the sea. He bent down and for a moment she thought he was washing his hands but he scooped up a handful of water and flung it at her. The cold spray landed on her face and neck, as shocking as an icy shower. She kicked some water back at him though most of it landed on her trouser leg. He retaliated by grabbing her foot, leaving her hopping and jumping as if a crab had bitten her. They were laughing like they used to laugh when they had their water fights on the beach in Troon as children.

"OK, OK. You win," she said, laughing.

"Send me the network spec," he said, taking her arm. She had a sudden flashback to when he would walk her to primary school. The careful way he would tuck her arm under his. Look right, look left and right again, then they would shout, 'All clear,' and walk across the road together.

"What about Benjy? In your letters you told me he's in Norway with that girl who used to work for you," he asked.

"Benjy and Nine spend most of their time in Norway running a seaweed business but they've kept the Skye Superfoods brand going and employ local people to run the farm here. They come over regularly."

"Margaret and the boys would like it here," he said, taking an outsized breath.

"Bring them next time," she said.

"I will," he said. The mention of Margaret and the boys had made him edgy again, as if he had suddenly remembered them. Beth could see Dougie was at the water's edge about to get into his boat.

"Off you go then. I'll tell Dougie goodbye from you."

"I'll be in touch soon, Beth."

"Good," she replied. She watched him trudge back up the dunes, his shoes in his hand. He stopped at the crest and turned and waved. His solid figure outlined in silhouette. She waved back and they both stood waving, as if reluctant to lose sight of each other. She continued to wave even after he had walked down the other side and there was nothing to see but the gulls wheeling overhead in the wide sky.

She turned towards where Dougie was waiting. "Jump in, lass," he said, pushing the boat clear of the land. She sat at the back of the boat, trailing her hand along the surface of the water, watching it break into droplets; enjoying the sound of the creak and groan of the oars in their shackles as Dougie rowed them further out.

"Happy families?" asked Dougie.

"I hope so," she replied.

He had brought the oars in and was about to haul in one of the oyster crates. "Poor bugger. Being locked up for two years."

"I think he'll be alright. I've got a plan."

"I can tell you're up to something, Beth. There's a look in your eye when you're onto an idea,"

"Which eye gives me away, Dougie? The good one or the bad one?" She leaned forward and he stroked her face.

"A unique combination of the two," he replied, kissing her lightly.

"Speaking to Alec made me realise how little I miss my old life in business; all that striving, competing, worrying. Am I doing enough? Am I good enough? What do people think of me? The more energy I put into trying to keep on top of it all, the harder it became to make sense of anything. But here. With you. There's space. Time. Everything feels easier."

"It's hard to feel important when surrounded by so much grandeur, harder still to feel reigned in under these vast skies," said Dougie, leaning over and putting the crate back in the water.

"I read in the paper that global warming will mean bacteria levels will rise to such an extents that in the future all mussels and oysters in the world will be poisonous for humans," said Beth.

"Thank goodness we don't live in the future. Remind me never to visit. Sounds like a horrible place," said Dougie, sitting back in the boat and taking up the oars.

"I used to live in the future a lot. I've no intention of doing that again."

Dougie stopped rowing, allowing the boat to drift on the incoming tide.

"I'm glad, though my motives are purely selfish. Being here with you now is like living a poem. I look at you and see the way your eyes darken as the light fades, how the freckles on your nose are getting lighter now the sun has lost its strength. I see the way your hair tumbles in the wind and how my hands want to reach out and stroke it but not to tame it. And I don't have to wish it lasting forever. Because here, in this very moment, it is forever."

Epilogue

It is with great sadness we announce today the death of Beth Colquhoun at the age of 62 years after a short illness. Beth was the Industry Attaché for the UK Trade mission in Singapore from 2005-2012 and then had a short spell as Chief Executive of The Agency in Scotland from 2012-2013. However, she will be best remembered as the mastermind behind Kandoo, an internet-based company responsible for realising the ambition of hundreds of businesses worldwide by matching ideas from young entrepreneurs with sources of funding. Companies such as Japones (Spain), Auditrali (Malaysia), Celltak (Australia), and The Gantting Group (Finland) are but a few of the household names that owe their start to Beth's vision. Last year she was made a Dame of the British Empire for her services to business development.

She was also the driving force of the global charity Funny Face, whose mission is to change societal attitudes towards facial disfigurement by funding both medical and holistic advances in diagnosis and treatment. Beth herself had a rare form of Bell's Palsy (Reynolds Syndrome) and was a role model and inspiration to the many thousands of people with whom she worked.

Beth Colquhoun never married but is survived by

her partner of 18 years, Douglas (Dougie) McKinnon, his son Benjy and daughter-in-law Nine, and their three children.